'*Man of Glass* thrusts the reader [...]
fourteenth-century northern villa[...]
Amalric, a young, thoughtful, cre[...]
his glazier father. Am's journey f[...]
Glazier and head of the househ[...]
tragedy, but always underpinned by hope and sustained by faith manifested through creative beauty. I thoroughly enjoyed the journey.'
Revd Alan Simpson, Secretary, Diocesan Advisory Committee for the Care of Churches

'What an epic journey! The medical bits gave *Man of Glass* a real punch and the sense of how horrific a pandemic like that must have been. I am a practising artist and craftsperson in stained glass. The craft of stained glass today follows the same basic methods and techniques as medieval glaziers, though our tools/kilns, etc have evolved. I can say that the descriptions of the materials, methods and tools described in *Man of Glass* ring true and have an authentic feel – especially Am's drive as an artist.'
Stained glass artist, West Yorkshire

'An enthralling read with believable characters. It is full of fascinating historical details about the creation of stained glass and the progress of the plague in a small Wolds village in mediaeval England. I could picture the place vividly. Religious faith of the time was described well. I liked the sense of community and could feel their isolation from the wider world despite being caught up in great events.'
Debi Burridge, retired librarian

'This book evokes most vividly what it must have been like to live at the time of the Black Death, with both its description of the fear and superstition surrounding the pestilence and the frustration of trying to find a cure. The author makes an excellent job of telling the story through the eyes of Amalric, a young man born with aspirations for a better life and a talent for creating stained-glass windows that could lift him out of poverty. Set in a Yorkshire village in the fourteenth century, this book successfully conveys the strength of the role of the church in the lives of people at that time. I was left wanting to know more about Amalric's future.'

Jean, Bamford Reading Group

'The vivid descriptions and storyline of this book immersed me in the fourteenth century. I was lost in the suffering brought about by the plague but then uplifted by the love and dedication of the family, the medic and the clergy. The book brought to life the struggle of the early doctors along with the wisdom of old remedies. Hope breaks through by the love for each other and for the church.'

Angel Culley, retired Head of Midwifery and Nursing at the Jessop Hospital for Women

MAN OF GLASS

When pestilence strikes, will
Amalric's dreams be shattered?

Andrea Sarginson

instant
apostle

First published in Great Britain in 2020

Instant Apostle
The Barn
1 Watford House Lane
Watford
Herts
WD17 1BJ

actual persons, living or dead, or actual events is purely coincidental.

British Library Cataloguing-in-Publication Data

A catalogue record for this book is available from the British Library.

This book and all other Instant Apostle books are available from Instant Apostle:

Website: www.instantapostle.com
Email: info@instantapostle.com

ISBN 978-1-912726-18-9

Printed in Great Britain.

I have come to understand the nature of glass[1]

Theophilus

---

[1] *On Divers Arts: The Foremost Medieval Treatise on Painting, Glassmaking and Metalwork*, John G Hawthorne and Cyril Stanley Smith (NY: Dover Publications Inc, 1979). Originally published by University of Chicago, 1963, translated from *De diversis artibus:* Theophilus (Roger of Helmarshausen), twelfth century.

Author's note

Much of *Man of Glass* is derived from my imagination, formed over years of interest in the medieval period. It is set in 1349 when the pestilence, now known as the Black Death, made its way up to the north of England from the south.

The village of Warren Horesby is fictitious but was inspired by the deserted East Yorkshire medieval village of Wharram Percy, now under the care of Historic England, and which has sizable remains of a church dating from the twelfth century.

Meaux Abbey is not fictitious but though once powerful, nothing now remains except grassed-over stones. Events occurring there were recorded by Thomas Burton, abbot from 1396 to 1399 and it is from a translation[2] of this I took events relating to the abbey in 1349. All characters are fictitious except for the abbot of Meaux Abbey. Hugh de Leven was abbot from 1339 to 1349. My portrayal of him is purely imagined. Swine Priory was a religious house of nuns, in North Yorkshire, south of Meaux Abbey. Again, little remains but both are scheduled monuments of Historic England.

The windows in York Minster can be seen today. The 'monkey' window is part of a much larger fourteenth-century

---

[2] 'Houses of Cistercian monks: Meaux', in *A History of the County of York: Volume 3*, ed William Page (London: Victoria County History, 1974), pp 146–149. *British History Online* http://www.british-history.ac.uk/vch/yorks/vol3/pp146-149 (accessed 26th September 2019). This article contains information translated from an original history of Meaux Abbey, 'Chronica Monasterii de Melsa', written by Thomas Burton, the Abbot of Meaux from 1396 to 1399.

one, the pilgrimage window, n25, in the north nave. The Cistercian windows, known as the Five Sisters' Window, n16, in the north transept north wall, date from the thirteenth century.

The technique of stained-glass window production is taken from *On Divers Arts: The Foremost Medieval Treatise on Painting, Glassmaking and Metalwork,* a translation of the twelfth-century Latin manuscript of Theophilus, who was probably a German monk.

The song lyrics are the author's own poetry.

The medieval practice of medicine has been both assumed and derived from many sources over the years, including my own personal experiences and that of medical and nursing personnel I know.

This story is a work of fiction and I apologise for any inaccuracies that may be found.

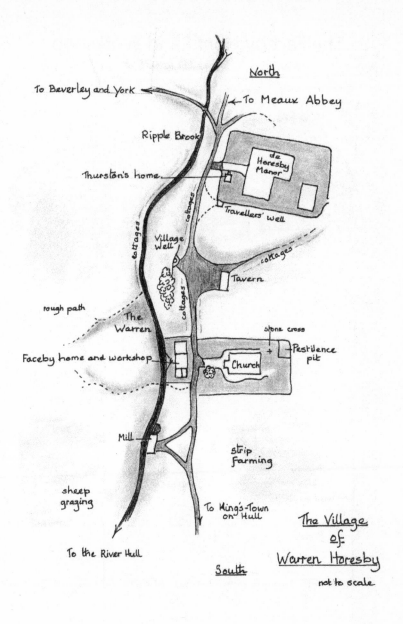

North

To Beverley and York

To Meaux Abbey

Ripple Brook

Thurston's home

de Horesby Manor

Travellers' well

cottages

Village Well

cottages

Tavern

cottages

rough path

The Warren

cottages

stone cross

Faceby home and workshop

Church

Pestilence pit

Mill

strip Farming

sheep grazing

To King's-Town on Hull

To the River Hull

South

The Village
of
Warren Horesby

not to scale

The Faceby Home and Workshop

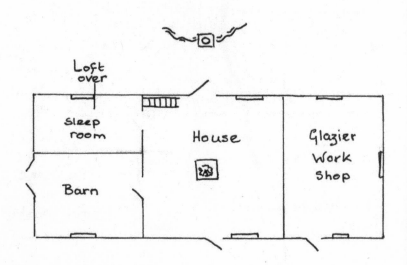

Part One

Rumour

Chapter One

East Riding of Yorkshire, early spring 1349

A few spluttering and stinking tallow candles added little light to the meagre glow of smouldering damp logs in the fireplace of the Warren Horesby tavern. A seated figure in coarse travel robes sat with hands tucked in wide sleeves to keep warm. His hood flopped forward, deeply shadowing his eyes. Around him huddled the men of the village, their own eyes and ears alert for signs that he might speak, for this man was different from other travellers: more withdrawn into himself, more sombre than the smiling monks or ebullient pilgrims who occasionally rested on their way north. A few of the men had recently seen his dark, solitary form by the gates of the manor but never before at the tavern.

A pot of drink, heat-sizzled with a poker from the fire, was thumped onto the table in front of him. Freckled, ginger-haired hands emerged from the sleeves. Long, refined fingers curled around the warm pot. Black cuffs showed at the wrists. He nodded his thanks. Eventually, after staring long into the fire, he began to speak with a southern brogue from the depths of his hood. He was on his way to Meaux Abbey, he said, only a few miles away, but the inclement weather had driven him to first take warming sustenance at the tavern. He raised his head and looked under the rim of his hood into the questioning, smoke-reddened eyes of the weary men before him and told a fearful tale: a tale of black flesh and death, of dreadful disease spreading up the country... spreading in the way that spilt ale flows into the crevices of a rough-hewn tavern table, inexorably and uncontrollably.

Motley clouds hovered over Warren Horesby like a giant sheep's fleece: wet, heavy and mucky from winter. Sodden clumps of grey rolled in a westerly direction obliterating the rising sun and threatening another downpour. Spring was hardly in evidence.

Amalric had heard the early morning church bell across the road while still in bed, but how long ago he couldn't tell: it could have been a cock's stride or a deer leap. All he knew was that the rustic clanking had driven into his head like a hammer on nails, forcing him to keep it on the pillow. Now, the dim light gave no clue as to the advancement of the morning. Desperate for fresh air instead of the stifling, stinking air of the sleep room, he staggered into the house, oblivious of things around him. At the doorway he lifted the latch and pulled back the door. Cool, damp air slapped his face. A sharp pain reverberated through his head as, forgetting to duck, he caught his forehead on the low lintel. Cursing, he pushed away a curtain of dark, shoulder-length hair and cupped his hand over a rising bump. Through the pain, he realised the day was not as advanced as he feared: the noisy, lumbering machinery of the mill at the lower end of the village was only just starting up. The steady clatter-clatter marked the beginning of the working day, just as the church bell marked the first prayers of the spiritual day. A heightened stink of animal and human waste nauseously wafted past him as village movement stirred the heavy air. Animals asserted themselves with mooing, baaing, snorting and clucking; tiny children's high-pitched voices cried out for attention and shutters clattered against wattle and daub.

Amalric found it hard to engage with the day. Last evening had been the first time he had drunk like a man. His day of birth some eighteen, maybe less, years ago had been a feeble excuse for the village men to drink copiously and his own father had been indulgent with him and them. The after-effects of strong ale, he now discovered, were far from pleasant: his dark eyes felt tender, watery; his tongue stuck to the roof of his mouth; his head hurt – both outside, as the bump rose, and inside. Overall, he felt at one with the dark, dank, dismal day. The only thing in his accessible consciousness was a jumbled mess of tavern talk and words that had frightened him then and wouldn't make sense now.

Usually at this time, Amalric would be in his father's glazing workshop, but with the weather so dull, the coloured glass would not show its full beauty for hours yet. He turned back into the house feeling a little less guilty about his lethargy. The light from the opened door caught the large rectangular shape of Molly the cow standing patiently by the wall, still offering her warmth as she had all night. The crumpled mess of his younger brother slumped over the table. He didn't bother to explore Edwin's condition further, suspecting that he had been out with the boys from the manor last evening, unconcerned that his elder brother was celebrating his manly age. Edwin would be in a dark mood, determined not to get involved in daily work, and best left alone.

Amalric closed the door behind himself. The light dimmed, leaving only that coming through open shutters. He saw his tall, slender but large-bosomed mother, Gundred, glancing occasionally with tight-lipped irritation at Edwin. The stockier little Nesta was keeping her eyes on the task of urging the fire into greater life. Its curling smoke from damp vegetation caught Amalric's dry throat, causing him to cough as he tried to grunt a general greeting. Nesta suppressed a giggle.

'It still dry out there, son?' asked his mother sharply.

Amalric nodded.

'Mm. I'd best be off to the well for right sure it'll rain again soon. And bein' first there saves on mindless chatter.' She pushed a strand of greying hair into her cap and lifted a small pot of ointment from a shelf and handed it to him. 'Arnica for the bump on your head. You're taller than you feel.' She gave a slight tweak of his cheek: it irritated him. He lifted her mantle from a hook, passed it to her and reopened the door. He saw her strong face was flushed. 'And shut the door to keep the heat in,' she said routinely, as she wrapped the mantle around herself and picked up her pails.

Amalric watched his mother walk up the road, pails swinging. Despite her preference to avoid mindless chatter, he knew she enjoyed her friends and their daily conversation. The world of women felt complex to him. His mother coped with five children and a husband better than any of the other mothers around. He knew she worried about him: his moods, his lack of confidence, his uncertainty of just about everything. She understood. He put his finger into the salve and at once appreciated the sensation of the smooth texture. Gently, he rubbed it onto the tender area of his forehead and felt it cool as the air passed over it. He sensed his mother's love so freely given, and loved her in return. He forgot his irritation and turned back into the house.

'Is Da up?' he asked of Nesta, by the brightening fire.

'No. Master Elias is still abed. Mistress says he's still heavy with ale.' She stood, wiped her hands on her rough apron and began another task.

Her cheeks were pink with heat, he noticed. 'Where's Matilde?'

'At a birthin',' she said pithily, beginning tasks that his elder sister would normally do.

Amalric became aware of other absences. 'And the twins?'

'Out back.'

Feeling both weary and unneeded, Amalric left the house and dropped down onto his haunches to lean against the cool outside wall of his home. The sound of giggling came lilting from the back garden. It came from the twins.

Berta skipped around the corner, her short tunic above plump bare legs, her dark, unruly curls bouncing. 'Hello, Mally.'

Amalric treasured her nickname of him. 'Hello, Berts. You may need to help get Molly into the barn. She looks a bit cow-lazy this morning and Nesta has her hands full.'

'I will, Mally. Bennet can finish the chickens. I'll see to Molly. "Mally and Molly, they're ever so jolly",' she sang, and skipped indoors.

'And shut the door to keep the heat in!'

Too young to do much more than take everything in their stride, the twins had been a constant joy to him since their birth eight or nine years ago – he wasn't exactly sure when they had been born. Their lively chatter and laughter always cheered him.

Amalric loved his home at the lower end of the village, on the edge and close to the road where travellers to and from the south passed. In front of him, across the road was the church. At present, it looked grey and rather forbidding but with sunlight and clement weather, it looked warm and inviting. Most mornings he would see his friend, Father Wilfrid, leaning on the gate after prayers, supping from his beaker, enjoying the first light of the day. But it was now too late – too late to talk about things that really mattered. The priest had no doubt set off on his daily rounds.

Amalric's reverie was brought to a sudden end by a commotion behind him inside the house. It evidenced a familiar disharmony and despite his instinct to turn away, he knew he had to face whatever was the cause. He sighed, stood and put his hand on the door latch, pushed slowly and bent to avoid hitting his head a second time. He suspected things might be being hurled but it was an angry child's voice that hit him, not objects. The voice came from Berta. Through the dimness, he could just make out that she was ineffectually pushing the perverse Molly on her rump with all her small might, trying to get her through the internal door into the barn. A steaming pile of dung shone fresh and malodourous on the impacted earth floor. Berta's dark curls pitched over her forehead as she angrily yelled at her brother Edwin to help. He now sat on a bench at the table more concerned with his fingernails than the rumpus in the room, a smirk playing on his face.

Amalric knew he must intervene to bring an end to the fuss but hesitated and was saved the effort by Bennet, Berta's twin, appearing through the back door from the garden, taking in the scene immediately. With his high-pitched young voice, he started rebuking Edwin, only to be slapped on the head in return and told to stay out of it. Berta's temper turned to hysteria and, protecting her brother, she jumped up and clawed at Edwin's face.

Amid the activity, Molly subsided into panic; mooed, kicked the table leg, knocked the breakfast platters asunder, narrowly missed the central hearth and Nesta, and hurtled into the barn away from the commotion.

Berta, with tears of hurt and frustration streaming down her face and legs streaked with cow dung, ran towards the warmth of the fire for comfort. Bennet followed. Black hair mingled as their heads bent together.

Amalric realised that Nesta had disappeared into the shadows.

Elias emerged from the sleep room, walking stiffly, his white hair tousled. He was forced to press himself against the wall in order to escape being crushed by the distressed Molly. He stood for a moment, shocked. Amalric stared at his father with concern. He saw his stooped back, shoulder and neck muscles taut with the effort of breathing and his deep pink complexion turning purple. His eyes, heavy from the liquor-induced deep sleep, peered through the gloom. All became silent. Amalric's own heart quickened.

Elias glared at Edwin, who was tense with antagonism, and at Amalric standing helpless and self-conscious by the door. A shake of his head aimed in Amalric's direction denoting despair was enough to cause his eldest son to feel like sobbing – but it was to Edwin that he gave most of his ire. He glowered at him, straightened his stooping back and moved closer to him. With effort, he puffed a night breath of stale ale and poor teeth into his third child's pale, handsome face and stared into his eyes.

'Time has come, Edwin, for you to do your full share round here,' he said with tight restraint. 'You're nothing but a hindrance to what anybody else needs to do. What with your fancy clothes, black tail at the back of your head like an ass' backside and posh friends with horses to take 'em all over! God knows where you go at night or get money from to mix with 'em. Soon we'll all have to face somethin' a lot worse than this endless bickerin'.' He raised his arm and pointed to the door. 'Be off out of here: go tend the sheep and their little uns by the sheep barn. They might be stuck in mud.' He waved his hand through the air in dismissal and relaxed, his vituperation extinguished.

Edwin wiped his hand over the blood oozing on his face, took his woollen cloak and sulkily grabbed a chunk of bread from the table. Amalric stood to the side of the open door and watched him slope out into the morning. But Edwin didn't head towards the sheep lands: he turned north towards the manor. Amalric decided not to tell this to his father, who looked unwell enough already after the morning's events. Knowing Edwin had disobeyed him would only add fuel to the flames. Amalric watched his father stamp out the back door, breathing heavily. He knew he had gone to find solace alone in the privy.

The privy was the wonder of the village. Amalric, too, often sought peace there. His grandfather, Old Elias, Elias' father, had dug a channel from the Ripple Brook which curved in an arc, passing close to and from their home. As a small boy, Amalric had gazed excitedly as foundation stones were set into the ground either side, at the point nearest their home, and a little hut of expensive wood erected on them. Inside, on a throne of wood, family members sat to allow their waste to plop into water and be washed away. It was not as grand as the garderobe he imagined at the manor, nor the nearest towns, but Amalric admired the sheer invention of it. Most other families had earth privies but quite often, people just wandered into a copse nearby. On the oak door of the privy were two beautiful carved, laughing faces – one at adult level and one low down for children. Those faces, it was said within the family, had been modelled on village priests, signifying their veiled concerns over all aspects of life.

'But Grandpa, why didn't you make one of them *your* face?' Amalric had asked as a very small boy.

'Because, lad, I have nowt but a bantam's idea of how I look,' was the reply. 'And anyway, tis more fittin'.'

The faces made Amalric feel happier at each visit.

Today, the little stream below the carved oak seat was running full. It may contain some village detritus from up the hill, but the occasional splashing of cold water on warm buttocks would be a blessing, serving to cool his father's distress. The comment about 'something a lot worse' had not escaped Amalric's clouded mind.

Matilde entered the house, tired from her birthing work. She looked around grimly, realising that something had happened. Silently and belligerently, she tucked her skirt into her belt to keep it off the floor, rolled her long sleeves to her elbows and began to help Nesta clear up.

Amalric smelled the scent of fresh herbs on his sister after cleaning herself from the birth. He wondered if it had been a difficult one, tiredness prompting her annoyance at the obvious commotion. Her exaggerated movements caused her freshly laundered cap, normally well placed to cover her dark curls, to slip. It had been her grandmother's and evidenced a sewing skill and grandeur of past fortunes. Amalric had, over years, watched her keep up its little repairs with fine stitches.

Essentially, Amalric felt sorry for his older sister. Sometimes when he came upon her alone, he would see a faraway look in her eyes. Occasionally, like today, she would be short-tempered. He had heard his parents discuss marriage for her, but no young man in Warren Horesby or nearby could match her sharp mind.

It frightened them away. She, like Amalric, had been educated by monks. Elias had been offered an abbey education for his two eldest boys as a reward for caring for the windows at Meaux Abbey, but Edwin had had no desire to sit at a desk. Matilde had pleaded to be sent instead. Amalric remembered his mother protesting, saying it was not right for a girl to do as much learning as a boy and it was a mother's place to educate girls. But Elias had given in to his daughter's insistence and now Gundred blamed him for Matilde's inability to find a husband – an educated wife being undesirable to the village dolts. Gundred found consolation, however, and more than a little secret pride in her eldest girl's healing and midwifery role in the village, her understanding of herbs and birthing being second only to Gundred's own. If marriage and children were not to be, then just being a skilled healer would be sustaining enough, she had said. Amalric was not so sure.

'I'll put this mess on the dung heap,' said Matilde through tight lips, brown eyes flashing as she swept past Amalric and went through the door.

Elias returned from the privy with a calmer demeanour and healthier complexion. Amalric felt bold enough to ask about the previous evening. The image was beginning to clear ever so slightly. Pots of ale had seemed to be everywhere – small rivers of it had run into thin wooden cracks. Faces had been stern. A stranger had talked.

'Er, Da… what was it that was said last night in the…?'

Elias interrupted him with raised hands, a sigh and a forced smile. 'How did you enjoy it, lad? Bit too much ale, eh? Best talk about it some other time.'

'Then come, Father, and instruct me on the day's doings,' he said a little flatly.

Elias sat down heavily on the bench beside his son, motivated by his eagerness to work. He was prevented from replying by Nesta, who appeared at his side with a large pan of porridge, ready to scoop a dollop into the wooden bowl in front of him. Amalric felt her presence but would not look at her. He had no need to look; he saw her well enough in his mind's eye. Her soft, brownish hair and large grey eyes, the black centres in them shining, reminded him of the little mice in the workshop for whom he secretly saved a little of their precious cheese. She was small but her imperfect face was full of character and laughter, with a smile that, when it was aimed at him, took his breath away. He dared not look at her in case his interest became obvious to both her and his father. His feelings were an embarrassment and he didn't know how to handle them. Nesta showed no emotion but moved to his side with the porridge pan in the crook of her arm, resting on her hip.

'Now, Am,' said Elias. 'What we have to do today is... Am?'

His son's attention was wandering. Nesta served the porridge to Amalric. The thick mass slopped into his bowl. She did not look him... but the tip of her long plait, pale at the end, fell forward and lightly touched his bare arm. He shivered as romantic thoughts broke through his lingering headache and distracted him: his father's words barely broke through.

'Yes, Da,' he answered automatically.

Elias grew frustrated. 'Stop daydreaming, Am! You're my apprentice, don't forget, and must needs listen.'

His son looked up, his eyes still wide and dreamy.

'In two days, the day after tomorrow, Am, we will be going to Meaux Abbey. Are you listening?'

'Er... yes, Da.' Amalric forced himself to be attentive.

'So... for this next two days, I want you and Ned to clear the workshop. Get rid of the bits of waste glass from them Manor House windows we've just finished, chalk the table afresh an' so on. Then...' He straightened and smiled triumphantly. 'We start somethin' new. We have to go to Meaux Abbey. I can't help feelin' a bit excited, like.'

His eyes sparkled with enthusiasm. Amalric noticed he looked younger.

'The Meaux monks have come round to thinkin' they'd like some new windows, 'appen a bit different from their usual ones.

It's alreet to have grisaille patterns, them circles and squares, grey lines in leaf shapes an' such, but a bit more colour is what they need, in my opinion. Anyway, it's all down to their beliefs an' nowt to do with me. I've heard tell, though, the abbot is thinking to have some figures – saints and the like. Quite a departure for Cistercians, if I'm not mistaken.'

Elias' enthusiasm fired Amalric. His eyes focused. 'That's great, Da.'

'We'll take Ned with us for a bit of a treat. Anyway, we may need his help if more work comes our way – raise him up a bit from workshop drudge to assistant, like.'

Amalric deflated. 'But the shutters; we wanted Ned to fix them. You know how they stick, especially the one on the window that looks up the street. You know how long he takes to do a job.'

'Well, he can fettle 'em today and tomorrow. I'm sure between you, you'll get everything done, son.' There was a note of impatience in Elias' voice.

Amalric had to learn to manage the workshop but was finding being masterful a struggle, even with someone as docile as Ned. He found him frustratingly slow. 'Oh... very well. It's a good idea to have him with us on the visit,' agreed Amalric, reluctantly.

At that moment Gundred opened the door and daylight flashed into the room. She put down her pails in the corner, took off her mantle and hung it up. She saw her daughter chopping herbs wearily and touched her arm. In that small gesture, Amalric saw the closeness of women and felt a little pang of jealousy.

'Hello, love,' said Elias, looking towards his wife. 'All well at the well?' He grinned at Amalric and burped.

'It's Lent,' said Gundred. 'You should have cut down on your drinking. Had none o' that strong stuff. That priest across the road is too lax! And you let our Am drink too much – you both staggered home! Most of the village men were the same. Strong ale is a pestilence, if you ask me!'

Amalric knew his mother was grateful for the soured ale she obtained from the tavern to make her copious amounts of medicinal vinegar. He sometimes enjoyed this banter of his parents. On the other hand, today it had a strained edge to it. Something had triggered his mother to mention pestilence.

'Aye, the pestilence seems to be spreadin',' said his father. 'There was a traveller from down south in the tavern. He didn't speak like us. Said he'd heard about it killin' all an' sundry. He'd not seen it himself, like. He'd come up here to work. Was on his way to Meaux Abbey for a few days. 'Appen was stayin' at the manor.'

'Oh, and what was he like?' said Gundred, sharpness in her voice.

'Hard to tell because he kept his hood on. He was a mite thin. I suppose he'd come to escape it.'

'It'll 'appen come to nowt,' said Gundred sharply. 'You don't want to listen to such tales. We've come through all sorts of pestilences afore.'

'Well,' responded Elias, 'they've hired a physician at the manor, expectin' him soon I've heard, so it must be bad 'cos you know how much they cost an' old Lord de Horesby wouldn't spend money for nowt.' A flash of realisation crossed Elias' face. 'Eh, maybe that was 'im! The physician!'

'What!' exclaimed Gundred. 'A higher-up share drink with you lot in that pokey, stinkin' tavern? I think not! But old Horesby would spend money to bump him up in society. Having your own physician looks proper. They're good to have around the table if high-ups come callin': all dressed in black and lookin' serious. Anyway, we don't need a physician round here. There's enough of us with healing sense to cope. And there's Father Wilfrid with his prayers. Pity old Horesby didn't employ somebody with skill enough to pull teeth, deal with farmin' injuries, stitch folk up and such. If he'd have thought of his tenants, that's what he would have done.'

'Aye, well that's as maybe but I'm getting reet fearful.'

Gundred closed the subject with, 'Well, what will be will be.'

'Wives... allus think they know best,' Elias muttered to Amalric and closed his eyes. His son noticed it with disquiet. There was something here that was not being said. 'Anyway,' Elias continued, 'I'm going up to the tavern again this evenin'... but not you, Am.'

Amalric felt excluded. If only he had been more of a man than a boy in the tavern, held his ale better, he would remember what the stranger alleged. He saw his mother's eyes narrow. He looked at Matilde but, clearly, she dare not question her mother's attitude. Anyway, there was the excitement of Meaux Abbey to come. He rose from the table and left the cloying atmosphere of the house for the workshop.

As Amalric entered the workshop, he thought about his grandfather. It was rare to have such a place in a village, but Old Elias had seen possibilities grow for glass windows in religious houses and the nascent curiosity of manorial lords – he had thus seized opportunities. What Amalric loved about the place was the redolence of the old man's ambition and love of beauty: the carefully ordered storage racks for glass, the large worktable, the little hearth in the corner to heat glass cutters. Amalric's father had followed on successfully and now Amalric's own ambition to work with coloured glass burned bright. However, as for everyone else, life had been difficult over the past years and work had fallen off. Now with the prospect of new Meaux Abbey windows, the business might have a resurgence.

Outside, a smart wooden sign, for those who could read, declared *Elias Faceby, Glazier.* Below it, beside the door, a coloured glass window showed an example of the glazier's trade. Amalric had made it. It was a source of wonder to him that his father should use his son's inexperienced work and not his own to declare his glazing business. It seemed to Amalric that it embodied parental trust and confidence and he admired his father for taking the risk.

Amalric had made the window two years previously as his intermediate apprentice piece for the Glaziers' Guild. It was very small in comparison with the huge coloured ones he had seen in religious buildings, being no taller than his arm was long, and half as wide, but it was just large enough to be a picture. He ran his hand lovingly over the smooth undulations of the glass surface and the dull lead cames and felt a love for his craft. Even now, the dull spring light passing through revealed amber, red, blue and green. In summer, the same colours would splash and smudge against the walls as the sun shone through. He called it his shepherd window.

Amalric wanted to do things with coloured glass. He didn't want to be simply a craftsman following other peoples' ideas, but an artist, inspired and inventive. But he wondered if it would ever be possible. Both his grandfather and father, while successful in monetary terms, had nurtured great creative ideas that had been limited by wars, weather, animal plagues and so on. Why should it be different for him? Couldn't making money also include being really inventive? Amalric's dreams wouldn't go away. In his imagination he made a huge coloured window for an important religious building, with scenes that told stories. But as always when moving his hands over his shepherd window, they rested eventually on one particular piece of glass… something always niggled him about *this* part of the window – and it wasn't just the clumsiness of inexperience. Why had his father allowed it? He longed to take the piece out of its leaded frame and change it.

An ale-induced stabbing pain in his head was sufficient to return him to the everyday. Two other windows were simply openings in the wall. Both had shutters with crossbars, now swollen with the wet weather. Amalric hoped one day to see clear glass in these windows but it was far too expensive even for glaziers to be profligate with its use. The result was a compromise, particularly at this time of the year: to stay warm and dark with them closed, or cool and light with them open. His father had once instructed him to nail thin woven wool to stop the breezes but the result had been too dim to work in.

Amalric stumbled his way to the back window and braced himself for the cool air that would enter the room as the crossbar slid off its hooks and the shutter reluctantly opened. The resultant view of the garden, which stretched to the brook, was always a pleasure: his mother's vegetable patch; the good laying chickens; a swill-filled pig in a pen; beehives at the far end; and Molly the cow. Amalric himself had set traps for rabbits, the odd badger and the fat rats that ran menacingly from the brook to invade their home. But best of all were the herbs planted near the back door and picked for cooking and healing. They were in neat rows, tended daily, with attempts made to protect them from the voracious rabbits by little fences. His mother had explained that most were used efficaciously for the four humours – blood, phlegm, yellow bile and black bile. Amalric knew nothing of these things, only that they required betony, hyssop, rue, chamomile and more. He loved to squeeze the leaves of sage and thyme, then smell his fingers. Bennet and Berta frequently ran amongst them and covered themselves in perfumes. Gundred always scolded them but with a smile and shining eyes. Away from the precious plantings was a small domed clay kiln for fixing paint on glass.

Amalric moved over to the window on the end wall that gave the view of the road. The crossbar would not budge. He heaved it with irritation. Suddenly, it gave way, shot up and clattered to the floor, catching his right pointing finger as he automatically put out hands to stop it. He saw blood begin to seep from a graze. Anger engulfed him. Ned should have attended to the sticking wood. Cuts were the blight of glaziers and he cursed Ned Tynel for being the cause of this new injury.

As he was sucking the wound, a small piece of glass on the table flashed in the light and distracted him. It was part of the debris from a window made for the solarium of Warren Horesby Manor showing the arms of Lord de Horesby. Amalric had reckoned it a rather boring job because the precise design of the shield offered no chance of invention. But, as always, he had enjoyed the colours. He picked up the piece and held it to the light. Cold from the early morning, it was like a piece of thin sheet ice over deep water; transparent but blue coloured, a deep sapphire. Glass was like jewels. He loved to make precious gems out of small waste pieces and spin tales to the twins, of kings and queens who might have worn them. He loved to watch their dark eyes grow large and their mouths drop open as they became enchanted by the mystery of colour. He peered through the glass to the March sky. The dark, lowering clouds of the north turned a glorious blue and he wondered at the magic needed to turn wood ash, sand and metallic powder into such a material: a material with a sublime smoothness but which, when broken, had the spikey edges that were responsible for most of the scars on his hands.

A sharp breeze suddenly blew. It lifted Amalric's hair. His dreaming was once more curtailed as the cold air reminded him to instruct Ned to shave some wood off the shutter bars. He baulked at the idea. Ned was two years younger than him but lumbering and slow. It would be easier to do the job himself. But his father was now insisting that with less than two years of his ten-year apprenticeship to go, he had to learn how to manage. Annoyance and fear of responsibility mingled in him, settling on thoughts of his brother Edwin who, like Ned, was two years younger and showed no sign of taking responsibility for anything. He gripped the glass: it pricked his palm. He winced and dropped it.

A whistled tune signalled Ned's imminent arrival. Amalric looked out of the open window and saw him ambling down the street carefree, the long point of his old-fashioned hood swinging from side to side hiding his straw-coloured, unwashed curls. Samson, his mangy ginger dog, padded as if on springs beside him, his tongue lolling happily over grimy teeth.

Without giving time for Ned to enter the workshop properly, Amalric blurted, 'Ned, I need you to attend to the shutter bars.' His exasperation showed as he lifted the bloodied hand in front of Ned's face. 'I could barely push them open this morning, they're so swollen from the wet. Some wood needs shaving off… please.'

Ned ignored the bungled attempt at authority and replied morosely, 'Aye.'

Amalric became hot and his face reddened. He silently berated himself. 'Please.' How could he say that so feebly? He felt slightly queasy.

Chapter Two

Next morning, the day was as dull as the previous one. Amalric morosely slouched out of the sleep room. His father's drink-laden snores had reverberated around the small room, forcing him to get out of bed. His mother, alone in the house, slammed bowls and beakers around without her normal efficiency, putting them down then moving them again absent-mindedly. She wiped the table with a damp cloth several times.

'Ma, is something wrong? You seem…'

'I'm sick of hearin' about the new pestilence. Your father came home last night in a right panic. Drink-sodden again. No doubt he'll have forgotten about it this mornin'.'

Amalric suspected he wouldn't.

'I don't hold with all this talk. I'll deal with it if it comes like I always have done – but, to be on the safe side, Nesta and I will do some cleanin'. We'll wash stuff and clear them droppin' insects from the thatch. A cockroach fell into your father's stew yesterday. Thankfully, he didn't notice it.'

A smile played on Amalric's lips. 'Do you think insects spread it, then?'

'No!' Gundred stood up straight, putting her hands on her lower back. 'He'll be thirsty and grouchy when he wakes. If he *must* drink too much at the tavern… well! He should know the strength of their special brews by now. If you help me fetch the water, he'll be able to have a whole bucket full to drink all to himself!' She laughed without her eyes joining in. 'Anyway, Am, I need lots of water today and I need you to help me get extra.'

'But Nesta could…'

'She'll be busy, *you'll* have to come with me.'

'I just thought, 'appen I could go with Nesta to save you work.' Amalric stood, expressionless.

'No!'

He felt put down. 'Right. I'll follow you shortly to help you back with the pails.'

'You'll have to run the gauntlet of those gossipin' women, mind. Tis woman's work but you needs learn about women. You're past bein' a boy and a man needs to know things.'

'Aye, Ma. Ned is often there helping his mother so *I'll* lend you *my* muscles for a while and feel gallant like a knight.' He gave an elegant but exaggerated bow.

Gundred responded by giving him a warm-hearted tap on the head with her rough hand.

'Yes, really low-born Ned may be, and simple, but he is good to his mother… and an honest worker for your father. It'd be a help if your brother Edwin could sometimes lend a hand like that. He's too old for his years – and as usual, he's nowhere to be seen at sun-up. We saw nowt of him yesterday.' She sighed. 'Anyroad, come by the well in a while. I'll take four pails. You can carry two back and I'll carry two with the yoke.'

Amalric was pleased to help his mother. She looked pale these days. After five children and one or two lost before they had chance to live, Amalric knew she had not been without suffering. Recently he had caught whispers between her and Matilde that suggested something about her age and time of life. His father had dismissed them as 'women's things', and Edwin had put his finger to his nose indicating he knew all about such secret things. But it was a mystery area to Amalric. Of course, he knew some things – the reason for the monthly washing of rags, for instance – but Edwin seemed to be aware of so much more.

Amalric opened the door for his mother.

'Close the door, keep the heat in.'

Again, he watched as she went up the hill. Standing there, he heard other doors slam as women left their homes mindful, like his mother, of keeping in the little heat that was inside. But today he noticed the slamming was more vigorous than usual. He suspected that after a second tavern night, drowsy husbands would annoy their women folk, hence the angry slammings aimed like darts at husbands' headaches. Yet, most of the village women tolerated their men's predilection for the tavern beverages. Heaven knows, such comfort kept them sweet, they said... if it wasn't too often. It all amused him.

Half way up the village road, Amalric saw figures draw in behind his mother. He easily recognised them from their backs as Ned's mother, Alice Tynel, and her friend, Myrtle Ashe. Myrtle always aroused apprehension within him, knowing as he did that she and his mother were long-time adversaries. With them were Myrtle's daughters. Amalric's mind filled with images of them. Constance, the younger, with a scabbed face and vacant look, and Liza, the elder, thirteen years or so. She had recently taken to wearing adult cast-offs which, even so, failed to hide thick ankles. He shuddered at the thought of her curtains of oily hair through which she peered at young men. Amalric himself had been the unwilling recipient of her precocious, lustful looks. The thought discomfited him intensely and he turned away.

It was a relief to look to the sky and assess the weather. There might be a downpour but what did that matter against the present beauty of God's heavens – grey clouds stretching eastward, ending in a golden contour with a streak of pure blue below – like his favourite blue glass? Obviously, somewhere the sun was shining but he knew it was unlikely to hold a promise for Warren Horesby. Sunshine was rare these days and could not raise the village from the damp place it had become. Had it not been for its nestling on the slopes of a valley, it would have suffered the indignities of frequent floods – as so many other villages had. As it was, only a few strips in the lower fields were

34

sometimes rendered waterlogged and useless for crops or grazing.

'You look as white as your worktable, my friend. I assume you still have a thick tongue and a heavy head on you from the evening before yesterday.'

The voice broke through his dreaming. Amalric followed the sound of the voice. Father Wilfrid was leaning on the church gate, just across the road from the Faceby home.

It was the priest's habit after morning prayers, weather permitting, to take his first hot drink of the day in this spot: while warming his arthritic hands on the smooth surface of his beaker, he could look up the hill and view the village and his flock. He himself was inconspicuous in the shade of a gnarled old yew tree and most folk rarely thought of his early morning presence. But not Amalric.

'Hello, Father Wilfrid. It's good to see you. I'm afraid I was too late out of bed yesterday to greet you.'

'Nay, lad. Like you, I'd had a goodly portion of ale the evening before and found it hard to lift my head from my pillow. The pillow's flat with age and my neck had neither the strength nor the will to lift my head from it in time for prayers. The poor verger had to see to the bell himself and, in fact, he looked no better than myself. We were there last evening as well and feel no better today. How are you feeling? Have you recovered after a day without ale?'

Amalric felt his face become hot. 'I'm fine.'

The priest tutted and smiled. 'It's alright, lad, I like more than a single beaker of ale myself. You'll soon be a man and will need to hold your drink and know when to stop. Hard times will come. You know you can always talk to me, don't you? In or out of the confessional. After all, I've known you since you gushed into the world, bloody and screaming.'

'Thank you, Father.' Amalric wished he could fully remember the evening in the tavern. The priest's sombre tone was perplexing and he was relieved when his voice took on a lighter edge.

'Would you like a drink of Adam's ale fresh from the well, to assuage your morning thirst? Water is no doubt best for you.' He grinned mischievously then said more seriously, 'Mind you, it tastes a bit tainted to me.'

Amalric laughed. 'No, thank you, Father. I'd… I'd better get on. My da's a bit indisposed, too, he's not up yet and… there's work to do and before that I have to help Mother with the pails.'

'Alright, lad. Off you go. The soul's enemy is idleness – as I believe St Benedict taught. And you may be wise not to drink; the taste really is poor.'

Amalric smiled his goodbye. He liked to chat to the priest each morning and afterwards watch him waddle down the path until the colour of his long cassock and the limestone walls became one in the shadows of the Saxon porch.

Amalric was grateful for the quiet that walking to the well offered. His thoughts amounted to contemplating his insecurities: the idea that life ahead seemed to be a blank, bleak, empty space; that his desire for romance and love would never be fulfilled; that his dreams of coloured windows would not come to fruition. Since his night in the tavern, his assured future as inheritor of his father's glazier business had suddenly evaporated like a morning mist but why, he couldn't remember. He felt afraid, of what, he didn't know. Only the tiny bright green specks of stoic little early spring flowers seemed to indicate a positive future.

When he arrived at the well, his mother was nowhere to be seen. Feeling thirsty, he lowered the well's pail deep down, raised it and scooped water into his hand, but it tasted foul. It was unusual. The water was well known for its purity. He tipped it away. The well had originated from a stream trickling out of the valley side. Long before present memory, it had been dug down deep to provide clean, sparkling water in even the worst drought. It probably accounted for the origin of the village. Now it was a deep hole, stone lined and topped with a superstructure of low stone walling and wood, and a flat wooden cover with a hinged section. Amalric hung his head far over the side. There was a foul stink. He looked around. Parts of a well-used pail lay on the ground, shattered into parts. No one had bothered to pick up the pieces for firewood. Under a bush in the nearby copse, he saw two wet, shiny, black objects. One seemed to be a dead bird, the other a large cat-like animal which spilled from a filthy log basket. Both wriggled with maggots and stank. Something had happened here. He looked further away and saw his mother and a couple of other women trudging towards the Manor House.

'Mother, what happened at the well? Where are you going?' Amalric asked when he caught up. His mother put down her pails. The other two women carried on.

'To the manor travellers' well. The water'll be clear there. There was devil's work at the village well.' She spoke quickly with a raised voice.

Amalric recognised anger in her. 'Devil's work?'

'Aye. And most of it Myrtle Ashe. The well top had been left open an' a bird had got in, followed by a cat. Both drowned and rotted. The stench was horrible. We must thank the Lord a child had not fallen in. It took Ned with his father's rope ladder to get 'em out. Caused a right to-do, it did. Myrtle stirred things up by saying the black animal was the devil in disguise an' the bird its helper. Then she said it was somthin' to do with pestilence. Well, you can imagine the commotion. Myrtle knew that word would stir things up. Some of the women went mad, throwin' pails all about, screamin'. I tried to calm things – told 'em it was just a cat an' a bird, the devil havin' better things to do. But that Myrtle takes a situation and wrings evil out of it.'

Gundred stopped to take a long breath. Amalric understood her anger.

'Come, son. Help me get water. I can get some for cleanin' from the brook behind us but it's got village waste in it an' it's not fit for drinkin', so we'll stock up at the manor travellers' well.'

Amalric arrived at the workshop before Ned Tynel but soon heard the familiar whistle.

'Mornin', Master Amalric,' Ned said as he opened the door, damp after a cursory wash and with a putrid aroma coming off his short tunic. 'Cool again, int it? It'll rain. The gardens still look waterlogged. Ma reckons that if the rain don't stop for a day or two we'll all die from a surfeit of water.'

'Mornin' Ned, you reek! And leave that flea-ridden beast outside.' Amalric suspected that Samson had had a good sniff, if not a lick, at the black corpses at the well.

'Aye. Sit there, Samson, outside the door, an' wait.' Samson obeyed. 'I 'ad to go down the well,' Ned said cheerfully, not realising that his young master knew. 'Ma made me. A bird an' a big rottin' cat was in it. Mistress Ashe said it was the devil in disguise an' we would rue the day we ignored it.'

Amalric curled his lips.

In the workshop, Ned began to dreamily pare excess wood off one of the crossbars. Amalric suspected that he would take off too much wood and when the hoped-for summer warmth dried it out, there would be rattles when the wind blew. But he hadn't the will to say something about it; there had been enough conflict today already. He turned to his shepherd window for distraction. He ran his long, thin, grazed finger over the smooth glass surface and traced the lead strips, called cames, which held the coloured pieces of glass together. He put his finger to his nose. It smelled clean, fresh with a metallic tang. In reality, the window lacked the finer skills of a master but, despite that, Amalric was proud of it and grateful for his father's confidence in him... or at least, he wanted to be.

It illustrated part of the Bible story that Father Wilfrid told every Christmas-time in the church and which the village folk enacted plays about. In it, a white angel hovered in a dark blue sky over two shepherds on a hill and pointed with one hand to a star in the sky and the other to the ground. The shepherds were being instructed to follow the star to find the Christ child, newly born and lying in a stable... but the hand pointing to the ground always bothered Amalric: it shouldn't be like that. It should point to the shepherds as tradition dictated, the way it was painted on the church walls. But Amalric had been instructed to do it that way by Old Elias, his grandfather, who had been a member of the examining committee of the Glaziers' Guild: a man who knew how to carve realistic faces on privy doors and make wonderful windows. How could the young Amalric disobey? Even his own father had approved the incongruity. Perversely, the old man had died soon afterwards. Amalric had worried that his chance of gaining his intermediate approval would be lost. However, the Guild had pronounced his window 'good', and granted him a pass. But the shame of passing despite creating something that was realistically wrong niggled at his pride and made him long to do something better... totally on his own. And what made it worse, Edwin taunted him, saying how surprised he was that his staid and boring elder brother had needed the help of an old man to pass.

An unexpected clicking of the door catch announced Amalric's father.

'I've decided to escape the women's stern faces and join you in here, Am. I don't know what's happened up at the well but your mother's in a reet dudgeon.'

He pulled his cloak tightly around himself and, ignoring Ned, joined his son in front of the coloured window. He put a hand on Amalric's shoulder and with his other hand also traced a lead came, the one that surrounded the glass piece with the questionable drawing.

'Eh, lad, your time'll come. With them Scots and French seen off, there's a chance for the country to settle at last. With you helping me, there might just be a chance to make some gradely windows for religious houses nearby.'

Amalric was not to be pacified. 'Aye. But why did I have to do this window Grandfather's way?' One day, he would insert a new piece of glass with a repositioned hand.

'Another time, lad. You've a lot to learn yet.'

The door clicked again. Berta popped her dark, curly head round the edge.

'Ma says come to breakfast.'

Elias turned and Amalric saw his father's face blanch as he looked at Berta. Something from his tavern evening stirred in Amalric's memory yet again. He watched as his father stretched out a rough hand and tumbled his little daughter's dark curls. She smiled and tugged at his jerkin.

'Come on, Da. Ma's got one of her angries on.'

'Bless you, Berta, my grand little girl.'

'Are you alright, Da?' said Amalric. Something was wrong.

'Aye, lad. Just lookin' at Berta. She's young, ain't she?'

'Yes, Da,' said Amalric.

Chapter Three

After the second day of clearing the workshop, Amalric and Ned were glad to set off with Elias to walk to Meaux Abbey. They were replete with Gundred's rich porridge and felt optimistic about new work. Amalric noted with some surprise that although the air was damp, rain was holding off. The route to Meaux went up the neat main road of the village, past the Manor House with its imposing surrounding stone walls and the little travellers' well, onto the rough pathways of the valley, through woods and up onto the breezy Holderness Plain. In the far distance lay the Yorkshire Wolds but today the hills were totally hidden, as were the farmlands, by the thick mist that washed everything into a laundered greyness. When they reached it, it forced the three of them to tread carefully so as not to be misled onto paths off the side of the road: paths which led temptingly into narrow little valleys dappled yellow with primroses and glinting with streamlets. Samson, however, was not constrained, scents being his vision. He left Ned's knees and ran in and out of the misty depths, exploring every tuft of grass and animal dropping with intensity. Every now and then, eyes bright with expectation, he dropped a stick in front of Ned to throw ahead.

Today Elias was taking advantage of the gentle pace forced upon them. The day was warming. The mist would disappear eventually and the minute balls of water clinging to their woollen cloaks would dry off. Their cold, wet feet would dry and warm up.

'Look 'ere, they'll soon be flowering,' called Elias to Amalric and Ned, having spotted short, dark green spikey leaves of Lenten lilies at the side of the path, as a pale light seeped through the mist and diffused over them. 'Your mother loves 'em, Am.'

His son only nodded. Their progress was too slow. Amalric was eager to get to Meaux and talk about windows. Ned, however, was thrilled and smiled broadly. The gentle pace suited him: he had never been this far out of Warren Horesby before.

'Aye, Master,' he said, 'and look at them little yellow uns. It's like they're creepin' out of the valley.'

'Aye. We'll pick some with roots for Gundred on our way back and she can put 'em in the back garden – and some for your mother, Ned. She'd like you to do that.'

Amalric dropped behind, thoughts swirling. He liked the idea of giving flowers to a woman. It was romantic. Flowers could say what words couldn't. This morning, he had so much wanted to be alone with his father on the walk to Meaux, to goad him into talking about relationships. Elias, when in the mood, would talk freely, and with a bit of persuasion would go on to talk about romance. His parents' conversations could be stormy but love always lay at the heart of their partnership. He knew that beyond the conventions of marriage, true love could bring excitement with a wife. Yet he lacked knowledge. It bothered him, especially with the strange sensations he experienced on seeing Nesta... a servant. His mother wouldn't like that! There were so many rules to abide by and so many old women who watched a young man's every move. It was difficult to know how to behave with a girl. His younger brother knew far more about love, but Amalric didn't want to be like him. Edwin took no heed of courtship conventions, nor the watchful busybodies. He'd discovered women with his drinking friends and their whores in nearby towns. His boasting sickened Amalric.

Elias' woollen cap, intended to keep the cold off his thinning hair, slipped back a little and his cloak loosened. His son recognised he was about to start reminiscing and was dismayed. The journey would take even longer. He dropped back further, sullen and brooding but not out of earshot. Ned had never heard Elias talk about his younger days and was an avid listener. With the joy of the elderly repeating stories of their youth, Elias told of how he had been a glazier's apprentice with Master Robert of York. Mischievously playing on Ned's gullibility, his hands vigorously amplified horrors, such as workers being cut in half by falling glass or tumbles from scaffolding high up the minster windows. Ned's eyes widened with amazement and revulsion, stopping in his tracks as he imagined the scenes in garish detail. Amalric caught up and saw Ned's pale face. Glancing at his father, he made a loud, exaggerated sigh. Elias seemed to take the hint, looked a little chastened and began to tell more realistic tales.

Meaux Abbey came into view as the little group cleared a small copse and rounded a bend. Ned gasped at the sight. The buildings rose out of the flat plain, pale and ethereal, with the abbey church tower rising higher than anything else as far as the eye could see – the last wisps of mist clung to its roof. The buildings shone clean and glinted in the fresh, weak sun. Elias said the last stone had been placed less than 100 years previously. Amalric saw tears in his father's eyes and recognised his devotion to the abbey. Even though he had served his apprenticeship in the grander minster and churches of York, and while his home church was in Warren Horesby, he knew his father's deeper spiritual thoughts rested at Meaux. He, Amalric, had developed no such spiritual affiliations; he simply wanted to make windows.

The villages around Meaux, such as Warren Horesby, had for years provided a constant supply of workers to serve the abbey. Today, men and women could be seen working with the lay brothers on the land outside the precinct: in the orchards where the first blossoms were peeking from tight buds, on sheep fields dotted with rounded, pregnant ewes, and by fish ponds.

The pathway that Amalric, Elias and Ned had travelled joined another much busier one where they met other folk shambling along, delivering provisions. Children sat on top of carts while their fathers and older sons, like Amalric and Ned, walked at the side or held on to the reins of lumbering animals. Young women walked with skirts hitched up in tight belts, their ankles showing, to avoid mud and animal droppings. Some had baskets on their heads. This roadway ended in a fine stone bridge over a moat which encircled the abbey precinct. Everyone eventually clattered over the bridge, barely disturbing the elegant swans below.

Once over the bridge and through the perimeter wall of the abbey church, the objective for new windows could be seen in its entirety, raised as it was on a small mound in the centre of the precinct, dominating all the other buildings. Colourful lichens patched over the old stones. Warren Horesby church was tiny and humble by comparison.

Amalric, Elias and Ned veered off the busy, manure-muddied trail to follow one formed of eggshell-smooth cobbles, neatly placed and shiny with moisture. It led to the western end of the church. There they found Abbot Hugh, hauling on the great wooden west door to close it. He turned, saw them and smiled.

'Welcome, my friends! Elias, how good to see you and with Amalric, too. You always make a good team.'

Elias whipped off his cap in respect.

Amalric was comfortably familiar with the Cistercian order and smiled at the senior cleric, but he knew that Ned would be confused – he would find the importance of Abbot Hugh hard to reconcile with the elderly man's grubby appearance of poverty. His long habit of loosely woven, coarse Yorkshire wool was creamy coloured but turned deep grey at the bottom where his sandled feet had splashed up mud. His tonsured head, however, did set him apart from normal folk – though the close-shaven, shiny pink central circle, surrounded by neat grey hair, was not at all like Christ's spikey, bloody crown of thorns which it was meant to represent. A small wooden cross on a fraying thin rope hung from his neck. Ned gaped.

'And who are these?' Abbot Hugh said, looking at Ned and his hound.

Elias placed a hand on Ned's shoulder. 'This is my young assistant, Ned Tynel, Abbot, a willing lad who tries hard,' he replied with an impish smile implying a degree of inability in him. 'The stinking bundle of mangy fur is his pet, Samson.'

Ned bowed his head nervously but Amalric noticed a slight smile in response to the abbot's vibrant grin, playful eye and deeply wrinkled face. He watched him finally won over when the elderly man stroked Samson behind an ear and the dog responded by leaning adoringly into the lanolin folds of the abbot's flowing garment.

'Well, it's wonderful to see you all,' said the abbot, enthusiastically. 'You have come at a good time. We're preparing the abbey church for Easter. Passion Sunday is, as you know, in only three days' time, and then, in two weeks, our Easter celebrations. It is but a short time in which to get everything done. We make everything spotless and glistening, and strip the altar bare for Good Friday and the crucifixion of our Lord. Then we have a good old celebration on the Sunday for His resurrection, the coming to renewed life.' He put a hand conspiratorially to the side of his mouth. 'More than a little abbey wine may be consumed, though as good Cistercians we ought not to imbibe to excess… but it is for medicinal purposes and cheers us no end.' He laughed loudly. 'For now, I may be able to offer you hot ale specially brewed for the season. It will be watered on account of it being Lent but good nevertheless.'

Elias smiled at this. The abbey hot ale was very much to his taste. He liked it strong but even so, today's weaker version would be welcome after the long walk. Amalric feared further delays.

'Come to the warm refectory, all of you, for refreshments. You must be weary from your journey... and stiff, eh, Elias?' His own aching bones clearly made him aware of others' infirmities. Abbot Hugh then looked at Amalric with a knowing expression. 'And there is someone there *you* may wish to meet.'

Chapter Four

The refectory was a large, simple building on the south side of the abbey cloister. Its stone roof and walls boasted little in the way of decoration, but the smell of wood smoke emanating from the slightly open door evidenced warmth even before Elias, Ned and Amalric entered. Without being told, Ned took a piece of rope from his jerkin and tied Samson to a metal loop set in the outside wall. The dog flopped down disconsolately. Once inside, the travellers saw a large central hearth burning brightly with logs. A few sleepy, elderly monks sat upon benches to the side. Nearby, a flight of steps went up to a low gallery, prompting memories for Amalric of his schooldays. When a pupil, he had seen this very room full of monks eating silently while listening to another in the gallery reading aloud from the Bible. He glanced at Ned. The young assistant's eyes were wide with amazement. This clean, homely room for many monks and visitors was so different from his own small, simple home.

At this time of day, no one sat at the long, scrubbed tables except a slim figure with a pile of manuscripts in front of him. He wore a long robe of finer wool than the abbot's, dyed black and closed at the neck and wrists. The edges of the neck and cuffs were noticeably sharp and unfrayed. His face was obscured by a thin ginger fringe that flopped over his brow as he bent forward and his finger traced words on a manuscript. A pot beaker of ale at his side stood untouched.

Abbot Hugh moved towards him. 'This is Thurston of Oxford, lately employed by your own Lord de Horesby as physician. He sits with manuscripts in the warmth rather than the cold library. Doctors of medicine feel the chill rather more than monks.' Abbot Hugh grinned but only momentarily. 'Old Horesby is fearful of the coming pestilence, it seems.'

Thurston did not look up.

'Thurston!' shouted the abbot. 'Leave your studies a moment, I pray; we have guests and you'll want to know them, I'm sure, seeing that you'll be living no more than a village-length apart.'

Eyes scowled through the fringe. 'Oh, I'm so sorry. I get lost in manuscripts.' The accent was not that of a northern man. Flustered, he rose to shake a hand cursorily with Elias. His other remained on the manuscript to keep the place. He then went back to his studies. Amalric, disappointed, had caught but a brief glimpse of the physician's face but thought he had seen a slight look of recognition pass briefly over it. The refined fingers, freckles and ginger hairs on the back of the hand looked vaguely familiar.

Abbot Hugh's mouth slipped from the curve of pleasantness to a straight line of disdain at the lack of good manners. 'Humph! Ah, here comes Father Luke. It's his turn to be the refectory server today.'

A tall monk wearing a habit that hung from youthful shoulders appeared silently, as if from nowhere. He carried a tray with a pottery jug, beakers and a plate of bread with sheep's cheese, which he placed on a table separate from the physician.

'Thank you, Luke,' said the abbot, and turned to the little group. 'Now, all of you, sit and eat. I must attend to my work. We will talk later, Elias.' He turned and left with a disapproving glance at Thurston.

They ate in silence, enjoying the warmth and mindful not to disturb the figure so obviously absorbed in his texts. Amalric knew his father was keen to discuss his ideas for new windows with the abbot, but also that ale and copious amounts of bread and cheese would lie heavily on his stomach. He would be slow to move. It would be beneficial for all their sakes for him to rest awhile.

'Am, go check on the workshop,' Elias said, unsurprisingly, 'I've not used it for a while. It perhaps needs tidyin'. Ned, go with him or have a wander round, see what an abbey feels like. I'll meet you both by and by in the church.'

Ned sped off with obvious relief, to untie Samson and explore. Amalric was pleased to see Ned speed away, hoping he would meet the lay brothers who were as uneducated as him. As manual workers and craftsmen, they were denied books and the finer points of worship but had a devoutness that matched Ned's own naïve view of faith. Ned would be comfortable with them.

Amalric went to the workshop. It was a lean-to structure on the south side of the abbey, open to the air save for low stone walls and a sloping, heather-thatched roof. The ground needed sweeping and spiders' webs swung grey with dust – but for now, all was in order and Amalric, in any case, was far more interested in the ginger-headed physician. He decided to act a little daringly. He jogged back to the refectory, where the quiet peace was being disturbed by the clattering sounds of food preparation. He seated himself abruptly on the bench opposite the doctor. Thurston had one hand covering an ear and the other tracing words on a page.

'Hello, again,' Amalric said, now slightly embarrassed at intruding.

The physician looked up. Hunched over the manuscript, Thurston had looked old but on seeing his smooth and freckled face, Amalric guessed him to be only ten years older than himself. Red-rimmed hazel eyes with pale lashes looked up and stared deeply into Amalric's own deep brown ones as if searching for something.

'Hello, again,' Amalric repeated, somewhat unnerved by the scrutiny and unable to hold the gaze himself.

'Oh... er... good day,' Thurston kept his finger marking his place. The vellum was dry and brown with age, the Latin script faded. Notes in a darker ink littered the margins of the page. Small sketches of human body parts were among them.

'I can read Latin,' blurted out Amalric.

'You can?' The hazel eyes widened.

'Yes, but not well.'

Thurston's brow raised with interest as Amalric's enthusiasm continued.

'When I was younger I was taught Latin by the monks here. I was allowed to look at some of the manuscripts but though I could read, I couldn't really understand what they were about – only the one we have at home.' He looked down at the page. It was upside down to him, but he was able to pick out a leg with dark marks and a scribble. 'Why would someone add notes and drawings to what is already written?'

'I think because, like me, they were researching disease. Spare vellum was in short supply and so they just made use of the spaces to keep their ideas and thoughts together in one place. Sometimes, I find them useful.'

'What are you looking at now?'

'It's a book about very ancient pestilences. Pestilences can come back after hundreds of years. See, someone has illustrated the disease the author is speaking of.' Thurston pointed to the leg, then at a chest with spots dotted all over it. 'But I can't make out the true nature of the diseases.' He sat back and sighed, eager to change the subject. 'How is it we will be living so close?'

'Well, our home and my father's glazing business is in Warren Horesby. Opposite the church.' Amalric relaxed, crossing his arms on the table and leaning forward to await further conversation.

'Ah. I have recently taken up residence in a little cottage in the grounds of Horesby Manor, near the gate. I've been doing some research here, as you see.' With effort, he thumped the heavy parchment pages shut. Dust puffed. 'I only qualified recently. I trained in physic at the University of Oxford. Coming from the south, I still feel an outsider. It will take me a while to learn how you speak. While I use the same language, you say words in a different way – add your own. But *your* own speech is clearer to me – it must be the Latin which has affected it.' He paused. 'I know little of life in this area. I have come to the abbey a few times before today but have ventured only once into your village, to the tavern – and that in bad weather and near darkness.'

Realisation dawned. Amalric was now sure that Thurston had recognised his father and most likely himself. 'Ah, so that's why...'

Thurston, on the other hand, was warming to his own subject. 'I believe the healing work of your village folk is mainly done by your women and the priest.'

'Aye, physic men are rarely seen where we live. My mother and sister have the healing skills and are proud of it. Father Wilfrid is good at some healing things but mainly tries to heal our souls... but I'm sure they'd all speak to *you*,' Amalric said and smiled, encouraged by the earnest, honest face to attempt irony.

Thurston became dour but spoke with increasing passion. 'I'm afraid they may need some help soon. A pestilence is working its way up the country. It has come from Normandy. Nothing is a barrier to it, not the sea, marshes, moors nor mountains, nothing. It has ravaged the south of England, moved up country, and I hear there may have been a few cases recently in King's-Town on Hull, but it could be hearsay.'

'Hull?' Amalric sat back. His mouth opened wordlessly. So close! Recent events whirred in his mind: the nebulous tavern talk, the incident at the well, his mother's reaction to his father's concerns.

'Yes.'

Thurston ignored Amalric's obvious shock and continued. 'Nothing to fear at the moment. In any case, it needs time to take hold before spreading wildly. Lord de Horesby is a man of foresight and is paying for my services in the hope that I may be able to save his family… if it comes… and additionally help his tenants. He fears for their work on his land. My fear is that I will not be able to stop it destroying wealthy families, let alone poor ones. That is why you find me here.'

Amalric found his voice. 'Have you found a cure?'

'Not yet. I've spent weeks searching the abbey's library: fifty books of physic! I hoped to find something to enlighten me as to a cure or preventative. Father Luke has helped me find the manuscripts and the infirmarer, a very experienced man, has helped me interpret the herbals. The religious orders have excellent knowledge of healing, you know. Both here and in Oxford, I have gone over Galen and Aristotle, and from before them, Hippocrates, looked at the works of obscure writers I've never heard of before and, because the disease is said to have started way back in Arab lands about ten years ago, I have looked at the Arab encyclopaedias translated into Latin…'

'But…'

Thurston was not to be diverted. He raised his arms dramatically with hopelessness.

'I've studied past movements of the planets. The humours. Faith. I have found accounts of disease that equate with this pestilence, and scores of spurious cures but I have found no *real* cure.'

Amalric looked at Thurston wide-eyed. The passionate outburst disturbed him… the ancient names, foreign lands… the concerned frown. His curiosity became a cold fear in his chest. What it all meant slithered into place like the slide of a new window into its frame. Ale into table cracks. They could all die.

'What's it like – this disease?' Amalric felt his face blanch.

'There, I have frightened you and for that I am sorry.' His companion's face had turned pale. 'My concerns run away with me sometimes and I forget that those without my knowledge become fearful. Please forgive me. The symptoms are bad but need not concern you.'

Amalric felt young, uneducated, inadequate before this cultured and knowledgeable man. Then... after a pause, Thurston slapped the table with the flat of both hands.

'So...'

Amalric was slightly startled.

'So, you were taught Latin! That is unusual for a tradesman.'

'Well, I'm not all that good... but it will help, in time, with Latin inscriptions in the windows I make.'

'Ah, yes. Windows. Mm. I know little of the art of glass but I have seen wonderful windows. Latin will be useful for you. We must spend some time conversing or reading in the language. You must show me the manuscript you say you have at home.'

Amalric began to feel the warmth of a new friendship. He nodded, smiling, and stood up from the bench. 'I have to meet my father in the church now; would you like to come... if you've finished your research, that is?'

'Yes, I would. The clatter of pans is disruptive to my thoughts and there is no more to learn, anyway,' Thurston admitted with reluctance. He ran his hand over the smooth leather cover. 'In fact, I'm going back to Horesby Manor this afternoon. But first, I need to collect my order of medications and herbs from the infirmary. I'll meet you in the abbey church and afterwards mayhap I could beg to be allowed to journey with you.'

'Aye. Of course.'

They left the refectory in silence – Amalric with a developing fear but ghoulish interest in the unknown, and Thurston, head bowed and deep in thought.

Amalric approached the abbey church, the place where monks worshipped many times a day. It was big, the largest building on the abbey site. It stood high and wide, like a sturdy rock, with windows to let in God's light. To Amalric it was unpretentious, with little superfluous ornamentation, beautifully proportioned – alive and splendid.

He saw Ned and Samson leave the company of a lay brother and watched them draw close. Ned's eyes were roaming from the high roof to the ground, his mouth open in amazement. Amalric waited for him by the west door, hoping he wouldn't miss his footing and fall over.

'Ee, Master Am, I've never seen owt like this afore. It's grand.'

Once more, Ned tied Samson to a ring. The dog slumped down by the west door, put his head on his front paws and was instantly asleep.

'Aye, it is. The whole building's in the shape of a cross. Just wait till you see the inside. See, there's a small door set into the big door here. We can go through it. You go first. Mind your head.'

The midday sun broke through clouds just as Ned, with bent knees, passed through the door. Before him on either side, light streamed through windows that soared upwards and narrowed in a curve to a point at the top. Men's voices sang. Amalric knew Ned had never seen such a sight nor heard such a sound before. It was all glorious, not at all like Warren Horesby church where the light was meagre and the singing without skill. Ned was captivated and unable to move further. He held his breath, and his eyes widened. Amalric tugged him forward. Ned looked down. He was puzzled.

'Ee, Master Amalric, me feet are disappearing into the floor.'

'No, Ned, it's just sunlight on shiny tiles. See, the pattern – circles within circles, and diamond shapes too, yellow, green and brown. All shining.'

'Oh, aye.' He shuffled with embarrassment.

Then Amalric prompted him to look further into the building. 'Do you see the cross shape? It's to honour Jesus' crucifixion.'

Ned's eyes scanned the stone walls, smoothed with grey plaster, forming a space representing the long shaft of a cross. Half way down, this was intersected by two wide aisles at right angles signifying the crossbeam.

'At the crossing there, you'll be able to look up and see the inside of the tower that we saw in the distance, long before we got here.'

Ned saw where the tower was, but for the moment was content to look at the fine wooden roof that covered the remainder of the building. Birds swooped high up around it, their chatter breaking through the singing.

Amalric continued. 'Beyond, at the top part of the cross, you can just make out the sanctuary where only the monks can go. There's a curved wall around a huge altar with a plain cloth, and plain gold candlesticks.'

Ned's eyes probed rapidly, forward, upward, side to side, to spaces beyond spaces with light coming from windows he couldn't actually see. He nodded agitatedly, unable to comment. His face began to look glum.

Amalric realised that the understated, elegant but monumental man-made beauty was unsettling Ned. He had only ever seen the uncomplicated space of Warren Horesby church.

'Come, let's look closer at a window.'

He grabbed at Ned's sleeve again and pulled him to a window where the sun shone through. Most of the glass was colourless and had interweaving geometric designs, but occasionally there was a tiny pale blue or green piece and, on some squares, there was a lightly painted leaf or flower. Ned's good eyes picked out a tiny Lenten lily.

'I wonder if Master Elias has seen it?' he said, eventually managing to speak.

'I wonder,' said Amalric, and smiled, aware that his father would know every inch of the windows.

'Ee! Master Amalric, this is the most beautiful building I've ever seen. If I go to 'eaven, I want it to be like this. Do you think I'll go to 'eaven or the other place? I'm real scared that I might go into the fiery furnace and burn for ever.' His eyes grew large with fear. 'I'm not clever; it makes me clumsy, lazy, I know — everybody says so.'

Ned's sudden realisation of himself tugged at Amalric's compassionate nature.

'Your heart is good, Ned. I'm sure you'll go to heaven. You might have a bit of time in Purgatory first, like most of us, but maybe that won't be so bad.'

Ned looked as though he wasn't so sure.

Amalric could see his father with Abbot Hugh under the central tower, looking relaxed and in good humour. They both stood near rough scaffolding holding a platform high up with freshly carved, creamy stonework upon it. From below, Amalric couldn't make out what the carving was, but he was surprised to see such finery in the church. He and Ned made their way towards them. As they drew near, the singing came to an end and they could hear Abbot Hugh and Elias talking. Their voices spread easily around the huge spaces. Whispers were as loud and clear as normal words.

'It would be good to have the saints in the windows around the nave and the Virgin Mary depicted as the queen of heaven and earth, in the choir area. Some windows in York Minster are very colourful but then those particular windows were by monks not of our order. There are some Cistercian windows there, though, from years back.'[3] The abbot was silent a while then spoke with tight lips and furrowed brow as if daring himself to go on. 'Elias, I'm beginning to feel that God would not have given us such colour if He had not wanted us to see His light through it. But... it goes against...' He bent and whispered a confidence to Elias, then said louder, 'I hear you can paint a colour on the glass.'

'Aye, Abbot Hugh,' said Elias with passion in his voice. 'There is a silver compound. When it's painted on glass and fired, it becomes yellow or brownish.'

'Oh, really?'

---

[3] The Five Sisters' Window (n16) thirteenth century, north wall of the north transept, York Minster.

Amalric smiled at the intelligent interest shown in his father's work.

'It means you can add colour without cutting a new piece of glass. To change blue to green or add shape, like. I've always liked to experiment, try things out. Not too much, mind. You 'ave to stick to the rules. Our Amalric is learned, thanks to you, and talented. In time, he'll be like me.'

A surge of pride swept through Amalric. It was a passing comment, but to be spoken of in such a way by his father to Abbot Hugh was praise indeed. Amalric greatly admired his father, his skill and love of beauty. With Abbot Hugh, Elias was an equal. Not just because their faith said that all men were equal but also because they were equal in stature in their individual worlds. The abbot was confident enough to share his innermost feelings with Amalric's father and his father likewise with the abbot; God and beauty united them.

'And we'll need more workspace. Make the workshop bigger… it's a big assignment. And the cost… it'll take a lot of glass,' said Elias as they drifted to seats by the wall of the nave, becoming animated as their conversation deepened. Abbot Hugh was nodding a great deal.

Amalric was thrilled. Windows! Big windows!

The singing started up again in the choir, drowning out the voices of Elias and the abbot. The beautiful sound bounced off the arches and pillars as monks' voices sang the 'Song of Mary'.[4] Ned and Amalric stood transfixed. The confidence of future work increased Amalric's pleasure. The music seemed to enter him. Then, gradually the singing began to be lost in another sound. It came gently at first and then louder. The choristers became silent. A rumbling came from somewhere distant, not overland, more like underground. Then the glass windows rattled, gently. This was a common sound on windy days in

---

[4] The 'Song of Mary' is an ancient Christian hymn taken from Luke's Gospel (1:46-55). It is Mary's hymn of praise to God, known as the Magnificat.

buildings like this, where the glass might have been loosely fitted into the stone, but this was different, unnerving, a continuous rattle, not coming and going like in a Yorkshire gale... and it was getting more forceful.

Everyone in the cathedral stood listening and watching... but for what? They didn't know. As they strained their ears for anything that would give a clue as to what was happening, the noise gave way to a closer, louder reverberation like a huge cart with massive, rumbling wheels being pulled by giant oxen up towards them from deep in the earth. The fine tiled pavement began to move up and down and side to side as if the cart was about to break through. Tiles cracked. Ned clung on to Amalric, screaming, and Amalric hung on to a broad stone pillar. He could see his father and the abbot blurring with a shaking movement. Monks were running and being thrown to the ground in a flurry of undyed wool. Birds flew frantically about, twittering angrily. Feathers drifted. Mice and rats squeaked and scurried out of their hiding holes. A splintering sound meant that glass somewhere was falling out of a window. Amalric heard the noise of cracking stone followed by a pain in his head. He felt suddenly sick. Then all became blackness for him.

Gradually the blackness surrounding Amalric became grey and he became aware of daylight through his eyelids. 'Amalric, Amalric,' someone called him. But his name became confused with the last words that the monks had sung – '*Deposuit potentes de sede et exaltavit humiles...*' He knew those words. 'Amalric!' The Latin words drifted away and he opened his eyes to see his father leaning over him with a blood-spotted kerchief in his hand. All around was chaos and on the floor lay fragments of stone and glass, sheets of parchment with words of hymns, candlesticks, cleaning brushes and buckets, and feathers from unhappy birds.

'Da, what happened?'

'An earth tremble, son. A big one. Big for this part of the world, anyway. You got hit with a piece of stone angel from the scaffolding platform. It wasn't very big but enough to knock you out. It's over there. Fortunately, as the angel fell, it hit the pillar and shattered into pieces. It was one of the bits of angel wing that hit you. I'm afraid you'll have bad bruises. See your blood here.' He waved the kerchief. 'Ned pushed you to one side and saved you from worse.'

Amalric put his hand to his head and felt a large bump, sticky with blood, next to the lessening one of a few days ago. He could see parts of a stone angel littering the floor tiles. Standing among the pieces was a quivering Ned, his face contorted with fear. A wild barking was heard.

'I must find Samson,' Ned stammered, but could not move.

Elias carried on, 'It's thrown the poor monks into a reet tizzy. They were tossed all over the choir, robes ending up around their waists. Some were in a reet predicament – showin' bare backsides!' Amalric recalled through his addled mind that out of frugality and simplicity the monks wore no undergarments beneath their robes. His father would have had seen unbecoming sights!

Abbot Hugh, with grazed hands and a torn habit sleeve, staggered through the chaos and swirling clouds of dust to his guests. 'My dear friends, how are you? Oh, Amalric, blood! Are you badly hurt? Thank God you have not all been killed. Come, leave the building at once lest the earth tremble again. You must go to the infirmary.'

Thurston appeared, shadowy in the swirling dust, and saw his new acquaintances staggering towards him and the small west door. Elias had his arms around Amalric, blood still slowly oozing from his head wound. Ned followed hesitantly, by this time shaking uncontrollably and with tears flowing down his cheeks. Thurston covered him with his cloak and held him in an effort to calm him as they walked. Samson was still tied up. His barking became furious when he saw Ned and strained to get to him. The sound pierced Amalric's head. The abbot untied the rope and Samson leapt at Ned, relief and joy obvious in his bounding strides and focused eyes. Ned staggered at the impact of his hound then hugged him tightly and buried his head in the mangy fur. The abbot guided them, over cobblestones no longer neat, to the infirmary. Like all the other buildings, it had suffered in the earth tremble but being sturdily built and low, had fared better than the church.

Amalric's wounds were cleaned and dressed by an infirmarer monk, hovered over by Thurston, and it was not long before he felt much better and his thoughts cleared. Afterwards, Father Luke served them again with ale as he had done in the refectory, but this time with shaking hands.

'I fear the worst,' said Abbot Hugh, looking at Elias. 'This was the biggest tremble I've felt in my long life. When the ground moves in this way and angels topple, it must be a portent. I really wonder, Elias, whether I ought not to have been talking to you about making elaborate windows with human figures. When the Cistercian order was formed, we swore a vow of poverty, simplicity and work. But our wool production has flourished and we have more money, so I wanted to beautify the church to thank God. The stone angel that fell was on the platform, new and ready to be slotted in: a fallen angel. Maybe I should remain with simple decoration.'

Elias remained silent.

'Do you know what the monks were singing when the ground began to shake?' Abbot Hugh answered his own question, *Deposuit potentes de sede et exaltavit humiles.*'

Elias looked blank.

Amalric, while resting, heard the conversation, understood and felt compelled to translate. 'He has brought down the powerful from their thrones, and lifted up the lowly.'[5]

'Yes, you are right,' said the abbot, astonishment breaking through his worried tone of voice. 'You have remembered that which we taught you. Good.' He turned to Elias with dismay. 'I

[5] Luke 1:52.

fear I have attempted to be too mighty and God is punishing me.'

'No… that can't be right, Hugh,' said Elias.

Amalric knew his father was about to challenge the abbot's beliefs. He could see it in his look of defiance. After all, the assignment was about to be lost. The opportunity to earn good money was slipping away, but more important perhaps to his ageing father would be the loss of a chance to make something of lasting beauty. Amalric felt indignation simmer within himself. It had seemed so good, big windows… now nothing.

Elias breathed deeply, holding in his disappointment. 'Why would God deny you the beauty of glass when His own light shines through it reet wonderfully, and why shouldn't His saints, who are nearer to God than we ordinary mortals, be depicted with that light shining through them?'

'Elias, Elias, I only know that God's message will be fully revealed in time. For now, we will pray for forgiveness, repair our church, heal the injured – I hope no one has been killed – and leave new windows until a later time.' The abbot studied his friend's crumpled face. 'I am sorry, Elias.' Then he turned to Amalric. 'I am sorry, Amalric, my boy; it would have been a good opportunity for you. You are upset. Have you pain? No. I see it is disappointment.'

Amalric wondered if he and his father had also wanted too much. Was it really wrong to want to create something simply beautiful?

Thurston added to the gloom. 'I have to say, the earth trembles worry me but not for the same reason. They can loosen all sorts of evil miasmas that drift upwards out of the earth's putrid bowels. It happened way beyond these lands, years ago. I fear not God's message in this, but further palls of disease that might have been released.'

Chapter Five

Five travellers left Meaux Abbey in twilight – Elias, Amalric, Ned, Samson and Thurston. With a rising moon, they made their way carefully on pathways strewn with branches weakened by age and brought down by the earth tremble. It was late to be journeying, but Thurston had insisted they wait until they were all well enough to walk home and, in any case, four and a dog would probably be enough to deter opportunist thieves. They were a sorry sight: Amalric with bandaged head; Ned, with Samson loping at his side and a thick woollen blanket from the abbey's guest house around his shoulders; Elias, grim-faced with bitter disappointment at returning without a commission, and Thurston, head down, pensively lost in thought.

By the time they approached Warren Horesby, the moon was high, suspended in a patch of starry sky. They wondered what damage they might make out. The first building they glimpsed was the Manor House. The moonlight glinted on the roof tiles, revealing dark spaces where one or two had fallen off. Further on, they had to step gingerly over stones where part of the old manor wall had collapsed. Brushing aside his fringe, Thurston peered through the gap and pointed to a small thatched cottage nestling among small bushes and weeds.

'I have been lucky; my new home seems to have been spared the effects of the tremble. I hope you find the same.' His eyes rested on Amalric. 'May I visit you on the morrow? I would like to check your health after your being knocked unconscious at the abbey.'

'Aye,' Amalric managed a slight grin. 'It'll be your first proper journey into the village. Our home is the last one, down at the bottom, opposite the church. You won't be able to miss it. It has a coloured window with a sign above.'

'You'll be very welcome,' confirmed Elias. 'New friends only bring good. Goodnight, doctor.'

Thurston smiled and lifted his robe slightly, revealing fine leather boots, and picked his way over debris to get to his home.

Elias, Amalric and Ned continued on downwards to the moonlit village where shadowy figures stoically tidied as best they could while the silvery light lasted.

Ned's mother, Alice Tynel, was the only person alert to travellers, peering anxiously from the dark doorway of her home. When she saw her son, she rushed out.

'Eee, right glad I am to see you, lad,' she said, as Ned staggered towards her. She ignored Elias and Amalric. 'We had a tremble here in the village today so I guessed you had one at Meaux. What with you gettin' those black creatures out of the well, then a tremble, I feared for what might have happened to you. There's been evil around here right enough. Come inside, lad.'

She put out her arms ready for a pale-faced Ned to fall into them, but as he was about to, he checked himself and turned to Amalric. He took a small piece of stone from inside his tunic.

'This is part of what hit you, Master Amalric. The stone shattered when it hit the ground.' It was a piece of angel's wing, the tip of one feather carved from creamy limestone. 'I thought you might care to have it.'

Amalric was stunned by the gesture. The stone was small enough to hold in the palm of his hand and though he could barely see it in the dimness, his sensitive fingertips could feel the feathered shape. 'Thank you, Ned. It's beautiful. And a reminder of today.'

Ned smiled, obviously pleased that his gift had been well-received. Then he allowed himself to be encircled by his mother, and they and Samson disappeared into the gloom of their home.

Amalric held up the little stone chipping in front of his father. 'Who would have thought that something so beautifully made could hold such danger for me? And who would have thought that Ned knew I would value the gift? He knows me better than I thought he did... and to my shame, this morning I harboured mean thoughts of him.'

'Aye, lad, but nothin' that a confession to Father Wilfrid won't put right, I'm sure.'

It amazed Amalric that such fine carving was intended for high up, where only God could see the exquisite workmanship. He could almost sense the calloused hands, with broken fingernails and stone dust beneath, that had carved it. If windows became taller, filling the spaces high up in church walls, would they be as exquisite for God alone?

At the bottom of the hill there was no obvious harm to the church or mill. In the moonlight they could see little damage to their own home. The loss of a little thatch and daub was all. A look into the deeply shadowed workshop showed no sign of obvious destruction there either.

'You'll check each glass sheet in daylight, eh, lad?' Elias said to his son. 'Your grandfather made good solid racks to hold glass steady but a rattlin' from the tremble might have cracked a few.'

Amalric nodded. He was feeling very tired.

Elias clicked open the house door. 'In you go, lad, let your mother see to you. You look as though you need some attention from 'er.' He sighed. 'I'd like to go to the tavern but there'll be nobody there this night. I might've been able to lighten the mood with talk of bare flesh on thin legs on full view in the abbey as the tremble struck. Strikes me we all need a laugh. Ee, but then, lad, you might've been killed.' He shuddered at the precariousness of life. 'I think I'll see 'ow the sheep have fared. There's enough moonlight. You go inside, lad, to your mother.'

Amalric knew the sheep would not have suffered unduly. Still, he knew his father would be reassured to see them: watching them gave him the conviction that life would continue in the way it had always done, watched over by Jesus Christ, the Good Shepherd.

Elias returned to the house but did not speak. Matilde was stirring the contents of a pot of ointment ready to fill smaller pots which littered the table – a sure sign that bumps and bruises had occurred among the village folk during the tremble. The twins hovered around Amalric with ghoulish interest, especially Berta. Gundred was fussing, lifting the bandage around his head.

'Well… two bumps now on this soft head of yours. What's this them monks put on your head? It doesn't look very helpful to me. There's nothin' on that dressing but a simple salve with no herbs. It's nowt like mine.'

'Ooo, there's a bump like an egg,' gloated Berta. She put a finger up to feel it but Gundred knocked it away. 'Go to bed, Berta, there'll be work to do tomorrow – clearin' up.'

Berta and Bennet both retreated, sulkily looking at Amalric under dark curls.

Amalric smiled bravely for them. Then, while glancing at Matilde, he said to his mother, 'Lord de Horesby's physician advised the monks.'

Matilde interrupted softly, just a little afraid to contradict her mother. 'Well, maybe, Ma, it will heal without herbs. I've heard that some of these doctors of physic have new ideas. They're very learned and must know more than we do.'

'Nonsense, girl!' Gundred was as annoyed by the comment as Matilde expected her to be. 'I've been learnin' about these things all my years since childhood, not just a few years at one of them new universities where they do more talkin' than learnin' on the job,' she said scathingly. 'This bruisin' needs attention, as well as some little cuts; marigold and arnica in beeswax is the stuff to soothe 'em. Maybe basil; that's good for black an' blue marks.' She scraped a walnut-sized lump of ointment from a jar held out by her daughter, spread it on a small square of old, clean cloth and slapped it firmly on Amalric's wounds. He sat meekly while she wound a coarse linen bandage round his head. It was good to feel like a small child again, but an adult part of him sensed Nesta in the shadows, busy at her chores.

Amalric sat by the fire. The earth tremble had only been spoken of briefly by his family so far. Like talk of the pestilence, it induced a fear for the future best left unsaid – at least in his mother's opinion. Outwardly, the late-evening ritual appeared normal. His father was dozing beside him with arms crossed and legs outstretched towards the warmth, the twins were asleep in the loft, Gundred and Matilde were wearily clearing pots of ointment from the table to leave space for breakfast. Nesta had gone to the barn to attend to Molly, settling the cow for the night: the evening air was warm and her heat was not needed in the house. It was a comfort to Amalric to know the members of the household were all safe after the tremble... all except Edwin, and no one knew where he was.

Unexpectedly, the door clattered open. Edwin staggered in. Aiming to sit on the bench by the table, he missed and fell heavily to the floor on his behind. He swore, and hauled himself clumsily up onto the bench end. No one else moved or spoke.

Edwin broke the silence. 'Father, give me shome money, I need shome.' Spittle spattered from his wet lips and shimmered as, caught by the firelight, it arced towards the ground.

Gundred looked at her wayward son, then questioningly at her husband.

Elias remained motionless, his legs still outstretched. He did not even look up but said quietly, 'There's no money for you... you drunken sot, and still nobbut a young un. Not until I see some sense in you. Not until you stay away from them manor boys will I give you money. You have to work for what I give you.' He paused slightly. 'Did you look on the sheep this mornin' as I told you?'

Amalric knew Edwin had not. The sight of his brother walking up the hill was enough to evidence his disobedience. Amalric's heart beat faster. He became tense; a bad scene was about to begin. He suspected that Edwin's day had been hunting followed by drinking and gambling with the Lord of the Manor's sons. The tremble would have meant no more than a passing incident. Elias raised his head and looked towards Edwin with narrowed eyes. Amalric realised that Edwin must have gambled successfully because he wore a short fitted jacket of green fine wool with fancy buttons – the new cotehardie that young men in towns were wearing to show off their rounded buttocks in tight hose. This one was far above the Faceby station. The sight of it must be irking their father.

Edwin replied unconvincingly, 'Of coursh, Da.'

At this, Elias heaved himself out of his low chair and pulled himself up to his full height. He kicked the chair. It slid on the floor. He stood momentarily to balance himself and then with his face grimacing he stepped wearily and stiffly towards Edwin.

Amalric found he could not move from his seat and sat completely still, distant, as if watching a village play.

Edwin began to slide on the bench away from his father but Elias, with a slow, deliberate movement, caught him by the collar of the cotehardie and pulled him up towards his face. With their noses nearly touching and Edwin hanging limply, Elias said in mock calmness, 'I don't think you did, son, because one of 'em is dead... not killed by the tremble but torn by teeth... reet sharp uns. It looks as though it was killed last night. The blood is old. Creatures 'ad been at it, 'appen manor dogs, and if you'd been to the pasture this mornin', you would've seen it and told me. Wouldn't you?'

Edwin began to choke. 'Da...' he hissed. 'Shtop.' His face was wet with sweat and dripping spittle.

Amalric felt sick.

'Not until you realise that there is no money for you until you alter your ways. My father before me and I have worked years to make somethin' of this family an' the business, and no moral weakling of a son is goin' to spoil our reputation, ruin us by wastin' it on useless lumps like them lads at the manor.' He tossed Edwin to the floor. Gundred winced as his hip caught the corner of the bench and moved to help him – but decided not to. Matilde carried on clearing the table but her hands shook.

'You wouldn't do that to your preshus Amalric,' Edwin spat out, glancing with evil at his brother. 'He'sh lucky. He'sh your favourite. Good with windowsh. Shtrong. Look at me, Father, I'm different! Look at me! What about me, me?' He slumped on the impacted earth, his momentary bravado spent.

Elias did as he was asked. He looked down upon the mess of his son. Dismay passed over his face.

The noise had penetrated into the loft above the sleep room. The twins' faces peered down through the opening. Elias responded to their giggles.

'Get back to bed, you two,' he yelled sharply without looking up.

Their faces disappeared back into the darkness.

In Amalric's battered head, he recognised Elias' traditional stance struggling against Edwin's ambitious, young outlook. He saw his father's righteous anger and his brother's pathetic, sulking attempt to defend himself. Instinctively, he stood and put out a hand to help Edwin up from the floor, but his brother pushed it sharply away. Elias made a soft puffing sound of contempt. Edwin then looked up at his father and, in the quietness, made a final mistake – he tried petulantly to make a joke of the circumstances.

'Well at leasht you can eat the sheep meat for Eashter. Ha! It's traditional. It's the sacrificial lamb… sacrificed like me.'

Elias roared. 'That's blasphemy. You'll rue the day, my lad, if you insult the Lord. Get off the floor and out of my sight!' He dropped heavily onto his chair.

No one else said a word. Edwin pushed himself from the ground and looked round at the others, giving Amalric a particularly penetrating glance. With his hand pressed to his hip, he turned and staggered through the doorway, his shoulder hitting the doorpost as he went. He disappeared into the darkness, leaving the door swinging on its hinges. Matilde got up to close it.

Amalric felt dizzy. His stomach churned. He saw flashes of light and the room began to swirl. Then he saw his mother's face peering at his own and heard her say from far away.

'Go to the sleep room, lad. You'll manage a bit of rest by yourself afore the rest of us need to sleep.'

He lay down on the mattress but no sooner had his head begun to settle than he heard an agitated mooing coming through the wall from the barn next door. At this time of the evening Molly was usually quiet. Then he remembered… Nesta was in the barn! His faintness forgotten, he staggered out of the sleep room into the house and then through the inside door to the barn. Matilde and Gundred looked up.

'Son… what are…?' Gundred's words went no further, as Elias shook his head at her and put a log on the fire, signifying that there must be no interference in this next round of the debacle.

In the barn, a rushlight threw meagre light on Molly the cow anxiously trampling around. A few chickens fluttered about her legs. A milking stool was on its side. Through the commotion Amalric could see Edwin behind the cow, grabbing Nesta by her arms, trying to pull her towards him. At once he realised that his suspicion had been correct. Edwin had come into the barn to amuse himself with her. Amalric stepped from side to side, unable to move around the panicking cow. The chickens became frantic. Dust flew. Then Nesta fell over backward onto straw, and through Molly's legs, Amalric saw a wet-grinning Edwin topple on top of her.

'Master Edwin, get off,' Nesta shrieked, trying to wriggle free from his weight.

Edwin's slurred speech showered her with more spittle. 'Come on, Neshy, give us a kish.' In an instant his head dropped to Nesta's neck and wet kisses dribbled on her. He felt for her smock and pulled it down.

'Ugh! Get off me! Please!' screamed Nesta.

Amalric, trapped behind the agitated cow, became incensed. His headache and pains disappeared in a red fury. He pushed on Molly's haunches as hard as he could to shift her. Mooing a complaint, she moved to one side. The scene suddenly opened up and Amalric lunged at an astonished Edwin, grabbing him by the hem of his cotehardie, pulling and forcing him to let go of Nesta. They tussled and threw punches at each other's faces. After hitting his brother's cheek, Amalric's fist carried on with the force of the lunge and crashed into the upright beam and he staggered back unbalanced, the pain going up his arm to his shoulder. Edwin caught his brother before he fell, put his arm around his neck and tightened it.

Nesta let out a small screech of fear as she saw Amalric's face grimace and his eyes become red. She pushed herself up from the floor and, regardless of the state of her clothing, grabbed Edwin's hair from behind, pulled his head back and poked her fingers into his eyes. Edwin, surprised, loosened his grip on his brother, whose superior strength was then able to overpower his own drunken attempts to choke him. Amalric threw Edwin to the ground, where he lay limp and inebriated, ridiculously spreadeagled over the milking stool. Amalric's hot fury turned to cold scorn. With his undamaged arm he dragged his brother to his feet by the front of his crumpled cotehardie. A fancy button flew off. He seemed light and weak. An old cow blanket sometimes used to cover Molly was nearby and this he thrust at Edwin and pushed him through the outer barn door. 'Sleep somewhere else tonight… and every night. I don't care where,' said Amalric breathlessly… and, to his embarrassment, tearfully.

Amalric turned to look at Nesta. Through moist eyes, he saw the shaking waves of her mouse-coloured hair, her moist grey eyes – the centres large and shiny – her wet cheeks and dripping nose.

Feelings similar to the ones he had had at breakfast were increasing wildly. He watched as she shakily grabbed at her clothing to cover herself. He knew she felt ashamed. He moved towards her; he could not help himself. He had to put his arms around her and draw her into his chest, to reassure her, to offer comfort. But as he put his arms out, she moved back from him. He was crushingly disappointed. His arms felt as if they had nowhere to go.

'Um... I hope you'll be alright now,' he said.

'Thank you, Master Amalric, I'll be fine. Thank you for rescuing me.'

'Well, if you hadn't nearly blinded Edwin, he would have choked me to...' He couldn't finish the sentence.

Nesta smoothed and secured her clothing and tucked her hair behind her ears to tidy it.

'You have straw in your hair. I'll pull it out.'

'Thank you.' Her eyes refused to meet his.

'I'll see you into the house.' He stood by the inner door of the barn and allowed her to go into the living area. He heard his mother snap, 'Go to bed, Nesta,' and through the dim light watched her go the servant's alcove by the workshop wall, where she pulled the curtain tightly closed.

Elias was silent and taut, drowning his thoughts in a hot ale. Matilde laid the table for the morning. Gundred looked knowingly at her son and silently placed a pot of ale on the table for him. Amalric downed it quickly and went off to the sleep room. He lowered himself to his mattress... and wept into his pillow.

The next morning, curled like a child, Amalric emerged into consciousness to the smell of herbs. His mother had sprinkled dried seeds and flowers onto his pillow to promote a healing slumber. He attempted to straighten his limbs and turn onto his back, but his body reacted in pain and stiffness. His head ached, and poking a finger underneath a bandage, he identified an egg-sized lump. He winced. Daylight stabbed his eyes as he tentatively half-opened them.

Getting up from the mattress was difficult. His shoulder hurt and his hand was swollen. Merely dressing in undershirt and hose was challenging. Lightly attired, he staggered into the house and squinted across the road through the unshuttered window. Father Wilfrid was not at the church gate – that meant the hour was quite late. He sighed with disappointment; a chat over yesterday's events would have been reassuring.

An urgent need forced him to stagger unsteadily outside to the privy. The small building seemed to be tilting. The carved faces lolled to one side. The door seemed to require more effort than usual and furthermore, as he entered, it pushed against him heavily, eager to close. Amalric's mind was not up to sorting the mystery. On leaving the privy, the door swung back onto his good hand, trapping his finger between door and doorframe. He kicked open the door angrily. Both his hands were now messed up as well as his head and his shoulder!

He went back to the house. It seemed strangely empty at first but Matilde appeared from the shadows.

'Come, have your porridge, brother.'

'Where's Nesta?' Amalric enquired, with an attempt at nonchalance.

'She's… had to go home,' said Matilde, hesitantly.

A surge of near panic spread through Amalric. 'But…'

'Her young brother came early. Banged on the door, he did. Said their mother was ill with rheumatics after all the wet weather an' couldn't manage. Their father has a bad chest. They're in danger of losing their home if they can't fulfil their dues to their manorial lord and…' she hesitated and spoke softly, 'and it seems her betrothed is waiting for her, as well.'

'Betrothed?' Amalric had to sit.

'Yes. We didn't know.' Matilde drew close to him. 'She's very lowly born, Am. She will needs marry to help secure their future. Ma said it was for the best. I think she's angry, fretting about last night. She wonders if Nesta… well, if she really is a good girl. You know… what with Edwin's feelings for her. Did she tempt him?' Matilde's question was to herself, not her brother.

Amalric felt his face sag.

Matilde gabbled on, seemingly aware of her brother's distress and eager for the tale to be told and over with. 'The poor lad started out before dawn. We had to let Nesta go but she looked very upset about leaving. We packed up a small sack of herbs and liniment for her to take. I gave her some good bread, eggs and honey from our hives. Being Lent, we can easily do without. It will do us good, anyway, to have less for a while. They're very hard-pressed in that hamlet up in the hills, you know.'

Amalric had never given much thought to Nesta's family and their poverty. Until now, he'd not even considered that Nesta had a home other than with the Facebys. Occasionally, he'd seen her gazing up to the hills when the sky was full of storms. Her hamlet was somewhere up there, just below the tops of the Wolds and seldom free of cloud. He struggled to remember what he had overheard when Nesta and Matilde had been talking. Something about poor weather and crops failing time and time again. Sheep had also been mentioned: always seeming to be ailing from foot rot and the like. He felt ashamed that he had cared so little.

'Then the tremble,' went on Matilde. 'I expect they felt it. No wonder her mother has taken bad. We gave them some porridge and let them go. I gave her my old shawl. It's fulled wool and pretty waterproof and she'll need…'

Amalric stopped listening to Matilde's chatter. He may have thought Nesta to be mouse-like but last evening proved that there was a hidden courage about her. She had not encouraged Edwin. She couldn't have but only he, Amalric, really knew. And now she was gone… and would marry. The day had started badly for him – but to have Nesta leave! To marry! What was it he was feeling for her? She was a servant, after all. His mother already doubted her. Perhaps it was for the best, he told himself, not really believing it. His emotions crashed like the spreading of cracks in glass before the pane shatters.

Matilde put her hand on his shoulder. 'Eat up, brother. Time heals.'

Chapter Six

Amalric decided to go to the workshop and wrapped a cloak around himself. He entered slowly and quietly so as not to assault his head with the unnecessary noise of clicking latch and clattering door. Ned was late. The windows remained shuttered. As he became accustomed to the dimness, Amalric saw his father by the shepherd window, his fingers dissolving into soft, reflected colours as he ran them over the glassy undulations. In the pronounced stooping of his father's back, it was clear that the previous day's events had exhausted him.

Alerted, Elias turned. 'This is a fine window, my boy. You have a gradely talent.'

'Good morning, Da,' his son said, flatly.

'Am, I know you're probably not feelin' good; in fact, you look reet badly.' He took a moment to take in his son's condition, but to Amalric's dismay, decided it was worth carrying on. 'But while we've a moment...'

'You're right. I feel like I'm near dying,' Amalric said, deliberately exaggerating his physical state. He found a stool under the table with one hand and with the other clutched his head at the increased pain brought on by bending. Once on the stool, he leaned forward with elbows on his knees and hands supporting his head, but that made his shoulder hurt, so he sat up straight. He tried to disguise his displeasure with an expressionless face.

'But while we've a moment,' his father repeated, still standing, 'I'd like to talk with you. I'm not feelin' too good myself.'

Amalric wondered momentarily if his father was anxious about his own health.

'Yesterday's trouble with Edwin has got me thinkin'. Your apprenticeship has not much time left to run, an' you've done well. When your grandfather set up this business, he had a bit of money and made more. The glass window business expanded. Then what with Scottish raids, an' war, an' famine an' the like, he never felt safe with money in our home. There were too many people only too ready to relieve him of it. He buried it, like lots of folk did. He confided its whereabouts to me. Well, roughly its whereabouts. I want to be able to use it when you've got your final approval to make us "Elias Faceby and..."' He stopped for a while, hoping the silence would raise in Amalric a thrilling anticipation. '"... Son, Master Glaziers".'

The attempt failed. The news was surprising and the subject important, but today Amalric wanted to simply wallow in self-pity and nurse his aches. In other words, to find some peace.

Elias carried on, ignoring the lad's fragile state. 'Edwin wants money now but I've not let on to him about the hoard. He wastes money. As it is, I don't know where he got what he's spent up to now. P'raps he's a good gambler or borrowed it. Anyroad, he's too young... maybe when he's older and more responsible. I just need to find it this comin' summer when the ground is soft an' warmer. You can help me dig for it.'

Money! Life was always about money. Creating magnificent windows was all that he, Amalric, wanted to get on with. Today he couldn't think about money.

Elias looked at his son and sighed. 'Aye Son, it's hard to take in anything else when you've been close to death, as you were yesterday. It was the first time for you, except when you had the diphtheria as a young un, but you won't remember owt about that. Aye, death is always close at hand. You'll meet it plenty more times in your future.'

Quiet fell like a sinking stone. Death close at hand. Amalric suddenly realised that his life could have been wiped out in an instant. He had not thought of that until now.

'Look, lad, I'm a bit worried that we didn't get the work promised us at Meaux. I was countin' on havin' a few new windows to make for 'em. It would've been a bit of extra money to put by. Mind you, the windows will need some repair and that might tide us over.' Elias paused a moment to think, then went on, 'Not only that, I've dreamed of putting a coloured window in yon church at my own expense, to thank God for my skill and good fortune in this village.' He looked through the shepherd window to the colourful wavy image of the church beyond. 'I won't earn money to do that now, not for a long time, so... finding that buried money...'

This at last meant something to Amalric. He understood. His da had dreams like his own. After yesterday's tremble, of course things would be held up. They would pass, but something else was troubling his father.

'Da, is there more that worries you?'

'Aye... there is summat else beside.' Elias looked into his eldest son's swollen, youthful eyes.

'Go on, Da,' said Amalric, beginning now to feel apprehensive.

'Despite what your ma says, I've been thinking about the pestilence what's comin' up the country. Abbot Hugh definitely took the tremble to be a warnin' from God an' the young physic man was worried. I know they both had the pestilence in mind. I'm not young any more. I often feel ill – headaches, chest aches an' the like. It would do me in if I caught it. It might do us all in.' He took a slightly laboured, whistling breath. 'But, as your mother says, we've always managed afore. It might be nowt or perhaps will 'ave burned itself out afore it gets up here – the devil gets tired before God does.'

Elias turned his attention back to the window and traced the lead came surrounding the glass piece with the wrongly pointing shepherd.

'So, lad, let's forget the pestilence. Nowt else we can do. Come summer, the tremble'll be forgotten, an' we'll both dig for the money.' He turned and smiled at his son.

Amalric managed a weak smile in return. 'Very well, Da, that's all fine with me.' But fear stirred within him.

'In the meantime, son, there's them shutters to see to, the glass to check for breakages and the privy to put right.'

'The privy?'

'Aye, it's leanin' backward after the tremble. It were obvious in daylight this mornin'. We'll end up in the brook if nowt's done about it. In your own time. You're not well at present.'

'Right, Da.' So it was the privy at fault and not his head. That's why the door kept swinging back. Amalric was relieved. A hysterical laugh bubbled in his throat then retreated.

'Go back to bed, lad.'

Amalric lay still on his mattress allowing his aches and pains to ease. Bennet and Berta were at the strips, weeding and scaring off the birds. Gundred and Matilde were out tidying and tending the vegetable garden. Ned had arrived at last and he and Elias were in the workshop. Edwin was still absent. The silence of the house, punctuated only by twittering birds in the thatch eaves, caused him to doze.

But his peace was not to last. A knock on the door disturbed him. A click of the latch and a voice far too jovial for Amalric's head said, 'Helloooo – physician visiting new patient.'

Amalric recognised the doctor's voice and rose slowly from the mattress and staggered into the house. He saw Thurston's ginger head and smiling face nosing around the edge of the door.

'Come in… please.'

It was exciting for Amalric to have a friend in the house. Thurston was obviously a person of learning. His doctor's robe of fine wool covered all but hands and head and sat elegantly on his slim frame. It contrasted markedly with his patient's crumpled linen undergarment, which exposed limbs and was open to half way down his chest.

'How are those bumps and bruises?' said Thurston cheerfully as his alert eyes swept over Amalric as if he were naked.

Amalric felt uncomfortable at the penetrating eyes, as he had in the abbey, and wondered if that gaze could see right through him. He had only experienced such a feeling before with one other person and that was Father Wilfrid – the priest who could see into the soul of all his parishioners.

Thurston was seemingly unaware of the effect he had on his patient but clearly noted Amalric's ailments. 'Oh! There's more damage than I saw yesterday. You must have been injured worse than I thought. Have you more under your shirt?'

'No, nothing. I had a fight with my brother.' It briefly surprised Amalric that the covered bruises had not been seen by the piercing eyes.

'What, on top of the day you had yesterday? You're lucky to look as good as you do and are not lying unconscious again. Sit at once.'

Amalric lowered himself gingerly onto the bench. 'Let me have a look at you. What's this?' said Thurston as he lifted the edge of the head bandage and saw ointment greasing over the lump.

'Marigold and arnica in beeswax. Mother swears by it. She doesn't rate physicians' knowledge very highly.'

'Well, given that she hasn't been tutored by men who swear by the 1,000-year-old ideas of Hippocrates and Galen… and who seem to think that the insides of pigs are the same as those of men, despite what is in front of their eyes, I'd say she could be correct in her thinking.' He laughed. 'Just the same, let me examine you properly.' Thurston peered into his leather satchel and pulled out an assortment of items. 'Pee into this jar please.'

'What?'

'Pee into this jar. Now. Be careful, glass is expensive, but then you know that.'

Amalric raised himself from the bench, lifted his garment and did as instructed. As the amber liquid flowed, he reflected on the glass-blowing skill required to make such a jar. He had seen it done.

The physician took the jar from him. 'Please sit again.' He held it up to the light and peered through the transparency. 'Mm… it's clear.' Then he held it against coloured discs painted on a chart, ranging from purple and dark red to the palest amber. Amalric's pee seemed to be somewhere towards the darker end of the amber range. Then Thurston dipped his right index finger into it, raised it to his mouth, closed his eyes and tasted it. He kept his eyes closed for a while and, on opening them, nodded satisfactorily to himself.

Amalric looked on, fascinated. 'Why on earth are you doing that?' He had used his own pee to mix with burned copper and ground glass to make paint for drawing details on glass before being fired. He also knew it was used to full wool in Beverley, to make it thick like his tunic, but this…?

'To assess your condition as recommended by the ancient Galen,' Thurston replied with a note of sarcasm, 'one must test for colour, clarity, thickness, sediment, odour, foam and, most unpleasant, taste. Yours does not taste sweet, it's not too acid nor too alkaline, it's as clear as well water and within the limits of balance with your four humours: blood, phlegm, yellow and black bile. However, though the colour is good, it is a little dark – you must take more fluid. Water rather than ale.'

'Mm. I've seen an animal called a monkey holding up a jar like yours in a window in York Minster. But I didn't know that was what he was doing.'

'Well, you do now,' said Thurston, a little sharply. 'The mention of monkey doctors always upsets me. I'm not sure of their meaning; it's as if physicians like myself are being laughed at, misunderstood. Many believe God alone heals. Well, in my view He needs people to help. That's what we physicians do. We learn and help. Anyway, had the window-makers ever seen a monkey? Pah!'

Amalric was shocked at the outburst and silently watched as Thurston took the jar to the open window, poured the contents outside, rinsed it with water from a jug, took a cloth, wiped it dry, wrapped the cloth around it and put it safely back in the satchel. Then he took a second chart, unfolded it and transferred his attention to pictures of heavenly bodies. Amalric dared to stand to look over his shoulder, mesmerised as always with pictures.

When Thurston finally folded the chart back up, he muttered, 'No problem there. Sit again, please.' He was now fully composed and once again the calm physician. He examined Amalric's head, his eyes and his joints and bruises. This time he followed it by looking at a small book. 'Hm. Nothing further to suggest hidden problems. No need to bleed you.'

He looked up and saw Amalric gazing at the small manuscript.

'I can see it's in Latin script,' said Amalric.

'Oh, yes, you read some Latin.' Thurston remembered and was clearly impressed. 'This is my *vade mecum*, it's where I check to make sure I've not missed anything. I'm not so confident in my own skills yet that I can leave a patient without checking to see if there is anything more I can do. It's what makes me so interested in new theories… always checking. This little book can be especially useful if I need to use techniques that I am not fully learned in, like cutting.' He browsed a few more pages. 'Mm,' he said. 'No lasting damage in you, I'm pleased to say. From now on, my special skills will not be needed; I will prescribe only your mother's care. But be sure not to rest as much as she will advise. Mothers like to nurse their sons and, in my experience, damage like this is best served with exercise once your headaches go. Keep your arm moving.' He packed his satchel.

'My father has a book. I told you about it,' said Amalric. 'My father was given it by a monk to thank him for repairing glass windows. It's called *On Divers Arts*, by Theophilus, who was a monk long ago. I'll show it to you.' He went to a cupboard set into the wattle and daub wall and pulled out the manuscript. He opened it to a section where the pages were browning and the edges worn. 'See, it contains all sorts of things a glazier should know. Mother thinks it's a magic book and says I needs be careful... of the devil or magic or something. It's a wonderful book! See the drawings in the margins.'

Thurston flicked over the pages. 'This is wonderful. How lucky you are to have it and be able to read it. And the little drawings must be very useful. If the drawings I've seen in physic manuscripts could tell me something about this coming pestilence they would be useful indeed. I've often seen those irritating monkeys you talked of in York Minster drawn by an untalented hand in books... they even have them in floor tiles in some places... but monkeys know nothing.'

'Can you tell me about it, Thurston – not the monkeys, but the pestilence? Why have we not seen the disease up here in the north? Mother says she'll deal with it if it comes.'

'Well, Am, I don't know what to say except that it's serious. It came over into England from Normandy, though the French say it came from Genoa. The Genoese say it came from the Turks, the Turks say from the great plains, and so on. It struck in England at Melcombe Regis on the south coast, in June last year. It arrived in Bristol in August, London in September, Winchester in October, and in January and February of this year it was throughout East Anglia and middle England. It's not far away, Amalric, possibly King's-Town on Hull, as I said yesterday. It hits towns very hard and many people have died. I've not seen it myself – I left Oxford before it arrived. Those who have seen it say it's a terrible illness. Death comes quickly.'

'But what's caused it?' Amalric found himself both scared and fascinated.

'Some say it's the planets. In March four years ago Saturn, Jupiter and Mars were in conjunction and the pestilence started on faraway continents about that time. I believe also that Jews are held to blame in some lands, even to whole communities being massacred for poisoning wells and such things. I have met but very few Jews and each was good and learned. I cannot believe they would cause such harm.'

Amalric remembered his mother's morning at the well, and his and Father Wilfrid's drink of tainted water.

Thurston continued. 'Myself, I favour the theory that wet weather and earth trembles have caused a change in the natural equilibrium, allowing pestilential miasmas to be released. The miasmas drift low and are attracted to stagnant pools, waste, dung heaps, and decaying corpses of animals. The big towns are the worst, where it's difficult to put dung straight onto the land, where privy emptying is often abominably slow, where butchers leave waste carcasses lying around and so on... It's the magistrates' responsibility to deal with such matters that affect the overall health of the populace. We physicians only deal on a one-to-one basis but we're not blind to the results of mismanagement. My guess is that around here, York and Beverley will suffer most, for their filth levels are high and their streets are crowded. Hull has many travellers and boatmen. The truth is, Amalric, it's beyond anyone to deal with it.' Thurston gazed at his hands in despair.

'Is there no cure, then?'

'No. Very, very few survive the disease, though some escape it altogether. It's a huge mystery.'

'What can we do, then? Should Mother and Matilde be doing something with their herbs? How will we recognise the illness?'

'Amalric, I cannot advise you, for as I have said, I've not seen it myself. It begins with feeling really ill and that is all I can say. The main thing, I believe, is to avoid contact with those who have it.'

'But surely that's difficult?'

'Yes, it is. The hospitals are preparing themselves for many sick patients... all gathered together in one place. I don't know if... Anyway, the monks and clergy of St Leonard's Hospital in York are even now increasing linen stores and medications to aid the body, while more clerics are being sought to heal the souls. They have 200 beds but I fear it will not be enough for York. Maybe they will build shacks to accommodate more.'

'Do they know how to cure it?'

'Certainly not! They look after the sick, those who have repented, that is, but don't look for cures. The soul is of greater importance to the brothers and sisters. They keep no records.'

Amalric was beginning to grasp the situation. His eyes were fixed on Thurston.

'Confidentially, Amalric, I fear that as the doctors and healers die, there will not be anyone left to care for the sick. Lord de Horesby has designed a leather suit to protect me; it covers my entire body including my head, with a pouch in the nose area to fill with sweet-smelling and medicinal herbs to counter the miasmas. He's had one made up in York. I've never come across such a garment before. I suspect it was very expensive. But he is a thinking man, for which I am grateful. He wishes to save me so I may save him and his family… but I don't believe I will be able to. For one thing, I will hardly be able to breathe when I'm wearing the suit, let alone minister to the sick.'

'Then… my mother won't be able to…'

'We can all only do our best to avoid any danger,' interrupted Thurston. 'I'm sorry, I shouldn't burden you with these things. I know such information is disturbing. As for myself, I feel alone here in the countryside where superstition, herbs and faith are what matter, not medicine. Medicine as taught in Oxford is anathema to the folk who have always healed themselves: it is not so much what a person dies of but how they die – reconciled with God and assured of a place in heaven.'

Thurston sagged, weary of the subject. He looked at Amalric standing by the table in front of the manuscript, goose pimples on his arms and slightly shivering in only his thin undershirt and hose. 'So… what of you, apart from your injuries? Have you a love interest? That always helps the heart, if not the whole body.'

Amalric was surprised at the sudden change of topic. He felt his face become hot and was unable to answer.

'Ah… I detect some embarrassment; I will leave the subject alone. You are cold, anyway, and need to keep warm.'

'No… It's alright. I just…'

'And I must leave now, my friend.'

'Of course.' Amalric really liked this man.

Thurston picked up his satchel and stood to leave. As he did so, Matilde entered through the door, slapping her bare feet on the floor. Her skirts were tucked into her apron waist to protect them from the mud of the garden and exposed her slim, mud-splattered ankles. Her capless hair hung loose in damp black ringlets and her grubby fingers held a bunch of freshly picked small, wizened parsnips. She sighed wearily and dropped them onto the table.

'My back aches. That soil is wet and heavy. I hoped leaving them over winter would see them fatten… but so many slugs, they eat just about everything… Oh!' She saw Thurston and recognised the garb of a doctor.

'Thurston, this is Matilde, my elder sister. Matilde, this is Dr Thurston from Horesby Manor.'

For a moment their eyes met. Matilde nodded and demurely looked downwards while Thurston scrutinised her. He shifted his weight from foot to foot, obviously seeking words to open a conversation.

'I believe your knowledge of herbs and medications is very good. Both you and your mother have an excellent reputation around here. I'd like to discuss the subject with you sometime.' Hesitation crept into his voice, 'That is… if you would allow me?'

Amalric looked on with interest. So, the physician had already heard of his sister. Here was someone who could be a match for her, but she was spirited: it may not go well, he thought.

'Aye, well, maybe. 'Appen we could teach each other a thing or two,' was Matilde's somewhat cool response, but the provocative way she dropped her skirt to cover her ankles spoke more about her interest in this man than either medicine or the laws of etiquette required.

Thurston smiled, bowed to her and left. Matilde managed a slight curtsy before turning away to attend to other chores more flushed and flustered than Amalric had ever seen. His mood lifted momentarily with the delightful thought that a liaison may be about to begin. However, the conversation with Thurston about the pestilence returned to trouble him. What little hope the physician had was in the study of diseases, the body's humours, the planets. Yet his mother put hers in plants. Maybe a visit to the parish priest would clear things up.

Chapter Seven

Late that afternoon, feeling a little better, Amalric wandered across the road to the parish church. He loved it. It brought out the artist in him. The green, rust and yellow lichens that scattered over it were, to him, daubs of paint put on by God's paintbrush. Once, as a young boy, he had mentioned this to Father Wilfrid and had felt foolish, but the priest had understood, pointing out that the lichens grew because of its age, decorating it like blemishes on an old person's face. Amalric knew of no stone building older nor stronger. It had withstood many troubles since the Saxons had laid the first stone.

He entered the church through a small porch at the west end of the long south wall, which sheltered a creaking, thick oak door. Once inside, he slumped onto a sloping ledge beside the door and for a moment was reminded of the old men and women who similarly perched each worship day to ease their legs and backs. His feet rested on brown-glazed clay tiles, dulled by mud from outside, and he felt their coolness spread through the thin worn soles of his calf-length boots. He never minded being in the church. Some villagers always seemed to fear God's wrath but Father Wilfrid had taught him from a young age not to be afraid, only obedient. A soft lingering smell of fragrant herbs played about him. He knew his headache now stood a chance of settling completely.

Amalric looked around and completely understood his father's desire to make a coloured window for the place. Originally, the church had very small glassless windows high up in the thick walls which offered a little light without allowing northern winds to blast too much on the worshippers below. But Amalric's grandfather had dispelled the gloom by knocking out stones to create larger windows lower down the walls. He had put glass in *all* the windows but it was not of the finest, being rather opaque and also, some was now loose in the stone grooves.

It would be wonderful to have at least one replaced by good, colourful glass. Even so, the afternoon light played through the old windows and was soft and gentle on Amalric's tender eyes.

Around him, painted walls offered tantalising, brightly coloured images of saints, Jesus Christ, Adam and Eve and, in the window reveals, seasonal scenes of farming and hunting. They came and went as sunlight and passing clouds threw them into clarity or shadow.

A burst of sun, unexpectedly bright, poured through a south window and lit up a painted figure of St Edmund on the nave wall opposite. He was Amalric's favourite saint. Multiple arrows pierced his body. Nevertheless, his expression was serene. Amalric wondered how anyone could endure such torture.

'St Edmund survived the arrows but was later beheaded – martyred because he wouldn't abandon his faith to heathen Vikings. He had hope in his own salvation, something we will all need soon.' Father Wilfrid emerged from the sanctuary where the gaudy colours of a painted low rood screen contrasted markedly with his leather-belted long, loose, grey garment of thick fulled wool. He waddled, round and pink-faced, down the nave in flapping sandals.

'Hello, young Amalric,' he said cheerfully. 'Well, not so young now, eh? Soon in partnership with your father, eh? I missed you this morning.' He saw the bruises. 'My word, Amalric, you're black and blue. Have you come to confess the sin of fighting, lad?'

'No, Father, I have not,' was the indignant reply. 'I was caught in the earth tremble at Meaux.' He felt it best not to mention the squabble with Edwin. 'But I was mean to Ned yesterday and I want to repent.'

'Well, that's good, lad. On your knees and praying for forgiveness should do it. You're both young, but... well... your backgrounds are different. It will happen from time to time. Human nature. Prayer is the solution. Pray to your favourite saint to intercede for you. St Edmund, isn't it?'

Amalric was comforted by Father Wilfrid's blunt common sense and knowledge of the human soul.

'But that earth tremble now,' the priest went on, '... a terrible thing indeed. A bad portent. Being Passiontide, I was checking our little wooden Easter sepulchre, there in the sanctuary, to free it of cobwebs and filthy bird and bat droppings, when everything shook...'

Amalric looked down the church. To him it was a miracle that the old and rickety painted cart holding a coffin-like tomb. and with curtains loose on their rods, had survived.

'... and our little Jesus, down from His cross to be dusted, fell without ceremony to the ground. In fact, He bounced!'

Amalric disguised a smile with tight lips.

'A very bad portent,' the priest repeated firmly, scowling at him. 'Bad that Jesus should suffer even more trials through my carelessness.'

Amalric recovered and stared at the little body. It was slightly longer than the length of a man's forearm and had arms that hinged outwards at the shoulders. Small holes gouged out of the wood indicated wounds caused by beating and crucifixion. The centre of the chest had a round hole with a crystal lid, which held the Easter host: the consecrated bread that became the body of Jesus. Amalric had seen this figure every year since childhood, taken down from the cross on Good Friday, placed in the sepulchre and left there until Easter Day, the day of Jesus' resurrection. Today the damaged little body had a more than usual significance for Amalric.

'Father, I need to speak with you about the pestilence.'

The priest's demeanour changed. His brow furrowed and his arthritic fingers nervously played with the metal cross that hung from a chain around his neck.

'I fear my few healing skills and prayers will be insufficient to hold the disease at bay.' As he spoke, Father Wilfrid gazed up to the roof and watched a small bird flying into the eaves. A small chirrup was heard, then silence. During its flight, the bird had lost a tiny feather, which was drifting to the ground. Father Wilfrid's eyes followed it to its resting place at the join of four tiles. Then he looked back to Amalric.

'I wish more people would ask about it. Mostly, the villagers seem to be ignoring the fact that the pestilence is likely to come here. They seem to think that they are sufficiently isolated to avoid it and able to live off the land without needing to go anywhere else or be near anyone else. That, and being too good to incur God's wrath. Because there is little crime, because they despise the lewd and raucous behaviour of the young folk and they work hard and because they are better than most villages at paying their dues to the manor, and to the church, they feel confident that God has no need to punish them.' The priest sighed. 'They are much mistaken.'

'Father, what about my brother's sins? I think he practises the lewd and raucous behaviour that they despise, and he spends money on frivolous, fashionable clothes.'

'It is such sinning that is the cause of this pestilence,' the priest reiterated. 'We should not forget that pleasure is a gift from God to be used wisely.'[6]

Amalric nodded.

'Each Sunday I implore my flock to pray as much as possible every day. It is the only way to gain God's forgiveness for the

---

[6] Derived from Ecclesiastes 3:13: 'it is God's gift that all should eat and drink and take pleasure in all their toil.'

sins committed by us all. It is up to your brother to do the same. You could try praying for him.'

Amalric ignored the idea. 'Father, why is God so mean?'

'It is not for us to judge Him, my boy. He judges us. There are those who believe the disease to be a sign that the end of the world is near, when we will all be judged. See… it is depicted for you on the west wall.'

Amalric looked. The Last Judgement was in shadow but the painted picture on the wall was well known to him: bodies falling to hell, others being saved and rising to heaven. It cautioned the congregation members every time they left church. It was the last image they saw before going back to their daily lives.

'Mind you, even now there are those who like to spread fear: village folk and some religious folk, too. I have heard of flagellants beyond England's shores walking around wailing and whipping themselves, sometimes with nails attached to the strings, going through the streets, half-naked, bleeding and calling for the forgiveness of sins, stirring up emotions.' The priest looked down at his large-jointed toes. 'I earnestly hope they will not come over to Britain. Some folk have already started creeping towards the cross – there is already enough hysteria.'

'Creeping towards the cross?'

'Aye. You'll know it when you see it.'

The priest's face grimaced with strong disapproval of this new ritual and he dismissively waved away thoughts of it.

'Look, Amalric, all I can advise is prayer – asking for the forgiveness of sins and practising abstinence from dubious pleasures, then hoping the disease will pass you by.'

Amalric considered his own dubious thoughts about Nesta, but let the priest continue.

'Actually, I'm looking to my superiors to lead the way on this. As early as last July, Archbishop Zouche of York sent a letter to all churches prescribing processions and masses to be held in towns and villages. I know he has personally found it difficult to reconcile God's favour at the Battles of Crécy and Calais and his own personal success at the Battle of Naseby against the Scots, with God's disfavour shown by the pestilence. If the Archbishop has trouble accounting for God's will, what chance do I or anyone else have?' He tutted with dismay. 'From what I've heard, even the most saintly and high-born of people fall ill; the king's daughter was struck down in France last year. I shall insist on processions throughout the period of our Lord's Passion and the saying of masses which people will have to attend. They will protest because they will not want to leave their gardens and land strips and sheep, but what else can I do?' He stopped. His eyes lowered. 'What can I do? What sins can be bad enough to cause this pestilence?'

Amalric was once again amazed at a passionate outburst over this coming disease but had no words in response. He simply bent to pick up the little feather from the tiles. It was soft, fluffy white at the base, brown at the curved tip, mouse-coloured. He put it into his pocket.

His curiosity wouldn't rest. 'But Father Wilfrid, if many people fall ill, how will day-to-day jobs be done? Will people starve again?'

'See the painted men by the windows, hunting and sowing seeds? It is all God's employment. God is a fact of life, Amalric, my boy. He is in control of everything and watches over us. There is little else anyone can do except answer when He calls. There is a season for all God's things. There will also be a season for the pestilence.'

The priest looked weary with the conversation and physically sagged as Thurston had sagged. He turned and moved away towards the altar with his head bowed and hands grasped behind his back. Amalric knew he was thinking. Often in the past, he had turned back to say something that as a boy, Amalric had found wise and weighty. He turned now.

'Am, I chose to be a parish priest rather than a monk. I never wanted to belong to a religious order, roaming around in beautiful buildings, cloisters, hampered by services at all times of the day and night, working on manuscripts. But... I admire their strong will and I pray like them. But I don't have answers and I look to them to give me some. My work is among the ordinary folk – those of this village especially. That's where the grit of life is. That's where I'm needed, even if most of the villagers don't know it... yet.'

Chapter Eight

Gundred rushed into the house, slammed the door behind her and dropped empty pails to the floor. She put her hands to her face. Amalric looked up from tending the morning fire. Matilde and Elias looked at her expectantly.

'Myrtle's daughter is dead,' she said, through her fingers. 'I could have saved her. She bled to death.'

'What? Liza Ashe?' asked Matilde.

'Aye.'

'And the baby?'

'Matilde, what's this about?' Amalric was perplexed.

'The girl was caught with child last summer. She wasn't fit enough to have a child. She was underfed and must have barely approached her menses.'

Amalric remembered Liza swathed in adult clothes.

Matilde pulled Gundred's hands from her face. 'And the child, Mother? What about the child? Why weren't we called?'

'Survived. A girl,' sniffed Gundred. 'A weaklin' of course. Tiny. Liza bled, went into a fit and bled to death.' Her voice trembled. 'I could have given her somethin' to stop it, the bleedin'. I was goin' to the well when I heard what was happenin'. I wanted to help, I really did. I stood at the Ashes' door ready to fetch my ergot but Myrtle said I'd not helped when they wanted it and that nothin' would persuade her to accept my useless potion now.'

'Mother,' said Matilde, 'calm yourself. Your potion might not have worked; it doesn't always. Don't take on.'

But Gundred had more to tell. ''Tis said she was ravished though I have my doubts. She was a fast little thing. Anyroad, now our family is being blamed.'

Amalric looked at his mother, his brow furrowed. 'Why? Why is she blaming us?'

'Well, for one thing, it suits Myrtle to imagine someone from this family gave the girl his seed.'

Amalric remembered Liza's lusty glances and how they had repulsed him. 'Well, it's not me!' Amalric knew his mother thought him too naïve, anyway. It vexed him.

'And for another thing, it's because I refused a few months back to give Myrtle somethin' for Liza to get rid of the child. She begged me. But she was too far gone, in my opinion. Too dangerous. She could have lost her life even then. But Myrtle said I owed it to her to try, our family bein' to blame. I spoke to Father Wilfrid about it at the time because the thought tortured me. He said any life was sacred. Killing the unborn is a mortal sin.' Gundred flopped to a seat and Matilde's arm went around her shoulders. 'But... as far as Myrtle's concerned, our family's at the root of her misfortune. Edwin's her target, I imagine.'

'No, Mother, not Edwin.' Matilde was always ready to defend her wayward brother. 'A tumble down the Snickelways of Beverley and York is more to his taste.'

'Aye. Myrtle never mentioned marriage – so I suppose Liza never told.'

At that moment, Berta descended tousle-headed down the ladder from the loft. Her brother peered over the edge.

'Somethin' wrong?' asked Berta. 'Only we heard shouting. Ma looks upset.'

Elias was stimulated to speak. 'Nothin' for you to worry about, love. Go back to bed. I think breakfast will be a bit late.'

Gundred sat heavily on the bench. 'Am, fetch the water from the well. I'm too upset to go back.'

'Right you are, Ma.' He felt nervous about going to the well: women there could be vicious. To his relief, it was late and deserted.

Breakfast was a silent affair. Bennet and Berta, not understanding the reason for long faces over the wooden bowls, skipped out to the garden when theirs were empty. When Matilde was clearing bowls away, Gundred's need to speak overcame her again.

'There'll be a vigil in church for Maundy Thursday so there'll need to be a funeral afore then. That's if our priest allows it, her havin' a bastard an' all. 'Tis said the girl managed a confession with Father Wilfrid on her deathbed but Myrtle is reckoned not to have heard it, though I expect she craned her neck to listen and sprained it with the effort. The girl had been silent all along about the father. She was always close to 'erself, you could never get much out of her except moody looks.'

'Now, love, don't speak ill of the dead,' interjected Elias.

Gundred ignored him. 'It'll have a bad effect on the village women. Especially them with daughters. They'll take sides – either that, or sit on the fence not speakin' to either me or Myrtle. Pregnancy in such a young lass is scandalous.'

Elias nodded, indicating that fathers of daughters would act similarly.

'I expect Father Wilfrid did what he could to shorten her time in Purgatory,' Gundred continued. '*Some* of her sins'll be forgiven.' She was near to angry tears. 'Trouble is, when Myrtle Ashe bears a grudge she's dangerous, even when she has no real proof.' Matilde touched her mother's arm in support.

Amalric sat morosely, his hands in front of him on the table.

The day after she had died, Myrtle's daughter was in a grave. Few in the village attended, put off by the circumstances, Myrtle's bitterness and her spitting obscenities to all who tried to comfort her. Amalric observed that only her friend Alice Tynel remained by her side.

On Maundy Thursday, Elias and Amalric left the workshop early to attend the Maundy Thursday Vigil. Amalric failed to see the relevance of it, given that village resentment seethed because it took folk away from vital spring work on the land. Even his mother and Matilde had claimed more important work to do.

The vigil began in the afternoon with a walking procession to ward off the coming pestilence, taking in two other villages and finishing inside Warren Horesby church. Dark clouds loomed as the group tramped the miles in gradually worsening weather. Church banners flapped and had to be rolled up for protection, shiny reliquaries were covered with cloth. A wind-blown mass was said on each of the village greens.

Once inside Warren Horesby church, the miseries carried on. Rain blew into the church porch and seeped inside under the great door, forming puddles. It lightly sprayed through gaps in windows onto the already soaked congregation. Folk were expected to look at the story of 'The Passion' on the walls but the paintings retreated into shadow, leaving the congregation to their own imaginings. They were familiar with the scenes, anyway: knew Judas kissed Jesus on the cheek to identify Him to soldiers and imagined his eyes burning into those of the gentle Jesus. They felt the pain of Jesus' beatings, heard His cries, smelled His sweat of fear.

Many shivered and wept into the obscure night. Amalric watched tears flow down his father's face. He saw him rock disturbingly backward and forward, but he himself experienced no such emotion and simply felt tired. He scrutinised Father Wilfrid's face during readings, prayers and silences and failed to see anything except a gloomy composure.

After the passage of seemingly endless hours, a lighter mood descended on the bedraggled congregation as sunrise began to glow through the east window. Gradually, the figures on the walls became visible again, their reds and ochres deepened. The rood screen glowed with the gold, green and red of paint. A creaking signified the opening of the church door and when the congregation turned, they saw through it a surprisingly clear dawn. Everyone straggled home to refresh themselves before returning for the Good Friday Mass: the crucifixion of Jesus.

Amalric expected the special annual mass to be gloomier than usual on account of the death of young Liza still reverberating around the village. His mother expected Myrtle to liken her daughter's death to a sacrifice.

'That woman will turn the situation to a triumph and will wallow in any sympathy shown to her! You mark my words!'

Along with most of the villagers, the Facebys arrived at the church early and waited outside to see Lord de Horesby arrive with his family. Church celebrations were usually something of a spectacle, the latest fashions being demonstrated, but this being the most serious day in the Christian calendar, clothing had to reflect it. Lord de Horesby and his wife came first, wearing black and smiling solemnly. Their two teenage sons and daughter grimaced rather than smiled, showing their disapproval of the rather old-fashioned, sombre, loose garments they had been forced to don. Clara, at the back, eyed the young men gazing at her. Amalric detected a haughtiness which signalled that no young man present was worthy of her, their social status being far below. Amalric found himself comparing her with the absent Nesta. They both reminded him of window glass: Nesta was transparent and reflected light, Clara was obscured by paint.

The villagers wore their usual clothes, cleaned and repaired for the day. Amalric himself had left behind his workday leather apron and wore a work shirt freshly laundered by his mother. He thought of Edwin and when he saw the de Horesby brothers, he got an inkling why his own brother sought their companionship. Even when looking dark and sombre, they swept into church with an elegance of status and fortune that no glazier would ever be able to match.

Lord and Lady de Horesby and their children made their way to the front of the church, at the left. They were the only people to have seats provided. Everyone else had to stand – except of course for the village weary and infirm, who perched on the stone benches around the sides.

The villagers jostled behind the Lord and his family. Elias, Matilde and the twins walked in behind Gundred as she elbowed her way to a place at the front right, across the aisle from the de Horesbys, which she felt was rightfully her family's, due to Elias being a man of business, and thus of elevated status. However, today was also a day to avoid Myrtle Ashe, whose social place was nearer the back and in whom, along with martyrdom, recrimination would be festering.

Amalric was slow to join his family and saw Ned alone by the yew tree. 'Why dawdle, Ned? Where're your parents?'

'Comin', Master Amalric. They're waitin' on the Ashes.'

Just then, a small group came through the gate and down the church path. Amalric saw Ned squirm. He had obviously tried to avoid the embarrassing scene they both now laid eyes on. On her hands and knees was Myrtle, crawling over stones and soil towards the door, her long skirt tucked into a twisted linen belt. Jacob Ashe followed unsteadily, holding his remaining daughter's hand. Behind them, Ned's mother, Alice Tynel, carried Liza's baby in her arms. Ned's father, Osbert Tynel, was by her side. Ned and Amalric stood to one side to let them pass. As they did so, Myrtle looked at Amalric; her bloodshot eyes glared perturbingly.

When she reached the porch, Myrtle stood and with some satisfaction looked at her bleeding knees. She spread the blood further down her shins. Then she went on her knees again. Amalric was shocked. So this was the new devotional act, 'creeping towards the cross', that Father Wilfrid had spoken of. The priest would probably be unaware that it was about to happen today. Jacob stepped in front of his wife to hold open the large oak door. At that moment, Father Wilfrid was solemnly walking up two steps to the front of the altar, which had been stripped bare of ornaments. His hands were clasped piously in front of him. The door creaked and clattered through the silence. At the top of the steps, the priest turned and over the heads of the congregation, saw the penitent at the far end of the aisle, tears streaming down her face and her bent body taut with agony. With narrowed eyes, the priest watched silently as she heaved herself upright and moved behind everyone else. She stood in obvious pain waiting for the worship to begin.

Jacob Ashe and young Constance made their way to the wall, where Jacob leaned heavily with humiliation on the stone bench. Of the congregation, only Amalric and Ned at the very back of church and the priest at the front had seen what had just gone on. Ned joined his parents. Amalric carried on to the front where he slipped in next to his father... but had all the while felt Myrtle's eyes follow him down the central aisle.

Father Wilfrid carried out the long mass with the solemnity Good Friday demanded. The Passion from St John's Gospel was read out in Latin by a visiting curate and, despite most folk being unable to understand, the serious and dramatic tone of his voice fixed the magnitude of it in their minds.

An elderly verger was then tasked with bringing a tall crucifix from the east wall behind the altar to the front. As he struggled, Amalric had time to look at the small swaying figure of Jesus and recall how the wounds had so affected him a few days before. He felt tense and emotional.

Everyone was invited to express their devotion by kissing the base of the cross. After the de Horesby family, the Facebys were first in the queue of villagers. As Gundred rose from her kissing, she turned to go back to her place and glanced down the church, past the queue. Her face blanched. Amalric knew she had seen Myrtle. Petulantly, Gundred allowed Elias to push her gently back to her place, where she stood staring forward, her breasts heaving. Matilde firmly took hold of the twins' shoulders, to keep them calm.

The Tynels made their way up the aisle. Alice, holding Myrtle's weakly mewling grandchild, had Osbert and Ned beside her. Jacob Ashe followed them, short of breath and looking a little blue around his nose and lips. Then... some way behind, splendidly alone, came Myrtle, crawling on hands and knees. With each painful movement, she moaned and asked the Virgin Mary, Jesus, the saints and God for forgiveness. She pleaded, she wept. Smudges of blood on the tiles trailed from the back of the church. As she passed Gundred, her eyes remained resolutely forward, looking only at the cross. Amalric saw a minute shake of the priest's head aimed at his mother, warning her to keep control of herself.

Father Wilfrid gestured with his hand for Myrtle to come forward to the cross. He said nothing as she heaved herself towards it and fell exhausted near the base after kissing it. She lay for a moment and Father Wilfrid was obliged to help her up. Amalric heard him whisper to her without his usual compassion that she need no longer creep. He said it was obvious to the whole congregation she had done enough to atone for her daughter's sin. Caring for the babe would be her duty from now on.

Myrtle's face took on an expression of supreme gratitude. However, she remained disabled and everyone could see it was impossible for her to retrace her steps to the back of the church. She slipped painfully next to Gundred, who was forced to move to the side to make room. Amalric knew his mother's anger would know no bounds. Her hands involuntarily rose to snatch at her adversary's white linen cap to pull it from her mischievous and pompous head! Only with great presence of mind was his father able to prevent her. Snatching a cap was like throwing a gauntlet down: it meant a duel. Female duels were not edifying to watch. Hadn't he, Amalric, been present at an altercation at the mill last autumn over who was entitled to the last bag of freshly milled flour? The bag had been torn and its precious contents wasted. He had seen several women walking home covered in flour, looking like ghosts.

Next came the moment when the crucified little body of Jesus was tenderly unhooked from the cross by Father Wilfrid. The consecrated host was placed in the little cavity in its chest, the embroidered curtains of the sepulchre were pulled to one side by a chosen member of the congregation and Jesus put to lie there in the tomb until Sunday. Many in the congregation became tearful. Myrtle's shoulders heaved and everyone heard her explosive sob.

When the service was over, Father Wilfrid stood in front of the altar facing his flock, hands resting over his belly, lumpy feet firmly apart, swollen ankles showing below his habit. His face was ashen. Slowly he cast his eyes over the people gathered in the nave. A low, collective mutter rippled about.

'I can no longer be silent,' the priest said. 'We are about to be faced with the terrible disease which you all know about but feel fairly confident will not strike here. My view is that it will. Recently we had an earthquake. God's displeasure was shown. It is close. Some of you will die. Each one of us must consider our own final days and make preparation. Look at the west wall and see what awaits those of us who have greatly sinned.'

A thick silence fell.

Then, as if to accentuate his words, Father Wilfrid took a crumpled parchment from his habit. It was a letter from the Pope to be read out in every church, stating that if a priest could not be found, any one of them could hear confession from a deathbed. Yes, they had all heard correctly: if there was no priest to be found, anyone could hear a confession from a deathbed. Amalric was horrified to think they could each soon be embracing a perilous closeness to God. So much so that they themselves could replace a priest and be sufficiently responsible for another's soul reaching Him.

Father Wilfrid, his bearing unchanged, allowed a few moments to let the severity of the information sink in. There was much shuffling. Stiff backs were stretched. Then, without a word, he motioned that the service was over and walked into the sanctuary where he knelt to pray.

Amalric was glad it was over. The church emptied. The de Horesby family were the first to leave but others at the front were obliged to wait till those at the back had shuffled out. Standing throughout, it had felt a very long time. He saw three people overwhelmed with revulsion at the news, holding hands to their mouths with bitter vomit rising, gagging as they struggled to the door. He saw that others had a great need simply to relieve themselves, clutching their clothing and running towards boundary trees.

Myrtle, however, mysteriously found enough strength and fortitude to push through the throng so that she was able to reach the de Horesbys and limp behind them. They ignored her. Amalric gaped at the nerve of her.

Outside, Elias took his son's sleeve and dragged him to seek out Jacob Ashe. They found him leaning against the church wall.

'Jacob, I'm reet sorry for you,' said Elias.

'Sorry. Sorry! That's no benefit to me.' It was an unusual outburst of vehemence for Jacob. He went on, 'My wife's as bitter as the cow's cud, I shall be ruined with the expense of a wet-nurse, my own health is failin' and my heart is breakin'. Your family is to blame, Elias. Can you do owt to help? No! *Sorry* won't help.' His face crumpled.

Amalric felt pity and helplessness of such intensity for the poor man that it shocked him. His father's sad face told him there was indeed nothing to be done.

Myrtle appeared and joined her distressed husband with only a glance at Elias and Amalric, the baby now in her arms. Her disability and piety were much lessened. Elias and Amalric stood back to let them go.

On Sunday, Easter Day, the wooden body of Jesus was to be resurrected triumphally from the Easter sepulchre in the church. On previous years the service had been festive but this time, Father Wilfrid's words on Good Friday had seeped through the village, somehow exposing death as a haunting spectre rather than a pause before the real joy of salvation.

Nevertheless, a celebration had been arranged for which Lord de Horesby had provided ale and food, set out already up the hill, in his barn. A lamb had been on the spit for hours already. Amalric's mouth watered at the very thought of the pleasure to come. His mother's mind wandered in a different direction.

'I wonder if Myrtle the martyr will be there?' she said to her daughter as they crossed the road to the church.

Amalric hoped that no one else could hear the cynical female spitefulness.

'Them knees will be bad today. Pourin' pus soon, I bet. She'll rue the day.'

Her son felt a momentary thrill – his mother was never lacklustre. In fact, her bold attitude to life lifted many a dull day.

The de Horesbys lived up to expectation. Clara wore a snug-fitting red gown with a casually draped thin leather belt around her small waist and, as before, glanced disdainfully at the village lads. Amalric felt, as most of the villagers did, that it was the boys who were most fashionable and colourful in their fitted blue and yellow particoloured cotehardies of fine wool and matching tight hose. Lord de Horesby and his wife remained reserved in sober, not quite so modern, clothing.

Myrtle and Jacob went to the back of the church. Their grandchild had been left with the expensive wet-nurse. Constance was again by her father's side. The Tynels hovered nearby. All went well with the service and though Father Wilfrid was solemn, he didn't mention the pestilence. Amalric was able to rejoice in being with his family without upset.

The Facebys were the last to leave the church and Amalric was not surprised to see the Ashe family some distance in front on the path. However, a limping Myrtle was showing impatience with her husband's sluggishness and his frequent stumbling. Constance dawdled behind them. Inevitably, the remaining congregants passed them, eager to eat, all except the Facebys. Myrtle obviously recognised their happy, chattering voices behind her and turned around to look. Amalric sensed trouble. Myrtle's emotions exploded. She quickly limped a few steps towards them. On reaching Gundred, she stretched out and pulled off Gundred's linen cap and threw it to the ground. She then grabbed a fistful of greying, darkish hair as it tumbled down. Gundred, surprised, came off balance and fell to the ground. Myrtle leapt on top. Shouts and blasphemies roared from the women. Amalric and the twins looked on in astonishment. Berta started to sob.

Bennet held her hand. His lips quivered. 'She will kill Mother!'

'No. No,' said Amalric to placate his little brother. 'Mother is strong. She will get the better of Mistress Ashe.'

Elias went to the women and struggled to separate them from a froth of top and undergarments, long, loose hair and a twist of legs. Jacob grabbed ineffectually at whatever came near his hands. Constance stood by him, rubbing frantically at scabs on her own face. There was a sound of ripping cloth.

Matilde, further behind, heard the commotion, looked and saw what was going on. Without thinking, she rushed forward and threw herself between the two women, pushing them apart, adding her strength to that of Elias. 'Mother! Mistress Ashe! Stop at once.'

Both fighting women then clawed at Matilde in an effort to remain in contact with each other but Matilde was strong and, with Elias, managed to separate them. Gundred stood trembling with the vehemence of the attack. Myrtle remained in a fighting frame of mind and with arms held back by a blue-tinged and breathless Jacob, she hawked and sent a gobbet of spittle flying at Gundred. The spittle ran gelatinously down the torn, freshly laundered white tucked linen top.

'Just wait, Gundred Faceby. Your family won't get away with it.' Myrtle's face twisted with hate. 'A curse on you!'

Spent with emotion and effort, Gundred looked down at her chest, then at Myrtle. Calmly, with her eyes squinting and her mouth turned down with revulsion, she wiped off the spittle with her finger and smeared it onto her adversary's own breast. 'And a curse on you, Myrtle,' she said, calmly.

Nothing more was said by the women. Amalric went to pick up his mother's cap. For once he was ashamed. It had been painful to see her brawling: his mother behaving like any other common village woman, and near the church. He glanced back, hoping the priest had not seen, but Father Wilfrid was at the porch door. His hands were clasped in front of his belly. He was shaking his head.

An arm went around Amalric's shoulder. 'Come on, lad,' said Elias, gently. 'Time to go. A bit of ale afore the celebration will cheer us. Let's off to the tavern while the communal lamb is roastin'.'

Gundred and Matilde heard and scowled at him.

A few days later, Matilde heard from women at the well that Jacob Ashe had died. His broken heart had failed him. It was no surprise. He had declined since the death of his daughter and coped increasingly badly with his malevolent wife. Gundred felt unable to visit Myrtle and weep over her husband's body, or to attend his funeral. Elias, though, defied her and told Amalric that he must also attend the death of a man from the village. It was a matter of honour. Amalric clasped his hands throughout the service and tried to put meaning onto the events of the past two weeks. He saw his father clutch his cap in one hand, and wipe a tear from his eye with the other.

Part Two

The Pestilence

Chapter Nine

Warren Horesby in May 1349 was tense with the threatened pestilence. Like the villagers, Amalric and his family followed two threads of advice: that of repentance and that of avoidance. With Father Wilfrid, they repented and curbed their desires. With Thurston's advice, they discouraged strangers from stopping as they passed through and they themselves promised not to journey into pestilential areas. As a consequence, the disease had, so far, not entered their huddled valley. Nor had it arrived in places to the east and north but it raged in both Beverley and York to the west.

When a message came from the Abbot of Meaux with regard to a window, Elias greeted the prospect with excitement. It would probably be only for repairs but offered opportunity for time away from the village, he gleefully told Amalric, and since the abbey was north and clear of disease, it was safe to travel. Amalric was not so sure and insisted they say prayers with Father Wilfrid before leaving.

As they rose onto the plain, the distant view opened up.

Elias stood and took a deep breath. 'By, that's grand! I'm reet glad Abbot Hugh sent for us; I'm bein' driven mad back there in the village. An' whether the job comes to summat or nowt, I can't pretend I'm not looking forward to a drop of excellent cool ale.'

'Aye, Da,' agreed Amalric, dolefully.

The Faceby home had not escaped the edginess. His mother without a servant girl was tired and perpetually short-tempered with his father. She frequently blamed him for some misdemeanour that he knew nothing of, while fanning her face to cool the flush which frequently appeared upon it. It worried him that she agitated about Myrtle's curse that had not yet been fulfilled. Matilde grumpily coped with most of the housework and the village healings, refusing help from Thurston when Amalric suggested it might be sought. The twins, feeling the tensions, often disappeared with Ned, whose knowledge lay more in wildlife than glass. Above all, Edwin's continuing absence hung about in the same way his grudging presence had done – unnervingly.

Window work had slowed and given Amalric time to mope. The thought of Nesta being betrothed had left him with an unaccountable sadness. Thurston was the only light in his dull life. They met occasionally and leaned against a fence or sat on a low stone wall to discuss matters beyond the circumscribed nature of the village. Among the all-pervasive wildflowers and buzzing insects, Thurston could not help but tell news of the pestilence. Amalric grew wiser with each conversation and worried, even though the fearsome disease had not appeared.

Now, in the monastery refectory, Amalric sat silently. Ale had been poured, golden, from a jug and he watched small bubbles on the surface of his drink volley little darts of colour as the sunlight touched them. The abbot had not yet spoken of the actual work he wanted Elias to do, only of his wish for coloured glass.

'Oh, Elias,' said Abbot Hugh, gazing dreamily into his beaker, 'to have coloured windows would be like having heaven outside. Just imagine how beautiful it would be with God's eternal light shining through into our church.'

'Aye, and through the saints, as I said before.'

'In Revelation, the Bible speaks of a city of "pure gold, clear as glass",[7] and precious stones: sapphire, emerald, amethyst. Elias, someday, I want my abbey to have those colours to show what rests before us if we are allowed into the Holy City.' The abbot lifted his beaker and looked at his friend over the top as he took a long draught. Then he put it on the table and wiped his lips on the sleeve of his habit.

'Now, Elias, hear me. I am prepared to ask God's forbearance to commission one window for the abbey church, a large coloured one in the east over the high altar.' The abbot scrutinised the face of his friend with amusement.

Elias stared across the table and pulled his ear. Amalric recognised his cautious excitement.

'What?'

'It will depict Mary, the mother of Jesus, in her glory, to be seen every morning. The Virgin Mary is very special to our order. We have an image of her as the queen of heaven and earth on the abbey seal. I would like her to be similarly shown in the window.'

Amalric's thoughts spun. Glass was molten sand, coloured with metal salts. It was not heaven. Yet he, Amalric, perfectly understood the image of heaven depicted in glass. The transparency, the colour. God's reflected light.

'Hugh,' said his father, 'it worries me that you feel like this. Is it not against your order? The warning you had with the earth tremble…'

'Ah, Elias, I will be honest with you. Though a monk, I am also a man and a man of greed at that. I confess my sins but it doesn't stop me sinning again, as with every man. This abbey is wealthy now. Our wool is sought after. Our management of crops is good. The poor are cared for. What should we do with

---

[7] Revelation 21:18: 'The wall is built of jasper, while the city is pure gold, clear as glass.'

our wealth but glorify God? And yes... maybe have a little pleasure ourselves, a little reward.'

Amalric listened. His father was interested, excitement growing.

Abbot Hugh continued. 'Life is more stable now. Raids from up north have ceased. There has not been another earth tremble and though I still fear the pestilence, it has bypassed us. Its absence is a good omen. Not only that, I have heard that other Cistercian monasteries are having highly coloured windows with saints without incurring God's wrath.'

The abbot placed both hands flat on the table, a satisfied look on his face. Elias waited.

'I want a window that will be admired. I want you to procure the best glass, my friend... to glorify God.' Then, remembering the earth tremble, the abbot said with mock seriousness, 'But we must be mindful not to be the source of too much envy, since our pride may go before our fall... again. I have at least reduced my ambition to one window only!' He laughed, grasped his beaker and banged it on the table. Then he stood. The matter was settled.

Elias stood and, over the table, shook the abbot's hand.

Amalric remained seated. He was at the same time overjoyed and horrified. He couldn't resist the urge to look up and speak.

'But the pestilence, Da? What if it comes? Shouldn't you wait?' He resisted speaking of death, but Thurston had convinced him of the awful fact that the disease would come and it would kill.

Elias threw him a warning glance, as did the abbot. He had overstepped the mark. Then the abbot smiled down on Amalric as if he were a child.

'God in His way will look after us. We sin little in this abbey. Our faith is strong. I feel my window will please God.' His smile broadened. 'The disease is in York even as we speak. You see, it has passed us by.'

Amalric felt sick with concern. He recalled a question of Father Wilfrid's, 'What sins can be bad enough to cause this pestilence?'

Sinning, to Amalric and his friend Thurston, was not the issue.

The abbot moved round the table and confidently slapped his old friend Elias on the back. Elias fell forward, tipping his beaker and spilling the last of his ale. It ran into a crack in the wood.

'But supplies? The glass? It'll take time. Suppliers won't be gettin' the stuff in, things have slowed so much,' worried Elias.

'Elias, do I have to tell you your job? There is so little work for the glaziers that the glass merchants in King's-Town on Hull have a surfeit, an excess of the most beautiful glass. I saw it last week on a visit there to one of our other monasteries. We must take this opportunity. It may be God-given.'

Amalric flinched. Hadn't Thurston mentioned King's-Town on Hull and the pestilence? Or had it now retreated from there?

Elias was invigorated. Amalric failed to share his zeal. It was Ned who caught his master's enthusiasm, standing with his mouth open in the workshop, happily shocked to see him return with a fire in his eyes.

From that day in May, Elias, Amalric and Ned laboured together. The first thing to be done was to clear the workshop beside the abbey church because the window had to be made on-site. It would be too large to make at Warren Horesby. When work eventually began in earnest, Elias, Amalric and Ned would stay there until the job was done, but for now, they moved between the two places.

The next task was to measure the stone frame of the abbey window and accurately draw its shape. It was a dangerous job, using ladders and wooden scaffolding. Amalric was given the task as he had a good head for heights. His resulting diagrams determined the spacing of the design and the amount of glass required.

Then it was drawing the figure of Mary and her child on a throne. Amalric watched his father competently draw basic lines with lead point on small chalk-whitened wooden boards to get the design and proportions just right, ready to transfer them as exact-sized drawings to the table, panel by panel. But as he watched, he felt uneasy with his father's style. The figure of Mary was old-fashioned, static, and her baby like a small adult. Her eyes were large but her gaze cold, the throne improbable. Given the chance, he would have experimented and tried something different. But what? He didn't know. Anyway, the design had been agreed with Abbot Hugh. It was traditional. How could he, a mere apprentice, make comments when they knew best?

Next, it was time to purchase the glass: amber for the throne, green for curtain drapes, white garments for the Virgin Mary to indicate her purity. For a background, Abbot Hugh particularly wanted expensive transparent blue glass, which he had first seen at St Denis and Chartres in France when a young man on a pilgrimage. 'Amalric,' he had said, 'if you never get as far as France, you must one day see the windows of Canterbury. They are equally magnificent. And then of course there are those in York and Beverley Minsters, where I first greatly admired your father's work. I want to have windows equally prestigious in my abbey: perhaps even more enviable.' He had laughed impishly.

Elias had responded with practicalities. 'Aye, but we need more than glass, Hugh. We need carpenters to make racks, tables and scaffolds, lead smelters to make lead cames, builders to make a kiln and see to the stone window surround, a blacksmith...'

'Yes, well, just go ahead and hire them,' the abbot had said, recklessly.

Amalric remained concerned. 'Da, we must be sure not to hire men from areas where the pestilence is present, or recently so.'

'Aye, son, you're right. We must be cautious.' But Elias was not in a frame of mind to be *very* cautious.

When their planning was complete, Elias and Amalric journeyed to King's-Town on Hull and a dockside warehouse. Abbot Hugh had recommended a particular merchant with a large amount of blue glass unclaimed since the pestilence. Elias was happy to comply, since he had bought many a glass sheet from the same man. On slow heavy horses borrowed from the abbey, they ambled south following the Hull River. It was a pleasant journey through valleys and glades. The air was warm and dry. Wayside blooms wafted in a soft breeze. Pollens drifted. Neither thought much about the pestilence since Thurston had assured them it was gone from the town, but when they approached it, seeking the road to the dock, their mood changed.

They were first unnerved by their horses' behaviour. The steady beasts hesitated and then became agitated. The reason became clear as both Elias and Amalric detected an obnoxious stench drifting on the air. It increased as they passed boarded-up homes and piles of reeking rubbish littering the roadside, waiting to be carted. It was a silent, brooding stink, hanging about on drooping, opportunist weeds and drifting from dark, dank Snickelways. Fresh air had been laid low by heavy, clinging miasmas.

Amalric thought of Thurston's prophetic words after the earthquake at Meaux, about such miasmas. He felt his face pale. He'd questioned the wisdom of the trip but that was weeks ago – neither of them thought that King's-Town on Hull would be like this. Not a word did they speak to each other but continued on. The horses became hard to hold but they cajoled them forward, the jingling of their harnesses obvious in the silence. In the town centre where the bustling market should have been, there were only a few small produce stalls, their linen shades hanging limp in the heavy air. The crowds they had expected to push against were absent. The few individuals seemed to be mainly young adults, grim-faced, walking or working with empty determination.

Elias and Amalric made their way to the docks. The stench intensified. A few trading ships were moored, and bobbed with anticipation, but only a few men attended to them. On the dockside, fresh produce rotted in sacks, left where they had been piled after unloading. Mysterious crates of who-knew-what lay for the taking. Among them were copious numbers of shiny, rotting dead rats. Some had been kicked into the water where their black, bloated bodies floated, feet-up. On the dock edge, a dog and cat lay dead with a mangled pigeon corpse between them. It was obvious to Amalric that the pestilence had struck more severely here than anywhere else in the town.

'Da, maybe we should leave.'

'Nay, son, the disease has gone. Things'll pick up 'ere soon. Docks are allus like this. Rats, dogs, cats allus around. Come, the warehouse is just over there.'

They dropped from their horses and led them to a tall wooden building. A large painted name indicated business success, but the dust on the sign and scattered empty crates outside suggested neglect.

'Old Silas should be there,' said Elias. 'I've traded with him for many a year.'

Amalric tied up the horses while Elias knocked on a small door set into a much larger one. They stood for a while before they heard the sound of bolts being pulled to one side. A younger person than Elias had anticipated opened the door.

'I've come to buy glass from Silas,' Elias said, getting to the point quickly.

'My father's dead,' the young man said, matter-of-factly. 'What glass do you want? The more you take, the cheaper each sheet'll be. I want to get rid and start over. The glass has been here awhile. My father bought it in afore the pestilence struck over the water. After that its production stopped.'

Amalric's unease increased at the young man's pragmatic attitude, but his father seemed distracted by thoughts of a bargain and was therefore unaffected.

'Is the pestilence still here, in Hull?' Amalric asked.

'Nay. It's long gone. My father was the last one to die. We thought it had passed but he was infirm and it caught him. Died here, in this warehouse. A few weeks back.'

Amalric shuddered. A few weeks didn't sound very long.

Elias interrupted the younger men's conversation, saying that any glass he ordered had to be coloured evenly throughout and clear enough to see through. Small samples of glass were brought for their inspection.

Amalric's fears were pushed aside, as he was transported to the nearest thing to heaven on earth for him – a myriad of coloured glass samples! They lay on a large table and his hands roamed over them, checking for thickness, holding them against the light, assessing transparency, putting one on top of another to see how the colour changed, putting his nose to them and sniffing in ecstasy. Even imperfect samples held a promise.

'See this, Da, the ripples, you could use these as folds in cloth. And these bubbles as pattern on cloth. And this streak as sunlight on gold. And this blue, Da, it's so pure.'

From the samples, they chose glass of the best quality from Bohemia and Normandy. There, large forests provided the special beech wood that was burned to ash and added to sand to make glass. From the warehouse, the glass would journey to Meaux Abbey via the Hull River, then ox cart. There was much to organise.

Amalric's anxieties about the future were pushed to the back of his mind by his father's enthusiasm. His ability to organise other workers even improved as he helped recruit talented artisans from hamlets between the abbey and Warren Horesby.

Chapter Ten

Amalric gazed down at his boots. They were messed up again and he would have to wipe the obnoxious slime off with grass. The soiling was the result of someone being caught short when suffering from the squits, leaving their excrement and vomit hidden in the greenery by the roadside. He should have taken note of the mass of buzzing flies. Parties of the poorest cottagers were paid to keep the village mess down but, clearly, they were not up to the job. He sighed.

While the pestilence had not appeared, the usual summer illnesses had. Besides complaints of the guts, Warren Horesby sweated and sneezed through seasonal colds and sore throats. Insect bites and stings were common and childhood illnesses stalked their little hosts. Matilde and Gundred were kept busy with ill folk. His sister admitted that help from the manor physician would be useful but Gundred disagreed, believing university knowledge was of little use to ordinary folk.

People began to believe the pestilence had bypassed them. In a village to the east of Warren Horesby, some wealthy villagers were so relieved, they commissioned a window for their church in gratitude to God, with an image of St Peter. Amalric considered them to be recklessly misguided but his father accepted the work, knowing it would be an excellent apprentice piece for his son. Elias wished he were wealthy enough to do the same for Warren Horesby church but, as

Amalric pointed out, God would, in any case, spread His beneficence to themselves, the creators of beauty. There would be time to make the window while they waited for the abbey glass to be delivered there.

Amalric prepared the table and started to draw the first lines of St Peter. Then news came that six crates of glass had arrived at Meaux Abbey. It was mid August. The small window would have to be held up for a day for the glass to be unpacked and checked. Then with Amalric finishing the small window and Elias finalising plans for the large one, the Faceby workshop would transfer to the abbey, working daily unless short days and freezing fingers made the handling of glass too dangerous. By the start of spring 1350, the large window would be completed, of that Amalric was almost certain.

A skylark hung over the plain, singing hollowly in the vast empty sky as the trio journeyed to the abbey for their one day of unpacking glass. Butterflies flickered glass-coloured wings around them.

'You'd best watch out for the blue glass, Am,' puffed Elias, wiping his sweating forehead. 'Unpack it last when you've got used to the work. It's three times the price of the colourless stuff.'

'Best *I* don't handle it, then, Master,' said Ned nasally, a summer cold lingering in his head. He was aware of his own clumsiness. 'Master Amalric has shown me that blue afore. When you hold it up, it's like looking into heaven... like God is up there.'

'Well, lad, I'll risk you handlin' it. I'm not one to deny you a glimpse of heaven.' Elias smiled at Ned's earnest, honest face. 'And you, Am, will have to be careful later cutting it into shapes; a slip of the grozin' iron'll be expensive, very expensive. But your young hands are stronger and more accurate than mine, nowadays, so I'll let you do most of it.'

'Aye, Da.'

119

As soon as they made their way into the abbey precinct, Elias hobbled over cobbles to seek Abbot Hugh. Amalric smiled tolerantly, knowing he would be hoping his friend, Abbot Hugh, would put away work in favour of an hour or two of relaxation. Ned and Amalric made their way to the abbey church south wall and adjacent glazing workshop. Two new wooden huts had been built, one to cut glass and the other to assemble panels. The large domed kiln looked clean and empty, ready to fuse paint and glass together. Amalric almost skipped with excitement.

One of the lay brothers was waiting for them, smiling, his full head of hair marking him out from the tonsured monks.

'My name is Mark,' he said, slightly bowing before them.

Ned jerked an uncertain bow in response – he'd met him on his previous visit. Amalric smiled a greeting.

'I had the crates of glass put into here.' Mark indicated the smaller hut. 'There is drink for you. There will be enough for the hound. I have permission to help you for the day, if you wish.'

Amalric nodded thanks.

'Aye, help would be gradely,' said Ned with a sniff, always glad to have a new friend.

'I've been working in the infirmary for days,' said Mark, moving to Ned's side companionably. 'We've got travellers in there who seem a bit ill, coughing all over the place and complaining of aches and pains. I don't much care for that kind of work, mopping hot brows and all. I'd rather be doing something like this.' He smiled broadly, his relief to be away from the nursing clear to see.

Amalric opened the creaking, new, rough-planked door and gazed in. Racks lined both sides of the hut. A small table was at the far corner and on top, a jug of water and beakers. Six wooden crates, half the size of coffins, were on the earthen floor. He took charge.

'Right, a drink, and then we'll get down to the unpacking. You and Brother Mark will unpack the crates and I will take each piece of glass from you and put it into the rack.' He had already decided that they would be stored in sequence like a rainbow. Red first, then amber and so on. Blue towards the end, then purple. 'And keep Samson out. If we trip over him, we'll likely break some glass.'

Samson, sensing something interesting, had crept into the hut and sniffed around but Ned took him by the rope around his neck and dragged him out. He was tied up to a small bush, where he was expected to doze in the warm shade.

None of the crates was labelled for colour, except the blue. It was thus doubly exciting for Ned to carefully lever each lid with a crowbar. A layer of sweet-smelling, golden straw was all that could be seen at first. Mark, who had never seen coloured glass before, pulled off the straw excitedly, eager to see what lay underneath. His eyes opened wide as he saw an undulating surface looking like water in a pool.

'Oh, my! This is so beautiful,' he cried, and opened his hand wide to touch the surface as if he expected his hand to sink into it. He looked surprised when his hand stopped on hardness.

'Help me lift it out,' said Ned, with a superior tone. 'It's only like the panes in yon church windows, but coloured. You'll see the colour when we lift it up.'

It was amber. As it was caught by a shaft of sunlight coming through the doorway, gold spread over the creamy new wood of the walls and across their faces. Mark was entranced.

Amalric inspected every sheet for cracks and, to himself, gloried in the splendour.

It was hot work. Amalric and Ned stripped off their thick woollen tunics, leaving only short hose secured with leather belts. Mark was not allowed to remove his clothing and Ned taunted him.

'I bet you're really hot, Brother Mark. It feels right free to have no tunic. See my muscles,' he said jokingly, 'and see my brown skin. Why don't you take your robe off? It stinks.' He laughed at Mark, who smiled sheepishly.

'You know I can't.' Mark's face grew redder.

Ned continued to mock. 'I saw you after the tremble when you fell and your habit was around your waist with nothin' underneath. I bet that's why you can't take it off.'

'Ned, stop teasing,' said Amalric. 'We need to get this job done.'

'I bet under that habit he's thinner than me an' I bet his muscles are just little tiny bulges.'

'Ned!'

But Mark was tolerant. 'You win, Ned. What I need is a Warren Horesby pot of stew. We eat many vegetables here.'

All three of them stopped to laugh.

Time sped by unnoticed. Amalric had not seen his father since they arrived but he didn't mind; managing a job himself was becoming easier and today was really pleasant work. Only the sixth crate remained to be emptied.

'The last crate. Not long now afore we can 'ave a mug of weak ale, eh, Mark?' said Ned, hoping this was true. His throat was dry. He put his crowbar under the wooden lid and pressed down to lever up the nails. With the first cracking of the wood, it was obvious that the straw was damp. A stench rose up which, even with an almost blocked nose, made Ned flinch backward and screw up his face.

'Ugh! Let's get this lid off, quick!'

Samson became aware of a new scent wafting from the hut. He pulled at his rope, barking. As the lid came away, the straw appeared a little soft, soggy, but the glass seemed unspoiled. As the sheets were lifted out to be put in the rack, the protective straw gave way to old clothing. Amalric reasoned that straw was in short supply in King's-Town on Hull because of poor harvests. Using it for packing was a waste, even for costly glass. Old clothing worked well enough to keep the brittle sheets separated and reduce the impact of the bumps from the road. Nor was he surprised, given earlier wet weather, to see it was damp and mildewed. The old garments had probably been gathered in the rain and stored in a corner of a warehouse without a chance to dry. As Ned and Mark carefully lifted out sheets of precious blue glass, they were unwrapped and the clothing thrown in a pile on the floor.

Ned came to the last piece of glass. It was protected by a pair of tattered hose, faded and stained to grey/brown. 'Phew, stinking!' he said, and pushed the bulky cloth to one side. Mark retched. Amalric heard and caught the stink but continued examining glass with particularly interesting imperfections that could be used with effect for the background. Outside, Samson's curiosity overcame him. He strained forward on his rope, broke off the branch to which it was tied and with rope and branch trailing, dived immediately into the hut. He nosed the stinking pile of cloth. At the same time, Ned lifted the sheet of glass from the crate, causing Samson to lift his snout. The dog detected an even more exciting stink and jumped in, catching the branch on his master's leg, knocking him off balance and causing him to drop the glass. The glass hit the side of the crate and shattered with a blue splash and a splintering sound over the floor... and over Mark's sandalled feet. He screamed.

Amalric, shocked at the sudden tumult, with great presence of mind put the sheet he was holding carefully into the rack for safety and turned to gaze with horror on the scene. He saw Samson, undeterred by the commotion he was causing, burying his snout into cloth. Then the dog raised his head triumphantly with a black furry mass in his teeth.

'Samson, out!' cried Ned.

The dog leapt out of the crate and ran outside with his prize drooping either side of his mouth... but shortly emitted a frantic whining sound. They all looked out. Samson was turning circles trying to knock dark insects from his shaggy coat. Then he rolled in the dust snapping his teeth. The black object lay on the ground.

Ned went to his dog. 'It's fleas. They've come from that black thing.' He kicked the black mass to identify it. 'Eee, look at that,' he said, as Mark came to his side. 'It must have been caught up in the cloth durin' the packin' and couldn't get out. It must have died of starvation. No wonder its fleas are hungry.'

Ned bent to grasp a tail and held up a large black rat. Amalric went to the door and remembered with unease the dockside in King's-Town on Hull and, further back, the black cat at the well. He, Mark and Ned stood mesmerised as the rat's rotting body swung gently, all the while slowly separating from the root of the tail until it suddenly plopped, a moist, putrid corpse, onto the dusty ground in front of them. Mark retched again. A few fleas jumped about, some landing on Ned's hands and bare chest. One or two jumped onto Mark's habit seeking exposed flesh and found his forearms below his rolled sleeves, his neck and face above the neckline of his habit. They both wriggled frantically as they tried to knock them off.

Amalric turned back into the hut and picked up the pieces of broken glass and gathered them into a pile and put them onto the table. Horror and despondency turned to silent anger at Ned's carelessness with the tying of his dog. He pictured his father's face red with anger. How would he tell him? His burgeoning confidence left him.

'Ugh! That was awful,' said Mark, slumping onto the top of one of the empty crates.

'Aye, it was,' said Ned, sitting with him. Samson was once more tied up, but more securely this time. 'It was the worst I've ever seen. We 'ave plenty of fleas about in our village, especially on animals, Samson has many, and if Ma don't clear our bedding out or the rushes on the floor for months we 'ave bugs, but I've never been attacked like this.'

Feeling faint, Mark had lowered his head onto his hands, only then to see his bloody feet. He tried hard not to vomit. A cold sweat glistened on his forehead.

'It's an omen!'

'Here, use this.' Ned gave Mark a rather mouldy piece of cloth with which to dab his cuts.

With Amalric, sternly silent and Ned and Brother Mark scratching, they walked to meet Elias. When they met, his son noticed an ale-induced unsteadiness.

'Eh, what ails you all?' Elias had trouble focusing. 'Eh, Ned, you seem to have fresh bites, stings or summat. Did you fall on a reet big wasps' nest, Ned, eh? And you, brother, you look proper ill.'

'Nay, Master,' said Ned. 'It was fleas in the glass packin'. They itch real bad.'

Mark said nothing. He just walked away in the direction of the infirmary.

'Amalric?' Elias asked, warily.

'Just a hard day, Da. You don't look so good yourself. Let's go home.' Now was not the time to give him bad news of broken glass. On one hand, it was only a single sheet but on the other, it was the most precious. But more important to Amalric was that he felt himself a failure again. But he had escaped the flea bites.

The following morning Ned didn't arrive at the workshop. Remembering his bites, Elias suggested that Gundred send Berta with some medications.

'Alice Tynel should have enough sense to deal with her own son and it's best not to interfere. Flea bites are common enough. If Alice needs help, she can surely get it from Myrtle.'

Gundred had rarely mentioned Myrtle's name since Easter. Now she said it with venom.

Bennet and Berta had no such reservations and were excited to see Ned covered in red hives. After breakfast, they ran eagerly up the road to the Tynel home.

Later, Berta was eager to tell her big brother about the visit. 'He looked so funny, Mally,' she said, her dark curls bobbing. 'You should see him. He's lying by the fire, wrigglin' all over with a prickly itch like this,' she demonstrated with exaggerated convulsive movements, 'and is covered in lumpy slime. He said it was a balm of his mother's. We sat next to him on his mattress, but it was dirty and some of the balm was meltin' and runnin' onto it. I didn't like it. It was stinky.' She pulled a funny, grimacing face and then smiled. 'But we told funny stories so he'd forget to scratch and stop feeling sick. Only we felt sick as well 'cos it was all so smelly. Ugh! I wouldn't want to live there. No, I wouldn't.'

'He's worried about Samson,' said Bennet more seriously, his little face screwed with concern. 'He ran off when they got home yesterday and hasn't been back. Ned's got a headache as well.'

On the third day after the trip to Meaux, Amalric had to leave work on the St Peter window to attend to his father's sheep. Elias had felt weary and had asked his son to lend a hand. It was a pleasant day and not too much of a chore. He walked back from the fields past the mill pond. A dragonfly flittered before him over the water and he saw its wings, rainbows flashing like thin glass in the sunlight. His eyes followed it under the overhanging greenery. He continued to watch in case it emerged, but became distracted by a large ginger furry-looking lump of something. His suspicions aroused, he grabbed it with his father's shepherd's crook, inching it to the edge. It was a swollen dog, its tongue protruding, large and unmoving. Samson! Samson was Ned's best friend. He wondered if the poor animal had drowned trying to ease himself of flea bites. He took hold of a leg and tried to pull it out onto the bank but the body was too slippery and heavy to get a grip. Anyway, it was perhaps best left hidden so that Ned would not have to face the news until he was well. Then he pushed Samson back deep underneath the vegetation. As it slid into watery shadows, Amalric said a prayer: you did that for friends. Poor Ned.

Ned became more ill. The twins were troubled after a second visit. They sought the consolation of their father and eldest brother in the workshop.

'Da…' said Bennet to his father, who was drawing on the large white table. 'We don't think Ned will be back working soon. He couldn't speak to us. He looks all lumpy and red and he aches all over… and he stinks. It's not the usual smell of that house. It's different today.'

Amalric stopped sharpening a piece of charcoal. Elias looked at his youngest son with a blank expression.

Berta, standing next to her twin and ever ready to enlarge her brother's account of a situation, added more information. 'His ma says his illness comes from the sin of taking off his tunic and making the lay brother jealous, 'cos he had to wear his long robe. He told his ma all about it. He's hot all over. He can't put his arms to his side either because he has lumps in his armpits.' She held out her arms to either side and flopped her head sideways in demonstration.

Amalric felt sick at the religious imagery.

'And his ears stick out 'cos of little lumps behind them. His nose is running. It's a really, really bad cold.'

'An' he has a tickle in his chest which makes him cough,' said Bennet, anxious to add something. 'But he always has that.'

Amalric recalled things Thurston had spoken of since the day he had met him at the abbey and later in friendly conversations. Things about the pestilence. Fear stung him.

Elias stayed calm. 'Then stay away from him because it may be somethin' catchin'.'

'But Da!'

'Stay away.'

The next day, Amalric was alone in the workshop. His father had approved his black line-drawing of St Peter on the tabletop and had given his son the responsibility of choosing colours and cutting glass. The first glass to be cut represented a fall of the saint's robe from his waist to hem; a narrow piece, to be roughly cut at first then carefully chipped away with a grozing iron to make the shape accurate. He chose purple as a suitable colour for Jesus' chief disciple and placed the sheet over the drawing on the whitewashed table. Black lines showed through the glass. Each piece had to fit just inside each separate shape so that there was room for lead cames to be pressed around the edge. The came was H-shaped to hold glass in both the upper and lower part of the H. In this way, one piece of glass would be held to another, eventually making a panel. Joints would be soldered to make them strong.

Amalric positioned the bubbles and undulations of the glass so that sunlight would catch them, giving texture and sparkle. Two cuts would make the basic shape. He stoked up the little hearth in the corner to heat up an iron cutting tool. It was normally Ned's job to keep the fire hot and Amalric was momentarily annoyed before remembering how ill he was. Soon the tip of the thin rod glowed red. He took a piece of leather to cover the end and pulled it from the fire, then delicately pressed it down on the glass where the drawn line started. The glass was hard and didn't crack. Quickly, and remembering Theophilus' instructions, he put a finger wetted with saliva onto the glass where the tool had been. A small crack appeared and immediately with the tool, he followed the drawn line. The glass snapped satisfyingly into two pieces at just the right place.

Next, the second line. He lifted the reheated iron and placed it at the edge of the glass. Suddenly, a scream tore through the air. Amalric's hand jumped and the hot iron slid across the surface, cracking the glass in the wrong place. He cursed and angrily looked up. Through the window he saw Ned's mother, Alice Tynel, running down the hill to the church. A few moments later he saw Father Wilfrid waddle up the hill as speedily as his thick ankles would allow, with her pulling at his sleeve. After a while, the priest returned slowly to the church and closed the door.

Amalric tried to continue his work but the commotion disrupted his flow. His progress with the window slowed, then stopped. The sun was lowering. He downed his tools and doused the hearth fire. Tomorrow morning, he would cut more glass. Maybe a pinkish piece for the saint's face, ready for his father, as the Master Glazier, to supervise the painting of the facial lines in the traditional, impassive manner. Then the piece would be fired in the kiln outside, so that the paint would become part of the glass.

It was Amalric's job to make the dark brown paint: a mix of green and blue glass ground between two porphyry stones, powdery burned copper and his own stale pee. It was a skilful job; the paint had to be just the right consistency to stay on the smooth surface. It struck him that it was strange to have a saint's facial expression fixed by paint. He asked himself how differently he would paint it if allowed to be inventive – smearing and scraping back the paint to make it more real. He longed to shape a smile, make a bumpy nose, raise an eyebrow.

Bending over the table had made Amalric's back ache and he stood and stretched. His hair was damp with the sweat of working and he pressed it back with the flat of his hands. He moved to the window to look up the village. The air was still and silent. Then he heard muffled words carried down the hill: 'He's dead. My one child, dead.' He saw Osbert Tynel grabbing at his agitated, distraught wife, Alice, obviously trying to calm her, but clearly his own distress was preventing him. Amalric watched, stunned, and could not believe what was happening. He sped out of the door and ran up the road. He reached them and tried to catch his breath to speak. Osbert Tynel, with rheumy red eyes glanced at him, managed to take control of his wife and pulled her away.

Fear tightened Amalric's chest. He stood, feeling foolish. Then he felt an urge to see his adored twins. The sun was almost set; Berta and Bennet would be in their beds in the low-roofed loft. He hastily went home and went straight to climb the ladder. He peered through the hole in the ceiling into the triangular space formed by the crook beams. He saw a last dusty shaft of evening sunlight spearing through a tiny window. It rested on their black hair. All seemed well but he could not rid himself of the sense of foreboding. He climbed down the ladder and went to his parents, who were both sitting at the table. His father glanced at him from under a furrowed brow. Amalric sensed a taut anxiety in both his parents and knew they were aware that Ned was dead. Nevertheless, he dared to broach the subject of visiting Ned's family again.

'No! You will not go,' said Elias, vehemently.

'But Da, he was your employee and my friend.'

'Aye, even so.'

Amalric was both sorry and guiltily relieved not to be allowed to visit the Tynel home, but needed to talk. 'Ma, do you think Ned's death was caused by the pes…?'

'No, son. Certainly not.'

His mother spoke sharply through a clenched jaw. He did not believe her. She always had trouble hiding how she really felt. He watched as she rubbed her hands over her cheeks, wiping something invisible away.

'You know what it's like in high summer, all sorts of insects are biting. Horseflies are vicious. Ned's illness may have come from one of 'em. You know how prone he was to that sort of thing: coughs, colds an' all. Best do as your father says.'

She moved to the fire and stirred the ever-present stew pot and pushed floating vegetables below the surface. There was comfort of sorts in the act of stirring. It made things come together. Her son refused to let the subject go, gnawing at it, wanting to open it up.

'Ned's bites came from fleas in a crate. Stinking clothes. A rat. Blue glass from France.' Hadn't Father Wilfrid and Thurston mentioned France and the pestilence? 'The French still don't like us for winning at Crécy and Calais, do they, Mother?'

'Am, that's more in your father's line,' said Gundred, with obvious impatience.

But he wanted the healing voice of his mother. He was desperate. A thought struck him. 'Ma… your curse on Myrtle. Could it have affected Ned, somehow? The Tynels are friends of the Ashes, after all?'

Gundred whipped round and threateningly brandished her long, thick wooden spoon at him. But she was unable to say anything. Tears welled in her eyes.

Chapter Eleven

Ned's funeral was held in Warren Horesby church the next day in the early evening, when the village harvesting had been done for the day. It had needed to be soon. His body had begun to stink remarkably quickly.

'It's because it's summer and hotter than usual,' Father Wilfrid said.

The smell of rosemary and other herbs in the church porch was strong: leaves, seeds and flowers had been strewn on the floor to be crushed by feet; a small cross made with stalks of herbs was nailed to the church door – all were intended to ward off disease. Amalric saw his mother's eyes linger on the herbs and knew she was trying to deny what she really knew.

Ned's body had been in the church all the previous night, in front of the altar. Alice and Osbert Tynel had watched over their son the entire time and were slumped on a bench, looking sunken and grey. During the funeral service, most villagers held kerchiefs to their mouths since the herbal perfumes failed to overcome the stench. The service was short. During it, Amalric looked up in an effort to hold back the tears: his father had warned him that he was too old to show much emotion. He saw little birds sitting on roof beams, lit by the remains of the day and by candles from below. One flapped its wings and a feather floated down, was wafted by the breath of congregants, brushed his cheek and landed on his tunic at his shoulder. He picked it off. Its softness saddened him.

Amalric and Elias wished to help carry Ned's wrapped body to the graveside but no one asked them. It was carried out on an old plank, covered by a precious embroidered cloth, by Osbert Tynel, Jacob Ashe and two others. They held it up with little effort. Alice Tynel staggered behind, supported by Myrtle: Myrtle would understand the loss of a child, since the death of her own eldest child, Gundred admitted to Amalric.

A few mourners gathered around a Ned-sized hole, dark and deep, in the graveyard. The Facebys' presence at the graveside was received with a hateful glare from Ned's mother. Father Wilfrid stood on the edge of the grave, hands holding a wooden crucifix. Beyond, someone had hung a wreath of summer flowers and leaves on the ancient stone cross which stood prominently at the north-eastern end of the graveyard. Amalric suspected it might have been Berta. He could see it had an artistic flair to it which he recognised. The freshness of the summer colours against the ancient stone, hundreds of years old, moved him in a way he couldn't describe. Berta was a sensitive girl. What with that and her healing interests, she would grow to be a formidable young woman, like Matilde. A pleasant thought. Then, for no reason, Edwin popped into his mind. He should have been there, with his family, for the death of a family assistant. The pleasant thought vanished.

Father Wilfrid sprinkled holy water and said words that Amalric found hard to take in. The priest's face was stern; the edges of his mouth tipped downwards into deep folds. Amalric sensed that the village was hovering at the start of a downward path. A dark path, the end of which was unknown, unvisited. All it needed was a slight push and they would tumble along it.

When Father Wilfrid had finished speaking, people picked soil from the mound at the graveside and threw small amounts over Ned's body as a symbol of respect and a final farewell, and then they left. Berta, with one hand, clung to Amalric and would not let him leave the graveside. In her other hand, she held a bunch of flowers, dry and gone to seed. He wondered what she wanted to do with them and was surprised when she threw them onto the almost-full grave. Why had she done that? Together in silence, they watched the sexton throw a last thin layer of soil over them. Berta looked up at Amalric, forestalling his question.

'Mally, they might grow. Like he'll come alive again but in a different way.'

Amalric said nothing; the lump in his throat was too large to allow speech.

On the path from the church, as folk made to scatter home, Alice Tynel hurried to catch the Faceby family. Her husband struggled after her in an effort to deflect a coming conflict.

She grabbed Gundred by the arm from behind and said calculatingly, 'This is your family's fault. It was the pestilence what got him, when he was workin' with your family.'

The few people around them stopped, horrified at the word 'pestilence' and waited for Gundred's response. Myrtle stood nearby, sneering.

'Don't be ridiculous,' snapped Gundred. Her instinct to deny the terrible accusation was strong. Her mantle slipped as her head spun round to face Alice. 'It was a surfeit of insect bites; fleas, horseflies and maybe... even bedbugs! And he was a weaklin'.'

Amalric suspected his mother would regret her outburst. Her heart would lurch when she realised her own fear had caused her to fling an undeserved insult on a poor woman who had the misfortune to lose a dear son.

Gundred lowered her voice. 'Anyway, the pestilence reached York and Beverley as far back as May, totally bypassing us; it can't have been the pestilence. Where would he have got it from? The only place they've all been is Meaux Abbey and nobody had it there and...' Her voice rose so all could hear. 'Elias an' Amalric ain't ill.' She stared defiantly at Alice, who then sank to the ground, weeping. Her husband struggled to bring her to her feet again.

Elias felt upset at his own wife's peevish reaction. 'Come on, time to go home. Everybody's reet upset today.'

Myrtle walked hurriedly past Gundred and Elias. She caught Gundred vengefully on the shoulder but made no sign of apology. Elias held his wife closer so she could not respond.

Standing by the church gate, Amalric watched Ned's parents walk slowly but stoically up the hill. There was a finality in the way they went, without looking back and appearing so much older than their years. It occurred to him that he might never see them again.

Bennet and Berta went to him, holding hands, tearful, not knowing quite what to do next. Amalric put an arm around both in an effort to console. They huddled to him. As he moved to guide them home, he glanced back and saw Thurston just outside the church porch. The physician had followed the funeral service, unnoticed by most people. Now he was talking to Matilde. Their conversation looked serious and conspiratorial. Amalric approved when Thurston put a hand on Matilde's shoulder because he suspected that had they not been within the precincts of the church, he would have attempted something more intimate. He hoped Matilde would have allowed him.

When Matilde arrived home, Amalric followed her into the barn, where he knew she would be milking Molly. 'I saw you by the church with Thurston, deep in conversation,' he said mischievously, a knowing grin playing on his face. 'I wondered if he might...'

'Don't be ridiculous, Am. Grow up,' she said. 'We were talking about the pes... about herbs and healing.'

Her dark, flashing eyes told him not to ask more. Amalric felt young and naïve.

Next morning, Amalric went to the workshop, after sharing a drink with Father Wilfrid, and went immediately to push up a shutter bar. When it came away easily in his hands, he thought of Ned whistling down the hill with Samson. It was hard to think he had been put in the ground only the day before.

A sound caught his ear behind him and he turned, surprised to see his father sniffing into a piece of rag. It was obvious he had something to say and had been waiting for his son.

'Er, son, I have… have reet bad news.' Elias tried to control quivering lips. 'There was a journeyman by the tavern last evenin'. We wouldn't let him in but he had a message for us. He'd been to Meaux Abbey askin' for work on their land. He had to ring the bell for a long time. A monk told him that six of them, including Abbot Hugh, had died suddenly, two days after we were there. All were buried on the same day.' He gulped. 'Dear God, Hugh was my friend.' He wiped his eyes. 'The monk asked him to call in to tell us and wanted to give him money for his pains, but the man wouldn't take it. Fearful, he was, that coins might spread it.'

Amalric could hardly believe it. 'Did they die of the pestilence, Da?'

'Aye, son, tis likely they did.'

'Oh, Da. Was the journeyman well?'

'Aye. I bought him a drink for his pains. He had to drink it outside, mind. Now nobody'll touch his beaker. It's still outside in the grass. Dogs are sniffin', of course.' Elias was silent for a while and Amalric waited for him to speak again. 'Why hasn't it come to me? I'm old. I sat with Hugh. I don't understand it.'

How could Amalric answer his father? Why hadn't he himself caught it? He'd been at the abbey with both Ned and Mark. Maybe it wasn't the pestilence.

With such terrifying news, neither he nor his father could contemplate a day's work. They left the workshop. Elias leaned on his son for support.

Inside the house, both Amalric and his father slumped at the table. The only noise was Gundred's clattering over breakfast preparation.

Matilde came in from the barn. 'I wish Nesta would come back. I'm too shocked at the news to have a care for milking.

Molly is better behaved for Nesta. I hope the milk doesn't dry up.' She looked meaningfully at her brother and attempted a grin. He knew she was playfully paying him back for his mischievous comment about Thurston. 'What do you say, Am, about Nesta?'

Gundred smiled. 'Am, put away that red face. Aye, we all miss her but no doubt she'll be married by now,' she said, glancing at her son. Despite her stance on the lower status of servants, she was obviously relieved at the breaking of tension among them all. 'Anyway, the twins should have finished their jobs by now and be in here. I expect somethin' has taken their fancy outside. Be a good lad and find them, please.'

Amalric strolled to the back of the building where they might as usual be giggling over feeding the chickens or pig.

'They're not to be found, Ma. Are you sure they're out of bed?'

'They'd better be,' she said, and stopped stirring the porridge. Wiping her hands on her rough pinafore, she strode towards the loft ladder, climbed and put her head through the hole in the ceiling. Amalric heard her sniff. She then continued up into the room. The expected ruckus did not come. A slight moan was heard. Matilde flashed a worried glance at Amalric. Then Gundred peered down through the hole. Despite being in the shadow of the thatched roof, it was clear that their mother was deathly pale.

'Matilde, I need to you to make up some potions with as much angelica and blessed thistle as we have. An' some basil an' rue.'

Gundred was calm, insistent in her way of speaking.

Without questioning her mother's command, Matilde replied, 'Yes, Ma.'

Amalric feared what this might mean. 'Matilde, what is it?' His sister didn't answer. 'Mother,' he called up into the darkness, 'shall I send for Thurston?'

Matilde looked up expectantly into the loft.

'You will not,' came the answer. 'We don't need fancy learnin'.'

Elias' head lowered towards the table.

The Faceby morning routine disintegrated. Amalric found himself walking up the main street of the village. Gundred and Matilde had shooed him and his father out of the way while they got on with caring for the twins. Muttering to himself, Elias had gone to the workshop to brood among the glass. Amalric had not wanted to follow. He needed to be outside in the fresh air and ordinary life of the village and he wanted answers to the questions buzzing in his head.

The August hot spell had cooled a little and he was surprised to see so few people taking advantage of the comfortable early temperature to complete strenuous summer jobs. The ones he did see were going about their daily jobs alone. Something was wrong. They had hunched shoulders, or a mantle pulled low over a face, or eyes staring ahead instead of seeking others to chat with. Normally, he hardly noticed the noise of the waterwheel turning down by the river but today the clatter-clatter intruded on the unusual quietness. Then he saw bunches of herbs hastily placed on the ground in front of doorways. With sudden clarity, he knew the tavern talk had spread and villagers feared that the pestilence had arrived, and he dreaded that everyone would hold his father responsible: the visit to Meaux Abbey, Alice Tynel's accusation at her son's funeral and the deaths of the abbey monks would be evidence enough. He knew, then, the twins' illness had to be kept secret for as long as possible.

Panic gripped him. It had all happened so quickly. One day, Ned and the monks were alive and the twins well; a few days later, death and illness had claimed and threatened. He had to know for certain whether or not the twins really had the disease. If they had, his mother was confident she could heal with her herbs. On the other hand, Thurston hoped to find answers in the writings of others and Father Wilfrid believed the cure lay in repentance. Would any of these work? Amalric needed to talk.

He decided to continue up the village, hoping to see his physician friend. He came to the well. Four women stood apart from each other as they took it in turns to draw the water. As he approached, they stopped and stared at him. Amalric waved and said 'Good morning' as cheerfully as he could, but they did not reply and fixed him with stony stares and vengeful hands on hips. Their animosity was palpable. He circled around them and went on his way.

As the crush of village homes thinned out, he heard, behind him, the shuffling tramp of men walking on the dirt road. He knew they would be on their way to harvesting for Lord de Horesby, to fulfil their dues. Unlike himself, they would be wearing short jerkins and hose which enabled them to walk quickly: his longer tunic and leather apron flapped below his knees and slowed him. They soon drew level, six men, each carefully keeping a space between himself and his companions. They had farming tools slung over their backs and, as they passed, one young man turned to face Amalric and drew his sickle from his thick-muscled shoulder. He held it with both rough hands in front of himself. The freshly sharpened blade glinted in the sunlight. Amalric stepped back and put up his hands in defence but could say nothing. One swipe would sweep a leg away.

An older man stepped forward. 'Come, Colin, he's nobbut a lad. Tis no fault of his.'

'Aye, it's as maybe, but he's his father's son, ain't he?'

'Just leave him be. Don't touch him.'

The men walked on, but Colin hung back and gave Amalric a malevolent look before turning back to join the others.

Amalric's upper lip wetted with sweat. It was the first time he had experienced hatred sufficient to kill him.

The manor appeared through trees at the top of the hill. Fresh patches of colour on the roof showed that roof tiles displaced by the earth tremor had been replaced. Smoke gently rose from the chimneys. It was something of a relief to see such calm normality. Then he saw the oddest of sights, a creature walking towards him clothed in an all-over leather robe and hood. Hazel eyes with pale lashes peered through holes in a leather mask above a large nosepiece. Amalric, again fearful, drew back to let the mysterious creature pass.

'Hello, Amalric.'

'Thurston?'

'Yes.'

Amalric bent down with relief, hands on knees and laughed almost hysterically. Thurston waited for his friend to calm down.

'What on earth are you dressed like that for?'

The muffled Thurston replied, 'It's the garment I told you about that Lord de Horesby purchased for me to wear in the event of the pestilence. I'm trying it out on his strict orders. "You must wear it, doctor",' he mimicked his patron, '"or I shall dismiss you." I call that a threat so I have obeyed. It's not a good time to be dismissed.' He looked back from where he had come. 'But we're almost out of sight of the manor; just walk a little with me on the road back to the village and I'll strip it off. He doesn't give me much credit for sense of my own, but then, he is a frightened man. Just recently he's taken to going off with his sons in a cart with bulging sacks, armed with swords and picks and spades. I believe he's been burying his wealth. The Manor House looked empty of valuable ornaments this morning when he summoned me. Mind you, I wouldn't trust those lads to keep the treasures safe. They like a good time too much. But the old boy trusts them. I like him, really.'

When the Manor House had disappeared behind trees, Thurston pulled off the mask and hood. His ginger hair was damp and ruffled, his face pink and moist.

'Phew! It's a hideous thing to wear. The leather is thin – no expense spared – but far too hot. The perfume of the herbs in the snout is overwhelming. I shall die of suffocation before the pestilence.' He took a deep breath. 'Lord de Horesby has heard about Ned's death and the ones at the abbey. There are one or two severe illnesses around, which he hopes are non-pestilential. I go to see if sore throats are something like diphtheria. Anyway, he insists I wear the garment to protect myself and him... just in case. Phew!' His face was becoming less pink. 'Now, then, Am. Have you come to see me? You look a bit pale yourself. Here, sit.'

Amalric was usually amused by Thurston's gabble of information but today his emotions were running too high to recognise humour. They sat down on a grassy bank by the road and he twisted a grass stalk around his fingers.

'I've just been threatened by workers on the road. One wielded his sickle at me – I feared I might lose a limb.'

'I've known of this before. Fear of the pestilence can be as great as the disease. But you are alright?'

'Yes. But... I'm fearful for my family... I think we have *it* at home.' To say 'pestilence' was to accept it. 'The twins are both ill.' His voice cracked. 'I need to be sure.' Amalric noticed an almost invisible recoil as his friend took in the news, then he smiled reassuringly.

'I'm surprised your family is affected by illness. You seem a healthy brood. Mayhap it's nothing too serious, just something brought on by normal summer miasmas. Did the twins meet with Ned when he was ill?'

'Yes. But Ned had only been to the abbey, where he'd not met with anyone ill. He only had flea bites and, oh yes, he'd lifted a dead rat.' Amalric's eyes widened with sudden remembrance. 'Oh, a dead black rat... and there was the dead black cat months ago. Could it be the devil's work, or the curses between Mother and Myrtle?'

Amalric scrutinised his friend's face, looking for a response, but his expression was blank. The hazel eyes were without emotion, unblinking. He'd slipped from friend to physician and was well practised in not giving away his thoughts until he was sure of the facts.

Thurston was dismissive. 'I know little of those things. Do they have sore throats? Prickling of the skin?'

'I... I don't know.'

'Who is looking after them?'

'Mother is looking after the twins by herself in the loft and won't allow anyone else to see them. Matilde is making up potions and passing them up the ladder to her. Matilde has seen them, though; she peeked in when Mother's back was turned.'

'What did she see?'

'She saw both the twins lying on their mattress. She said they were too tired to move, looked flushed and had a rash. Both have swellings which are painful... under their arms... and there is a smell which is hard to describe, sweet but pungent; it makes you want to retch.'

Amalric saw emotion come back into his friend's face with an alarming furrow of his brow. He waited in silence for him to speak.

'Is anyone else ill at your home... Matilde?'

'No.'

'Well, my dear Am, I can understand your fear. It may be the pestilence but I can't be certain. Usually, after the first few cases it takes a while to get a tight hold. There's a lull of some days. In that first period, one is never sure that it is not simply a summer illness. If it is the pestilence, then your mother is right not to let anyone else see them, for it is fearfully contagious. If there are no black areas on them, then whatever the illness is, it has not progressed too far at the moment.'

Amalric breathed in sharply. 'Black areas?'

'Yes. Am, I'm sorry but it is best to be forewarned, then you can face it. With the pestilence, the body will likely show signs of dying – black areas.'

'But what can Mother do to prevent it... and their dying?'

'Am, I don't know. Maybe nothing.' Thurston's hands went up in a gesture of hopelessness. 'I can visit them if you wish, but she is experienced with the healing herbs and will be no worse than I at treating this. She may even be better; love and compassion are great healers. All my knowledge from the ancient healers, newer philosophies, the planets, bleeding, I believe to be mostly ineffective – and as for balancing the humours when every humour is acting against each other – I have no idea how to deal with it. For myself, I have to come to terms with my lack of ability, and simply learn.'

Amalric slumped. He felt beyond weeping. He thought of the twins, their dark heads with bobbing curls so often close together, laughing. He was desperately worried for his family and himself, and here was his friend, his learned friend, with no ability to cure. He gave Thurston a rueful look.

'I'm sorry, Am, I'm afraid I think of this disease as a battle to be fought. I must learn to fight. We all must. For myself, I am one alone with no close family. I can take risks. But you and your family are my friends. One thing I can prescribe is a painkilling potion perhaps stronger than any of your mother's. It's a mixture of opium and henbane that the surgeons often use to relieve the pain of cutting. It's quite expensive, the special opium comes from Persia, but Lord de Horesby is generously letting me have some for village use. It also induces sleep. I have a phial here in my bag. You must take some home. I have spent two days making up the concoction and I shall be giving it to anyone who suffers.' He hesitated. 'It may help death come more easily, if the illness goes that far.'

Amalric's face crumpled as he looked at the little glass bottle: so little against a devastating disease. 'I can't bear to think it might. But if it does, then how will the twins have the strength for absolution? What will Father Wilfrid say if they're too drowsy from this concoction to make confession?'

'Am, I cannot be all things to all people. I try to cure bodies, or at least make bodies more comfortable. Perhaps you should talk these matters over with Father Wilfrid. Your parents would be consoled by the thought that you had confided in a priest. Come to think of it, maybe I should see Father Wilfrid. I may suggest we join forces in a spirit and body assault to fight this dreadful disease together – that is, if he stays. I have heard that some clergy flee.'

Chapter Twelve

They walked on to the village together – Thurston with the leather suit draped over one shoulder and Amalric edgy with worry. As they came to the church, they heard the clanking of spades and voices. The sound led them behind the old stone building to Father Wilfrid, sleeves rolled up, busy supervising sextons digging up green turf.

Berta's wreath was still on the Saxon cross, its colours fading. Despite his worries, Amalric became distracted by a compulsion to remove it, so that the exquisite carvings he knew to be there would be fully revealed. He placed the wreath on the ground and traced the stone art with his fingers. Stone was so unlike glass, impervious to light; it was solid sand, yet sand made glass.

'See here, Thurston,' he called. 'It's Jesus healing the blind man. See His fingers on the eyes.' Amalric marvelled at how the carver had managed to fit so much into the small space.

Thurston nodded with mild interest.

'Now, Amalric, my boy, dreaming again!' Father Wilfrid raised a plump bare arm in recognition and pleasure. Amalric jumped with surprise, his little reverie shattered.

'Ah, and Master Physician too. It's good to see you both.' The priest unrolled his sleeves. 'Come into the church where we can talk.' Inside it was cool. They hunched on the stone benches. Thurston let his suit drop heavily to the tiled floor. For once, Amalric found the painted figures too bright. His head dropped to his chest. Father Wilfrid rubbed his own aching knees.

'The Archbishop,' the priest said, 'has given all village clergy instruction to enlarge the graveyards and dig pits in anticipation of pestilence. Let's hope it's just a precaution. I've chosen the north-east corner – cool but facing the place of resurrection. I recall Jeremiah Chapter 9:22: 'Thus says the LORD: "Human corpses shall fall like dung upon the open field, like sheaves behind the reaper, and no one shall gather them.'"' He sighed. 'I hope my lower limbs will cope.'

They reminded Amalric of two tree trunks, gnarled, rooted, mud-spattered.

'I could give you a liniment,' said Thurston.

'Thank you,' smiled the priest, 'but I will spurn your kindly offer. I have one from Amalric's mother. Good it is, too.'

'I'm sure it is. When I have time, I will study these country remedies.'

'Anyway,' went on Father Wilfrid, 'the gossips say Ned had the disease but I'm not convinced of it. I've not caught it, though when I visited, a sheet covered all of him except his face. Mm. Last evening, I heard, they had it at Meaux. Some deaths. I cannot ignore it any longer. Oh, I've tried to,' he tutted. 'There, you see... I am just like my flock, denying and fearful at the same time.'

Thurston opened his mouth to speak but was interrupted.

'Father Wilfrid! We have the pestilence at home!' blurted Amalric impatiently, head now raised and feeling inadequate beside these knowledgeable men. 'Thurston has confirmed the signs. I don't know what to do.' He was a frightened child.

'Well, not confirmed, more suspected,' said Thurston, calmly.

Amalric shifted his feet, petulantly. Anger replaced fear. He screwed his fingers into his palms to keep control of himself.

'Oh, my boy, I am so sorry,' said the priest and rested his hand on Amalric's shoulder. 'Who is it? Your father, for he was at Meaux with Ned? But so were you! I believe the abbot died and the young lay brother, Mark, who helped…'

'Brother Mark! But he and Ned only had flea bites. There was a black rat, though, like the black cat at the well. Was it a demon? Is it the devil causing this or Ma and Myrtle's curses? Oh…'

'Amalric, be calm. Who is it at your home?'

'It's the twins! Mother is insisting on nursing them herself. She won't let anyone else near them. They're so young. Thurston has given me a potion that may help them to be peaceful. Only… I don't want them to die without confession and the Last Rites. And I don't want you to become ill through visiting. And Father is slumped at the table, what with Ned, the news from the abbey and now his youngest. And what if Mother catches it and dies? And Edwin is gone and doesn't know and our servant, Nesta, is… Nesta is away in the hills.' Tears seeped into his eyes. 'And I fear what will happen when it's realised that we have the pestilence at home. I have already seen hatred in the eyes of…'

'Am, Am, be at peace! It may yet not be the pestilence. I'll pop my own head around the door and see what I can do. I will sort their confession and Last Rites if need be. They will not die unshriven.'

'But if it is the… you may fear and leave.'

'No. I love my flock too much to leave them in a real hour of need. Some clerics have deserted their flock. Archbishop Zouche left York to escape the pestilence which raged there and left poor Hugh of Damascus in charge, without a choice. Mind you, we are better off with Damascus, as he's a practical thinker.'

'Father, we may all die,' said Amalric, anxious to keep the conversation on his own concerns.

'If we do, then we will all be together. And yes, I am fighting the urge within me to leave and be safe. I cannot deny it. But where would I be safe? Up in the hills or on a deserted beach up in Northumberland, talking to no one and denying my calling?' The priest thought for a moment and a smile played on his lips. He spoke calmly. 'You know, in some ways, I shall feel a sense of relief if the pestilence is here among us. I've predicted its arrival for a long time. I think I will have the strength to stay. My reason for being on this earth may at last be clear. People will need me.' He turned to Thurston. 'Physician, I am glad you are here. We must try to avoid panic.'

'I'll help whenever I'm not needed at the manor. We'll need to work together, Father. I'll help you sort a plan for the village.'

'That is good of you. I cannot expect Lord de Horesby to come into the hotbed: he'll wish to save his heritage by isolating his family and servants from the rest of us. He has a personal chaplain but I believe the fellow to be...' He searched for a word. 'Cautious. The walls of the manor will prevent intruders and I suspect the gate will be firmly locked and guarded. At least he is allowing you to be here, which is brave of him.'

'Yes, but only as long as I wear this hideous garb!' Thurston held out the garment so that the priest could see it in its entirety.

'My, my, you will need courage to wear that as well as courage to deal with the sick.' He smiled at his own humour. 'It will fall to me to organise things in the village should it come to pass, but we shall work together as much as we can; you caring for the person who is sick and I caring for the person who is a sinner. Now, Amalric,' Father Wilfrid turned to his unhappy young friend, 'these sudden happenings are almost too much for a sensitive lad like you, but you will have to be strong. Go home now, where you will be needed.'

Amalric felt put down by the priest's condescending tone. He left him and the doctor to their discussion. Funny how he was reminded of Samson at that moment: the mangy dog, straining at the piece of rope, eager to be involved yet incapable of helping, only able to give love.

The next morning with Matilde and Gundred busy, Amalric reluctantly milked Molly in the barn. He took the pail with its creamy liquid into the house through the internal door. All was silent. Matilde, responding to his footsteps, appeared out of the fire-smoked shadows. As she grasped the handle to take the pail, she glanced at him with meaningful eyes.

'Mother says there are black marks on their bodies. She's rummaging through pots of ointment. She's trying everything she knows. She's hysterical. I've never seen her like this before.'

'Shall I fetch Thurston?'

'No, she still will not have him.'

'But we have his potion for their pain. Don't let them suffer, Mat. Give her the potion.'

'She will not use it.'

'Please, Matilde. Please. It will work. I know.' Amalric stared into his sister's eyes and saw her nascent faith in the physician, her compassion and, most of all, her resolve to disobey her mother.

Matilde nodded, filled two beakers with a small amount of milk and dripped potion into each one. She ascended the loft ladder. For a while there was silence, then from through the hatch came loud protestations from Gundred.

'It is the magic of physic. I will not.'

'No, Mother, it's merely a mix of herbs. I've heard of it myself. We use the same herbs but these are from another country.'

'I will not.'

'You must.'

A groan came from one of the children. Then an anguished wail from Gundred.

'Give it them, then!'

A little later, all was silent. Things calmed for a while.

Death frightened Amalric: the kind of death that this would be. The only dying he had seen was that of his grandfather. With his family around him, life had gone out of him like a soft puff of air: a sighing, a relaxing. His wrinkled eyelids had gently closed over large black pupils and his soul had drifted away. The priest had been present and the Last Rites, the anointing and all those proper things had been done. It had been a good death. But this? How could this be a good death for the twins when the pestilence caused great pain for them and overwhelming fear in others? It seemed to Amalric that this death would be a selfish, brutal, tugging away from life, not a safe going. He would never see his beloved twin siblings again.

Father Wilfrid, true to his word, visited but Gundred would not allow him to climb into the loft. From the ladder, he bellowed questions to the twins about repenting their sins but neither was able to answer. The priest left the house despondent after putting a comforting hand on Amalric's trembling shoulder.

That evening, Amalric sat on his haunches outside, leaning against the front wall of the workshop with his head bowed. At a door click, he looked up and saw Matilde emerging from the house, tears dripping from her nose and chin, unable to do more than lean on the doorpost for support. Amalric knew the worst had happened and went to her. They hugged and cried together.

Spurning all help, Gundred washed her two dead children and wrapped them in the cloths that each wife kept for the purpose. Matilde simply handed the things she needed up to the loft. Amalric and his father, feeling helpless, retreated to the workshop and Amalric lit the hearth for warmth as the day cooled into night: the extravagance of it ignored. They took no heed of passing time. Elias slumped forward a little. Amalric put out an arm to save him from falling towards the heat and noticed that his father slavered spittle down his jerkin and his face sagged ever so slightly on one side.

'Come, Da, I'll take you to lie down.' They both staggered together back into the house.

Next morning, Elias remained in bed with his face to the wall. Matilde and Amalric stood by helplessly as, early in the morning, their mother dragged the two small wrapped bodies from the loft. Her face was stony white, her jaw tight. Amalric was conscious of the hideous indignity of her struggle as the bodies bumped down the ladder. She carried each one out of the house across the road to the cool church.

Gundred stayed in the church all day beside her children's little bodies. Father Wilfrid braved the stink and pottered around her, comforting her at her vigil and saying prayers. Amalric heard her wails from across the road at home – he had never felt so helpless and distraught, longing to be with his mother. His imaginings were worse than being there – in his mind, he saw wrinkled cloths wrapping worm-ridden, rotting bodies. It was redolent of the painted Lazarus on the church wall, rising from his tomb. As a child, he had peered at it with horror rather than comfort. Cynically he thought now, no one will come to raise the twins as Jesus had Lazarus.

Amalric again felt the absence of his brother. Edwin would no doubt have had bitter words to cut across the grief and relieve the weighty tension.

The twins' burial ceremony was, like Ned's, in the early evening. A few small family groups came into the church but most loitered further away, too fearful to be close and too ashamed to stay away. Previously a fuss would have been made with flowers and gifts of food to tide a family over the period of mourning. But now, with three unusual deaths, the pestilence threatened again. From now on, fear would be the enemy of friendship – Amalric realised that. It was not easy to think of others' needs when just giving comfort to a friend held the risk of death.

The ones who were at the funeral wrapped themselves protectively in brown cloaks, almost hiding their identity. Everyone hoped desperately the cause had been a summer childhood illness but the stink from the twins' bodies worried them. It hung about the church, tempered only a little by fragrant herbs. Thurston hovered outside, a pillar of slender blackness, spurned by Gundred.

As Father Wilfrid solemnly spoke, Elias was supported by the arms of Amalric, and Gundred by Matilde's. Afterwards, the twins were laid side by side in the family plot in the central part of the graveyard, their feet towards the east ready for the day of resurrection. Before the final soil covered them, Amalric threw flowers that had gone to seed on top. Remembering how Berta had done the same for Ned, he had hastily picked them from around the church before the burial. He hoped they would grow, resurrect. Then, through the dusk, he went to seek the wreath Berta had made for Ned. It was still where he had placed it on the ground by the stone cross. Despite all its fresh green life having totally desiccated to crisp brown, he picked it up, took it to the twins' grave and laid it on top.

The following morning, Gundred wasted no time in furiously washing down the loft with rosemary in water and any other herbs that might be effective in killing disease. She spread rosemary leaves and finally burned herbs to purify the space. Amalric and Matilde, though forbidden to help, stood beneath the loft opening, hoping the thatch would not be set alight. Their mother then washed herself in the back garden with rosemary, rue and other herbs in clear water fetched from the village well by Amalric. All this was in an effort to remove any lingering pestilence, but the sweet, pungent smell lingered around the building no matter what she did. It lingered on her arms from carrying her children. She began to sniff her nose down her arms frequently. Amalric looked to Matilde, who just shook her head despairingly.

When Gundred finally finished her tasks, she allowed herself to weep again: long wailing cries. Amalric feared that his mother's standing in the village would never be regained: she had failed to be allowed to save Liza, a curse was on her from Myrtle Ashe, and pride in her own healing skills fell before the immense failure to heal her own children.

The Faceby household carried on in a miserable way. Grief hung heavily. Amalric stood in the workshop, despondently staring at the faceless St Peter on the table, hindered in his work because his father could not raise himself to supervise the painting. It would have to wait. As for the work for Meaux Abbey, Abbot Hugh, the man who dared to look upon glass to glorify God and embellish the abbey church, was dead. The chance to create something big and beautiful had slipped away. Amalric ran his fingers over the shiny, smooth, blank face. Peter, Jesus' rock, had no life in him.

At the side of the face was a small piece of bread. That it was there surprised Amalric. It had been part of a hasty meal taken when he was cutting St Peter's robe. But it seemed long ago, even though in reality it was only a few days. It was as though time had been swallowed up by a mist which changed everything. He picked up the bread and it fell into crumbs. Just then, sensing food, a mouse poked its nose through a crack low in the wall, sniffed for danger and, sensing none, emerged timorously. Amalric idly threw the crumbs to it. The little creature scampered towards them, unafraid. He watched as it nibbled. The sun played on the soft brown fur. Grief and longing mingled in his own chest and he knew he had to find solace in the open.

He went around the back of the house and trod purposely over chamomile, thyme and sage. Perfume rose. He stepped over the privy stream, passed the small domed kiln, scattered the hens, ran his hand over the back of the sow as she ate scraps at the edge of the pigpen and slapped Molly's brown rump. Each of these animals was silent and morose as if missing the twins. He walked past the vegetable garden where his mother and Matilde had worked hard but which already showed signs of neglect: rabbits had been attracted by the tempting leaves. They had hopped over stepping stones from their steep warren at the far side of the brook and negotiated the fences and hedges intended to keep them out. Over countless years, failed attempts had been made to rid the village of them and, giving in, it had finally been named after them. The twins had spent many hours hunting the rabbits with Ned. Ma's rabbit pies were good.

Edwin too had hunted at the warren. Who would keep them down now?

Passing the hives, Amalric strode through a gap in the garden hedge to the Ripple Brook. He enjoyed its urgency, its babble and wildness. In the parts where it poured over a rock in a thick shining mass, it reminded him of molten glass. He had seen colourless glass made and he marvelled at how it flowed like a slow river and solidified, capturing a moment of transparent beauty in a way that the ever-moving river could not... except when it froze. He loved glass. He loved the way that it could be changed from colourless to glowing colours with the addition of metal compounds, cobalt, lead, iron, sulphur, copper and more. He especially liked the way the sun's rays, with passing hours, moved over and through the soft undulations, changing the appearance of a window and of a room.

There was no doubt that glass, coloured or colourless, plain or painted, with figures or patterns, was especially fitting for abbey windows. Why, he wondered, did some monks think it distracting and others that it held a deeper understanding of God? Maybe one day he would know enough to form his own opinion. It was the one thing his father's Theophilus manuscript did not tell him. For years now he had poured over the ancient sheets of vellum, fascinated. The Latin text held almost everything an apprentice of glazing needed to know about glass. The twins had laughed at his studiousness.

He looked closer at the water. Things were never what they seemed at first glance. His mother had been reluctant to collect water from the brook, since it collected the village detritus as it flowed near many houses before reaching the Faceby home. The contents of night pots, cooking waste, wood shavings, animal manure, dead rats, all swirled in its depths.

He was about to turn and leave, when something made him look up: a rustle of grass, a flutter of cloth. A figure was working its way down the steep warren diagonally on a thin path towards the far side of the brook. He blinked and made out that it was a small, young woman.

'Nesta?' he called tentatively. Then louder, 'Nesta?'

'Hello, there, Master Amalric. How wonderful to see you,' she shouted. 'I've just come on a short visit.'

'No! Don't come.' He was alarmed. 'Oh, Nesta, I want to see you but we may have the pestilence. To even look at me is probably dangerous. Bennet and Berta died and were buried a couple of days ago – I can barely remember when.'

'Dead. The twins.' Nesta blanched. 'Oh, Lord!' She hovered by the brook side, clearly unsure of what to do. Her lips quivered.

Amalric felt he couldn't cope if she cried. He hastily spoke. 'Ned died first. The Meaux Abbey monks have it. Abbot Hugh is dead. Oh, Nesta, just tell me all is well with you and then go. Please, please don't cross the river. I couldn't bear it if you...' Amalric struggled to control his feelings. Nesta looked so pretty. Her clean mouse-coloured hair, bleached paler by the summer sun, flowed loosely about her, and her grey, rough woollen over-tunic had obviously been washed. Slung round her neck were her shoes and he suspected that she had walked mainly barefoot to keep them mud-free. A bolt of sheer pleasure caused him to smile, but at the same time, he realised that with his whole heart, he wanted Nesta to stay safe.

'Master Amalric, you look tired and sad. I took the opportunity to come because the summer work has slackened. Mother is improving but not able to do much yet. My brother and sister are getting old enough to help out... but Father can't do much.'

'And you are betrothed. You must go home. Stay safe.'

Nesta's eyed flashed. 'I am *not* betrothed. I'm supposed to be but I can't stand the lad. He's a dolt.'

Relief exploded in Amalric's chest.

'Master Amalric, the pestilence has not reached us, our hamlet is very isolated. No one passes by and people rarely leave to travel anywhere else. I haven't seen a priest for months so I suppose I'm damned anyway. And the twins... you must be... I'll come.'

'Nesta, please go.' Amalric was becoming irritated at her chatter. He was feeling torn in two. Through the air, his hands pushed her away.

Nesta understood. 'I will go,' she said abruptly. 'But I shall be back in one week. I'll settle up at home, then come. One week. Yes, one week.'

He saw her determination. 'No, Nesta. You musn't.' But he knew she would.

'Give my love to your family.' She looked searchingly at Amalric. 'I'll pray for the souls of the twins.' She turned to go, then turned back again and waved.

Amalric stood transfixed as he watched her go, his emotions swinging as she trudged back up the hill with her hair still blowing about her shoulders. Not betrothed! A relief, but why? Everything felt muddled: the awful loss of the twins mixing with inappropriate feelings for a servant. What would his mother say when she knew he had persuaded the one person she would accept assistance from to leave? Nesta would be back in one week. He had to let her stay then for his mother's sake. Best to say nothing till that day. He pulled himself up from the grassy bank to go home.

At the house door, he noiselessly lifted the latch, bowed his head under the low lintel and entered softly. Matilde's back was to him as she bent over the fire stirring a pot. He was surprised to see that her cap had fallen from her head and lay on the floor. He could see her black hair scraped back and tied into a rough untidy plait. This was unusual; normally Matilde was fastidious in her appearance.

'Matilde?'

She turned abruptly. 'Am, where have you been?' Her eyes were red, her expression frantic. 'Mother is ill. She collapsed. I put her to bed in the sleep room.'

Amalric stopped dead. Mother? No. *She* couldn't be ill. 'Maybe it's exhaustion from caring for the twins,' he said, trying to put off thoughts he did not want to think. 'She's not young. It must have been hard work... then the grief. I'll go to her.' He stepped forward but stopped at the sleep room door as his nose picked up a pungent smell.

'No, Am! She's ill from the pestilence.' Matilde's words hung in the air, a finality to them. 'You and Father must stay in the workshop.'

'What? No,' he protested. 'I'll fetch Thurston.'

'Am, you know Mother would not have Thurston attend her. Please do as I say. If you don't take heed of me, we will all die. This really is the pestilence. You may tell Thurston that, in time. You should tell him. She has the buboes – great swellings under her arms, her neck, red, purple. No blackness yet. I held Ma closely as she fainted at the table, smelled her breath. I may be doomed even as I speak. Take Father, stay in the workshop, milk Molly, take food from the barn store and don't have contact with us. I'll speak to you with the door ajar and you can pass food through to me.'

Elias had been present when his wife collapsed but Matilde had not let him near her. The Master Glazier, a successful, capable man, now stood helpless in the corner with his face ashen and drooping a little more on the same side as before. His hands rubbed together as if trying to restore feeling. Amalric pushed down the horrific thought that everyone was leaving him and took his father by the hand to lead him into the workshop. The hand felt limp. The old man needed to lie down. That morning, before Gundred had taken ill, Matilde had put the sleep room mattresses out to air at the back of the house. Amalric fetched two into the workshop and placed them on the floor.

Later, with his father resting on a mattress, Amalric went to the barn to milk Molly. As if recognising his mood, she stood quietly for him. He sat on a little three-legged stool with the pail between his knees and put his head on the cow's velvety soft, warm flank. She turned her head to him and the large black eyes with long lashes blinked slowly. It was comforting to have his flesh on the warm brown animal. He worked away, shooting the milk into the wooden pail. A tabby cat, alerted by the noise of squirting milk, sauntered in. She lived on the numerous village rodents and birds but liked to come for a daily drink. Amalric aimed a jet of milk at her and she stood balancing on her back legs with her white front paws waving to keep balance as she batted at the stream and caught the milk in her mouth. When she'd had enough, she scurried off. Amalric wondered if in feeding the cat, he had given her the energy to kill rodents and birds... the little sparrows? It reminded him of something Father Wilfrid had once said, that not one sparrow falls to the ground without God knowing.[8] Who deserved to live? Was it the bird or the cat? What a strange thing life... and death... was.

He lifted the full pail and took it to the house. He opened the door slightly, passed the milk through and put it on the floor for Matilde to give to his mother.

'I'll go give Thurston the news,' he said, before closing the door.

---

[8] Derived from Matthew 10:29: 'Are not two sparrows sold for a penny? Yet not one of them will fall to the ground apart from your Father.'

Chapter Thirteen

It was a hard trudge up the hill and Amalric didn't know whether he passed anyone else or not – his thoughts were too encompassing to note anything except where he trod. He found the manor gates closed but not locked. He felt nervous about walking in but he placed his hand on the wood and gingerly pushed one open. He was relieved to see Thurston leaving his cottage.

'Thurston!'

'Hello, Am,' came the shouted reply as he turned. 'Wonderful to see you but I'm called to the manor urgently. Later perhaps. I'll call…'

'It's just a message from Matilde.'

Thurston stopped.

'She says to let you know Mother has it, the illness. She's certain. The buboes. But don't come. She insists.'

His friend mouthed a blasphemy, horror in his eyes.

Later that day, Amalric knew the creamy milk he had taken into the house had been worthless when he heard his mother's retching and vomiting.

The following day, early morning light seeped dull grey through the cracks in the workshop shutters. The shepherd window was dim and colourless. Amalric's head ached from listening to the sounds coming through the thin wall throughout the night. Just before dawn his mother's cries of pain increased and Matilde's entreaties to drink Thurston's potions became frantic.

Then came the moment Amalric had been waiting for. Matilde asked Amalric to fetch Father Wilfrid, but above all not to let him into their home. He ran to the church; it was still early but the priest was not there. Panic was becoming a familiar companion. Amalric was beside himself with anxiety. His mother needed confession and the Last Rites; the quality of her afterlife depended on it. What should he do? Father Wilfrid had said in extreme situations others could do it if a priest wasn't available. But how did one do it? Over his young life he had never taken much notice of that sort of thing. Maybe Matilde would be better suited, being a midwife; she'd perhaps had to do it for dying mothers and babies. Thankfully he saw the old priest struggling down the road. The hem of his habit dipped from side to side as he limped. His cross swung from his neck with the same tilting motion. Amalric was startled by the priest's ashen face.

'Father Wilfrid, are you ill?'

'No, my son, just very, very weary. What can I do for you?'

'Oh, Father, it's Mother. She's mortally ill. Matilde has sent me to ask you to call. It's for her soul...' he ventured, as if Father Wilfrid didn't know.

'Then before I go to rest, I will see her.'

Matilde peered past the edge of the door. 'Father Wilfrid, stay outside, please. Just tell me what to do so Mother may gain absolution from her sins and I will do it... it is she who wishes it.'

'No, Matilde. Amalric and Elias must stay away but I will come in. In any case, I've already...' He checked himself. 'I'm not going to fail another member of your family. To die well is important. I didn't see the twins. Your mother is a good woman. She deserves to die well, with the hope of salvation.' Before going inside, he glanced at the distraught young man before him and couldn't help but say dismally what was clearly at the forefront of his mind. 'Am, my boy, lots of souls will be similarly at risk... dying one way or another.'

Amalric looked into the sympathetic, tired eyes of his friend, searching for the wisdom he often found there.

The priest carried on, 'You know, lad, it is the gift of God to be saved – by grace and through faith.[9] Your mother had faith. Trust your own heart, answer your soul's longings.'

Amalric answered his soul's longing to be with his mother. He stood helpless by the sleep room doorway, watching as Father Wilfrid gave his mother the Last Rites. When it came to the anointing of her body, Matilde helped by pulling back the bedcloth from her neck and, as she did so, Gundred gave a high-pitched scream of pain. Amalric winced on seeing the tight swollen buboes and black blotches. The priest recoiled and gasped. Amalric stepped back, horrified. Disturbed by the noise and commotion, Elias staggered from somewhere to join them and pushed his way forward. The part of his face which could move freely contorted as he saw his wife's body partly exposed and dying. He inhaled sharply, groaned and dropped to his knees. The empty phial of Thurston's potion slipped from an unseen place and rattled over the floor.

Gundred died holding out her arms as if seeking her young twins. She smiled as if they had come to her.

'Purgatory will be a short stay for her,' consoled Father Wilfrid.

'Edwin should have been here,' mouthed Amalric, inaudibly: he didn't wish to add fuel to the emotions of others but his anger and concern for Edwin had, at that moment, been sucked into the red anger and fear that now churned in himself.

The priest acted quickly: the sextons were dispatched to fetch a simple coffin, just a box, from the village carpenter. Father Wilfrid loved and admired Gundred – her status deserved a coffin rather than her body wrapped merely in a

---

[9] Derived from Ephesians 2:8-9.

sheet and carried, unstable, on the body-cart. And anyway, her death, at least, had to be admitted to the villagers, if not the cause.

'Father Wilfrid, not burial yet, please,' pleaded Amalric. He knew Thurston had advised the priest to bury the same day as death to prevent the build-up of miasmas around the body which could affect other people – but surely it would not apply to his mother?

'Oh, Am, I'm doing what I can. It's late August and bad for miasmas, I believe. Your mother's body was… and, well, your friend Thurston says…'

'But it's Ma.'

The priest put an arm around his shoulders and hugged him like a son.

Father Wilfrid helped Matilde place Gundred's body inside the box. She had wrapped it firmly but already the bindings were dampening. Amalric nailed the lid and Father Wilfrid commented that a sealed coffin kept its secrets better than an open one. Uncertainty was best for the village at the moment. Again, the hope was that a common summer infectious disease would be blamed.

The sextons, however, were wise in the ways of death and found their work unusually repugnant. The aroma emanating through cracks in the wood was uncommonly foul-smelling. The men's mouths twisted in suspicious distaste as they wheeled the coffin on the body-cart to the church. The priest had to remind them that August was a month of stinks and if they did not carry out their duties to the dead with reverence, the resulting effect on their own time in Purgatory could be disastrous. But Amalric knew that soon their gossip would spread.

'Come, lad, be a mourner,' coaxed Father Wilfrid with avuncular concern. 'I too am truly heart-weary. The vigil will be short and we'll bury your mother within a respectable time. I'm sorry Elias and Matilde are incapable of attending the vigil with you.'

The sun was still quite high above the horizon when Gundred's coffin was taken from the church to the graveyard. It had to be wheeled there; no one else save the two sextons was there to help carry it.

'Oh, Edwin.' Amalric resignedly followed the coffin alone. He was dismayed at this callous decision to have death and burial so close together. He had last seen his mother at her Last Rites, then she was quickly and anonymously shrouded in white. It was hard to believe she had gone.

True to form, the sextons had gossiped. Villagers, whom Gundred had known all her life, were mere guarded, shadowy figures by the church gate, brown cloaks again tightly wrapped.

'This could be the last person I put into a family plot for a long time,' said Father Wilfrid, out of hearing of the sextons. 'Others will likely have to go in the pit. Be silent awhile, my boy, tell no one.'

Amalric watched his mother lowered speedily by the nervous sextons into the Faceby family's grave, beside the twins. He then realised he'd forgotten to bring flowers in seed as he had done for Berta and Bennet. He walked away from the graveside, distraught and lonely.

In the far corner of the churchyard, a huge mound of soil, indicating the pit for the pestilential dead, caught his eye. It would go some way, Amalric thought, to resolving village conflicts and jealousies as folk lay together in death.

Days went by. No one else suffered the disease. Thurston had warned about the pestilence arriving with a few cases followed by a lull and then a big outbreak. Amalric remembered and waited, thinking he might well be the next victim, but he wasn't worried, because he was empty, vacant inside, save for anger: the twins and his mother had been taken quickly from him without goodbyes, hugs or kisses; he was having to care for his father, who was sinking more and more within himself, and Thurston had not appeared to help. Father Wilfrid had hastily buried his mother and so, feeling resentful, he had not been to a church service nor even met the priest in the early mornings. Now his ire was aimed at Matilde. She had recovered sufficiently to clean as her mother had done after the twins, but now she was morose and lethargic. The fire lay cold in the hearth. Without its smoke, it was easy to see her wilting exhausted on the bench. She weakly waved a hand indicating he should leave her alone. She had aged. Her black hair fell lank and her face lacked any colour. In just a few days her clothing had begun to hang off her.

Amalric's anger softened.

Matilde responded to his gaze. 'Am, I'm weary. I ache all over. My skin pricks like the devil's little arrows being shot.'

'Then rest. I'll light a fire and make a broth. We'll have to manage with stale bread, though.'

Amalric swiftly and efficiently killed a precious laying chicken. The strangeness of life and death struck him again: even in normal daily life, death was all around. After plucking, he broke the carcass roughly into pieces and threw them into the pot, adding a few corn grains, an onion and a carrot. He made a fire and hung the pot over it. Soon the smell of cooking chicken filled the house. It wafted outside and into the workshop through the open shutters. It roused Elias from the workshop and he shuffled droopingly into the house.

The three of them sat silently, eating hard bread softened by the broth. A few stray chicken feathers littered the table and Elias picked at them with his one useful hand. All night, Amalric kept the fire going. There was an unseasonable chill and he had to keep his father and sister warm and also heat comforting ale for them.

Amalric was about early next day. The first thing he did was to stoke up the fire and cook porridge for breakfast. More wood needed to be cut, the animals to be fed. The jobs seemed endless, just for the three of them to survive. He looked in on his sister in the sleep room. She looked flushed.

'Am, I'm so tired. I hurt all over. I have it, I am sure. Go away,' she sobbed. 'Go away.'

Her brother was shocked. 'You can't have, it's caught quickly. It's been a while since Ma died.' Then he remembered Thurston's words, 'There's a lull of some days.' Amalric wanted to scream; he was distraught. Now his sister. He told himself to remain calm, it may not be the disease – how many times would he say this before he really believed it? How do you face death yourself? Can you really not protect other people – the ones you love?

Then he suddenly remembered Nesta! This was the day she said she would visit again. One week after her last visit. If he didn't go to meet her, she might come to their home. He had to warn Nesta to stay away, stay over the brook. Someone must have a chance of survival! She would arrive no doubt by mid-morning. There was still time to prevent her coming.

He reached the riverbank just in time to calm his breathing and pounding heart. Nesta came over the hill and waved cheerfully when she saw him. As she drew close, he could see her face and her beautiful smile. Something melted for a moment inside him.

He shouted over the noise of the water. 'Nesta, Mother is dead and Matilde is showing signs of the pestilence today. You must go home. This is the last you will see of me. I have to look after Matilde and then I will catch it. Go. Go! Please! Oh, please!' He waved his arms as if to push her away again.

With that, Nesta wordlessly heaved up her skirts and tucked them into the girdle around her waist. As she did so, a pack on her back swung forward and Amalric realised she meant to stay. She stepped impetuously onto the stepping stones and her short, sturdy legs carried her over. On the last stone she slipped a little and Amalric, waiting, caught her in his arms. He felt as if he were dissolving into her. Her hair smelled sweet and clean. Summer freckles dotted her cheeks and nose. Then she pulled away from him. A pink flush rose from her neck to her cheeks.

'Nesta,' he said sadly, 'this could be certain death for you.'

'Maybe, but my sister Mary is old enough to care for the family now, under Mother's instruction, of course. We've paid our tenant dues. I'm your servant. I love your family, Master Amalric, and I'm ready to share my life with you. Don't push me away. Let me help. I may still be young but I'm strong and capable.' She rolled her sleeves to show her tanned, firm arms and grinned.

Amalric had to smile. Nesta was determined to stay. He gave in. What else could he do? It was a risk, but one that Nesta was more than willing to take. They walked back to the house side by side.

When they opened the door, they saw Matilde standing stiffly by the dying fire. Sweat ran down her face, damp hair fell over her shoulders. Her head was leaning to one side. Both arms were held out to the sides and her legs were wide apart. Amalric felt a frenzied, inappropriate, giggle rising in his throat on seeing her comic pose.

'Matilde – what are you do…?'

'They hurt, oh, they hurt,' she stridently cried. The thin linen of her undergarment bulged at her armpits and groin.

Nesta was horrified. 'Master Amalric! This is really bad. Go fetch Master Thurston.'

'I… I can't, he… he works for Lord de Horesby. Mother and Matilde wouldn't let me fetch him before. We must look after her ourselves.'

'Master Amalric, go fetch Master Thurston… and the priest.' Nesta was loud and insistent. 'They are your friends.' Her voice softened. 'Come on, Mistress, let's get you to lie down on your mattress.' She guided Matilde gently into the sleep room and pulled her hair aside to cool her face, revealing in Matilde's neck a large bulging mass. 'Oh, my!' she said involuntarily. 'You poor thing. Amalric – go!'

Amalric responded to Nesta's firm tone. Sick with fear, he ran out of the house and up the hill to the manor. He arrived at the gates. They were locked. He rang the bell. No one came.

Should he climb over? He rang again. Then a servant slowly shuffled towards the gate.

'Aye?'

'Doctor Thurston, please.'

'Ee's busy.'

'Then give him a message. Please.'

'Aye?'

'Tell him Matilde is ill.'

'Aye. Matilde is ill.'

Amalric ran back down the hill without hope that the message would be passed on. He went to the church and found the priest at prayer. Breathlessly he tried to interrupt the flow of Latin.

'Now then, Am, whatever it is, it can wait for God to listen to my pleas for this village. He has waited days to see you.' He muttered on prayerfully for a short while, then stopped and looked up.

Amalric stepped from foot to foot and added guilt to his impatience. 'Please, Father, sorry, Father. Matilde is ill with the pestilence and I have left her with Nesta, but we don't know what to do. Nesta told me to fetch Thurston, but he's busy.'

'Ah! So, physic is missing and you've come to see if faith can step in and help the situation.'

'No, Father!' Amalric was dismayed by the priest's sarcasm. 'Nesta said I should tell you.'

'Ah, the girl is back. Good, you need her.' He pushed himself erect, hands on knees. 'I'm sorry, lad. I'm an old and cynical priest, forgive me. Thurston *is* busy. The Lord's sons stupidly went off to York and caught the pestilence. I expect it still lingered in Snickelways. I gave them Last Rites. That's where I'd been when you met me coming down the High Street when your mother was ill. Lord de Horesby's own chaplain had run off. I suspected he would. Some use *his* vows, huh! That's why Thurston's busy – I expect it's spread throughout the manor but I've not heard.'

Amalric stood unmoving.

'But there is more I have to tell, that concerns you.' The priest took a sighing breath. 'Edwin was with the sons in York, and not only that, visited our tavern last night. One brave soul told me Edwin looked ill: pale and sweating. They ran him out of the village.'

'Oh no!' Amalric could hardly believe his brother had actually been so close. 'He was back here and they ran him off? Did they tell him about Ma and the twins?'

'I don't think so. They were frightened. Forgive them if you can.'

'Why didn't he come home?'

'I don't know, and I don't know where he is now, my boy. But people do strange things when the pestilence is about.'

Father Wilfrid allowed his young friend time to absorb the news. Amalric struggled to make sense of it. So far, only the Tynels and Facebys had suffered the pestilence but now it was at the manor. Had the sons died? Edwin had recklessly been to the tavern. No wonder, thought Amalric, the villagers were suspicious of the Facebys, in the light of twisted evidence but no facts.

Father Wilfrid wrapped an arm around his young friend's shoulders. 'So, Nesta is back, eh?' He winked knowingly. 'Come, let's visit her and your sister.'

Chapter Fourteen

Amalric and Father Wilfrid left the church. The day was warm, heavy and still. Rutted dry mud on the road was the only evidence of earlier wet months. Dust coated their footwear, rendering it almost the same colour as the parched soil. Desiccated flower heads clung to stiff stalks. A single, twittering bird echoed. How was it, Amalric wondered, that at such a time, his eyes and ears should be intensely aware of normal things – or the lack of them? Which was it? All or nothing? He felt a dreadful expectation and knew instinctively, this was probably the calm before a violent storm.

On reaching the Faceby door, Father Wilfrid hesitated momentarily, then grasped the latch and went in. The shutters were closed to keep out prying eyes of villagers as they passed. A few early evening light beams filtered through. He made his way to the sleep room. Amalric heard him greet Nesta, then mutter prayers. When he emerged, the priest repeated bluntly that a lay person may receive final confession. Amalric was terrified.

The priest spied Elias in the shadows, huddled on a stool in a corner. A random light beam glistened on his wet, drooping mouth.

'Eh, Elias, old son. Sad times, eh?' The priest's face clouded with sympathy as Elias mouthed empty words and plaintively held out his good hand to touch Amalric every time he passed by. 'Er... Amalric, shall I take your father into the church? The sextons have spread herbs. It smells delightful. It will calm him.'

Amalric was overcome with gratitude. 'Oh, Father Wilfrid, that would be wonderful – this situation is so bad for him. He's not been himself lately. He's got a bit of a palsy on one side of his face, also a hand, and he seems a bit confused. I would like to have him sit outside, though I fear he may wander off, but mainly I fear that the villagers' suspicions will overcome them and blame him for Ned's death, the twins and Mother.'

'Aye, lad. I can understand your fears. One more sighting of illness in your family would confirm the pestilence's grip. I could do nothing to avoid panic then. So... Elias will be safe in the church. No one will dare harm him there. I will make him a mattress near the sanctuary with me.'

'Thank you, Father Wilfrid. But your own safety...?'

'No matter. Push him out to me and, before we go, I will bless your house.'

The village busybodies watched the strange sight of Elias, with his woollen cap screwed into his hands, standing weakly by the side of Father Wilfrid, who shouted a blessing and sprinkled holy water on the Faceby home. The folk would hopefully realise that the old man was alive, not dead of the pestilence as many of them feared, and that the priest was not administering Last Rites but something more positive: hope.

A knock came to the door and, on opening it, Nesta was horrified to see a creature in a hideous garb. A smell of herbs wafted about.

'Argh! It's the Grim Reaper come for Matilde. It's too soon!'

The creature was also astonished to see her. 'Oh, hello, you must be Nesta. Your master has told me of you,' a muffled voice said.

Nesta didn't recognise the voice and stood somewhere between fainting and crying.

Amalric could not help but be both relieved and slightly amused. He stifled a hysterical laugh that threatened to explode. Surprisingly, his message had been passed on.

'It's my friend Thurston, Nesta. No need to fear. He's a physician.' He turned. 'Stay out there, my friend, we will talk over the threshold.'

'No, Am,' said Thurston, pushing past him. 'I've been in contact with too much to hold back now. I'll disrobe. I'm hot and weary in this thing. It's done no good to protect the manor from the disease and I need to be close to Matilde to examine her.'

He took off his cloak and laid it on the bench. His long black robe had been abandoned in favour of a thin grey one with sleeves rolled up and the neck open. Amalric noticed staining on the front.

Thurston first examined Matilde's pee, lately passed into the night pot and brought to him by Nesta. It was a small quantity and very dark. He did not taste it. Then with the help of Nesta, he gently cut away Matilde's clothing with a kitchen knife to expose the lumps in her armpits and groin and the larger one in her neck. She screamed with pain. Thurston's face crumpled and Amalric noticed the effort of will required to recompose it into that of an objective physician.

'Ah… such buboes!'

Amalric stood by, realising abjectly what his mother and the twins had suffered. The swollen mounds looked red and angry. Matilde's body was covered in a livid red rash and she sweated profusely, wetting the wool and straw mattress so that it gave off an animal and rotten grass stink… and added to that, the sweet, pungent smell coming from Matilde's own body. It was almost more than any of them could do to avoid retching.

'Am, I can do no more yet at the manor. I may, though, be able to do something here. Matilde is very ill but she is not showing black marks, the harbingers of death. I will not give up on her.'

Amalric watched his friend's moving lips and darting eyes as he worked through a plan in his mind.

'I must work with Nesta, for there are things only another woman should do. She will be a good nurse and I will need you in the background to keep the fire going, provide some broth, that sort of thing... and comfort Nesta: she will be distressed and may become ill herself. We all may.'

'Aye, at least there'll be purpose to my day.' A feeling of hope seeped into Amalric despite Thurston's gloomy last words. Matilde had the slimmest of chances and there was distracting work to be done.

'First of all, Amalric,' said Thurston in a professional, confident voice, 'open the shutters. Clean fresh air must flow in and out but not from the south. The disease has come up from the south and may be blown by the wind. No sense adding more. Keep the fire going. Fetch clean water from the well, not river water. Then tear up pieces of cloth – thin bits of old linen will do nicely – some to the size of a large cabbage leaf and some much smaller, and an old sheet into strips for bandages. Boil all of them clean. Fetch honey from your mother's hives and store it in pots.'

Thurston was clearly in his element: instructions flowed. With the shutters open, fresh air and light poured in. He turned to Nesta. 'Now, I want you to make up a large quantity of poultice mixture with medications that I will give you from my bag. Do you have stale bread and cooked onions in the house?'

'Yes,' interrupted Amalric. 'Only stale bread!'

'Good! Make it into crumbs, Nesta, and mix them with hot water, the onions and the medications and then wrap some of the mixture into each of the five larger pieces of cloth and put one on top of each bubo. Replace with five more as they cool.' He took a deep breath. 'What I am attempting to do is this... with the hot poultices, I hope to pull the pus inside the buboes nearer to the surface. When it is as close as it will come, I shall lance the buboes with my knife, it's very sharp, and the pus will out. Pus is good, I believe, so don't be afraid of it. It will bring with it all the evils of the pestilence. We are lucky to be in the month of Virgo. If it were the period of Sagittarius, I would hesitate to do this. Although… I might attempt it, given the alternative.'

The house became a hive of activity. Nesta worked diligently. Matilde's screams were awful as the hot poultices were put on her painful swellings. Neighbours heard: some tried to peer through the house windows as they passed to the mill, but most watched from a distance, not daring to go close. Their fear mingled with curiosity and concern but not one of them knew for sure what was happening in the Faceby home. Only Father Wilfrid came close and dared to peer through the open shutters. Amalric managed to wave while he was stoking the fire, boiling water or cooking broth.

Towards evening, Thurston had to leave Nesta and Amalric with Matilde in order to minister to his patients at the manor. He assured them he would be back as soon as possible but they were nervous in his absence. A crucial time was developing for Matilde. Three buboes were beginning to bulge: the largest one in her neck, one in her armpit and one in her groin, each with dark red centres and inflamed edges. The remaining ones simmered on without coming to a head. She became hot and then cold. They found themselves covering her with blankets to keep her warm and then stripping them off to cool her down with water wiped over her burning skin. She became delirious and imagined arrows being shot at her by the devil's helpers. 'Tis their arrows,' she rambled hoarsely. She had a raging thirst but her throat was sore and swollen; it was difficult for her to drink. It seemed a long night but Nesta and Amalric worked on in companionship. Amalric felt strangely contented and wondered how he could feel like this when the situation was so appalling.

A drizzly dawn arrived. Amalric was relieved to hear the normal sounds of church bell, mill wheel, birds chattering, cocks crowing and animals waking. He saw movement outside as men silently began to take advantage of the damp morning to work on the softened land... but each walking alone. When they had all passed, he stepped outside for a breath of fresh air and saw Thurston striding down the hill. His forced cheerful 'good mornings' as he passed women at their doors brought only sullen nods. Amalric knew the villagers resented his friendship with his own family. Perhaps they rightly suspected he was giving medical care? Why would a physician have compassion for those who could not pay him, when his true loyalties should be with the Lord of the Manor? But above all, he was a physician. Yet, what Thurston learned about this disease would serve all people in the future. The villagers may never understand that.

Amalric opened the door for Thurston. The stink of the pestilence hit his nostrils hard and he retched. 'I'm sorry, Am, Nesta,' he said, as he wiped away saliva on his grey sleeve, 'but I am human, you know.'

'You should be wearing your suit,' said Nesta.

'Damn the suit. How is Matilde?' He feared she may have died.

'Three buboes are bulging horribly,' said Nesta. 'In fact, they look ready to pop.'

'Then let's help them,' said Thurston. 'Am, stand by the sleep room door in case we need you. You will have to ignore society's rules; Matilde will care nothing of you seeing her naked.'

Matilde's breath rasped in and out, as the bubo in her neck pressed onto her windpipe and obstructed her breathing. She rolled on her mattress, grasping at her neck. The bedclothes were damp, stinking. Thurston saw before him a Matilde he hardly knew. Her face was livid, her eyes bulged and her body was covered in a red rash. Her skin was hot to the touch. To prepare her for what was to come next, Thurston gave her a large dose of his special potion, drip by drip on her swollen tongue. While waiting for it to work, he and Nesta worked

174

quietly around her. They slid the mattress, with Matilde on it, away from the wall so they could work on either side. They put cloths to soak in a bowl of vinegar solution and smaller cloths into a bowl of honey. Lastly, Thurston took out a knife from his bag and laid it on a large piece of cloth on the floor by the mattress. Then they were ready. Thurston knelt at the side of Matilde.

Nesta gently pulled the sheet away from Matilde's naked body exposing the three buboes which bulged large. Their earlier red appearance had turned to purple. The skin over them was taut and shiny. The largest was in her neck and pushed her head grotesquely to the right. Thurston examined them with the wide-eyed Nesta at his side. He touched them with the flat of his fingers and could feel the pressure of the fluid inside the bubo. He felt for the area where the skin was thinnest – in the middle of the rounded swelling. Matilde did not react.

'We must get this poison out. We shall have to leave the buboes that have not responded to the poultices and hope that enough of the poison to effect a cure comes out of the others.'

Thurston decided to start with the bubo in her armpit, the one that might be easiest to 'pop'. The neck he would leave until last. He asked Nesta to hold Matilde's right arm up and above her head. The skin over the bubo pulled tautly. He then put his left hand over the swelling, spread his fingers, took the knife and pressed the point firmly into the tense skin between his finger and thumb. Almost at once a burst of grey pus mixed with blood shot out of the wound into the air and splattered onto the floor. Both he and Nesta retched at the stench. Nesta turned away and vomited as silently as she could onto the floor at the side. It puddled noxiously but she pulled part of the bedding over it. Thurston carried on, his mind deep into his task. He enlarged the wound and washed it out with vinegar. Then he stuffed the cavity with the cloth soaked in honey. 'A good balance,' he said. 'Sweet honey with the sour of pus.'

Amalric watched by the door with his hand over his mouth, disgusted and fascinated at the same time. He was amazed that someone could be so bold as to assault a person like that – stab into their flesh to release bad things.

Then, disregarding Nesta's attempts to maintain her mistress's modesty, Thurston prepared himself to repeat the lancing for Matilde's groin bubo. It was large, forcing her leg to the side.

Amalric found it hard to watch and turned aside: it was too close to the secret, womanly part of his sister. Thurston seemed to have no such regard, yet he heard him say to Nesta, 'This is so close to all that matters in marriage and childbirth. Scars might change her prospects drastically. And here nearby, under the pulsing, is blood. I must miss it.'

Nesta was silent.

Thurston stabbed the purple swelling. Pus poured out. He stopped for a moment. Sweat beaded on his forehead. Then, again, he enlarged the wound and cleaned out the cavity.

Last was the bubo in Matilde's neck. 'This one is the most difficult to deal with,' he said to himself.

Amalric had turned back to the scene. He saw more perspiration on his friend's forehead. It dripped from his nose. His grey garment darkened in the centre of his chest, across his shoulders and down his back. 'This neck anatomy is complicated,' Thurston muttered, as if reminding himself of past lessons. He straightened himself from kneeling, stood and put his hands to his aching back. He bit his bottom lip. 'If my knife slips into her windpipe, what then can I do? Nothing. Breathing is life.'

Amalric had become fascinated and recalled the manuscripts at the abbey that Thurston had studied. His friend's mind was now in that academic world, recalling things, assessing the situation.

'Also, there are more areas of pulsing blood.' Thurston felt around Matilde's neck. 'What they do exactly I don't know, but if I cut them, they won't stop bleeding until all the blood is gone. Then there are the mysterious thin white strings that have something to do with feeling and movement. There are also strips of muscle like meat.' Thurston knelt again at Matilde's side. 'This neck bubo, if lanced, is likely to affect her appearance later with tight scars… if she lives. Women care about their appearance. I want to be confident that I am doing the right thing.' He sat back on his heels. He clearly needed more time to compose himself. He muttered on. 'After all, this is surgeon's work and I am a physician, not very learned in the unsavoury work of treating such massive carbuncles as these buboes.'

He continued to mutter for a while, then picked up the knife that had pierced the other buboes. Amalric noted a slight trembling of his hand. It hovered over the bulging mass… was it throbbing? If it held blood, Matilde could bleed to death. Any chance of saving her would be gone.

Thurston's confidence drained from him. Perspiration emerged afresh on his brow.

Nesta turned to him and their eyes met. She understood his fear. 'Pray, Master Thurston.'

'Dear God, help me,' asked Thurston.

Amalric wiped tears away with the back of his hand.

Finally, Thurston's confidence returned. He picked up a wad of cloth and laid it down ready to plunge into the wound if necessary. His hand relaxed. He adjusted the knife so it was held as a scribe would his pen, with poise and assurance as if about to write a text. The knife penetrated the bubo. Again, the foul pus spurted out, grey and stinking. Only a few streaks of blood followed. Matilde gasped as the pressure on her airway was relieved. Thurston fell back on his heels and sighed thankfully. He wiped the knife blade on an already dirty cloth to save the clean ones for dressings. Then he dealt with the raw cavity in Matilde's neck, as he had the others. He looked at Nesta.

'Look, I'm trembling again, Nesta. Me, a doctor of physic. Like priests, we work for God but with different knowledge. We know the body better than the soul which it contains, rather than knowing the soul through which God governs it. I needed reminding about God.'

Amalric felt light-headed. He stood with a wet, ashen face, swaying at the sight of the raw nakedness of Matilde as she lay on the mattress gently moaning, with three holes in her flesh stuffed with cloth and her arms and legs splayed out. She looked damp, open and helpless. Pus puddled sluggishly on the floor; some spattered the wall. Doctor's tools lay in disarray and both Thurston and Nesta were filthy and moist. The air around them was warm and fetid. To Amalric, it was a farm scene and reminded him of a mauled animal or a hard animal birthing. He gulped back the acid taste rising in his throat. This was the pestilence. All that Father Wilfrid and Thurston had feared was in this room. Now he knew the sight, the sound, the stench of it.

Matilde lay silently. Amalric nervously wondered if the painkilling potion had been too strong. Thurston tweaked Matilde's ear. She moaned, showing she was simply deeply asleep.

Thurston washed away the filth from his hands and some from his garment so that he was clean enough to return to the manor. But one thing the physician had to do first was add to his *vade mecum* what he had done. 'Am, mayhap future lives will depend on what I've learned this day. I hope I've learned to cure the pestilence – always, or just sometimes.'

Amalric came to sit by him. He was surprised to see how shaken the physician was. The pages closed.

'Am, I'm sorry for the things you saw today. I wonder if this pestilence will stretch us all beyond human boundaries. I certainly felt stretched beyond my own abilities and knowledge today. My assault on your sister's body…' He stopped.

Amalric saw how tortured Thurston was. This man loved his sister.

'I wanted so much to cure Matilde but I have to acknowledge that my medical expertise was inadequate. I've not been a doctor long enough. I've been reduced to experimentation. Oh, Am! What a thing to say to you. It's your sister. You are still young.'

'My friend, I'm much grown lately. You have studied and found nothing to help. You did more than anyone else would have dared. I have great need to be grateful, whatever the outcome.'

'Aye, I hope so. But even though I asked God for help, I feel I'm fighting against His will for her life. That is sinful.'

'Maybe God has allowed you to fight.'

'Mm. God's intentions will become clear soon enough, I suppose.'

Amalric watched the physician pack up his things and then go slowly up the road back to the manor.

Chapter Fifteen

Next morning, Matilde's thirst was prodigious and Thurston had said she must drink as much as possible – her pee needed to be pale. Nesta insisted on going to the well early for fresh water. Amalric wondered at the wisdom of it, knowing she would meet many of the village women. He waited anxiously. She returned tearful and trembling.

'Mistress Myrtle Ashe is evil,' she blurted out to him, closing the door behind her with relief. 'A few women were there, all standing separate, like. I tried hard to be polite and said "good day" to them all. Mistress Ashe was spiteful. She asked how you and Matilde were keepin', sayin' they'd not seen any of the Facebys for a few days. She said, "Sad about your Mistress Gundred".' Nesta imitated her toadying voice so well that Amalric found it hard not to smile. 'But she didn't look sad at all. Then the other women tried to say how sorry they were but she shut them up with a look. "Gundred's own concoctions didn't work, then," she said, "on the twins or herself." I tried to say she probably died from a broken heart, after her twins dyin'. Then she asked what all the screaming had been about lately, an' the visits from the doctor and the priest. She said we were behavin' like la-di-da folk. I told her it was to offer consolation after the deaths of the twins and Mistress Gundred. I said Mistress Matilde had been very upset and weepin'… ever so loud. Then she said, "And how is Master Edwin with his fever?"

She knew the men had thrown him out of the tavern. I said, I didn't know. That we hadn't seen him. That he'd not been home. After that, nobody helped me lift the full bucket from the well like they usually do. I felt clumsy, what with bein' small. The water spilled and wet my clothes. From now on I'll fetch water at night by moonlight when village doors are closed.'

Matilde continued to improve. Nesta changed the three dressings, washed the bubo cavities with vinegar and renewed the honeyed cloths. The deep wounds began to look clean and signs of healthy tissue began to appear. But Thurston had warned that the healing would be long and leave scars. The two remaining unlanced buboes in Matilde's groin and armpit had not matured into pus-filled volcanoes like the others but even started to subside. Thurston was not needed any more.

Up the hill, the physician carried on his work at the manor with mixed feelings. Amalric met him briefly one afternoon and learned he felt elated on one hand and extremely depressed on the other.

'I've cured Matilde of the pestilence but not Lord de Horesby's sons. Now his wife has buboes. They will not come to a head, so I cannot lance them. Black patches litter her body.'

Amalric winced at the thought. 'Go on.'

'Not only that, the sons' manservant died in a matter of hours after showing symptoms. But this time it was different: he had a cough that brought up blood and racked his body until there seemed no more blood left in him. I couldn't decide whether this was the pestilence or something different. Lord de Horesby is distraught, and who can blame him? He's spent good money on me, there are only about 100 physicians in England, just to have me fail him. Had he not been grieving so much he might have told me to leave. And why, after all the contact I've had with the sick, am I not dead? And why are you and your priest not dead?'

Father Wilfrid had to finally admit to the villagers that the pestilence was among them when he was called to the younger daughter of Myrtle Ashe. The disease took her in a matter of hours. Father Wilfrid had seen the buboes and the black flesh, and smelled the stink – so unlike the usual smell of death.

The villagers had to be warned immediately. The plan that the priest had devised with the physician had to begin. He called the villagers together on the green in front of the church at mid-morning. Amalric left the workshop and stood at the back, his arms folded inside his leather apron top.

The weather confirmed the mood: still, heavy, the sky sickly with low cloud, yellow and thunderous. A few birds in the yew tree dared to twitter, then stopped. The miller had stopped grinding wheat. The silence was expectant. Father Wilfrid looked sorrowfully on the people before him. Many he had known from birth, he had buried their loved ones... but this was different. His voice carried, clear and decisive through the quiet.

'We have the pestilence in our village.' Some heads nodded. 'No person is to blame. There must be no recriminations. It is God's will. Carry on those tasks needed to live, but there must be no more gatherings of people. Stay close only with your own family, no groups of friends. No evenings at the tavern or gossiping at the well.' He looked around at his flock. Amalric saw his face cloud.

'The church building will close. All services will be conducted in the open, standing apart from each other. Seek your own remedies. Lord de Horesby's physician will help us when he can.' A murmur of doubt went around. The priest ignored it and carried on. 'Burials will be in the pit behind the church. Many of you will have to make sacrifices.'

Amalric saw villagers flinch, knowing that they didn't fully understand what was meant by sacrifices. Nor did he, really. None of them had experienced such a pestilence, but certainly lives would be lost; burials would be with little ceremony;

livelihoods could fade away and some families might not exist any more.

'Go now,' continued the priest. 'Put your affairs in order. Keep your faith. Above all – repent. I'll take confessions each evening on the church green under the yew tree.'

The crowd dispersed in silence. Amalric returned to his workshop and from the window watched as a sexton went up the hill with the church body-cart. His mouth and nose were covered with a cloth that held herbs, the dry, thin stalks of which protruded from the sides. A little while later, he returned with Constance's body. Myrtle followed alone. They disappeared round the back of the church where, no doubt, Father Wilfrid would be waiting.

Amalric left the window, reflecting that nothing would alter the fact that Constance Ashe was the first to be laid without ceremony in the pestilence pit. He imagined her small, white, tightly wrapped body against the dark soil of the large hole. His own loss welled up. He remembered the fight between his mother and Myrtle and the curse they had flung between them. If this was a curse, it was beyond reason. But then curses were. He knew from now on, the trundled death cart was going to be a familiar sight across from his home: a flat cart with wrapped bodies, a stench, a few mourners weeping, followed by silence. How long would Father Wilfrid last? Amalric shivered with dread.

Later, when sweeping dust out of the workshop doorway, he saw Myrtle running from the back of the church, through the gate towards his workshop, shouting indistinctly. Her tangled hair streamed behind her, loose from her mantle. Her fists shook in his direction. As she came closer he heard her more clearly. He stopped his sweeping.

'She poisoned the well. She skulked there in the night. She let the devil in. I saw 'er. My daughter drank the water. Nesta 'as killed my daughter.'

It was as if an arrow had hit Amalric's heart. His broom clattered to the floor as he ran out.

'No, Mistress Ashe, Nesta has not. She could not. It was the pestilence. No one has control over it.'

At that moment, Father Wilfrid appeared from the back of the church. Seeing the commotion, he rushed forward. 'Myrtle Ashe, go home at once. Repent of your sins. Now go.' He pointed to her cottage up the road.

Myrtle had visibly sagged at the priest's voice. She turned to walk home… but not before giving Amalric a backward glance of seething resentment that he suspected would not be calmed.

'Oh, my boy,' said Father Wilfrid, his face showing great dismay as his eyes followed Myrtle, 'this is only the beginning, I fear.'

At that moment, Elias staggered out of the church door and stood uncertainly, letting his eyes get used to the light.

'Go back in, Elias.' The old man obeyed. 'I'll keep your father with me a little longer,' said the priest, 'to allow you to think how to handle this resentment. His confusion is such that it will have little effect on his addled brain. He will sit quietly enough in the church with the saints for company. How is Matilde?'

'Improving, Father, we think. We daren't be too confident. I have since been thinking of the martyrs on the church wall, such as St Edmund, the one with arrows sticking out of him. Nesta and I haven't succumbed yet, and for that I'm also grateful. I'm just hanging on hopefully.'

'Ah well, the great St Paul said, "But if we hope for what we do not see, we wait for it with patience."[10] Keep your faith, my boy. I suspect it is little, but it will grow. Sometimes hope is all we have. So, have hope, my boy. It's never wasted. I hope. But I also fear that as much as I discourage groups of people, my church will eventually become a meeting place of panic,

---

[10] St Paul's letter to the Romans 8:25.

grumbles and hysteria. People will need to see the saints, the Passion, all those things painted on the walls and looking so calm. I'll keep the door closed as much as I can, especially now as your father is there, but prayer will become selfish, passionate entreaties to God, just as it has in London where the disease still lingers. News has come that flagellants arrived there at Michaelmas adding even more fuel to the fires of panic, with their naked flogged and bleeding bodies. Thankfully, Myrtle Ashe's creeping-towards-the-cross incident didn't escalate among the villagers, but who knows how people will react now in the face of such terror.'

The confidential way in which Father Wilfrid spoke to him caused Amalric to feel more like a full man than a boy. A responsible man. It was clear that while God would order things eventually, faith alone was not enough: God needed capable hands and hearts on earth to see this through.

Amalric went into the house. Nesta was outside at the back, washing Matilde's stained bedding in a tub over a small fire. Not wanting to interfere with woman's work, he went back into the house. He felt a little lost without Nesta about him, and looked for comfort in planning how to carry on the glazing business now that his father seemed incapable. He decided to seek inspiration from the Theophilus manuscript. He went to the cupboard in the wattle and daub wall and took it out. For a while he sat at the table peering over the book, absorbed in its detail. It fired his dreams and he became lost in imagined colour and composition, reflections and pictures.

After a while, intruding on his thoughts, came an excited chattering sound, low at first, then louder. With his curiosity aroused, he went to the door, opened it and saw a crowd of people walking down the road in a long line. He thought at first it was one of the processions organised by Father Wilfrid to hold the pestilence at bay and wondered if he should join it, but as his eyes focused to the distance, he saw a red flickering light. It was small at first, but as the crowd drew nearer, he could see two men holding flaming torches. Myrtle Ashe stood between them. His heart could not at first believe what his head was telling him. He looked back into the house – Nesta was just struggling in from the garden with a wet blanket to dry in front of the hearth.

'Best not to leave this dryin' outside,' she was mumbling to herself. 'Some of them birds drop a fearful waste, and anyway, it looks like thundery rain is comin': there's black clouds kissin' the hills.' She was surprised to see Amalric looking agitated. He grasped her shoulders to make her turn back. The water from the heavy wool blanket dripped over his feet.

'Nesta, get out! Get out!' He pushed her. 'Go!'

'What?'

'They're coming to burn the house. Get out! Through the garden.'

Just then they heard Myrtle scream wildly, 'She poisoned the well. She let the devil in. Burn the devil's helper and the evil in the house.'

Nesta found it difficult to understand what was happening and before she could turn to run, she saw her mistress coming out of the sleep room, having been wakened by the commotion. She was naked except for bandages and a thin sheet around her shoulders. Painfully, she turned her head and dark-circled, unseeing eyes followed the noise. Matilde then staggered from side to side through the house, past the central fireplace. The bandages holding her wound dressings began to unravel. Nesta, holding onto the heavy dripping blanket, failed to grab hold of her and she reached the doorway.

The crowd stopped immediately when they saw Matilde draped in the creamy-white of trailing bandages. Amalric realised that to them, she probably resembled a painting on the wall of their church.

'She's risen from the dead,' said a shocked villager at the front. 'She looks like Lazarus comin' out of the tomb. It's blasphemy. There's evil here. God's being mocked.'

Matilde stood in the doorway, still like a statue. Amalric and Nesta, behind her, saw the twisted, hate-filled faces of their neighbours. Nesta heaved the blanket to one arm and grabbed Matilde's wrist with her free hand. Amalric moved in front of Matilde and gestured ineffectively for the crowd to back off. Beyond them he glimpsed Father Wilfrid running from the church, his garments flying and his plump abdomen bouncing with the effort. His cry to 'Stop!' was heard as the first flaming torch was flung. Amalric brushed Matilde aside while watching it travel through the doorway into the house. On reaching it, it was easy to stamp out the flames, but the next left the hand of a villager and went out of sight as it curved in a golden arc onto the heather-thatched roof.

'You fools! You fools!' the priest cried, as he pushed his way to the front of the crowd with both his hands pointing to the flames taking hold. 'What did I say? No recriminations. The pestilence is God's work, not man's. It's punishment for behaviour such as this. And stay apart from each other, I said.'

Amalric rushed and watched flames lick over the roof searching for dry patches, free to spread in the still air. The warm weather had dried much of the surface thatch, and the central fire smoke had dried the interior under-thatch, but earlier constant wet weather had left parts of the middle layers damp. This halted some of the spread, but the flames easily found the driest parts.

'Go fetch your pails and get water from the brook and save as much as you can – that is, if you want any respite at all from time in Purgatory,' the priest yelled. 'Damn you all to hell!'

Amalric felt helpless and stood with Matilde and Nesta outside. The patches of damp thatch were causing a great deal of smoke and Amalric could not see clearly where the flames were. He feared that if the fire spread uncontrollably, the workshop would go up in flames but there was little he could do… but with the Theophilus manuscript he could start again. Yes, he had that hope. At least it was safe in the cupboard in the corner. No, it wasn't! It was on the table in the house under the flaming thatched roof!

'The Theophilus!' he cried.

Nesta at once realised what he meant. 'No, Am. No!' She let go of Matilde and clung to his tunic but Amalric pulled away. 'Then put this over your head,' she cried, and flung the wet blanket over him.

Amalric disappeared into the house. Through flames beginning to take hold of some furniture, he saw the manuscript on the table and put out his hands to grab it. Then he heard a rushing sound. Flames fell from the roof all around him. A momentary glass kiln brilliance. Then smoke and choking. He had to run, run, run... run towards the familiar figure in the priestly habit.

'Amalric. Amalric. Come, my boy, come.'

Then he was under the yew tree in the softness of Nesta.

'I have it,' he said, his throat rasping.

'Oh, my dear boy. You're safe,' said Father Wilfrid. The priest's eyes blinked hard.

The wet blanket had saved Amalric from the worst of falling, flaming thatch. Under the scorched wool he clutched the Theophilus manuscript.

'Oh, your legs, Master Amalric,' he heard Nesta say, and felt her shaking as she held him.

Pain began to grip his lower limbs. He looked down and saw skin melting from them as blisters appeared. Smoke was in his throat and he felt the need to cough violently. Then he saw Father Wilfrid's anxious face peering at his own. 'Why did they do this?' he asked between coughing spasms.

'The villagers are like frightened sheep, my boy. Many follow a strong person, being unable to think rationally for themselves. They followed Myrtle Ashe. They're looking for someone to blame for the pestilence and, as you know, think it was your family. Now... most of them are feeling ashamed and have turned to fetching water to put out the fire. At least the fire is limited to the centre of the building.' He looked down. 'But your legs, Amalric. They're burned. They must hurt dreadfully.'

Father Wilfrid grabbed one of the villagers by the sleeve as he was passing, taking water to the fire. He took the bucket from him and told him to go for the manor physician. 'There will be added years in Purgatory if you do not go,' he threatened. 'Go!' He pointed up the road and the man reluctantly sloped off. The priest then gently poured the water onto Amalric's legs and the charred remnants of his hose.

With Amalric safe, Nesta remembered Matilde. 'Father, have you seen Matilde?'

'Er... no.'

'Matilde?' asked Amalric.

'I'll see how things are with your house. You must have somewhere to take Amalric. He must not stay out here.'

'What's wrong? Matilde?' Amalric grew agitated.

'Amalric,' said Father Wilfrid, gently. 'I'm afraid Matilde is missing.'

'Not... in the house? Oh, no.'

'My boy, I'll find out,' The priest hobbled off. After what seemed an interminably long time, he came back.

'Your sister is not inside, Am,' reported Father Wilfrid. 'She must have run off. No doubt we will find her.'

Amalric took in the news. Not in the house did not mean safe. 'But Father Wilfrid, where is she?'

'I don't know. I'll look for her soon. In the meantime, you need a home. The barn and sleep room are in reasonable condition and if the smell of burned materials and the blackness is ignored, they are useable. There is much debris on the floors. The walls at the front have partly fallen down. Much of your oak furniture has resisted the flames and is merely scorched. Luckily, your store cupboard is unharmed.'

Amalric looked at Father Wilfrid. There was more to come.

'I'm afraid the village rebels have recklessly broken much glass in your workshop, possibly adding jealousy to their recriminations. The drawing on the table is destroyed.'

The wanton destruction added to Amalric's distress.

'Am, I'm sorry, lad.' It was all the priest could say. Comfort was not his to give at the moment.

Amalric observed Father Wilfrid as through a fog, cajoling and threatening the villagers to clear the building. As the fire-damaged parts cooled, smoking remains of thatch were swept away. Items that were burned and useless went into a pile in the garden. Molly was milked – she had mooed so much that no one could put up with the noise until she was comfortable and her routine re-established. The milk was left in pots. Ale and water were put by the side of Nesta and Amalric as they huddled under the yew tree. No one was prepared to offer more comfort than this to help: the belief that the Facebys had caused the pestilence to come to the village was too strong to overcome.

By twilight, when some order was returning to the scene, Father Wilfrid worried that Matilde might be wandering naked somewhere. He took his leave of Nesta and Amalric, promising to return with any news he had. He began his search by walking up the road, the most often travelled route out of the village. Nesta and Amalric watched him go. He disappeared into a grey veil of drifting smoke that lingered on the hill.

Chapter Sixteen

Rain began to drizzle. Remaining smoking embers sizzled out. On the ground under the yew tree, Amalric lay dry but shaking, still cradled in Nesta's own shaking arms. His legs stretched out in front of him. His hose had largely burned off and from his knees to his ankles, his legs were covered in charred grey skin, some of it peeling away and some of it hideous blisters filled with fluid. His boots had protected his feet. He was almost unconscious with the pain now, but continued to cling tightly to the Theophilus manuscript. He had a rasping cough. Nesta's mouse-brown hair, grey with dust, fanned over his face. He saw through the hair that her own face was pale and striped with wet, sooty streaks. Her eyes were red and a bleak expression showed clearly that she had no idea what to do next.

Amalric felt himself floating. Drifting away. He heard Nesta begin to weep. Then the shadow of Thurston's form came towards them. Tiny water droplets on his grey robe paled him into ghostliness. It was as a dream, hard to comprehend, vague.

'Oh, my dear Nesta. This is really terrible. What has happened? Was the fire deliberately started?'

Amalric calmed a little on hearing his friend's familiar voice.

'I had a message from a man sent to the manor but he didn't stay. I'm sorry I'm late, but it's an awful situation at the manor. So many are ill. We must get Amalric inside before the dew falls heavily, but first he must drink.'

Amalric felt a beaker put to his lips. Cool liquid washed over his raw throat.

'Nesta, where is Matilde?'

'Oh, Thurston, we don't know,' she said, between sobs. 'When people came down the road with torches, she roused herself and appeared at the doorway. She frightened them. Her bandages were fallin' off. They thought she was risen from the dead like Lazarus. We don't know where she is.'

'Did she go back into the house?'

'Father Wilfrid searched there, but didn't find her.'

Amalric felt his friend fall silent for a moment.

'I'll go have a look around, see if it's possible to get Am inside somewhere.'

More silence. Thurston returned. 'The sleep room roof is intact. Am, we'll get you in there to rest. We must have you in the building. These blisters are wet and so to keep the healing balance, we must keep you in a dry room.' He turned to Nesta. 'With those burns, he will feel the cold intensely. Keep him as warm as you can. Stay by him, he will need you.'

Nesta nodded. Amalric smiled his gratitude – he knew Nesta would stay by his side. He felt drowsy.

'Am, it's getting too dark to examine you. I'll leave you my potion for the pain. You will have a raging thirst so drink plenty of water, milk and ale. Here is my cloak to cover you, to help keep you warm.' Thurston turned again to Nesta. 'If you find the means, put a warm poultice on his chest to help him breathe the noxious smoke away. I'm afraid his condition will worsen before he recovers. I think you will be safe from now on.' He bit his bottom lip. 'I hope Matilde returns soon.'

As Thurston turned to leave, Father Wilfrid returned, grubby and tired. Amalric roused and noticed a brief hopeful look on the physician's face.

'Stay a moment, physician, I have news.'

Thurston, Nesta and the dreamy Amalric looked expectantly at him.

'The light was failing but as I got to the well and stood to get my breath, I saw Myrtle Ashe drinking from the well pail. She seemed unable to stand up straight. Hunched shoulders. Maybe in pain – I don't know. She looked to have a fever. Rash on her face. Sweating.'

Thurston nodded knowingly.

'Anyway, she turned to me with that evil look she has and said, "I expect yer lookin' for her – Lazarus – Matilde Faceby."' The priest continued. 'She said she'd seen a near-naked woman walking past the brook, back yonder – seen her going down to the river. Then she looked defiantly at me. Those eyes of hers! She smiled peevishly and spat out words designed to cause us misery, "I expect she's drowned." Then, she gathered her strength and began to limp away to her home. I watched her go. I was shocked at her vehemence. Then after a few paces she turned back and said, "See, priest, I've got it. You an' your faith can do nowt."'

Another silence fell. Father Wilfrid was the first to break it.

'Would you believe? I felt sorry for her.' He shook his head in dismay, then turned his attention back to Amalric. 'My boy, I'm so sorry. But you know what Myrtle Ashe is like, she throws poisoned words as if they were devil's arrows. Her words may not be the truth. I've been to the river and seen nothing. Have hope, my boy.' He turned to Thurston. 'Physician, you look awful. All this news… it seems to have broken even you. Let's get the lad here safely into shelter, and then come to the church with me and we will find succour in the saints together.'

Two dry mattresses were laid side by side in the sleep room. Amalric was carried into his damaged home and laid down with Thurston's cloak covering him, just as the first clap of thunder broke over the village.

The following day was fresher after the storm. The sky was blue. Sunshine reflected off damp vegetation. The Faceby home was cool. Puddles scattered the central part of the building, the house, and ash and debris floated in them. It stank of smoke and burned items. Nesta had been able to make Amalric a hot drink and porridge on a small fire in the hearth, which was open to the sky. She had stayed at her master's side all night and he had heard her say her prayers, thanking God for the sleep room's escape from destruction and for the store cupboard's strong oak doors that held flames back from provisions... and Master Amalric's deliverance from death.

Amalric's vagueness was replaced by an odd combination of pain and clarity. When his friend Thurston walked in, he found his appearance upsetting. His grey robe was further stained, clearly unwashed since attending to Matilde. He stank of sweat; his hair was unkempt. Red eyes and dark circles pointed to exhaustion and sleepless nights.

'Nesta has managed well, Am. You are a lucky man.' Thurston lowered himself wearily onto a charred stool.

In that phrase, 'a lucky man', Amalric detected a deeper meaning and it had to do with Matilde: his friend was keenly feeling her loss.

'This is a brutal happening for you, Am. The pestilence is not only a disease, it's social mayhem. Yesterday evening in the church, I looked at the saints and wondered where the philosophy of physic fits with faith. Can either of them do anything to stop this? I'm shocked to realise that despite saving your sister, she might have since died from something so cruel as the misguided vengeance of the villagers. And here you are, also a victim. And in the church with his palsied face and lazy limbs, is your father.'

Amalric had completely forgotten his father.

Nesta came to Thurston's side with a beaker of thin, warm ale. 'Master Thurston, are you alright?' she said, on seeing his slumped figure.

'Yes, I'm fine. Just weary.'

'Tell me what to do to heal the master's legs and then leave us. You're busy with the pestilence and I can manage. Besides, you look exhausted. I have Molly for milk, some laying chickens, the beehives and all the greenery still in the garden, though it's rabbit-nibbled and damaged from scorched wood bein' roughly thrown about, but nature's good and it'll recover again. If there's any news, any at all, I'll let you know.'

'Aye.' Thurston's voice answered dully.

'What do I have to do, Master Thurston, for Master Amalric?' she repeated.

'Oh - I'll examine him.'

Amalric's too-bright eyes looked at him. He moaned softly with every movement Thurston encouraged him to make. Every now and then a choking cough racked him but Nesta had put a thick, warm pad of herbs mixed with soft clay soil and wrapped in a singed cloth on his chest. Thurston marvelled at its heat-retaining properties.

'Has he coughed blood, Nesta?'

'A little.'

'The pestilence sometimes shows in coughing. Avoid the spittle if you can. Now… these legs. Well it's good to see that your boots protected your feet. Come Nesta, let me show you what you need to know.'

Nesta looked on, wide-eyed. Her master was content to listen.

'See here,' instructed Thurston, 'the skin is pink, lightly burned, but if I press, it goes white. I take my hand off and the pink returns. Now – here are blisters, large ones like bags of water, which we need to burst in a moment. They are like these here, that have burst already, with the skin peeling off leaving it raw and oozing fluid: they are very sensitive.' Thurston touched the raw area, causing Amalric to wince. 'They are on the surface and will heal quickly. Now, see here, here and here.' He pointed to more areas, which to Nesta didn't seem too bad. Nor to Amalric because they didn't hurt when pressed. But Thurston was particularly interested in the largest of these just below the knee. 'When I press this area, it will not change from the white colour. I believe this and the two similar smaller ones to be quite deep burns and will need a lot of watchfulness. Eventually, with good care, most of the burns will probably heal satisfactorily…

but with scars… always assuming, of course, the pestilence does not intervene first.'

For now, the large watery blisters that wobbled needed to be burst. Amalric gulped a light draught of painkiller that was insufficient to bring on a deep sleep. Thurston then knelt by the mattress and out of his satchel took a knife. Amalric saw the small, sharp blade glinting and became nervous. His friend made no movement.

'What's delaying you, Thurston?'

'A thought came to me but left quickly before I had time to understand it… Now I feel dreadfully fatigued.' Thurston's arms fell to his side and his fingers opened so that the knife clattered to the floor. 'I lanced Matilde's buboes with that blade and released foul, blood-stained pus, the poison of the pestilence. It's a good tool,' he said, looking down at the knife and wiping sweat from his upper lip with his tongue. 'I don't know what frolicked in my mind just then? Nesta, do you have a cooking knife that has survived the fire?'

'Aye. An old one that has a charred handle but is still sharp.'

'That will do.' Thurston shook his arm. 'There, the feeling is coming back. I can't think why my arms lost their use. I just felt that somehow it was wrong to use the other knife.' He looked confident again. 'Am, you will not feel this.'

Amalric felt afraid of the kitchen knife but hardly had time to protest before Thurston had painlessly popped the first blister at the base with its point. Fluid ran out. It was clear and straw-coloured. More blisters were popped. Thurston leaned back on his heels and sighed with relief. Nesta wrapped Amalric's legs in vinegar-soaked cloths.

'Nesta, if the burned areas are not healing very well, if they have pus and the edges look red and angry, that is the time to put on honey-soaked cloths like we did for Matilde.' Thurston sighed again. 'Then if that does not work, other than bleeding, I cannot offer more.' He gave Nesta more painkilling potion in case Amalric could bear the pain no longer. 'I know your own knowledge of herbs and skill will suffice to keep Amalric comfortable, but burns can turn bad.'

A short stillness of unsaid words hovered between the three of them.

'I must go,' Thurston continued. 'I will have much work to do from now on and will probably be unable to visit for a while.' He laid a hand on Amalric's shoulder. 'Heal well, my friend.' Then he moved to go to what remained of the house doorway. 'Oh, I almost forgot.' He picked up his knife from the floor and put it into his satchel.

'God be with you,' said Nesta.

'Aye.'

Amalric's condition deteriorated as the effect of the burns took hold. Time lost its shape. Along with visions of overwhelming fire, singed manuscripts and heightened colours of broken glass, there were moments when he saw Nesta bending over him, her soft face full of concern, and he heard the occasional creaking settlings of burned timber, smelled the scorching of wood and cried out in fear for his legs.

Every now and then something different roused him, or a voice other than Nesta's was heard.

An old man's face hovered. It had a grey, unkempt beard, straggly hair and stinking breath. Spittle dripped.

'Da?'

He heard Nesta's sharp voice: 'Master Elias, come out of there. Your son is resting. He's not well. Father Wilfrid has brought you home. He's a very busy man. You must sit by the fire. Yes, I know it doesn't look like your home.'

'Da! Da!' Amalric called.

'Rest now,' said Nesta.

The firm, steady voice of Father Wilfrid broke through to him. 'Amalric, my boy, keep your mind on St Edmund. The arrows which pierced his legs.'

'His legs? My legs? The pain.'

'Remember, they didn't kill him, my boy.'

Chapter Seventeen

A space of time passed. Amalric was aware of voices again. Was Father Wilfrid talking to Nesta?

'Your hands are busy at the moment… have not enough time to care… work with your two men will be very hard.'

'Two men and one other life!' Was that Nesta talking?

One day, he heard a high-pitched cry. A tiny cry. What was it? It recurred. A small animal?

'It was a sin.' Who said that? Father Wilfrid?

Sin. Sin. Sinning. The word 'sinning' went round and round in Amalric's head.

'Nesta… Nesta!' he called. 'Who is sinning? Edwin?'

'It's nothing, Master Amalric. Please rest.' Nesta was tired and irritated. 'Do as I say.'

Then Father Wilfrid. 'The nuns from Swine Priory…'

'Nesta!' Amalric shouted. 'What is it? Are you weeping? What is it about Swine Priory? I won't go. Am I dying?' He could understand nothing.

As the initial shock from the burning passed away, Amalric became more aware of his situation. Embarrassment at his own helplessness became a problem. Since being small, he had required no one to attend to his personal needs and it was hard for him to accept that he was like a child again. He could see that Nesta, too, felt shy and awkward at first, but she told him that she had looked after her own two brothers and knew quite well the ways of young men. She found efficient ways for him to cope with washing and his waste. Yet... as days went on, he began to recognise the simple joy that the touch of her capable hands on his painful body gave him. At those times, he felt a shapeless longing he had never before experienced.

Good sleep was hard to come by, tortured as he was by the thought that his family had been the target of so much hate – enough to burn them out of existence. And the loss of his mother, the twins, Edwin and Matilde. Their absences crushed like a weight on his chest and in his head. When a fitful sleep eventually descended, yellow flickering images of the fire came back to him and he felt smoke suffocating him – he coughed and coughed. His sweating hand sought Nesta's in the space between their two mattresses and she, in an exhausted deep sleep, always put her hand into his. Then for a short while he slept soundly.

Away in the sleep room, Amalric could not see what Nesta was doing when she was not at his side, but he knew she had the care of his father. He heard her encourage him to go to the privy and wash each morning. She prevented him from roaming to find Gundred by making little sweetmeats, persuading him to sit by the damaged wall in the glow of the autumn sun, or sing songs with her. Amalric enjoyed the songs too. They stirred him, warmed him, settled him:

> Of every kind of tree, the oak is this land's fairest,
> Its bowers stoop towards my love, to touch her heart,
> the rarest.[11]

Amalric's small burns began to heal. But the deeper ones worsened – one near his knee especially. He began to feel very hot, then cold. A feeling of being trapped grew upon him, as if enclosed in a bubble, floating on a sea of warm pain. He felt a shadowy Nesta place pads of cool moss under his legs. She

---

[11] Author's original work, inspired by fourteenth-century poetry.

diligently applied honey dressings to the wounds, but it was a bitter treatment: flies and wasps were all around him, hovering, tickling and buzzing incessantly. He saw her wave away as many as possible and try to keep him covered with a large cloth, worrying he may be stung. But he wanted to tear off the sheet, the blanket, the sticky bandages – they trapped him.

One morning, Amalric felt more awake. He watched Nesta remove a sticky dressing from his leg ready to apply a fresh one and saw her face blanch. Her cry upset him. He raised himself on his elbows and looked at his legs.

'I'll be in the grave soon, I'm dying,' he cried. 'Black patches! The pestilence! Oh, Nesta!'

Panic seemed to arise in her. 'No, no. It can't be. Be still. I'll clean your legs.' She brought a bowl and cloths. As she gently wiped the black areas, he watched her face twist with revulsion. Then she stayed her hand. 'You're not in the grave, Master Am. Rest now,' she said, and gently rewrapped his legs.

Days later, Amalric, in a drifting sleep, was awakened by a clatter and voices.

'I'm sorry to surprise you. You've dropped your spoon.'

'Master Thurston! Oh, my, you look so thin! Exhausted.'

'And you look so weary. Carry on, Nesta, till you've finished feeding Elias.'

'Come in.'

'I shouldn't.'

'Thurston, come in, please!' shouted Amalric, anxious to see his friend.

'No, Am, I've been in too many bad places.'

'Please. The happiness of our minds is surely good medicine. Anyway, I'm dying. Black skin. The pestilence is here as I speak. I shall need Father Wil…'

'Oh. Nesta didn't say.' Thurston came into the room. His eyes burned into his friend's face for a moment, professionally examining him. With one hand, he wafted flies away, while gently pulling bandages from Amalric's legs with the other.

Thurston's face registered shock.

'Nesta!' he called. 'How can you have allowed this to happen?'

Amalric lifted himself on his elbows again and looked at his leg. The largest burn by his knee looked like a piece of black leather. It had shrunk away from the surrounding skin and, horrifyingly, undulated. Something soft and white moved at the edges. 'I told you so,' he gasped. 'I'm as good as in the grave already.'

Nesta hurried into the room.

Thurston glared at her. 'What's all this? These maggots?'

Amalric saw Nesta's eyes blaze and her childish years surface. She stamped her foot and shouted petulantly, 'My da says wrigglers clean the skin. They eat dead flesh. He puts 'em on sheep sores when they're hound-bitten an' it festers. I feared Master Amalric would die anyway, he was so ill, so when I saw the wrigglers, I left 'em there just to see if he was like sheep an' they'd do the same job on him.'

Thurston did not respond. He tugged at the moss. 'And this vegetation? It's soaking wet.'

'We use it at home 'cos it holds a lot of wet stuff when we have no cloths. I can't keep up with Master Amalric's mucky sheets – the wet, the pus an' all. An' what with all the washin' I have to do for Master Elias, it's all so…'

Amalric was bemused by the conversation. In truth, he didn't *feel* as if he was dying, even though the evidence was before him.

He watched Nesta give way to tears, wailing into the corner of her apron. He felt her hurt, her anger and fatigue of the past days.

'I didn't know what to do,' she said. 'When I saw the black, I thought Master Amalric was dying of pestilence, but there were no buboes like Mistress Matilde had.' Calming down, but with a quivering lip, she said, 'I did what you said with honey but I couldn't keep the flies off. I was so tired. They must have laid their eggs in the dead flesh. I feared Master Amalric would die. I couldn't bare another one dyin' – not him! I thought anything was worth tryin'.'

Amalric became more alert. She had said, 'Not him!'

'You should have asked me to call,' snapped Thurston. 'I'm in the village often enough.'

Nesta's own irritation increased. She shouted, 'I only saw you afar when I was at the well an' you looked – look – so tired, so busy! See – you're filthy. And 'appen you carry the pestilence.'

Thurston sagged. 'I'm sorry!' He turned from Nesta's distress to Amalric's clear, wide-open eyes and gentle breathing, then his attention turned to the burns. With tips of his fingers, Thurston lifted the edge of the black, dead, leathery skin from the largest burn close to Amalric's knee, and found it came away easily, revealing a moving white mass of small worm-like creatures below.

'Bring me vinegar and a cloth.'

Nesta did so and watched him wipe the creatures off the burn, away to the floor where they wriggled helplessly.

Amalric strained to see. 'What are you doing?'

'Quiet, Am.'

A soft doughy material was left behind on the burn which was cleaned away with the vinegar cloth. Below this, the flesh was soft, raw, clean and pink and the edges of the wound seemed to be growing inwards. Thurston peered closer. 'Can it be?' he muttered. 'Is the deep burn healing?' He lightly pressed with his fingers. The raw area felt healthily firm.

Nesta recovered from her outburst but felt embarrassingly chastised. Sniffing softly, she began to clean up the mess from the floor, dropping the maggots into a bowl. She went to remove a few stragglers from Amalric's legs.

'I'll throw 'em on the fire; I don't want 'em to turn to flies. We've had enough of them already.'

Thurston now looked embarrassed. 'Err… no. Leave some on the wound. Nesta, I'm sorry. I think the maggots are working like on your father's sheep.' He smiled contritely. 'The burns seem to be healing. The wounds are looking clean. You have done good work here. *I* might have learned something today.' He put his freckled hand to his chin and stroked his stubbly ginger beard. 'I'll have to think about this. I've heard of it before, but it is not scientific. More to do with local healers. Mm... House maggots eating putrefying human flesh... for benefit?'

Amalric saw Nesta's face beam like a forgiven child. He felt relieved for her. She was giving her all for him and his father.

'So... we may tell Master Amalric that he is not in his grave bein' eaten by worms?' she asked of the physician.

'Yes, we can!'

All three laughed.

'You are a lucky young man, Amalric. I hope I haven't brought more ills upon you simply by being here.'

Amalric, Elias and Nesta escaped the pestilence's grip, despite Thurston's fears for them.

The fever left Amalric entirely as the maggots continued to do their work and drove him to distraction with itching. The warmth of the night was the worst time. Only when Nesta changed his dressing pads and the maggots were lifted off did he get a short spell of relief.

With a clearer mind, Amalric's thoughts turned to Matilde and Edwin.

'We don't know where they are,' said Nesta to his questioning.

Amalric had a vague memory of being told that Matilde was nowhere to be found after the fire.

'Matilde disappeared. Mistress Ashe saw her and told Father Wilfrid it was likely she had drowned in the brook.'

Amalric remembered.

Nesta could not soften the words. 'We've all been too busy to search for her.'

Amalric's face didn't alter. 'And Edwin? He had a fever.'

'I've heard nothing.'

Amalric felt distraught and helpless. 'Then tell me all that has gone on in the village since I was burned.'

So she did, but not quite everything. One thing could wait, or even never be told.

While Amalric had lain in confusion and pain in the sleep room, Nesta had watched Warren Horesby readying for the coming storm. Amalric knew the process that people frequently went through to survive epidemics, but this time, Nesta's accounts showed it to be more virulent. His own mother had failed. Like all the healers, she'd had no experience of buboes, no experience of a disease that could kill so quickly – when a person could simply suddenly fall and die by the roadside.

'Everybody was ever so busy, Master Amalric, after the fire. Everything seemed really urgent,' said Nesta. 'The mill churned out as many bags of flour as the miller could manage, then it stopped. Lots of animals were tethered in garden plots. Carts with night soil and manure were put on the land to leave room for it to pile again in gardens. I went to the well at night, fearin' the women, but I saw a stream of 'em in daytime with every bowl, jug and pail they owned, to store fresh water in. I heard from a manor servant that Lord de Horesby was mindful of the needs of us villagers and tried to build up a stock of food in his big barn, but had found supplies hard to find.'

Nesta's most disturbing tales were when the pestilence hit.

'Every time I heard the body-cart, I rushed to the window.' Her wet eyes glistened. 'A couple of days after the fire, the first cart trundled down the road. I knew it was a pestilence death because the two mourners looked so fearful an' they had their faces covered. I couldn't make out who'd died. The body wrappings were a bit stained but neatly done. The next day there were two cart journeys and then it got more 'n' more. Then the bodies came unwrapped with their arms an' legs bouncin'. One sexton disappeared an' then the other disappeared so that folk had to wheel the cart themselves.'

Amalric listened without breaking into Nesta's tirade. It was important for her to speak of the harrowing scenes, to unburden herself of what she had seen.

'Oh, Master Amalric, I watched from here, each cart goin' through the gate, under the yew tree and round to the pit at the back. I imagined everyone bein' tipped into that dark place.' She lifted her apron to wipe her tears. 'It's been awful. Now everythin' is so quiet.'

Amalric listened for familiar sounds coming through the sleep room window but heard none save the birds and animals. 'Nesta, is anyone left?'

'Aye, but I've seen very few. An' they looked so weary. Mainly folk of our age. Not many old ones like your da. I haven't heard children cry. I think everyone that's left is lonely.'

He imagined the remaining folk drifting like shadows on the paths. 'Have you seen Father Wilfrid or Thurston?'

'Aye, but not for a while. I watched Father Wilfrid limping to and fro. Sometimes, when I was out, I saw him standing by doors or windows saying prayers from as far away as he could manage. Sometimes I even saw him hold a hand. I never saw him standin' at the church gate. One mornin' as he passed by here, he told me that he was makin' a list of all the deaths, beginnin' with Ned.'

It was a consolation to Amalric that no one would be forgotten. 'And Thurston?'

'I didn't see him often. I think he was busy at the manor but he did see some folk in the village. I've only seen him once since your legs had wrigglers.'

She giggled and Amalric laughed with her. It relieved the strain of listening to such bad news.

'When I last saw him, he said to tell you his experience with Matilde had made him able to cure one other villager.'

'Oh, that's good.'

'But no more.'

There was only dismal news for Amalric to receive. After so many deaths, it was clear from closed doors that the remaining villagers felt medicine and faith could not help them, preferring to die unencumbered by medical or religious rituals in which they had not the energy to indulge.

One day, when Elias had wandered off, Nesta found him by the manor gate. A single servant there told her that only Lord de Horesby, his daughter Clara and a few servants had totally escaped the pestilence. She saw the estate land unworked and spoiled with weeds. Thurston remained, it seemed, in his little cottage, seldom leaving it. Opposite the Faceby home, the church too stood listless, its door firmly closed.

Amalric continued to heal, but slowly. Occasionally, leaning heavily on Nesta, he struggled to the door and sat watching for signs of Warren Horesby's resurrection. It was slow in coming.

By something over one moon's passage since the major onslaught of the pestilence, the village had descended into a doldrum – silent and motionless. Amalric could not bother to add up the weeks and was content to measure it roughly.

Nature's perfumes lay dormant under the putrid reek of the great miasma. A myriad of heavy, rotten odours wafted down the village. They struck his nostrils and sank into his lungs. They warned travellers to stay away. No one passed the Faceby home.

Few homes had smoke twirling through the thatch. He surmised that ownerless animals had pulled free of their tethers and fowl had wandered away, searching for food on the strips or up in the hills.

Morning sounds were absent. No church bell signalled prayers. No mill clatterings announced the working day. Amalric observed, thankfully, that birds still bobbed and twittered normally, delighted by autumnal berries.

Nesta told him how she had to walk gingerly up to the well.

'There's carcasses of dead dogs, cats and rats all over,' she stressed. 'Not only in horrid, shadowy places but openly on the road, left to rot. Some of the cats, black ones, have a straw cross placed on their slimy fur.' She grimaced. 'I think it might be 'cos someone thought it had somethin' to do with the devil rather than it dyin' from starvation. Or maybe it was killed, specially. And,' she found the next sentence difficult to say, 'there's a swollen human body lying on the main road. I can't see who it is – was. Carrion crows, feral dogs and rats are at it – sniffin' an' pullin'.' She gagged at the thought. 'Ugh! You can see the skeleton more every day.'

Amalric hoped, as he knew Nesta did, that it was not someone they both loved. He felt really sorry for Nesta having to face such terrible things and he was glad she found comfort at the church. Leaning against the old, solid east wall with morning light on her face, she had discovered a kind of peace in its unchanging nature. And ghastly though it was, she told him, the pestilence pit represented for her the souls of those lost to the disease – their trials, their redemption. She therefore felt herself nearer to God. For him, the pit resembled the picture of hell painted on the west wall of the church – bodies tumbling down into it, arms and legs waving a resistance. Punishment for sins.

Part Three

Aftermath

Chapter Eighteen

Days drifted on. One morning, Amalric was surprised to waken to outside sounds: shutters opening, footsteps on the road, a distant voice, hammering from the mill. He turned over in bed, ignoring the returned familiarity, and reached out for Nesta. She was not there. Up to now, she had been on hand through the night to help him, but of late, she had risen before he had fully wakened. He missed her softness. She made him feel warm, comfortable but excited. He wanted the pleasure of her smooth limbs, her shiny grey eyes and long brown lashes looking into his own eyes. He wanted to enjoy her unrestrained smile and gesturing hands. Now that he was recovering, he felt himself less of a patient and more of a man.

'Where are you, Nesta?'

She called from the house. 'Can you hear Master Amalric, the village is comin' back to life? Can you hear? The stink ain't so bad today. I think I'll just go to the church for a while.'

He pictured her, grasping her mantle, wrapping it around herself, then walking barefoot across to the church.

He rose from his mattress and went into the house. He stood by the damaged wall and understood why Nesta wanted to be at the church. A pink sun misted over the building and the moist yew tree leaves caught the radiance. He watched her reach the end of the path, expecting her to carry on to the east end, but she hovered by the porch, then surprisingly, entered. The door was hidden from view by the porch wall and he assumed that Father Wilfrid had opened it to start services again. Amalric grew absurdly joyous. To see his old friend would mean a new start to everything. Maybe he would appear at the gate soon with his beaker and his first drink of the day. How wonderful that would be. Amalric rushed to put on his hose and jerkin over his underclothes. But as he stood with one leg in his hose, he heard Nesta shouting at him.

'Master Amalric! Master Amalric!'

He looked out. Nesta was waving frantically from the porch. He quickly continued dressing and hobbled on painful legs over the road, through the gate, past the yew tree. Nesta ran towards him, regardless of bare feet on rough ground. She was agitated, her face white.

'Oh, Master Amalric,' she gasped. Her mantle was loose on her shoulders. She pulled him by his jerkin. 'You have to come inside the church.'

Amalric allowed himself to be dragged to the open church door. Inside, crisp dead leaves moved with the draught. Amalric desperately hoped to see Father Wilfrid standing with hands on his paunch, laughing, 'Come in, my boy.' But there was nothing, only sunbeams holding dust moats in the air, rodent droppings on the floor, items of worship and some bits of old rag in the sanctuary. A bird twittered in the roof.

'Nesta, there's nothing here.'

'That's what I thought. I came in, quiet like, in case Father Wilfrid was at prayer. When I couldn't see him... I called out but there was no answer. It was odd that the door was open but no one inside. Then I saw the bundle of rags, over there beyond the screen, in front of the altar. Come with me, Master Amalric. I daren't go into the sanctuary alone.'

Dry leather sandals, with mottled, swollen feet, poked from beneath the rags. Amalric recognised them as Father Wilfrid's. His tattered priest's habit covered the shape of a motionless body. Beside it, water from two tipped beakers glinted on the floor of the sanctuary and dripped down the step.

'What shall we do, Master Amalric? I daren't touch him – he's a priest.'

'Leave him.' This was the pestilence's last hammer blow. Just a little while ago Amalric thought the disease had gone, moved on. Now here it was again. His friend, comforter and wise adviser was dead. Like a sudden storm, a wail broke from the constant grief lodged in his chest. Every sorrow of the past weeks gathered within the death of this dear man.

Feeling intensely angry, Amalric staggered to the image of St Edmund on the nave wall. The flat, impassive painted face looked straight ahead. The arrowed legs stood unmoving. At that moment he hated St Edmund. Denouncing the saint's ability to help, he pummelled on the cold limbs with fists. Finally, beaten by the unyielding wall, he slumped to the ground.

Amalric felt, rather than saw, Nesta tentatively approach him. She wiped away his tears with her hand and put an arm around his broad shoulders. In that moment, Amalric looked at Nesta and felt all his anger, all his love, everything, sweep cleansingly towards her. Calmed, he resigned himself to his fate.

'Well, Nesta, this is surely the end for us. The pestilence has returned. We must prepare ourselves.'

'Maybe, but I don't think…'

'Nesta, if you are going to be hopeful, it's pointless. Death will come.'

Nesta ignored Amalric's dismal protest and went to the priest's body. 'I think our priest died of somethin' else. He looks so peaceful. Come and see.'

Amalric hauled himself up slowly, thinking Nesta would be mistaken. She had pulled back the priest's hood. Turned to one side on the cold floor, the recognisable face was pale, bluish, the eyes half-closed, relaxed. Calm. There was no sign of the agony that preceded pestilential deaths. No obvious lumps in his neck like Matilde's. No bloody spittle around his mouth. No blackness.

Amalric became animated. 'Let's look for black marks and buboes on the rest of his body.' He knelt and began to lift Father Wilfrid's habit.

'Am, we can't,' said Nesta horrified. 'He's a priest.' She stepped back, her hands to her mouth.

'Then I'll do it alone. He would understand.'

Amalric pulled back the priest's habit and looked for signs of disease. He felt the cool flesh for lumps. There were no black areas. He found nothing, just a pathetically wasted body, hard swollen knees and pitted, swollen ankles. He sat back on his haunches.

'Nesta, I believe he simply felt exhausted and lay down by the altar to die. He wasn't pestilential. See the two beakers... he wanted me to join him for a morning drink... it must have just been too much for his worn-out body.'

Words failed them. They sat on the cold tiles and found each other's hands. Around them the solemn shadows of the church gave way to full sunlight. The painted figures burst into triumphal colour. St Edmund's passive image showed nothing of the beating he had received.

'Nesta, we should tell the village about Father Wilfrid. Come.'

As they left the church Amalric felt strangely comforted, as if the priest were merely out of sight. His remembered voice whispered in his head, 'Have hope, my boy.' Amalric turned to Nesta. 'I'll do something for this church one day, as my father wished to do, and know Father Wilfrid is smiling at me again.'

As quickly as Amalric's painful legs would allow, he and Nesta went to tell the news to the villagers. Knocking on doors was a hard task. Many, many stayed firmly shut. Some were gingerly opened. Grief was obvious in those remaining – drooping wet eyes, pallid skin and thin bodies. Amalric realised with horror that he too must look the same. But strangely, the news of this final blow stirred people. It was agreed that whatever the actual cause of their priest's death, the pestilence was still responsible.

It had simply worn him out. But even in death, he worked for them. He brought them back together through mourning for him and discussing how he had worked tirelessly for them through their bleakest days.

Only Horesby Manor remained untouched by the news. No one dared venture beyond the boundary wall, where no movement had been seen for some time.

Amalric and Nesta watched Father Wilfrid being placed ceremoniously into the pestilence pit behind his church, to join his flock in death. Fear had, at first, been on the faces of the men who gently lifted him from the church but, by now, some things had become more important than one's own death. People came from all over the valley and stood crowding the graveyard. Simple prayers were said over the wrapped body by an elderly villager, just as Father Wilfrid had said they may when no other priest could be found.

Yet for all the crowd, and Nesta holding his hand, Amalric felt lonely. Others had insisted on dealing with the priest's body for their own atonement, and he had felt pushed out, physically weak and unable to argue. Yet he was beginning to realise that sometimes, others had to lead… Nesta had led him to recovery. He threw seeded flowers into the pit.

One week after the death of Father Wilfrid, Amalric tentatively thought about the glazing business, even though his legs were still troublesome. Some areas had not quite healed, especially the deep burn on his calf. His knee pulled tight with contracting scars and he limped because of it.

In the workshop, everything was sooty blackness from smoke. He crunched on shards of glass that littered the floor after the villager's resentful rampage, weeks before. Thankfully, his shepherd window was still intact but smoke had settled greasily on the glass, making it almost impenetrable to the morning light. The big table, racks and little hearth and tools were fine. Ingredients for chalk whitener were safe out the back along with lead cames. As for glass? Well, while no large sheets remained, he could make use of small pieces. The St Peter drawing had gone but he could start to draw again as soon as the workshop was clean.

Three fearless field mice appeared and ventured in front of him. A family. Of his own family, only he and his father had survived. The noses twitched and beady eyes looked up at him hopefully. Their soft brown fur shone smooth. Nesta! She had family too! The realisation came to him like a thunderclap. He stumbled back quickly to the house, where she was busily preparing their first meal of the day.

'Nesta, I have been so selfish; you should go home to your hamlet to see what's happened to your family. They'll be worrying about you.'

Nesta stopped stirring. 'I suppose you're right, but I can't leave you. You're still not well, especially in the night, and Master Elias is a real handful. I'm still your servant.' She recommenced stirring the pot.

'But don't you want to know how your family's fared?'

'Oh, of course I do.' Her eyes watered. She sniffed. She stopped stirring again.

'Then go. Da and I will be fine. You must go. I shall miss you. But this morning, the birds are singing and mice are in the workshop, just as they've always been.'

'Master Amalric, I worry that some of the villagers will still think your father brought the pestilence from Meaux, force you to leave. Will you be here when I come back?'

'I shall not leave. Any one of them could have brought it. It *had* to come. I think they know that now. And… I've been thinking – I'll deal with our repairs and then start up the glass business again.'

'But that will cost money. Perhaps I could take in washing or…'

Amalric was too excited to listen. 'Father has some money hidden somewhere. I hope it wasn't lost in the fire. Also, I must journey to Meaux Abbey. The pestilence will have passed on by now and I must see if work remains for me to do. Then there are the sheep to gather. There's no telling where they may have roamed.' He sighed at the enormity of it all. 'I have lots to do. I have to build a new life, Nesta. I'll make plans while you're away. But you need to know what's happened to your family. You won't worry then.'

He was enjoying the feeling of concern he had for Nesta but her expression puzzled him. The grey depths of her eyes gave little away.

'Master Amalric...' she hesitated. 'We both know that there are women in Warren Horesby and beyond without husbands now. They'll need to find a man to support them and some of them quickly – those that have children. You may marry soon.'

'Even so, Nesta, you'll always be our servant.' That wasn't what he wanted to say.

'Master Amalric, you must do as you wish... as you need.'

Nesta was serious while Amalric covered his emotions with flippancy. 'And anyway... you might still find a suitor in your own village. You may not want to come back.'

The expression on Nesta's face became one that Amalric couldn't interpret. A thick silence fell between them. Nesta looked at the floor. Amalric knew something else was coming.

'Master Amalric, I am a servant. Your injuries are much improved. I will most likely return and then I'll sleep in the corner... as servants do.'

Amalric decided to go to Meaux Abbey on the day after Nesta had left. He started early, hoping his father would be safe for the day. He'd left food and ensured all ways out had been securely closed.

As he passed by the Manor House, he recalled a long-ago journey with his father to York Minster where he had first seen the window with a monkey and a doctor's flask. He looked through the open gate to Thurston's little stone cottage beyond. The door was closed. He didn't stop, fearing what he may find.

It was hard to walk. The scars around his knees pulled and tore; blood trickled down his calves. It took until midday to reach the abbey. It looked disconcertingly beautiful and golden in the autumn light. A silence like thick honey filled the air. Animals roamed alone. Four swans glided angelically in the moat. The bridge was empty of carts. Amalric wearily limped to the precinct. No clamour was there either but sheep roamed in the small gardens and among the buildings. A lone bell began to ring for the noontime service of sext. It sounded strangely hollow and eerie.

Following the clanking noise, he came to a lone monk pulling on the rope that led up to the top of the church bell tower. He was the monk who had provided food and drink when he'd been there with his father and Ned in spring, when the earth tremble had struck. When he had met Thurston. Images flooded into his mind. It was as if years ago, not months. The monk now sagged with exhaustion. His previously smart tonsured hair was sparse and untidy, his habit grubby.

'Father Luke?'

'Yes, it is I, Father Luke.' Skeletal fingers let go of the rope. 'Amalric Faceby, is that you?'

'Yes! How good to see you, Father.' The urge to embrace was great.

'Yes.' Luke also beamed his pleasure and held out his arms.

The two clasped each other, glad to be with another survivor from the past.

'Oh, Amalric, we have had a dreadful time. All our prayers, supplications and penances failed to prevent the pestilence arriving. The abbot was among the first to go. He and five others died on the same day and within the month twenty-two monks and six lay brethren had gone. Fifty people would come to our services, now we have ten.[12] Now, as you see, here in

---

[12] These figures were taken from 'Houses of Cistercian monks: Meaux', in *A History of the County of York: Volume 3*, ed William Page, pp 146–149.

October, we are severely reduced. I ring the bell for each service but barely raise anyone.' He waved a hand to indicate the empty abbey precinct. 'We remaining few are tired and dispirited. We don't know how to carry on. We have dug graves until our backs are nearly broken. I wonder why those of us left have been spared.'

Amalric waited patiently as Father Luke rapidly related his experiences of the past weeks.

'I've not been able to discern God's plan in this. Much seems unfair. Our infirmarer died among the sick, while another monk ran off to live as a hermit on the moors and has survived. My understanding of my faith has been severely challenged.' He stopped and took a deep breath. His speech slowed. 'Anyway, Amalric, on a more cheerful note, let us forget the dreary bell and the sext service – no one else will come – and rejoice that we have each survived. I see that your legs pain you. What has happened?'

Amalric pulled up his hose. His scars showed, red and weeping.

'No, do not tell me yet. Come, let us find some abbey ale and then sit and converse. There may even be some wine. God will need to see us care for each other. Your legs need some attention. If needs be, I'll put soothing dressings on them.'

Amalric realised that no new work was likely to come his way from the abbey for a while, but he promised to look over the windows every now and then to keep them safe from falling out. How could he not, when despite all that had happened, the glinting sun on the glass there still thrilled him? But he must find other, bigger, commissions.

The journey home was easier. It had been good to talk with Father Luke. The herbal ointment and potion had relieved the discomfort of his legs. Seeing the glass, maintained so long by his father, made him think about his own final Glaziers' Guild approval. Now his father was unable to work, would there be any other guild members left to approve his work? He felt young, inexperienced.

Chapter Nineteen

Amalric examined the makeshift roof repairs of sparse tree branches, heather and old cloths that the reluctant, guilty villagers had erected weeks ago after the fire at the insistence of Father Wilfrid. They were failing to keep off the rain. Large drips frequently plopped onto the impacted earth floor. Autumn had advanced and there was little in the house to prevent cold air from seeping in. The thought of money frequently occupied Amalric's mind. His home and the glazier business depended on it.

Elias sat by the hearth slightly shivering, the lax skin of his face trembling. Blueness tipped his fingers and nose. His grey hair was unkempt and he dribbled spittle. His tunic front was food-stained. It hadn't taken long for Amalric, now on his own with his father, to realise how much Nesta had tended him.

He settled on a stool by his father in front of the dying fire and threw on a log. It sent up sparks but temporarily dimmed the redness. Slowly, fresh flames took hold and the log began to burn. The bright light roused Elias and he droopily looked at his son.

'Da, I know that life is hard for you at present,' Amalric spoke slowly to ensure the words would penetrate the clouded mind, 'but I need your help to rebuild our lives. Before all our troubles, you told me that Grandpa had hidden some money away. You didn't want Edwin to get his hands on it. Well...

Edwin's gone. I need the money to restart the glazier business. There's no new work for us at Meaux Abbey but perhaps, when the churches and abbeys get back to life, there'll be work, somewhere. Maybe only a few glaziers are left. I may find work and without a final Glaziers' Guild approval I might not get far, but I have to start trying.'

Elias tipped his head to one side. He seemed to be listening.

'Tomorrow, I'm going to clean up the workshop. There are lots of new things I'll need, hog's hair brushes, glass, maybe an assistant...'

A large drip of water fell onto Elias' head. It dripped through his grimy hair, down his forehead to the side of his nose. He put out his tongue in a weak attempt to lick it from his upper lip.

His son smiled. 'And we need to repair our home; we need a roof.'

Amalric waited a while to let the first batch of information sink into Elias' mind. The fire crackled. Then he slowly and emphatically said, 'Da, I need that hidden money you said we could use.' He took a deep breath and sighed. Had it all gone over his father's head? 'Da, you must know where Grandpa hid it. You must remember something.'

Elias stared into the flames. Then he slowly became animated, as if a memory was being poured into him, waking him up. His hands waved about and he struggled to speak. 'Angel!' he spluttered. 'Angel, angel, angel!'

'What do you mean, Da?'

'Aaan... gel,' Elias said adamantly, and then wilted. The memory drained out. The light in his eyes dimmed and he stared into the fire once more. The flames became a glow.

Amalric knew people sometimes saw angels before they died. He wondered if this was happening to his father. 'Angel' meant nothing to Amalric.

Amalric needed to go outside for fresh air, away from smoke. It was dusk. The church, the rock of consolation, drew him. Autumn breezes had piled dry leaves in front of the porch. They drifted and rustled when he pushed on the door. Unoiled hinges squeaked their resistance. There had been no activity in the church since the funeral of Father Wilfrid. On that day, there had been flowers, but now only spikey brown stems remained in pots in the sanctuary. Dust, dead flies, bat and bird droppings scattered the floor. As so often, a bird twittered somewhere in the roof. A feather drifted down. Amalric shivered. He passed further down the darkening church and stood in front of the wooden altar. Like the floor, its surface was scattered with the debris of passing time.

Among it was the little wooden figure of Jesus that Father Wilfrid had dusted for Easter, now carelessly placed as if someone had started to tidy up before running out of enthusiasm. His artist's fingers moved over it, feeling the raised wood grain. The rough carved little wounds disturbed him like a memory forgotten, but the emotion remaining.

The colours of the familiar figures on the walls dimmed almost into monochrome and he couldn't help thinking they were waiting for something to make them relevant again. He could almost feel their breath, hear them whisper. St Edmund drew him as usual. The face was passive. One shadowed painted arrow pierced a leg where Amalric's own deepest burn had not yet fully healed. He ran the flat of his hands over it. The wall was smooth, cool. Other arrows penetrated where Matilde had been tortured by the buboes and where Thurston had pierced them with a knife. Why had he, Amalric, beaten his hands on those arrowed legs after Father Wilfrid had died? The saint had suffered enough. He looked up: in the gloom, the eyes which gazed stoically forward now seemed to be lowered to meet his own. Changing light did that, he knew. Yet he felt that St Edmund understood. Their wounds were similar – St Edmund's, Matilde's, his own. The saint hadn't given up! Still gazing at St Edmund's eyes, he imagined him to be saying, 'My wounds are your beginning' – silent words that meant the past was to be built on, not repeated.

Then he became aware of more familiar words, 'Have hope, my boy.'

'Father Wilfrid?' He involuntarily called out and immediately felt foolish to be answering a voice that was only in his mind.

Amalric rapidly left the church, berating himself for hearing imagined silent voices. He must still be unwell! He stood to regain his breath with hands on knees. Oh, how he missed Father Wilfrid and the way he had always seemed to appear from the shadows just when he was needed, a little plump figure in a coarse, long robe, fat feet in sandals. Well, he would have hope. He would have a new beginning.

The next morning Amalric went into the workshop. The shepherd window would be his starting point for cleaning up. There was a small crack low down but the lead came was stable: the glass wouldn't fall out. The worst problem was the greasy soot. Searching under the table, he found a pot of his mother's special cleaning balm. His father used it for the final touch after new glass had been installed. The resulting sparkle was always glorious. He rubbed the soft paste sparingly over the sooty glass with a dry cloth and wondered what he would do when it was all used up. Only his mother and Matilde had known the recipe, and neither he nor his father had bothered to ask how it had been made.

With the shepherd window brought back to life, it occurred to him that his father might enjoy being in the familiarity of the workshop.

'Come on, Da,' Amalric said, as he led his tottering father in through the workshop door, hand in hand. On seeing the shepherd window, tears came into Elias' eyes. The beauty of the glass and its reflections spreading around the untidy workshop stirred old feelings. Amalric had to put a stool under him before he crumpled to the ground.

Elias became animated. 'Angel! Angel!' He leaned forward and lifted his tired arm and hand with a huge puffing exertion to point to a tree.

Amalric had a moment's insight. When making the window, he had been inspired by the rabbit warren hill beyond the Ripple Brook. In glass and glass paint, he had depicted it and a young birch tree which grew on top.

'Da? Da, did Grandpa make me change the angel's hand for a reason? Is… is the angel pointing to where money is buried?'

Elias nodded, his energy almost gone.

Amalric was stunned. 'Er… but where… exactly?'

A whisper was all Elias could raise. 'Reet close.'

Amalric's eyes followed. He put his nose to the glass. The angel seemed to be pointing to the side of the birch tree. Then he realised the angelic finger end almost touched a smudge of paint, like a slip of the brush. It was where a broom bush grew now – he knew it. Once small, after years of growth it was now larger, as was the birch tree it nestled beside.

'Is that smudge the broom? Did you or Grandpa paint that when I wasn't looking, before it was fired?' No answer came, but Elias' mouth showed just the suggestion of a smile.

Amalric mulled over the idea of buried treasure. Surely such a thing was unlikely. Yet he had heard tales that years back in raids, wars and famine, people often buried money for security. He remembered Thurston telling him he had seen Lord de Horesby and his boys go off with laden sacks and spades. Would his resourceful Grandpa have done it too? But why would he want the message in glass? To be permanent in fickle times? Clear to someone who could not read? The idea was preposterous. Even if it were true, the myriad entangling roots would be impossible to dig through. Yet the chance that money was there would not leave his mind.

That night Amalric raised himself from his mattress when the village was still. His shadowy form tramped painfully up the hill with a spade and sack, his way lit by sporadic moonlight. At the top, the birch tree wafted its branches delicately. But where to start digging? He must avoid the top of the hill: anyone not sleeping and looking out in a clear moment would be able to see him silhouetted against the sky. His grandfather would have also thought of that. Perhaps best to start between the bush and the tree where the ground sloped away from the village view.

Amalric first lifted the damp autumnal turf, heaving up the grass roots. He had no idea what he was looking for: was it coins in a rotted sack, a leather pouch? The pressure needed to push on the spade caused his legs pain and as time wore on it was all he could do not to cry out. He sweated and cursed. The moon kept going behind clouds, jauntily mocking his efforts, but the birch leaves softly stroked his face and moved encouragingly over his bent back. Would he have to dig around the whole broom bush? What if the broom was on top of the treasure, closely holding it to itself in tangled, knotted roots? It began to seem a hopeless task.

When the sky began to turn from black to ultramarine, Amalric sat wearily, almost weeping with disappointment. Roots were exposed; turf and damp soil littered the ground. Tomorrow he would have to come again and dig on the more exposed side and risk being seen. He threw the shovel with annoyance onto the bare earth. There was a clunk. He struggled up. Clearing more soil, he hit a hard surface, the top of a wooden box. Reinvigorated, he bent to feel it. It was hard oak and, of course, his grandfather would use hard wood to delay rotting. He worked his shovel around it, loosening the soil. It came out with a slurping sound. The box fitted easily into his sack. With a sense of relief, he tidied up the ground, and replaced the turf. Then with aching and sore legs he tried to saunter home casually, looking as if he had been out early, merely seeking mushrooms.

Back home, Amalric lifted the door latch as quietly as he could but unexpectedly found his father sitting by the cold fire waiting for his son. The old man watched as the box lid was easily prised open. In the early light, they saw it was full of old coins made dull with damp. Elias pursed his lips and gave a slight nod. Amalric decided to put the box in the cupboard that was set into the wattle and daub, accompanying the Theophilus manuscript. However unlikely the window message had seemed, he now had money.

Next morning, despite his intentions to sort the leaking roof, Amalric was excitedly distracted by the thought of working in coloured glass again. Nothing had been heard from the congregation which had first commissioned the St Peter window, only that the village had been badly hit by the pestilence. His plan was to make the window but in a new style of his own devising – he was feeling the freedom of being on his own. He would redraw the figure but make it smaller and set it in a wooden frame. Then he would carry it to a few churches or manor houses as a sample piece. Only small pieces of glass remained after the villagers' reckless rampage in the workshop, so there would have to be more joins in the glass than was usual. In any case, a smaller figure would allow smaller glass pieces to be used. One long purple piece for the fall of St Peter's robe was out of the question; it would have to be two. The greater number of lead cames necessary to hold small pieces together would spoil the simplicity but it couldn't be helped. Crucially, there was a yellow piece large enough for a halo. He prepared his table as Theophilus instructed. With a knife, he scraped dust from a piece of chalk so it fell over the table, then sprinkled water on it everywhere, and rubbed with a cloth to give a smooth whiteness.

Yet, try as he might, Amalric found it hard to maintain his enthusiasm. His freedom to create felt hindered by grief. Images circulated in his mind: colourful, full of movement, but he couldn't translate them into a new style for glass. The only way to move on was to give up creating something new and go back to the style where his father had left off, before the pestilence hit. Dreams of new designs were for the future – far ahead. For now, it was better, for a demonstration piece, to draw St Peter as his father would have done.

Eventually, a finished line image of St Peter was on the table. Black on stark white. Amalric had found the task laborious, routine, without the bubbling excitement he loved. St Peter had the usual upright posture, and wide eyes in an otherwise expressionless face. The drawing was good, he knew it was, but nevertheless unsatisfying. Lacklustre. And those eyes, why did they look so unseeing? Still, in coloured glass, there would be at least a sparse vitality.

A sound in the distance penetrated his thoughts. Was it his name being called? It got louder. Strangely, it sounded joyous, even excited.

'Master Amalric, come out here.' It was Nesta!

A grin spread across his face. Nesta was coming home! He went to the back of the building and saw her little figure skipping down the warren. But two others, whose outlines he could not recognise, trailed behind. Her family members? His eyes strained. One was a thin man in worn, fashionable clothing. The other was a woman in a gown that entirely covered her body. Her head tipped to one side and she had thin hair blowing out from a cap. Nesta held back when she got to the water's edge, letting the others step gingerly over the stepping stones. Suddenly Amalric felt the pain of his scars. His knees buckled and almost gave way.

'Edwin? Matilde? What... what is this?' he shouted over the brook's gurgling.

'Hello, Amalric,' gasped Matilde breathlessly, as she struggled jadedly up the low bank. The journey had been arduous for her but she had enough energy to draw him to her. Amalric gloried in her sisterly embrace but felt her skeletal shoulders and the scars in her neck.

Edwin stood by, sheepishly, holding two freshly killed rabbits but saying nothing. When Matilde let go, Edwin hugged him with one arm and less enthusiasm than their sister.

'I'll miss them, brother,' he said, flatly.

Amalric knew who he meant. Saying names made grief take shape. He felt a pang of pity for his proud and reckless brother.

His youthful face looked narrower and older, his youthful contours thinner, and the ass' tail scraggy. His swagger had gone.

'When I left here to walk home,' said Nesta, 'I went the longer way – it's easier walkin' – an' passed the old sheep barn. I saw signs of life, scraps of food, animal bones... that sort of thing, and dared myself to find out who was inside. I was scared but found these two.'

Amalric was charmed by her vivacity. She seemed happy. He wondered if she was really betrothed this time.

'It seems that durin' the fire, Matilde wandered off to the barn. Edwin was already there! He'd escaped to it when the villagers ran him out of town fearin' the pestilence, but it turned out to be a bad cold. Well, he looked after Matilde and fed her – you know how good at huntin' he is. She managed her wounds as best she could but they healed badly. Anyway, when I found 'em both, I persuaded 'em to come with me to my family up at the hamlet. These past days have been spent cleanin' and restin' them. When I first saw 'em, phew, what a stink!' She drew breath at last. 'Well... Mother wasn't too pleased at first, fearing the pestilence, which still hasn't arrived there, but she soon enjoyed carin' for 'em. Her achin' bones seemed to be cured for a while.' Nesta's excitement calmed. 'Oh, Master Amalric!' she exclaimed and put her hands on her hips and sighed happily.

Amalric managed to ask blithely, 'And are you betrothed?'

'Huh. No. I told you before – the lads are dolts!'

He nodded and hid his immense relief.

On their entering, Elias lifted his head, but failed to recognise his two lost children and regarded them as unwanted visitors. 'Gundred! Gundred! Folk 'ere. Come. See to 'em!'

Matilde's face creased when she saw her father so cross at their presence and incapable of doing anything except sitting by the fire. Amalric noticed that Edwin remained unmoved and slunk to the barn. Matilde went to rest in the sleep room.

Amalric sat with Elias by the fire, watching Nesta's strong, small hands deftly skinning the two rabbits to make a stew. He noticed both the expertise and gentle reverence with which she carried out her task, and the soft expression on her face. He wondered if she was saddened by the death of the creatures. It deeply moved him in a way he could not explain to himself.

By the time the dismembered rabbits had been laid into a large pot with the last of the year's herbs from the garden, Amalric felt emboldened to put right something that had bothered him. He would be back, he told Nesta, before the rabbits had cooked.

With unease churning in him, he went to the manor, the scars on his legs tight and pulling all the way up the hill. He ventured through the gateway. Sheep roamed aimlessly. On reaching Thurston's cottage, he parted weeds and kicked animal droppings from the step. Then he knocked apprehensively. There was no answer. He lifted the latch and slowly opened the door. He put his head through and a stale body stink hit his nostrils. He expected to see at best nothing and at worst a corpse, but what he saw was his friend bending over a small table in the sparse room, as if asleep. A tipped flagon was on a table among crumbs and a small portion of dry cheese. More flagons scattered the floor among his physician's equipment. A bed was against one wall

The sudden shaft of light disturbed Thurston. He lifted his head, then rose in surprise.

'My friend,' said Amalric, 'what's happened to you? You're living worse than a hermit… apart from the wine.'

Amalric saw dull red eyes staring in amazement at him, a pale, haggard face, a shabby, rusty beard and a forehead with deep furrows extending into a new bald patch. His long grey garment hung loose and stained.

'Oh, Am!' Thurston grappled at the reality of a visitor. 'I'm sorry you see me like this. Lately, I've felt too drained of energy to go back to the village… to see what had happened to you all. I couldn't face… no matter! I assumed you were dead! The pestilence raged so greatly. You had so many problems. I thought... How did you...?'

'As you see, I'm not dead.'

'I don't know what to say.' The physician's eyes moved over his bag, roughly thrown to the floor, a cracked urine flask, empty small potion bottles and scattered manuscripts including his *vade mecum*. Then he bent to pick up several parchment sheets with his own writing on them. Amalric's eyes followed his sporadic movements. 'I had grand ideas... to find a cure. I found nothing.' He threw the parchment sheets to the floor again. 'But the disease won, whatever I tried to do. I have seen some awful things... awful things.'

Amalric let Thurston carry on.

'Two people survived, Matilde and one other, a village man. He then killed himself because all his family died. Matilde ran off and drowned.'

'But...' Amalric tried to interject.

'I failed. I failed my master, Lord de Horesby, I failed the village folk, your family when you needed me, and especially Matilde.' Thurston hesitated and then said more quietly, 'I failed God, yet I am left alive.' He took a sobbing breath. 'I'm a physician but I'm deprived of curing.'

Amalric put a hand on his friend's bony arm.

Thurston continued quickly. 'People will think in their ignorance that I saved myself by some magic or other. I did not. Something enabled me, and you also, I see, to escape the disease and I have no idea what it is.' He stopped speaking, thought and then asked, 'Father Wilfrid?'

'Dead, I'm afraid, but not of the pestilence. We believe he just wore out. Look Thurston, like Father Wilfrid, you did your very best... all is not hopeless...'

'I feel it to be,' Thurston interrupted. 'Hopeless.' His eyes scanned Amalric, who felt discomfited by their piercing, puffed tiredness. 'Ah... Am, you look different. Older. Legs bad? You look as though you need a drink.' He lifted up the flagon from the table. 'I have been given permission by Lord de Horesby to

230

take enough wine for my needs. There are few at the manor to consume the large quantity in the cellar. Lord de Horesby and his daughter. A few servants.'

'Lord de Horesby – ah, yes. Nesta told me.'

'Yes, but a recluse. His daughter mopes around the manor.' Thurston peered into the flagon. 'Oh dear… I'll get another.'

Amalric declined the wine with a wave of his hand, 'Don't drink more wine, save it. Come for a meal with me and Da. Bring some wine with you. It will be a change from ale for us. Come on.' Thurston did not smell too clean. 'Mm, maybe a wash at the well before we leave, and perhaps change into your old black gown.'

Chapter Twenty

Amalric opened the door of the house and cheerfully said to the occupants, 'Look who's here.' Nesta was by the fire. Edwin was slumped over the table. Matilde sat beside Elias with her hand on his and the tilt of her head towards him.

They all looked to the door. Every movement stopped as they grappled to recognise the ginger-haired, black-garmented man standing in front of a grinning Amalric.

Thurston seemed embarrassed. The visual scrutiny appeared to upset him. He ran his hands over the bald patch and thinning hair. He clearly had no idea what to do next. He looked at Matilde, then back to Amalric.

'Why did you not tell me?' He looked angry. 'I can't...'

The homely atmosphere broke like brittle glass. Edwin sighed sardonically. Matilde turned her eyes from Thurston. Amalric immediately felt his own naivety. How stupid he was to think he could mend all that had passed with a surprise visit, a meal of rabbit stew and wine. Such things were for easier times. Recent events ran too deep. He ran his eyes over everyone. It was a stalemate, an impasse. He stood helpless and young. No one spoke.

Then a resolute voice broke the silence. 'Come, sit, Master Thurston. We'll tell you how it is that Mistress Matilde and Master Edwin came back.' Nesta flashed an outraged look at Amalric.

Thurston dropped heavily to the bench. Amalric noted with hidden delight how, from time to time, his eyes rested on Matilde and hers on him. No one spoke while Nesta told her tale. Then, when she had finished, she busied herself with servant duties. Amalric caught glimpses of her through the smoky dimness, but was too pleased to be with his family and friend to wonder how she might be feeling.

The wine had its effect. It warmed their blood and Nesta's meal filled them. Elias dozed by the fire, while around the table, Amalric, Matilde, Edwin and Thurston talked far into the night, almost to dawn. Each expressed their wonder at escaping death, their fears, their sufferings, their tentative hopes for the future. For Amalric, it meant God had been lenient. It was as if they had all been allowed to come back from the dead.

A horizontal strip of light blue sky was broadening way beyond the church when Amalric walked home with Thurston, having left Edwin and Matilde sprawled in the sleep room, Elias snoring by the fire and Nesta in her curtained corner.

He regretted behaving like a mischievous child earlier. 'Thurston, I'm sorry. It was a juvenile trick to play. It must have been a great shock to see Matilde, Edwin and Da suddenly like that.'

'And Nesta.'

'Aye.'

'No matter, Am.' They walked silently, watching their steps to avoid barely visible stones and debris. As the manor came into view, Thurston spoke.

'Am, I'm so glad to have seen Matilde. My heart aches for her.'

'Aye, she's suffered, there's no doubt. But she had eyes for you alright.' Amalric felt himself being playful again and stopped talking.

Thurston looked down thoughtfully as he walked on. There was an air of awkwardness about him. 'With your permission,

Am, I would like to… court her… err… you know what I mean.'

Amalric became stern. This was serious. 'Do you pity her?' He had to be blunt. 'Are you sorry about her scars – her head being pulled to one side? If you are, she won't allow that. I know my sister. She will not accept pity.'

'Am, I'm responsible for how she is. Wounded. She can never be as active as she was before the pestilence. She told me of the scars in her armpits and groin. They'll make her joints stiff and her neck will always be on one side.'

'You cured her! She's alive! You don't have an obligation. She won't stand for that!'

'No, Am, I love her. When I thought she had gone, my life was empty. When I saw her this evening, something flooded into me. You may understand. It was like colour after greyness, light after darkness. My life can have meaning again. I know it. I just need to recover my mind. Get cleaned up. I know my feelings for her will not change. I have loved her since I saw her with muddy feet and parsnips in her hand.'

'Then why ask me, Thurston? Father's still the head of the household.'

'Am, things are different now. You and I both know he is incapable of any decisions. You must take control. You are now responsible for your family.'

The fact hit Amalric hard. 'Aye, but I'm reet scared to admit it.' His father's word 'reet' had popped into his mind – it seemed appropriate, natural. They stood silently for a few moments.

'Well, what do you say?'

Amalric had never experienced such talk. Father Wilfrid had spoken generally of love between man and woman, sanctified by God… but now he, the eldest son, had the power to say 'yes' or 'no' to this older, learned man.

'Oh, Thurston, I'm no more my sister's keeper than of the rabbits in the warren. All I can say is, I'd be happy to have you as my brother.' He slapped Thurston on the shoulder.

By the time they reached the manor gate, Thurston's demeanour was again thoughtful.

'Am, I feel bound to say something else. I know I've not seen you for a while and maybe my mind is not recovered enough for you to take heed of me but… beware of Edwin. From what you have told me before, his motives are hard to discern. He is devious. Despite being away from you and suffering a hard time, he may not have changed. He will be hard to control. He will always be a man of fashion, aspiring to a higher class.'

The morning was cold. Amalric pulled his cloak around himself. He was taken aback by Thurston's interference in his affairs.

'Aye,' was all Amalric replied. They parted. He was disturbed by Thurston's talk. Who was he to say how he, Amalric, should treat his own brother? It was one thing taking over the workshop, but another being head of the whole family. Then a further realisation presented – as such, he would need to marry. Nesta's words about the husbandless village women would have to be considered… but not yet.

Walking back down the hill, Amalric thought of his damaged home and makeshift roof. Now, with his father's money, he could think about repairs. The glazier business would give him a living. Edwin, with persuasion, could deal with the strip farming and sheep – Thurston had to be wrong about him. Nesta would keep the house, garden and livestock. Matilde and Thurston would marry and live nearby. He himself would marry. All would be well.

As he drew nearer, Amalric's smugness disappeared – all was not right in the house. From outside, he pulled back a piece of tattered linen which hung in the charred window space. The light hardly penetrated but he just made out two shadowy male figures grappling over something. He rushed in.

'Edwin, what's going on? Da! You're too ill to be fighting.'

It was clear that Edwin was trying to wrestle a box from his distraught father, who held it tight with his one good arm. Elias' palsied arm swung helplessly. The Theophilus manuscript was on the floor.

Elias saw Amalric and let out a wail, 'Aaaam!'

With his father's attention diverted, Edwin pushed the old man and at the same time wrenched the box from him. Elias staggered and fell to the ground backward, hitting his head on the cold, rough, blackened stones of the hearth. His body twitched, then relaxed. Blood seeped slowly from the back of his head through tangled hair, forming a pool. It soaked gradually into the impacted soil of the floor.

Edwin stood motionless with the box in his hand. It was empty. The lid had fallen off and spilled coins to the floor as Elias fell. Some had rolled into the blood.

Amalric knelt by his father, calling to him, his hands lifting the bloody head to rest on his thighs. Elias' eyes refused to focus, their black centres large. Amalric knew he was dead. A desolation engulfed him, impinging again on the mass of grief already there. Bending over, he wrapped his arms round his father's head. Tears soaked the old man's face. Amalric moaned softly, feeling his childhood drift away with his father's soul. Then, with the realisation that his father had not confessed his sins, came fear for what might happen to him in the afterlife. Would it mean endless years in Purgatory atoning for sins? He felt once again Father Wilfrid's absence.

'Do you confess your sins, Da? Of course you do. May your sins be forgiven you, Da.' Oh, what were the proper words?

Matilde and Nesta had been wakened by the commotion.

Matilde took in the scene. 'No!' Her face became white as linen as she pushed Amalric to one side and knelt beside her father. She put her healing hands on the lifeless cheeks.

Nesta stood by, immobilised by the shock.

'It's ended now, Mat. All ended...' said Amalric, standing. 'Ended with father dying like this. Edwin has finished it for us all.' Amalric glared hatefully at his brother, wanting to beat him into the ground but unable to move. Matilde then stood and coaxed Edwin to the bench, where he sat with the empty box still in his hands. In that moment, Amalric's anger flared even for Matilde. He held it down as best he could, concentrating on Edwin, the cowering youth protected by their sister.

'Edwin,' said Amalric, 'your greed has killed our father.' Thurston's recent words played in his mind.

'No – I found…'

'I will not hear excuses, Edwin.'

Nesta watched from the shadows until her practicality took over. She pushed Amalric to sit on the bench a little distance from Edwin. She wiped his hands clean of blood then covered Elias' body with his own cloak. She cajoled Matilde to help clear the mess and replace the coins in the box. The Theophilus manuscript was returned to its place. None of them was yet able to contemplate moving the old man, and they sat staring at the bizarre scene – the corpse with bare blue feet peeping from underneath a fulled woollen cloak. In death, grotesquely similar to Father Wilfrid.

The day passed to mid-morning. Edwin left the house. A little later, Amalric went to the workshop intending to make decisions on how to deal with the new situation. As he turned towards the workshop door, he noticed it was slightly open. Through the thin gap he could see Edwin with a livid face, loose hair flying, angrily rubbing at the whitened tabletop with a damp cloth. The drawn head and shoulders of St Peter had already been wiped away.

A wave of furnace rage sparked in Amalric. He charged through the door and sprang at Edwin, putting his artistic fingers tightly round his neck. Edwin though, this time, had the greater strength, pulled them away and pushed Amalric against the shepherd window. The sudden force of the impact caused the window to bow outwards, stretching the lead cames and loosening some of the glass. As Amalric slid to the floor below the window, winded, he heard the dismal tinkling of falling glass.

'I found the money!' shouted Edwin. 'I was looking around to see what was left in the house after the fire. I found it. In any case, why should you have it? Glass. Huh! Even your precious shepherd window wasn't right, was it? Look at it now. In bits.' His lips twisted in a smirk. 'Why do you want to be like Da? What use is it to be just like him?' He pointed to the white table. 'That saint was staring at nothing. Things've changed over this year, Amalric – I can't be like Da. I don't want to spend my life with bits of glass, or sheep, or crops. I'm not like you.'

Blasphemies exploded from Edwin. Amalric was shocked. Had it come to this? Such dreadful profanity – but clearly, Edwin had no care about that.

'I have to start over again, Am, be what I really want to be. There's opportunities out there 'cos weaker folk are dead.' Edwin stood with hands on slim hips, chin raised in defiance.

Amalric had no words to say. He limped to the door and bumped into a startled Nesta as she was entering, seeking them both. He pushed her to one side. 'See what he's done now, really ruined everything!'

Nesta continued into the workshop.

He heard her say, 'Master Edwin? Some food is ready… and drink… then we must do something about the master.'

Amalric turned back to her with a bitter expression and pointing finger. 'Don't be kind to him, Nesta – you above anyone has a reason not to be kind. Remember the barn!'

Amalric took the money box and put it back in the cupboard with the Theophilus, believing Edwin would not attempt to steal it again during daylight. Then he went outside to look at the damage to his shepherd window.

He looked at the bent lead cames bowing out of the window frame, and the pieces of glass suspended in the dry weeds below. Most held their original shape. Daylight reflected off some and penetrated others, colouring the weeds with jewel colours. Somehow, in his mind, their beauty contrasted with Edwin's menace. How was it that his brother could arouse the sympathy of Nesta no matter what he had done? Frustration, anger and sadness forced him to stride off to the brook. There he watched water cascade thickly and lucidly, like molten glass, over the stones. The sight of it cooled his temper. Maybe Edwin had just found the money, but clearly he wanted to keep it, or some of it. It galled Amalric to think that Edwin could see that the pestilence had changed everything and new opportunities were there to be seized, while he, Amalric, only saw a need to re-establish the past by carrying on as before, too afraid to try new things.

Edwin had unwittingly made him think differently about the future. Amalric now knew for certain that the old imagery was not expressive enough to convey all that had happened. Death was always close but never so grasping. The survivors were all emerging into a new world. Amalric had to be a part of it. 'My wounds are your beginning.' St Edmund's imagined, silent words slid again into his mind. Bad times had to be built on, not repeated. Would his father want him to follow the old ways blindly? Hadn't he and his father before him been adventurous with their talents? Drawing St Peter in his father's style, the old style, had been laborious, uninspired, dull. Edwin had been right to destroy it. 'Have hope, my boy.'

Having found a new but brittle purpose, Amalric returned, alert, into the house. His father's body still lay on the ground, covered by his own cloak. Matilde sat fatigued in a corner. Nesta was putting a stew pot over the fire. Edwin was eating a bowl of porridge.

'Am, I... I don't know what to say. I'm a fool,' Edwin grovelled.

'Aye.'

'I wasn't searching for Da's money, you know. I found it in the cupboard by chance. I merely looked to see what was in there.'

'In the dark?' Amalric suspected that seeing the money would have been like a flash of light in Edwin's head as he saw an opportunity for new clothes, a horse and adventures in the towns.

'Father saw me and grasped it with that one good hand of his. Nesta and Matilde know I wouldn't steal the money.'

Nesta's face turned red.

Amalric's eyes narrowed. 'Nesta has no reason to defend you! What you mean is, you weren't wily enough. Father caught you stealing the money.'

'No, Am. How could you think that? I've changed.'

'Changed! You'll never change. You don't even now realise the harm you've done. It's not just father lying here going cold, it's all that's gone before.' Amalric's confident mood shattered into seething, angry resentment. 'Years of thinking about yourself and what you want. What with the young Ashe girl and all…'

'The young Ashe girl?' Edwin looked surprised.

Nesta and Matilde's eyes widened.

'Aye,' replied Amalric, as bitter thoughts held in for so long were about to be released. 'It was the start of…'

'Stop,' said Matilde, suddenly. 'Listen!'

A whistling sound was heard in the distance. Such a sound had not been heard since Ned died. Matilde stood and looked out. Amalric followed her to the charred window. Thurston was coming down the street. He was close. He looked clean; his ginger beard had been shaved off. A new physician's black garment had been brought out of storage. It flapped deep black, creased, soft around his legs. In his hands he held a bunch of autumn flowers. Amalric looked angrily at Edwin but stayed silent. Edwin stared back at him and his eyes filled with fear. He turned as if to run off but his brother grabbed his sleeve.

'No, don't run away from us – this time, stay!' Amalric was firm, strong. Talk of the Ashe girl would have to wait. He was glad: such things would be better said later, more calmly.

'But Thurston will… '

Amalric knew that Thurston would immediately see the covered body by the hearth and guess what had happened. Any excuse his brother might try to give was no match for the physician's superior intellect.

'He will know what happened and I will be hanged!' said Edwin.

'No!' Amalric still clung to Edwin and pulled him closer. His breath puffed into his brother's pale face. 'God knows, this is the last straw. I want our family to survive. We have all been through hell but we can start again and you must recognise me as head of this household. And you must allow me to take care of Da's money. It must be used for us all... for us all,' he emphasised.

Thurston breezed into the house, his face aglow with smiles. 'Good day to you!' he cried aloud. 'Your physician friend is here to offer the health of a grand day.'

No one replied to the jocular words. The physician stood perplexed at the response and peered through the dusty sunbeams coming through the window. His eyes rested on the cloak by the hearth, and the blue feet. His nose twitched at the smell of death and blood. He looked around.

'Is it Elias?'

Amalric suddenly realised that Thurston must have seen the bowed cames and the shattered glass as he came past the workshop window. There was also his father's blood still on his hose. He rapidly found words that he hoped would satisfy the physician. 'Good morning, Thurston. As you can see, we've had a difficult morning.'

Amalric felt rather than saw Edwin's expression. He knew there would be a glint of fear in his eyes.

'Father fell on the hearth stones and hit his head. He died immediately,' said Amalric.

Thurston looked quizzically at all their faces. Amalric saw the lover's demeanour become that of physician.

'Well, I'd better take a look at him.'

Edwin didn't move. Thurston put the flowers on the table and Matilde's eyes followed them. Then he bent down to pull back the cloak and saw Elias' unresponsive face, the unseeing eyes. He turned the head to one side to reveal a wound where he'd fallen heavily on the hearth stones, then turned the body slightly, looking for other signs that may have caused death. He looked at the stains on the impacted earth floor.

'Your father died some hours ago. See, here is the cause.' He slipped his hand gently under Elias' head, pointing out the soft spongey dent on the back.

Amalric felt sick.

'The fall has damaged his skull. In his condition, it wouldn't have taken much of a knock to kill him. He died quickly and without pain.' Thurston's face drooped with sorrow. 'A fine man. It's a dreadfully sad day.' He replaced the cloak and tucked it under the body. 'Amalric, I wonder if I might have a word with you: perhaps in the workshop.'

Edwin involuntarily sucked in a breath. Thurston heard and looked at him. Their eyes met but Edwin turned away quickly, his face blanching. Amalric shook his head at Edwin almost imperceptibly but he felt sure that Thurston had caught it. His friend went out in a manner which forced Amalric to follow. Once inside the workshop, the physician went to the damaged coloured window, then turned and saw the drawing on the table, half of it obviously erased by a frantic hand. His face showed no surprise.

Amalric's heart beat fast.

'Amalric, I'm sadder than I can convey about your father, but... and I wish I had not to say this... but something's been happening in this house and I expect it has something to do with these.' He held out a hand with two bloodied coins in the palm. 'I found these under your father's body. I suspect that there was a struggle of some sort.' He stood up straight and important. Amalric saw a man completely held by the honesty of his profession. 'You must realise I cannot condone unlawful death.'

Amalric wondered what exactly he meant by that.

'And you must promise me,' continued Thurston, 'that you will do something about Edwin... now. You must be strong, otherwise he will ruin you. It is up to you how you deal with the situation.'

He slapped the coins onto the worktable and with a wave of his hand, signalled the end of the conversation. Then, from the table, he took the cloth that had expunged St Peter, wiped his bloodied hands, threw it down and turned rapidly to leave. 'I bid you good day.'

His long robe swirled about him. Amalric observed the crease of a clean boot at the ankle as he walked away, and thought of Pontius Pilate at Christ's trial. Had Thurston washed his hands of them? Would his father's death be reported to the magistrates?

Back in the house he found Edwin at the table, his head in his hands. The earthy smell of Thurston's autumn blooms wafted from a pot on the table. Matilde's hands trembled as she caressed the thin blooms. Her eyes were wet. Amalric wondered if tears would ever stop.

Chapter Twenty-one

Elias had to be buried. Amalric journeyed to Meaux Abbey to speak to Father Luke to ask if he would be the priest at his father's funeral. It was an even harder journey this time: sadness rested in his scarred legs and made it difficult to put one in front of the other.

'Of course I'll help with your father... but it's not the pestilence back again, is it?'

'No, Father Luke.'

The look of horror that had flitted across the monk's face became one of relief and compassion.

'There was trouble in the house and he... he fell on the hearth... hit his head. He died so suddenly. No confession, Last Rites, nothing. I fear he will spend a very long time in Purgatory. I'm so worried: he died unable to confess his sins.'

'So, he died unshriven?' said Father Luke with finality. 'If you would like to make confession?' He obviously preferred not to hear more outside the confessional.

Amalric looked down at his boots. 'Er, no. I couldn't. Not yet.'

'In time, maybe? Till then, don't worry yourself. He will have company. So many have died from the pestilence without making peace with God. Even our own brethren. We say prayers. For a man like your father, Purgatory will no doubt be short.'

Amalric nodded, thankful.

'But it must be soon. The weather is quite warm.'

'We've put him in the church where it's cool.'

'You know, Am, none of us know how soon we will die, as the last weeks have shown. But God is compassionate... and you are living. To live as well as we can is the greatest gift we can give the dead. We will do our best for him.'

Father Luke broke into a slight smile and put an arm around Amalric's shoulders. 'Now, rest and cheer yourself. I have some good news. Lord de Horesby has asked me to be the temporary priest for Warren Horesby. This will be until things get back to normal when another priest is found.' His smile broadened, lighting up his face. 'I must say I'm looking forward to it. There is little I can do here. The abbey is recovering, but slowly. Our new abbot feels I would be better serving a ravaged village. So... you will see me often. I look forward to seeing the paintings on the walls of your church. I believe they are splendid.'

It was good news for Amalric. The faith of Warren Horesby had been overturned in the past few months and leadership and instruction from a man of faith was sorely needed.

'But first, let's sort out your father's funeral.'

Amalric, Matilde, Edwin and Nesta stood in church at midday and looked unhappily at Elias' coffin. It had been filled with copious amounts of fragrant herbs in an attempt to avoid an aroma redolent of the pestilence. Spikey stalks poked through inadequate joints. The only available carpenter had done his best but was barely an apprentice: the wood was roughly sawn, and corners skewed. The respected and talented Master Glazier deserved better.

The funeral service was a short, mournful occasion with only a few villagers attending. Amalric hoped Thurston would come. Matilde kept looking back every time the church door creaked, but it was only the wind.

Father Luke asked God to have mercy on the unshriven man, saying that though he was not prepared for death, his life had been an example to others and as a worker in glass he had sought to glorify God. He asked that Elias be allowed a short time in Purgatory and be brought eventually into the bliss that would last for ever.

Two youthful sextons carried Elias' coffin to a freshly dug grave next to Gundred and the twins. Since they had died of the pestilence, it was thought unwise to open their plot. Elias could not lie with his wife and children. Amalric looked into the dark depths at thin roots and worms and remembered the wrigglers on his burned legs, kept there by Nesta to save him. He threw seeded flowers into the grave. Everyone needed to be assured of resurrection.

Edwin, Matilde and Nesta left the graveyard, leaving Amalric to linger by the graveside. He hoped to see the black figure of Thurston hovering by the church wall, but he did not. While Elias was alive, there was at least some continuity with the past. Now, everything seemed to have stopped. He couldn't perceive a time beyond now. Building on the past seemed a hollow ambition. His eyes wandered over to Ned's grave. Little plants were showing through the soil – Berta's dried seeds, perhaps, now growing but staying low, waiting for spring. He set off running to catch up with his brother and sister.

'Well, Edwin, we'd better start tidying things at home,' said Amalric, breathlessly. 'The work is heavy – clearing the floor of blood, the animal pens, the roof needs fixing...' The list in his mind grew longer.

'Not today, brother. I'm off up to the manor to see what's happening there.'

Amalric stayed silent. Disappointed.

As he crossed the road, he was distracted by a group of four young women a short distance away – hovering to show sympathy for his family, he thought. He waved a thanks. But what if... what was it Nesta had said? What if they were looking for husbands? He and Edwin were fair game. He knew that at least two of the women had lost their men to the pestilence. One was looking especially provocatively at him, her skirt slightly raised above a slim ankle. Where were the nosey old women who used to watch and control the lust of the young? He was reminded of Liza and how he had been the recipient of her lustful looks at the well, before Easter – months ago, when she would have been with-child, her eyes staring at him through curtains of oily hair. He shivered.

Safely back in the house, Amalric mulled over his brother's grasping need for money. The money his father died for had to be hidden securely. But where?

'Am,' said Matilde. 'Would you clear the blood from the floor, round the hearth? It nauseates me.'

With the first thud of his spade into the stained, impacted soil, it struck Amalric that to hide the money under Edwin's nose might be amusing. He removed the outer rim of hearth stones, dug away, and made a large hole.

Edwin did not return that night.

The morning after, Amalric leaned against the house wall and contemplated the creamy church against a glass-blue sky, the dark green mass of the yew tree and a robin bobbing near to him, baring its red breast. 'Have hope, my boy.' He suddenly realised, despite the loss of his father, he was ready to work with coloured glass. Really ready.

In the workshop, he cleaned the table of all traces of St Peter. Before doing any new glass work, he had to repair his shepherd window. He carefully levered it with the wooden frame out of the wall and carried it to the table. One or two loose pieces of glass dropped as he turned it to horizontal and lowered it down. All the glass remaining in the frame had to come out of the damaged lead cames. The glass that had already fallen would be reused unless too broken, in which case, new glass would have to be cut. The restored window would have a repositioned angel's hand pointing to shepherds and not to a bush, as he had promised himself.

A soft click disturbed him. He looked up, surprised. Nesta walked in carrying a beaker.

'Good morning, Master Amalric. I know you used to have a drink with Father Wilfrid, so I brought you one to ease you into the day.' She put the beaker on the table.

Amalric's hand curled round the beaker. Sometimes it was as if Nesta could read his mind. He took a drink of the warm, fresh well water. While he, Matilde and Edwin had been absorbed by their grief, quietly and efficiently, Nesta had continued the running of their home.

He saw her glance at the table. 'Stay, Nesta. I'll show you the glass.'

'No, I've chores to do.' She left. A slight perfume of thyme went with her.

Pensively, Amalric turned to the window, empty of its man-made colours. He adored glass as if it were part of himself, and sometimes he wondered if it was sinful to care about it so much. He looked through the empty space to the church beyond. What was it that Father Wilfrid had once said? Ah, yes, 'it is God's gift that all should... take pleasure in all their toil.'[13] A sudden understanding hit him – God's world was the basis of everything. Man-made colours and patterns only enhanced what God had given in the first place. God had given people knowledge and talent to make them. He now knew, felt far more deeply than before, that his windows must be for the glory of God: complementing God's world. He set to work with renewed vigour. It absorbed him and lifted his mood.

A cough startled him. Glass piece in hand, Amalric looked up and only just recognised the strained face of the Lord of the Manor at the window, head and shoulders framed as in a portrait. He had not given Lord de Horesby a thought for a while and was dazed by the unusual and even slightly comic scene.

---

[13] Ecclesiastes 3:13.

'Good day, sir,' he said, hesitantly.

Lord de Horesby looked through at the tangled lead and glass on the table and at the glinting in the young glazier's hand. 'Good day, Amalric,' he said in a gravelly voice. 'How are you? You seem to be healing. I heard about your misfortunes, and then your father… very sad. A good man. It seems we have all lost someone.' He blinked hard to clear his eyes, and coughed again. 'Humph! I'm here at last to see how the village has fared after the pestilence. People are low. I've managed to organise a party of men, the few that there are, to clear up the mess. There's at least one rotting corpse to shift.' He grimaced at the thought. 'And a few dead dogs, cats, rats. I fear the men will lack enthusiasm. I see the mill has started up, though the grain is small in quantity: the harvest has suffered. Fowl are everywhere.' He rubbed at a bird dropping on his shoulder. 'I'm going next to Father Luke to see how he has settled in the church. There needs to be a few stern services, confessions and such.'

Amalric wondered where this blather was leading.

'Anyway, what we need is to get some commerce back in this village: people aren't passing through.' Lord de Horesby's eyes circled the empty window disappointedly. 'Mm, a pity about this.' His hand gestured at the broken glass. 'I suppose you are closing down?'

'Not at all, sir. Come inside, sir. Would you like some refreshment?' If he said yes, what could he give him? Did Nesta have ale put by? He didn't know.

'Thank you. I'll come in and sit but have no refreshment.'

Inside, Amalric, relieved, was able to view his visitor. The long tunic on his short, stocky body gave way to modernity with a buttoned front opening. It was of the finest wool, expensive and only slightly grubby. A fine linen shirt peeped above the neck. His shoes were of soft leather. Well-cut hair framed his shaved face. A perfume of roses hung about him. It was obvious that some of his servants had survived the pestilence. Amalric in contrast wore old hose, a holed woollen jerkin and a stained, long leather apron. Straggly black hair framed his black stubbled face. *His* perfume was a whiff of the home barn and sweat. Beside the noble lord, Amalric felt distinctively inferior. No wonder his brother envied people such as him. But Lord de Horesby, like everyone else, had suffered: his face looked yellowish, older than Amalric remembered. The lines were deeper, his eyes watery and rimmed with red, his hair greyer. The fine clothes draped loosely.

Lord de Horesby looked over the workshop. He picked up a piece of glass from the table and held it to the light. Blue reflected onto his face, giving it a greenish hue. 'Not closing down but struggling to keep going, eh?'

'Well, er, your Lordship, I'm trying to keep going,' Amalric said, cautiously. 'We've had more than a few setbacks but I hope to make progress soon. I'm about to repair this window...' Then an idea struck him. 'Sir, if I may speak boldly.'

'Aye, let's hear it. I'm looking for ideas.'

Amalric pulled a dusty stool from under the table. 'Please take a seat.' Lord de Horesby lowered himself slowly down. 'Well, you see, sir, with my father now gone, I have no glazing master with whom to complete my apprenticeship. If I could make a new window for our village church, it would be an example of what I can do and, if it is good, with a recommendation from yourself, the Glaziers' Guild may allow me my final approval. It would be almost a year early but given the state of things... Then I would be a craftsman able to seek work honestly. I could employ people from our village. There is a young carpenter, for instance, who, with a bit more learning, could make frames, tables, carts. I would bring some work back to the village.'

The lord's eyes momentarily ignited with enthusiasm. 'That is an excellent plan. I'll go to the church when I leave here. I'll speak with Father Luke and tell him of your intention. I can help with financing the project.'

Amalric could hardly believe his ears. The future suddenly had possibilities. It gave him confidence to pursue yet another fresh idea. 'Thank you, but… there is also something else.' This needed courage.

'Oh, yes?'

A deep breath. 'My brother, Edwin.'

'Edwin!' In an instant, admiration changed to exasperation. Lord de Horesby leapt from his stool. 'Come now, Amalric, surely you don't want me to have anything to do with him. He led my sons astray with his drinking, gambling and women. I've no doubt they picked up the pestilence from the Snickelways in York or Beverley. Those dark alleyways must have harboured the disease in their thick, disgusting miasmas. Your brother had the luck of the devil, I believe, and escaped it. Why he didn't catch it, I cannot think. Now I only have my daughter to help me with the estate and it's no job for a woman.' Lord de Horesby shook his head. 'She doesn't seem to mind, though, strong-headed vixen that she is.' He drew breath. 'Edwin, pah! Young ruffian! Never cared for anyone but himself as far as I can see.'

'Yes, but Lord…'

'Don't "yes-but" me, Amalric.' He looked fierce, the watery eyes blazed and he made a sweeping gesture with his hand. 'I want nothing to do with him. He came up to the manor last evening. I found him with my daughter.'

Amalric persisted, trying to eliminate the scene of Edwin and Clara playing in his mind. 'But, Lord de Horesby, Edwin is like he is because he cannot live the life he wants. He loves to hunt, to fish, to ride and to mix with like-minded people. He'll never be a hand-worker on a farm or in a glass workshop.'

Lord de Horesby turned away but Amalric pushed in front of him.

'You have no man to help you run your estate and possibly a few house servants. I've seen your estate land. It's unkempt, overgrown. There'll be few villagers left to give help and fulfil their dues – who will organise them? As you said, they are low.'

'Well, my daughter…'

'And the venison will be out of control, the game birds, your sheep, dogs roaming… What if you made Edwin a gamekeeper, or woodward to look after the forest? I'm sure if he could fulfil a life nearer to what he would like, the responsibility would tame him. He would become a man, a responsible man.'

'He's too young. You know that. What is he, something over sixteen, seventeen?'

'But there aren't many older men healthy enough to step into the positions. Things have changed. Everyone has to take risks now.'

'Risks? Listen, lad, you're on thin ice. I've heard things. The death of your father was, let's say, unusual. I may have to look into it.'

So, Thurston had reported it. Amalric felt his face turn pale. His courage plummeted. He dared not challenge the haughty lifted chin.

The tirade continued. 'I've heard things about his death. Not entirely an accident. Suspicious.' Lord de Horesby suddenly looked weary. 'But today is not the time. I must go.' His shoulders sagged as he looked Amalric in the face. 'Your father would be disappointed. Just maybe, just maybe you are not so different from your brother.'

He put a hand up in front of Amalric's face in dismissal of the subject and walked out of the workshop, grunting. A white dust patch the size of the workshop stool was on the back of his long tunic.

Amalric was crushed. He knew he had grossly overstepped his position. Never in his life had he spoken so boldly to one of higher rank, nor had he ever argued so strongly on behalf of his brother. His own nerve had surprised him. But now his name would be tainted along with Edwin's, and he might be involved in a suspicious death. But to be told his father would be disappointed in him – that was the most stinging of all.

As Amalric sat despondently in the workshop, another figure appeared at the window space, but this time it did not seem disturbingly amusing. The expression on Father Luke's face was actually joyous. The tall monk was properly tonsured and wearing a new, unbleached habit which, even from two bodies' distance, stank heavily of sheep grease.

'So... a coloured church window, Am. How wonderful!'

Amalric's mouth opened. He was dumbfounded. 'Have you seen Lord de Horesby?'

'Yes. Just now. He said you might get guild approval early. What might be the subject of the window? I've heard that some wealthy religious buildings are thinking about judgement and punishment in hell as a grim reminder of the sins which led to the pestilence. Some of the painted demons I've seen in the past on my travels... ugh! So ugly! Far too much red, like the disease itself. Much too fearful and gloomy, in my opinion. Unnecessary.'

So Lord de Horesby hadn't forgotten the window. Amalric laughed.

'I think we need a subject that speaks of resurrection, new life,' said Father Luke. 'People have been through enough already. Surely God will look kindly on us all if we are more hopeful. Lord de Horesby thinks I need to give stern sermons but just at the moment, I've not got it in me to do that.'

Amalric thought of Father Wilfrid, and nodded delightedly. 'Yes, one of hope. Which window will it be? I favour the one on the east wall!'

'The perfect position! But nothing too bold. Keep it plain.'

Amalric recognised Father Luke's austere view of decoration, which contrasted with what had been Father Wilfrid's more liberal stance.

'And you'll have to be sure to please the old man because he was in two minds about you. It was like he didn't know whether to praise or damn you.'

'Oh. Err... did Lord de Horesby mention Edwin to you?'

'No. Why?'

'No reason.'

Chapter Twenty-two

Amalric set to repairing his shepherd window with vigour. With it finished, he cleared the worktable of the past by thickly layering fresh white chalk upon it, ready for a new design to be drawn. The east window was large enough to hold two figures about half human size, but the subject was a problem. Edwin had been right. To merely copy Da after all that had happened was going back, not forward. His long fingers stroked the smooth tabletop. Here he would be creative. Here all his ideas would fuse into new images. The vacancy of white would be filled with black lines and then coloured glass. He just needed inspiration.

Amalric pondered over the worktable until the sun began to set behind the warren, sending a soft glow seeping through the workshop. Then, to better enjoy the hollow noises of twilight – the settling of birds, animals and insects – he left the workshop and stood outside. An arrowhead of squawking geese passed overhead. Down the hill a little, he saw Nesta walking dreamily up from the mill. The deep pink of sunset embraced her. With one arm she carried a bag of flour, held to one side on her hip as if carrying a child. With the other, she held up her skirt and looked down in order to take each step carefully along the neglected path. As she drew closer, he heard her singing softly:

All this year I've sought my love, I cannot find him
yet,
My dreams of love die in my heart, a stone within it
set...[14]

He knew the words – a popular song. As she approached, he grew oddly agitated.

'Hello, Nesta.'

She was startled. 'Oh, Master Amalric, you gave me a fright. What are you doing there? It must be too dark to work.'

'I'm just enjoying the twilight. Here, let me take that.' He opened the house door; no one else was inside. He took the bag of flour and put it on the table. Then he turned back to her and gazed at her face. It was a village face – ruddy, expressive. Wisps of hair curled around its edges. A long plait twisted above her forehead. A dark violet line under her grey eyes revealed fatigue.

Amalric stooped to place fingers lightly under each eye. He traced the violet onto her cheeks and softly cupped her face in his scarred glazier's hands. She let him do it without flinching. Then he bent to kiss her tenderly. Any ambiguous desire he had once felt deepened into something more refined, artistic in its beauty, taking time to form.

Then Nesta pulled away. 'Master Amalric! No.'

'Nesta, I'm sorry. You're tired. I feel... oh, I don't know!' He felt a red heat rise up from his neck to his cheeks. 'Call me, Am,' he said, slightly annoyed and hurt. 'After dressing my burns, you know every part of me. You've been an amazing servant.'

The word 'servant', so innocently spoken, ruined his attempt at romance.

Nesta visibly crumpled, as if the stoical endurance that had sustained her had finally cracked. She sat on the bench. Tears welled into her eyes. Her nose ran and Amalric offered her a

---

[14] Author's original work, inspired by fourteenth-century poetry.

cloth. She blew. Her response had not been what he'd expected. Was she happy or angry at his advance? Or was she, like him, confused by swirling emotions? He tentatively grasped her shoulders and looked into her teary eyes. His insides felt like melting meat jelly, trembling, running away out of him. He felt a desire to hold her as close as possible. Not to possess her but to love her.

'Oh, Master Amal... Am, you just think of what *you* want – to use a servant girl. You're just like Master Edwin.'

He was horrified. 'No, Nesta. I'm not. I saved you from him, remember.'

'For yourself!' she spat out indignantly.

Twice now, Amalric had been compared with his brother.

'Nesta, I...' He found no more words.

'Master Amalric... I'm weary. I need to store this flour.'

In the dim light, she picked up the bag and left.

Planning the new window eventually alleviated Amalric's embarrassment with Nesta and, after a few days, they were able to sit companionably by the fire. Nesta sat peeling vegetables. Water splashed with each chunk thrown into the pot. Amalric watched flying drops catch the firelight.

'I need inspiration, Nesta. I agreed with Father Luke that the window would be about "hope". You know, admitting that the pestilence happened but looking more to the future than the past.'

'Mm.'

'That made me think of Christ's resurrection, but bursting from the tomb doesn't feel quite right. There's a scene on the wall of the church already, anyway, and of Lazarus, but I don't want to approach *that* subject – it would bring back too many memories of Matilde.' He sighed. His sister was in the garden where he'd seen her wearily tidying the herbs. She was thin and not fully recovered from her ordeal with the pestilence. Her movements were stiff and laboured.

Nesta stopped peeling and put her hands, with the knife, in her lap. 'Ah, well… maybe I have an idea. New life…'

'Aye.'

'Yes. I have an idea.'

'Oh, and what's that?' Amalric looked at her. He enjoyed indulging her but prepared himself to mock her suggestion. He wriggled his stool closer to her.

'There's no need to do that, you can hear perfectly well from where you were.'

'Sorry.' He wriggled back.

'An Annunciation,' said Nesta, matter-of-factly.

Amalric was disappointed. 'My apprentice window was an Annunciation. I really don't want to do it again.'

'No, not "Annunciation to the Shepherds" but to the Virgin Mary. New life. New start for humankind. The angel Gabriel telling Mary that she is to have a child who will be the "Son of God".'[15]

Amalric's face stared at the bobbing vegetables, thoughts of mocking completely gone. There was an Annunciation to the Virgin Mary on the south wall of the church but it was simplistic, emotionally cold. He could use the same traditional symbolism in his window but change the style: keep the angel on the left, Mary on the right, a pot of white lilies to indicate purity, a hovering dove for the Holy Spirit – but bring it all more alive, vivid. Creative ideas rushed into his mind. His face broke into a wide grin. 'Nesta, you're right.'

He leaned forward, cupped his hand round her cheeks and gave her a kiss – a kiss of gratitude. She smiled. The subject certainly fitted creation ideas, new life. It was a theme of hope.

'How did you think of that?'

'Well, I hope one day to have a child, new life of my own.' Nesta waved her knife to emphasise her point. 'You see, such news for a woman is astonishin', frightenin' even. It can ruin a

---

[15] See Luke 1:26-35.

woman's life if it's out of wedlock – she can be rejected even by her own family. She can live a life of pain afterwards, or even die if the birthin' doesn't go well. I feel that women have hope in the Virgin. A child born successfully within true love is a wonderful thing.'

Amalric knew Nesta adored the picture of the Virgin and Child on the church wall and had seen her face glow as she crossed herself in front of it.

'So... do you want to have a child of your own?'

'Of course, but it's somethin' to wait for. I fear that the pestilence devil may still be lurking and will taint our bodies and deform children. I've seen terrible things happen to animals at my hamlet when disease or a curse has affected 'em.'

Amalric nodded, remembering the curses of Myrtle and his mother.

'I'm still young for babies, you know. I need to have more life before I risk havin' a child. And anyway, only Matilde remains of the village midwives. And...' she added emphatically, 'I'd have to be married.' Then she added tentatively, 'And you Master... er... Am? What about marriage?'

'Me?'

'Yes. You will needs marry. A craftsman has to have a wife.'

Amalric felt Nesta was being too bold, yet there was a delicacy in her conversation. She was, in fact, fragile in the matter of love and babies. She could shatter like glass but if she were leaded to him, she would be strong. He knew it.

'I don't know.' It was all he could reply.

Amalric's creative inspiration blossomed. The words Nesta had spoken had made him understand the enormity of the angel's words to the Virgin Mary: the commitment to new life, the exquisiteness of joy amid troubled times, the tension of what was to be. He now felt more deeply than ever the significance of coloured glass in telling Bible stories, and the importance of being creative for God.

He spent days in the workshop, inspired. He had the Theophilus manuscript by his side as he drew his design on the table. He took the written advice and drew carefully, because when fitting all the drawn, painted pieces together, the shadows and highlights had to match. The content was traditional but the way he drew was new.

As with his apprentice window, he created an angel but in a new style. It was how he imagined one to be – a smiling angel, dropping lightly from heaven to the ground in front of Mary, who recoiled in fear as she realised the enormity of God's message. Hovering between them was a dove representing God's Holy Spirit and in a vase at Mary's side, white lilies indicating her purity. A scroll wound around her feet with words in Latin: *ecce virgo concipiet et pariet filium.*[16]

The glass would be blue for Mary's gown, green for grass, and the background pink and amber for the glow of sunset. The angel's wings would be yellow and his flowing garment white, like the dove. The faces of both Mary and the angel would be pale pink and their haloes white, with yellow edges from silver stain. It was exciting!

With the drawing finished, Amalric invited Father Luke into the workshop to view his design. He wondered what the Cistercian might make of it. Would he have to start again?

The monk peered at it for a long time.

'Father Luke, is something wrong? Is it not good?'

'It's wonderful, Am. I'm not used to looking at drawings for windows. Forgive me. It takes me time to work it out. I am Cistercian, after all.' Father Luke grinned. 'But your figures live. Can you put that into coloured glass?'

The young glazier breathed a sigh of relief. 'Yes, and with these colours.' He placed samples of coloured glass on the drawing.

---

[16] Matthew 1:23: 'the virgin shall conceive and bear a son'.

'A bit more colourful than I'm comfortable with, but wonderful and appropriate for your village community. And truly a new start.' Father Luke's eyes were lively. 'How fitting if your window could be made ready for the special day of 25th March, the day we celebrate the Annunciation to Mary. The village would get a huge boost. We could ask Lord de Horesby to help pay for a party for villagers and his staff and family. Meeting of the social ranks is something we should start to do in this new time of ours. What do you say?'

'Oh, but Father Luke, even if Lord de Horesby pays, there is little new glass around.'

'Amalric, have you forgotten where much glass is stored?'

'The glass at Meaux Abbey! Of course!'

'I suggest we visit Meaux as soon as possible. I think the new abbot is strict and anxious to see the decadent glass removed. Better go soon before he gets rid of it in a fit of displeasure.' He took an excited breath. 'Then... in due course you will get your approval, reinstate your business, and, in time, you will make a name for yourself and find much work. Who knows, soon you may be able to exercise your imagination and make little red demons.' Luke threw back his head and laughed. 'God is at work here, my friend.' He slapped Amalric on the back.

The new Abbot of Meaux *was* anxious to get rid of the glass. 'Take it, take it,' he said to Amalric, waving his hands impatiently. 'Using it to convince your villagers that Christ was conceived as a human being to live among them will be more useful than it remaining here as a reminder of foolish pride in a building. Our Abbot Hugh was most unwise.'

'But there is the matter of payment. I can't...'

'No problem there, lad. Our records show that your father had not been paid for his labour for quite some time. I cannot deceive you. Take the glass in payment. As I said, our Abbot Hugh was most unwise.'

As he walked to the glass store, Amalric brooded over the abbot's remark: his father not paid, the abbot unwise, yet now he would have more glass of his own than he had ever dreamed of. Good coming out of bad. How he wished he could discuss it with Father Wilfrid. Surely there would be a phrase of St Benedict's to make sense of it.

When he opened the door of the glass store, daylight flooded in and a horrible musty stink hit his nose. It was obvious that it came from an old cloth, dotted black with mould, on the little table. He ignored it and went straightway to the wooden rack. All the glass seemed to be there. It was exhilarating. He pulled out a sheet of amber for the sheer pleasure of seeing the colour. The new window, being at the east end of Warren Horesby church, behind the altar, would be seen by everyone. Many times, he had been in church with the morning sun coming blindingly through the present east window. Father Wilfrid had been a dark silhouette against it. In future, the morning sun would cause shafts of coloured light to fall on the walls, floor and priest. The sun would not blind the congregation. Yet it was a daunting prospect.

He stepped back and leaned on the table, moving the cloth as he did so. Small pieces of blue glass tinkled to the floor. It jogged a painful memory. He perspired as he recalled Samson leaping into a crate and Ned dropping a sheet of blue glass. Poor Ned. Amalric put the small pieces of glass into his satchel to use as jewels in the new window or to grind up as an ingredient in paint. Then he remembered Ned and his father entranced by spring flowers on the road to the abbey, Samson bounding along with flopping tongue. Some parts of the past seemed so sunny, full of friends and family, the problems so small. Such memories were beginning to uphold him.

Father Luke arranged a hand cart to take away a first load of glass. Soon Amalric would have his own cart from his grandfather's money, and an assistant. This was now the real start of his new life.

Chapter Twenty-three

On his return to Warren Horesby, Amalric, despite his initial optimism, faced the possibility that his ideas could only be achieved after an enormous struggle. The weak late autumn sun rose and set over a dull, lifeless community. The gradual return of the village to a semblance of its former life could not conceal the heartbreak of the pestilence hanging over Warren Horesby. It seemed that many, many of the village folk had perished – somewhere between two-thirds and three-quarters, mainly the young and old. Numbers were irrelevant.

Hand-to-mouth daily living was kept going but without enthusiasm. Lord de Horesby's attempt to rally workers to clean up after the pestilence had been only a mild success: the road through the village was still littered with debris and creeping weeds, while animal dung stayed where it had dropped and gathered flies. The odd animal corpse rotted into oblivion where it had been kicked out of the way. The cart which had collected and deposited bodies stood unclaimed by the pestilence pit, where its last journey had ended. Daily gatherings around the well lacked the chatter of opinionated women, and the tavern benches and stools were empty of ale-full village men and interesting travellers.

Grief had settled like an invisible shroud, tight and stifling, wrapping the village in indolent misery.

Each day, Amalric pushed lesser problems aside and drove himself to finish the new window in time for Father Luke's service of the Annunciation. He excitedly anticipated the cutting of glass into shapes. Then would come the most adventurous part: the painting of faces – the smile of the angel and the shocked expression of Mary. He would also paint blades of grass, a Lenten lily, a mouse maybe. Then the paint would be fused with the glass in the kiln. Lastly, he would lead the pieces into panels and finally into one whole window.

For the cutting of glass, and the painting, he wanted a clear mind, no distracting thoughts: the work was delicate and mistakes were costly. It was time to call on Thurston at the manor to heal the rift caused by the awkward circumstances of his father's death. He needed to talk about things. He wanted to unburden his conscience.

Amalric strode up the hill and into the manor grounds, still overgrown and littered with sheep and other animal droppings. He found Thurston, his angular back towards him, outside the cottage earnestly tending sad-looking herbs.

Cautiously, he said softly, 'Er… hello, my friend.'

Thurston spun round on hearing the familiar voice. The extraordinarily broad grin on his face told Amalric all he wanted to know. But he looked tired, older. The bald patch had grown larger, and the remaining ginger hair was thinning.

'Come in. Come in. How are you?'

The cottage was tidier than at Amalric's last visit and they were able to sit together on two new chairs at the table. Wine was nowhere to be seen.

'I'm working hard at making a window, but because of that I need to get something off my chest, Thurston. Maybe you can guess.'

Thurston's face set into the familiar man-of-physic expression – a step back to normality. 'Go on.'

It was a relief to Amalric to give an account of his father's death.

Thurston nodded as he listened. Then he gave a shrug of his shoulders and spoke slowly, his eyes looking down at his hands. 'It must be really difficult to curb Edwin's excesses... as I so pompously suggested you should. Oxford university life is removed from the ordinary life of villages and my young home life was very privileged.' He smiled gently, apologetically. 'It is taking me some time to understand this northern country life.'

Amalric relaxed his shoulders. So even Thurston needed to make excuses for his own behaviour.

'But you did report Da's death to Lord de Horesby? What will happen to us?'

'Yes, I did. I had to. But he has since said nothing to me about it. I feel sure it can be put behind us.'

They both remained silent in thought for a while; then Thurston said hesitantly, 'How is Matilde?'

'Her head is tipped to one side and her tight scars make it hard for her to move her arm and leg easily. She is not the person she was. She is so quiet and morose. She pushes her hair into her cap very often, unnecessarily, as though it irritates her. Oh, Thurston, what has this pestilence done to us all?'

'Dreadful things. Sometimes, surviving can be the hardest thing of all. It will take time for us all to recover.'

Back home, Amalric stepped into the house and saw his brother dreamily staring into the fire and felt envious of his tenacity when pursuing desires, unconcerned with the outcome. Edwin looked up, and his expression turned to one of probing: his brows lifted, his dark, downy chin jutted forward.

Amalric responded. 'With that look on your face, I expect you want money? Clothes, women, is it?'

'Please Am,' he toadied, 'you can see how tattered my present clothes are and how ill they fit. They stink of sheep.'

Amalric felt a rare sympathy for his brother's predicament: his clothes *were* tattered and he *had*, albeit reluctantly, tended the family sheep. 'Aye, you're right.' He fumbled around his belt. 'You need to smarten up. Here take this.'

A small purse of money was thrust into Edwin's hand. Shock and pleasure led him to leave immediately, scampering out of the door like a young deer. Probably going to Beverley for a day or two, Amalric thought. His sudden generosity felt like a pain inflicted to cover up another pain. A pain for a pain.

When his brother finally arrived home two days later, Amalric had to admit that Edwin looked good, dressed in the new fashion: a short, leather-belted, green woollen cotehardie that fitted the curves of his burgeoning manly figure, all covered by a knee-length cloak and with red hose and pointed toe shoes showing below. They would have cost more than Amalric had given him. Perhaps it had come from gambling or was borrowed. Amalric felt a pang of annoyance and even envy. He knew his own large workman's frame would never look so good, no matter what he wore. If his brother was a young deer, he himself was a young mule. The next day, Edwin was once more away from home. Amalric had no idea where he was. He returned late.

The morning after, a knock came early at the house door. Nesta was confronted by a breathless young stranger dressed in an old, rather ill-fitting, livery suit of Lord de Horesby.

'Lord de Horesby, demands, err...' he paused and cleared his throat... requests the company of Master Faceby at the manor just after noon today.' The boy breathed out a sigh of relief. Nesta put a beaker of thin ale into his hand.

'I'm new at this,' he said, apologetically.

Amalric had no option but to obey. It was with a feeling of apprehension that he cleaned himself up and tied back his lengthening hair. He spat on his shoe leather to remove the chalk dust.

He set off with his heart beating heavily and the pull up the hill still stretching the scars on his legs. He walked through the gate, past Thurston's cottage and down the drive to the Manor House. The large building loomed before him: two storeys of stone and brick with three pointed roofs above. Wattle and daub outhouses were scattered around like chicks around a mother hen.

Only a few villagers of status were ever invited into the Manor House. His father had been one of them: summoned to attend the Lord's court where affairs of the village were aired in public and decisions made. Amalric himself had been privileged a year ago to help his father fit windows in the solarium, but that was then, this was now and, oh, so different. Then, he was a sheepish youth protected by his father. Now, he was on his own, in a man's capacity. His knees shook slightly and his throat dried.

A bronze knocker shone dully in the centre of the great oak door: an animal's head with a flowing mane. In its pointed teeth, it held a thick bronze ring. Amalric lifted the ring gingerly, feeling that somehow the animal would growl. He let the ring fall. To his surprise, it merely knocked loudly, breaking the quiet air. The door was slowly heaved back into the shadowy interior by Lord de Horesby himself. Amalric could just make out an angry face puffing and blowing above a brown high-necked collar.

'Amalric Faceby!' Lord de Horesby shouted from the dimness, causing the young glazier to step back sharply. 'Come in! I've no spare servant to attend the door. Most of 'em gone… one way or another.'

Amalric stepped into the large hall.

'Come. Sit.'

The hall was high ceilinged, the chair tall backed, the table polished but marked with dried food, the fire in the hearth meagre. A beaker of ale was pushed towards him.

'Drink!'

Amalric took a sip, not daring to flout the order.

'Now… that young brother of yours defies explanation!'

Amalric was surprised with the speed at which the lord got to the point. 'Err… what has he…?'

'He was here yesterday looking every inch the fashionable, confident man and I have to say it, lover!' Lord de Horesby grimaced in distaste. 'He has spent time with my daughter and she has been giggling like a three-year-old.' His expression softened. 'How I miss my wife. I don't know how to make a young woman like her behave when I'm in competition with that young varmint. Our old governess died; she would have known what to do. I take it you gave him the money for those clothes he was wearing and he didn't steal it, or gamble?'

'Yes. I... No. Well...'

'I've been thinking, though only God knows if I'm a foolish old man.'

Whatever Lord de Horesby was wanting to say was hard for him. Amalric saw that the older man was struggling with something he found distasteful: he furrowed his brow, twisted his mouth, looked upwards rather than at Amalric. Eventually, he outlined a plan to which Amalric could only foolishly nod with surprise and acceptance. At the end, Amalric dared to say one more thing.

'My father's death, Lord de Horesby... I... it was...'

Lord de Horesby, as before, raised his hand in dismissal of the subject and impatiently huffed out of the room, leaving Amalric standing embarrassingly alone. He made his own way out.

Thurston was sitting by his doorway reading as Amalric strode past the cottage on his way back to the gate. The physician looked up.

'You look as though life has just thrown something else at you,' he said.

'It has...' Amalric was about to tell his friend of Lord de Horesby's plan but noticed that his face looked paler and drawn. 'But Thurston, what ails you?'

'I saw Matilde today, sitting by the well. She is still very weak. We talked for a while. Then I... I asked if she would consider being my... my companion. I couldn't help but ask, Am. She looked so...' He looked up at the sky as if to hold back the impending wateriness in his eyes. 'I felt a while ago she would have said yes. Even today I swear she had a care for me, but she really spurned me, Am.' His eyes dropped back to his friend. 'I was really shocked. She was adamant. She said she could have nothing to do with me. She believes she must have been evil to have survived the pestilence and live in such pain and discomfort afterwards. "It's a living hell," she said, and being so badly scarred she believes she couldn't be a proper wife to any man. The awful scar in her groin, her twisted neck, the underarm scar that pulls her breast taught. Her constant weariness.' A tear ran down Thurston's cheek. 'I did that to her. I did that.'

'But you cured her, Thurston. She lives.'

'Ah, but in my zeal to cure, I gave her a pitiable life. I explained that I could help her and in time most of the pain would go.' His physician's ways took over. 'The buboes were large and deep. Such lancing as I did needs time to heal properly. It always results in tightening scars and...'

'Forget the physic rant, Thurston, just get on with your story. Please.'

'Sorry. But she just turned away and said no one could help. I put my arm around her, but she was unyielding and shrugged me off. I had to watch her walk away. I could help, though, Am. And she could help me. She is the only woman I could discuss my work with. She understands what I do. Now I fear for her sanity: she is so unhappy. Her family losses and the results of her own illness seem too much to tolerate.' He bit his bottom lip, apparently in an attempt to hold back more moisture in his eyes.

Yet more tears, thought Amalric, and reflected on how strange it was that one's own happiness was not complete unless loved ones were also happy. He left Thurston alone, looking broken.

When Amalric arrived home, Edwin was sitting sullenly drinking ale at the table. Nesta worked around him, preparing food. Matilde was helping but she was clearly exhausted. Against the health and busy ease of Nesta, she looked an unhappy, silent figure. Amalric looked at them both. He marvelled at the difference between the sisterly love he had for Matilde and the feelings he had for Nesta.

Amalric wanted to talk to Matilde about Thurston but had another thing to do first. He went to sit beside Edwin and thought how he might gain the upper hand before his news sent Edwin reactively running away.

He poured himself ale from a jug and spoke quietly. 'I need your help, brother, to repair this house. We need to pull together.'

Edwin looked down to his hands, bored. He picked at his nails. His groomed shoulder-length hair, loose from its tie, fell over his face.

'Lord de Horesby called me to see him up at the manor today.'

Edwin lifted his head. Concern flashed in his eyes.

'He told me he was prepared to take a risk... that if I guarantee your good behaviour and loyalty, he has a mind to make you his apprentice gamekeeper or woodward... even, eventually, reeve... but that's a long time ahead and, anyway, the village would need to approve.'

A stunned silence hung in the air. Nesta and Matilde stopped the meal preparations and stood open-mouthed. Edwin's dark hair trembled over his beaker. After a moment, he raised his head and stared at his brother. Amalric had never seen Edwin stunned like this and he gloried in the moment.

Nesta and Matilde stood listening apprehensively.

'The reeve!' Edwin was clearly not sure he had heard right. 'Lord de Horesby's... reeve?'

'Well, not yet, of course. Start with the lower jobs first as apprentice. In time, you might oversee his manorial lands:

organising planting, animal stocks, dealing with finances, collecting debts, hiring labour, renting out land.'

'Am, stop!' Edwin's usual confidence distilled rapidly into uncertainty.

'It's a bold risk on his part, but you could become vital to his estate.'

Edwin flicked his hair back. His voice cracked. 'But I'm not old enough. Not experienced enough for all that!'

'Well, you're good with horses. You can hunt. You move easily from village to town.' Amalric swept his arm over the meagre room. 'You enjoy the manor life better than this. In any case, Lord de Horesby would send you to learn on other estates where the pestilence has not caused so much devastation. His own sons are gone, otherwise he would be doing the same with them... It's work you would revel in.'

Edwin nodded. Then his eyes narrowed as suspicion began to set in. 'But why?'

Amalric ignored the question. 'But to go with my blessing, I will require that this house be repaired first and you'll have to help me with the new window for the church. None of that will take long if you put your back to it. If you fail, Edwin... Lord De Horesby will need to see signs that you are faithful, well behaved and a good worker. No more loose women or gambling. If you prove yourself, I will be obliged to guarantee you. If you betray our trust, his and mine, he will have you with the magistrates and imprisoned.'

Edwin shook his head. He was now speechless, his mouth opening and closing like a fish. Amalric put his chin deep into his pot of ale to hide the grin that he was helpless to avoid. This was a massive thing to consider. The leap across the social order was enormous for his brother, and the Faceby family.

'But I'm not, not, not of his station, I will not...'

'Be accepted? Times have changed, Edwin, as you have been at pains to point out to me. Land needs to be organised or we'll all starve. Here's your chance to manage rather than labour manually.' He let the information sink in. 'Oh, and yes... I nearly forgot…' Amalric smiled mischievously. 'Furthermore, Lord de Horesby's daughter, Clara, has a fancy for you, as you well know, and he'll look kindly on your relationship if you prove yourself chaste. No more nights out in Beverley. He hopes it'll calm you both down. Maybe offer a betrothal.'

Edwin became angry. 'You jest!' he spluttered. 'This is a plot to contain me. Well done, Am. You've finally got the better of me. I believed you.'

Amalric could not help it… an explosive laugh broke from him.

Edwin leapt up. His hand shot towards Amalric who, still sitting, ducked to avoid a slap on the face. 'None of this is true. You lie. It's a final attempt to make me more like you. Weak!' Blasphemies ripped from Edwin's mouth.

Amalric was shocked at himself. He had blithely been the cause of his brother's sacrilegious response. It was a dreadful thing to have done. Childish again! He guiltily watched his brother charge out of the house.

Matilde glared at Amalric with distaste.

'Matilde. It's the truth. Do I ever lie? I know it's hard to believe. Lord de Horesby really has offered Edwin all that I spoke of. I know it may be a last resort for the lord – his only way to keep his daughter calm and his land working – but it is the truth!'

'Then why tell Edwin so bluntly? You knew how he would react. You could have given him more time to absorb it, told me first. Am, you need to grow up!'

'You'd better go after him,' said Amalric sulkily, and stood aside as Matilde limped out as quickly as she could to find their younger brother, her non-judgemental love spurring her on. The reckless Edwin now faced a man's job and a sweetheart, even though he could not yet believe it. Amalric guessed he would be frightened and not able to understand why his principled and far too sensible brother and Lord de Horesby wanted to help him.

Despite his little triumph, Amalric felt bruised. Edwin would reach for social heights and money in all things, while he himself would pursue the merit and misfortunes of bringing glory to God and, in love, likely lower his social standing.

Chapter Twenty-four

Matilde appeared back in the house, where Amalric was waiting for her.

'Matilde,' he said, after she flopped onto a stool by the fire. 'I've seen Thurston.'

'Am, I've had enough of you for today, leave me be.'

'He looks ill. Could you not bring yourself to hear what he has to say?'

'I said – leave me be. I'm tired.'

'But…'

'I know what he has to say. He wants to marry me.' Matilde spoke impassively.

'So?'

Matilde lifted a log and put it onto the fire. Her mouth moved as emotions began to surface.

'So I'm scarred. I hurt. I believe I can't be a real wife.'

'But he needs a companion. Someone he can talk to about his work. You could do that.' Amalric was determined to carry on.

'Well, I can't. And it's none of your business. Thurston's work is not my concern, so there's an end to it.'

Suddenly Father Luke stood breathlessly in the doorway.

'Thurston is leaving!' he said with agitation. 'I can't say why, but I've just taken confession from him and it was hard for him to speak. He's going to his cottage to collect his belongings and will be gone. He's in no state to be trudging the countryside.'

'Why?' said Matilde, her face animated and concerned.

The priest opened his mouth to speak but Amalric butted in. 'Guilt.'

Matilde spun back to face Amalric, lank hair whipping loose from her cap.

'Guilt. Why?'

'Guilt at not being able to cure people, I suppose, given his learning and Oxford training. He's disillusioned. He's totally disheartened. He's had too many failures.'

'He cured me… and at least one other,' she said, defiantly.

Amalric was exasperated. 'Yes, but the other killed himself, facing eternal damnation rather than continue to live as he was. And he thinks he didn't bring *you* back to a full life. He knows how unhappy it has made you.' His patience was running out. 'He's reet miserable, Matilde.' Amalric's mouth twisted slightly as he experienced the mix of tolerance and exasperation he had known in his father. 'But with you by his side, he'd be a great physician! You were meant for each other.'

There was a pause. Both were shocked at his outburst. They glared at each other. Amalric felt a tightness in his throat as if his heart was rising up to choke him.

'Matilde.' His tone became softer, more controlled. 'Thurston needs you for what you are. Not just a companion. He loves you; loves you as you are now and all that means. I think I know about these things too. How love changes us.'

'Oh, Am!'

'Thurston would be understanding. He would be gentle and kind with you.'

Matilde's face agitated with tumbling thoughts, then became the clearest and most open Amalric had seen since the pestilence. She turned to the priest. 'Back to the manor, you said?'

'I saw him going up the road,' Father Luke replied. 'He said he would then follow Hull River to the coast. I fear he may be thinking of going over the sea.'

'That means he will have to pass by here!' Amalric looked at Matilde.

She looked back at him, and grabbed her thick mantle. 'I can't wait. I must go now.'

Nesta had heard what was being said and had quietly packed up Matilde's few belongings into a shawl, throwing in some bread and cheese and her fine linen caps. Then she had tied the corners. She pushed it into her mistress' arms without speaking. Amalric fumbled in his waist purse, pulled out coins and thrust them into her hand. She nodded thanks, hugged him and turned to the doorway and sped away. Regardless of her scars, she struggled up the road limping, hobbling from side to side with the speed of it. Amalric sensed how her body felt to her. Scarred and crippled. She and he were both changed from how they had been just before Easter when it all began. He watched until she disappeared, then waited to see her come down the hill with Thurston. But they did not.

Amalric spent a sleepless night worrying about Matilde. He had to assume she had caught up with Thurston, otherwise she would have returned. If only they had both passed by, waved – anything that would help him know they were together. They must have gone on the new path bypassing the village road which was trod during the pestilence. Why hadn't he thought of that? He could have met them. This new parting, even with his consent, was really hard to take. He rose early, guilt eating at him for pressing Matilde into running after Thurston, anger at Nesta for making it easy by packing up the shawl. Cold air had gathered in the house and outside a pale frost softened the rich, late autumn colours. How would she cope? Winter was coming on. Edwin too had not reappeared. But he wasn't worth the worry as he needed to assimilate his recent news before he returned.

He knew that Nesta, too, would have worried most of the night and he was glad to hear the light hiss of her breathing coming from behind her curtain in the corner. The singular sound in the hollowness of the room seemed to affirm the emptiness of his home. He thought of Matilde stirring the pot on the hearth as their mother had, and mixing ointments. Now there would be no one to help with healings and birthings in the village.

A sound shot into the quiet from somewhere low down. A stifled sob. Amalric whirled around and in the dimness by the barn door, saw a shadowed figure sitting on the floor leaning against the wall. At first he could not make out who it was and hoped it was Matilde, but she would never have sat on the floor.

'Edwin? Is that you?'

The reply came back. 'Aye.'

Amalric heard anguish in his brother's voice.

'She's gone Am, hasn't she? I saw her running to the manor. Was it after Thurston? She's not come back. She won't come back.'

Amalric knew better than to delve into his brother's thoughts but said softly, 'Come, let's get the fire lit and help Nesta by making the porridge.'

Three members then occupied the Faceby home and Amalric recognised that their relationships were improving, if a little uneasily. Edwin still dressed extravagantly and continued to spend the occasional hour at the manor, courting Clara. Amalric persuaded him to deal with the repair of the house and was amazed when Edwin began to show a surprising talent for organising. He employed builders to mend the holes in the wattle and daub walls, a local thatcher to replace the roof and the young village carpenter to make new window frames, shutters and a door. Amalric was even more surprised to find Nesta and his brother working well together, to bring the house back to a comfortable living space. Tables and chairs were restored, their charred parts planed away. A new fireside chair was purchased.

Amalric paid out money from his purse for it all, but it would soon be necessary to dig up some more of grandfather's money from its hiding place by the hearth, and he was still a little nervous about that: the disturbed earth would be obvious.

The making of the Annunciation window was a great joy for Amalric, but at the back of his mind, he worried about his place among other glaziers. His father had been well known in the trade so, even before finishing the window, before the weather threw its winter worst, it was time to seek out old acquaintances in Beverley: those who were still alive and working for the minster. It would embed him more within the trade and he'd find out the prospects of new work. He would also need to go to York: crucially, he had to put his name forward to the Glaziers' Guild to become a member. Lord de Horesby had promised to contact the Masters himself, but he had to lodge his own request for assessment.

Travelling cost money and there was not enough in his purse. One day, in Edwin's absence, he removed the outer hearth stones and dug up the box. He removed a few coins and replaced it, but it took longer than expected and he had to rapidly put back the soil, stamp it down and replace the stones. The different colour of newly turned earth showed beyond the stone.

Edwin walked in to find Amalric sitting at the table. 'Your face is flushed, brother. Hard work or are you sickening?' he smirked.

Amalric said nothing.

Amalric stood outside by the new front door. 'See, Nesta, I've purchased a donkey for my travels. I got her from old Ma Aikin up the hill. It was her husband's but he died.'

'Oh, Am,' said Nesta. 'Can you handle her? She looks a bit cantankerous. She has a mean look in her eye.'

The donkey heehawed and pounded her hooves on the hard ground. The sound alerted Edwin and he appeared from the garden. His face showed surprise.

'Yes, she's a stubborn beast,' confirmed Edwin as he ran his hand over her flank. 'But she'll serve you well, brother. Good choice.'

Amalric knew Edwin would have chosen a horse: an expensive horse. 'Well, she was cheap. She didn't have a name, only Donkey, so I'm calling her Myrtle.'

Nesta and Edwin laughed out loud.

'Am, that's evil of you,' said Nesta.

Amalric laughed too. It was so good to laugh.

'Oh, Master Am, I'll miss you. I'd better go and prepare food for you. The sooner you leave, the sooner you'll be back. Have you got saddlebags?'

'Aye. They came with Myrtle. Plenty of room.'

The following day was cold and wet. Nesta put parcels of food into the saddlebag and also her favourite shawl.

Edwin had said little but Amalric was cautiously confident he would be a brother to Nesta: he was growing up and now had passion only for Clara Horesby. Money was another matter. He didn't know if the changed soil by the hearth had been noticed by Edwin.

'Take good care of Nesta, brother. I trust you. The future of our family depends on you – and your own future at the manor.'

Edwin squirmed a little. 'Aye,' he muttered.

The brothers shook hands.

Amalric dared to give Nesta a peck on the cheek. She didn't recoil from him. Then he put on his deep-brimmed felted-wool hat, threw his cloak around his shoulders, shrugged to adjust it and took hold of Myrtle's rein. The look of envy on Edwin's face didn't escape him. Nesta stayed watching until he waved from the well.

Amalric spent two weeks away. Beverley had fared badly during the pestilence. In the minster workshop it was as he suspected, largely youngish lads like himself who were left to carry on their fathers' trades. A very few older men remained: it was they who had the knowledge, if not the energy, to add stability.

In the evenings, he joined them for ale and cider. It usually started with sadness at the loss of comrades but ended with drunken rejoicing that past glaziers would be together in Purgatory, making beautiful rainbow-coloured windows to earn a sooner release into heaven. And in heaven, that is where they would see God's ultimate colours and beauty. Amalric had a headache some mornings but, each night, Nesta's fragrant shawl softened his pillow and reminded him of her.

Then he arrived in York. It was a damp, cold place. It looked busy at first, as if the pestilence had never happened. He worked his way through stalls of food, blacksmith products, live animals, pretty ribbons and old clothing. Women stood in the entrances to the Snickelways tempting passers-by with a show of bare ankle, knee or bosom. He thought of Edwin. Yet behind the normal façade, the buildings and streets had the same dismal, unkempt appearance he had seen in King's-Town on Hull with his father, and more recently in Beverley. Many were locked up with great locks, bars and wooden boards: both merchant houses and hovels. The odd shutter swung dangerously on its hinges but no one bothered. He saw the hospital that Thurston had told him about, with hastily erected huts for the huge numbers of victims, now empty. Over it all towered the minster. Beautiful. Commanding. He went in.

The glass-filled windows were magnificent. Five old ones were slimly tall, elegant with grey grisaille and just a tiny bit of colour, similar to the Cistercian ones at Meaux. Later windows reflected strong colours on to the unswept floor. He quickly found the little monkeys he remembered, low in one window, and the one holding the doctor's urine flask. He saw an image of the Virgin Mary and felt Nesta in his heart. He saw his whole world in coloured glass.

Near to the minster was the Glaziers' Guild. Amalric went inside and left his request for assessment with the recorder, a middle-aged man with frenzied eyes sitting behind a dusty desk. He nodded as Amalric spoke, and recorded his request in a manuscript. It was an unremarkable experience.

Amalric was glad to leave York. He despised the desperate attempts to regain normality when too much of the disaster was left behind. The place was almost too big to clean up. He tramped disgustedly with Myrtle through cold, foul, stinking puddles as he left.

Amalric arrived home in the late afternoon. He walked beside Myrtle to lighten her load and speed her up. Through the gathering dusk he saw Nesta outside the Faceby home, sweeping. She saw him and waved enthusiastically. At first, he expected her to drop her broom, hitch up her skirt and run to him baring her ankles, but he realised that would be wrong. He waved back.

Then he came to her. 'Nesta, I've missed you. Your shawl was a surprise and so comforting. I fell asleep on it every night.' He pecked her cheek.

She was a little tearful and speechless. Amalric had to speak first.

'Is Edwin home?'

'No. He's at the tavern. He's been good to me in your absence, Master Am. You have no need to worry on that account. He deserves his fun sometimes.'

'Aye.'

'There is a meal for you, of warm ale, bread, fresh cheese and honey. Come inside.'

'Oh, Nesta. It is so good to see you, really good.' His arms wanted to hold her. Only she could give him the comfort he needed after being in the foul towns. 'Will you sit by me while I eat? My legs hurt. It's been a long day, I've walked a good way to save Myrtle, she's a little old and cranky.' He tried to speak lightly.

Nesta wanted to be near him; he could sense it. They sat together at the table but they were shy of each other.

With the coming of daylight, Amalric went on his knees to look at the soil near the hearth stones. It looked disturbed. It saddened him.

Later that morning he was in the workshop when Edwin sauntered in. Amalric fought the urge to say something about the buried money but instead saw a chance to gain his brother's help first.

'Ah, Edwin. Could you arrange for a wooden frame to be made to surround a small coloured window for me, and two boards of a size to be carried on Myrtle?'

Edwin's face evidenced an internal struggle. 'Why?'

'It's not enough to work for the monasteries and minsters, I should move into merchant and manor houses,' explained Amalric. 'When the Annunciation window is finished, I'll need to travel around and show a sample of my work. Maybe a St Peter. That's what the frame is for, and the boards for drawn designs.'

At the words 'manor houses', Edwin's face visibly changed to one of interest. Amalric was learning how to persuade his brother to help with jobs. Manor houses meant rising above one's station. It meant excitement and possibilities. Amalric hadn't forgotten the look of envy in his brother's eyes as he left for Beverley and York.

'Yes, I'll get that sorted for you. I'll make the frame myself. I know enough to do that. And… I'll come along with you if it will help and even shout out your business if you'd allow me.'

Amalric smiled. Success! In spare moments by rushlight in the evenings, he started to sketch new ideas on the wooden boards so that if… when… the glazing business picked up, he would have designs to hand – though not always biblical subjects, but flowers and animals. He knew that at York and Beverley Minsters, huge new windows were tentatively being considered and he so much wanted to be good enough for them when the time came.

Edwin worked at making frames but after a while found that his tools needed some attention from the blacksmith. Perhaps new tools, even. A new plane, chisels. Amalric responded carefully to his brother's request.

'If you need the tools, you must have them, but I haven't enough money in my purse. I'll have to get more from Grandfather's money. Come with me and bring a spade.' He scrutinised his brother's face but saw no emotion.

They returned to the house. Edwin went straight to the hearth. Amalric followed, not at all surprised; it merely confirmed his suspicions. 'The soil has been disturbed,' he said in mock surprise, looking directly at Edwin. 'It was smoother than this when I left.'

Edwin, still without a hint of emotion, prised up the outer hearth stones and dug into the soft earth. The spade clunked on the box lid. He lifted out the whole box and opened it. The lid clattered to the floor. He held it for Amalric to see.

'See, brother, I can resist. I found the box when you were away but took nothing from it. You knew I had found it. You think little of me. But I can be responsible.'

Amalric was speechless for a moment. From now on he could not hide the money. The amount of trust on each side had been equalled out. He drew out some coins.

'Here, go buy your tools.'

'*Our* tools, Am. *Our* tools.'

'Aye.' Was Edwin at last feeling the bond of family? Amalric's contrition turned almost to pleasure.

Chapter Twenty-five

Amalric glanced through the back window of the workshop. Shivering celandines littered the garden with sunshine yellow. His mother would have loved the sight of them. He blew on his cold hands and his breath flowed grey and nervous on the air. He hardly dared turn back to watch Lord de Horesby hovering over glass shapes on the white table, trying to make out the picture they would eventually become. He looked back and saw the ageing man running a finger over the details fired permanently onto the glass. The wing of the angel especially held his attention. He stroked it gently as if actually touching a feather. Once or twice he picked up a piece of glass and held it up to see the cold early spring light shining through. He held the blue longest. Amalric had named the colour 'Ned's blue'. This time, it reflected on a pinker complexion. Amalric himself was particularly gratified with the painted faces of the angel Gabriel and Mary. Mary's mouth was open in surprise. The angel smiled. Lord de Horesby's mouth had twitched on seeing them. Amalric thought it best not to mention that Mary was modelled on Nesta and the angel on Ned.

Lord de Horesby huffed and scrutinised. A fear niggled at Amalric: what if Lord de Horesby could not move away from more traditional imagery? What if the Master Glaziers didn't want innovation? 'Have hope, my boy.'

Lord de Horesby carefully put down the piece of blue glass in its place on the table, stood and stretched upwards with his hands on his aching lower back while muttering a long, 'Mmm.' He left the workshop, his cape swishing around him, and motioned to Amalric to give him a leg up onto his horse. His new calf leather boots slipped easily into the stirrups.

'Now then, Amalric,' he said, looking down from high up. 'I returned yesterday from the Glaziers' Guild in York. The Master Glaziers will come to Warren Horesby to assess your window on 25th March. Don't look so shocked: I know it will be the day of the Annunciation celebration when it will be blessed and dedicated. Might as well get it all over in one day, eh? I trust your window will be ready?'

'Oh, er, well I…'

'Don't look so put out, lad. I know it will be a hard day for you but there aren't many Masters left after the pestilence hit York and they want to do as much as they can in one journey around the area. The window had better be good: God knows I've praised you enough to them. Otherwise I will lose face.'

As usual, Lord de Horesby left little room for Amalric's own words.

'Well, I'll do my b…'

'That's right, lad. I'll see to the refreshments for the Masters and for the village celebration. Now I must be off. I don't want to meet that brother of yours, I see enough of him at the manor, fawning over Clara. But he seems to be behaving himself. Good day!'

He turned his horse and was gone.

Amalric went back into the workshop, breathless with the visit. He needed to gather his thoughts. It had been hard work getting to this stage. The weather had been cold and he'd often thought of Father Wilfrid by the church first thing in the morning, with his beaker of heated water, offering both warmth and comfort. Occasionally, he had fired up the little hearth to add heat to the room but, even so, sometimes his fingers were too cold to cut the brittle glass or paint delicate areas. The daylight hours had been short and the temptation to work through the dusk had sometimes been great. It had occasionally resulted in a costly mistake: like Ned, he had dropped one piece and seen it shatter on the floor. His fingers showed more small, old cuts than in the long days of summer. Nesta had sympathised. Edwin had tut-tutted sarcastically. Now after all the demanding work, Lord de Horesby had left without comment on the window.

Even without Lord de Horesby's spoken approval, it was time to permanently fit all the pieces of glass together. Each piece, surrounded by a lead came, would be held in place on the table with a few nails at the edge. Then, again with Theophilus' advice, he would secure the joints where the lead cames touched each other, with tin smeared over with a hot iron. The glass would be held firm, sufficient to make a panel. Each panel would link with those above and below, to make the complete window. Then it would be slotted into stone grooves in the east window of the church. Finally, to hold it securely and prevent strong Yorkshire east winds from the sea blowing the window inwards, thin iron bars would be fixed across the window and little copper ties, soldered to some of the lead, would be twisted around them.

But before finishing the window completely, he had a fancy to paint something on a small glass piece to show that he, Amalric, had made the window: a little mark that would be his signature. He didn't know any other glaziers who did this: it would be another innovation, another risk.

On 25th March, the Warren Horesby church bell clanged through the fresh spring air, calling villagers and folk from valley hamlets to the service of the Annunciation. It was midday. Amalric rushed across the road to the church where the congregation was already settled. Inside, perfumed smoke clouded the air. He had only ever smelled traces of the precious frankincense in Meaux Abbey and York Minster. It was glorious. Father Luke was obviously responsible for this special addition to the service.

The church looked beautiful. It had been scrupulously cleaned, then decorated with early primroses, early Lenten lilies and new green leaves. Shifting sunlight flowed erratically through windows. The painted pictures on the walls responded by glowing with colour as the pale light moved over them. Somewhere in the roof beams, as usual, little birds twittered excitedly. Feathers fluttered down.

Peering through the fragrant mist, Amalric was saddened to see a far smaller congregation than in previous years. The absence of so many familiar faces shocked him. Lately he'd been too busy getting the window finished to attend church services frequently and it had allowed his mind to forget the village losses. Now, on this special day of celebration, the congregation showed little in the way of joy. Looking around, he saw anxious faces, and hands twisting with nervousness. There was the occasional deep sigh and stifled sob. The reason, he knew, was the reverential atmosphere, causing emotions pushed down for months, to surface. He felt the same. The opportunity of sheer pleasure felt undeserved, as if letting down the dead when they had given up their lives. Other celebratory days, saints' days, Christmas, had come and gone without pleasure: services had been solemn, whereas this day marked a turning point. A renewal.

Amalric patted dust from his new tunic, hastily put on. He had given the window a final polish only an hour before, just in time. He was weary and nervous. Nesta and Edwin were already in their places, on the right at the front of the church. He joined them, standing beside Nesta, and couldn't help but remember how different things had been almost one year before with his mother, father and the twins, Ned and Father Wilfrid. And where was Matilde at this very moment? And Thurston? He felt a want of them all. He sought Nesta's hand. She held his tightly.

The church bell stopped clanging. A shuffling at the back of the church signalled the arrival of Lord de Horesby, his daughter and two Master Glaziers. They walked down the aisle and settled themselves at the front of the congregation on the left, opposite the Facebys. Edwin immediately moved over to slip in beside Clara, who beamed at him.

Amalric turned to look at the two Master Glaziers. They had arrived late in the village and, like the villagers, hadn't seen Amalric's window, covered as it was with a linen drape. They stood silently but cast their eyes over the walls. He wondered if they had seen the painting of the Annunciation high up on the south wall as they came in. It was traditional, simple, with no emotion on either the Virgin's or the angel Gabriel's part.

The church darkened as heavy clouds rolled in. Amalric became even more nervous. He began to tremble. It might mean that when the linen cover was dropped, the window would be in semi-darkness. He wished the Masters could have seen the window in a good light before now. It could all go horribly wrong. They were likely to say 'not approved'. He squeezed Nesta's hand, hard. 'Have hope, my boy.'

The service began. Father Luke spoke of the Annunciation as a symbol showing the promise of a new life, a saviour. Together with the new window illustrating the event, it emphasised that carrying on with hope was the best thing they could all do to honour the departed.

When it came to the dedication of the window, the linen cover was pulled ceremoniously away. The colours looked deep and brooding. The painted expressive faces could hardly be seen. To Amalric, it was obvious that clouds obscured the sun but, to most of the village folk, the window was a disappointment. It was first greeted by silence as they tried to take it in and then with a murmur as they swapped comments. Father Luke ignored them and dedicated the window to God with prayers. The incense faded away.

Amalric began to panic. Had his innovative design been a horrible mistake? Had he been too arrogant about his own creativity? Clearly, what was obvious to him was not so obvious to others whose experience of coloured glass was limited – this congregation knew only his small shepherd window, which they had disinterestedly passed by. Most of them had never been to Beverley or York. The congregants had long been familiar with the pictures on the walls of the church and the Bible stories they illustrated, so why should they appreciate the same in coloured glass? It was an extravagance. And although the depiction was different, maybe they had had enough change of late.

The service ended. The congregation filed out to walk the short distance to the greater excitement of the mill barn feast. Edwin walked with Clara de Horesby. Nesta left Amalric's side and hovered in the shadows by the door. Lord de Horesby, with the visiting Master Glaziers, went behind the wooden altar to stand close to the east window.

Amalric stood with Father Luke in the centre of the nave, watching the Masters put their noses to the lower part of the window. He watched as they climbed a short ladder at the side to lean over and look at the higher parts. They occasionally ran their fingers over the glass and felt the joints of the lead cames.

'Am, all is not lost,' said Father Luke, warmed to compassion by Amalric's wilting face. 'The village folk will understand the window in time. It's new to them. Beautiful objects can be hard to take when you've seen few of them.' One of the Masters put his hand on his chin and rubbed his beard. 'As for the Masters, here, they are experienced men and you must put your trust in them.'

'Aye. But Father, it all seems hopeless. I've tried so hard to do the right things but now I feel it may have all been a waste of time, a mistake. I have been too determined to make a change. Father Wilfrid always said "Have hope," but...'

Just then, Lord de Horesby motioned Amalric to join him and the Master Glaziers. Amalric's soiled workman boots made an obvious sliding sound on the tiles and cut through the silence as the three figures stood facing him, waiting. The sumptuous cloaks of the Master Glaziers hung heavy over colourful tunics. Above embroidered collars, their faces gave nothing away. As he approached, they all turned to face the new window. Clouds scurried; colour came and went. Amalric stood nervous and despondent.

'Now, Amalric Faceby, a question,' said one. 'What do you mean by making a window that moves away from the accepted style? The faces show... err, expression. You have included a mouse, a small Lenten lily. Mary is wearing a blue robe: it's unusual in these parts – blue is for sky... is it not?'

Amalric felt sick. He had gone too far but all he could do was defend himself. 'Well, sir, we have all been through a really bad time, what with the pestilence and the hard times before that, famine, sheep disease, wars...'

'Yes, get on with it.'

'Well, I thought that, as Father Luke said, we needed new life, a resurrection. So, I started with a new style.' He suddenly felt confident, had nothing to lose. He had become a new man: one day he could be the equal of these Masters. His voice rose, became more certain. 'The main traditional elements are there – the angel, the dove – but you see, sir, there is no point in creating new things in an old style. It doesn't uplift, nor move forward into the future. We must search out a good future, not dwell in the dying glow of the past. I have plans, sir, but they are about making windows that say something, that tell stories, that have real faces on the figures, like these have. When people look back in years to come, I want them to see *our* story in *our* windows. I want God to use my images to communicate with people. I want to make big windows for religious houses, small windows for homes... and the blue of the robe? Well, the most expensive, finest glass is fitting for the Virgin... is it not?'

The Master Glazier held up his hand. 'Enough, lad, enough.' He looked at the other Master Glazier. 'I think you had a question to ask.'

'Yes. Now, lad, what are those marks in the lower corner on that piece of blue glass at the bottom there?'

'It's my family name, the year and a little motif that will become my emblem, my sign.'

'Well we don't normally do that sort of thing. It smacks of pride and pride is a sin. Not good for a church, eh?' He looked back at Father Luke, expecting a nod of confirmation but receiving none.

'On the contrary, sir. It is most suitable,' replied Amalric, now more sure of himself. His shoulders went back. He took a breath. 'It's for two things: firstly, to honour my father to whom I was apprenticed; secondly, my life so far has centred around the people of this village, this church and my love of coloured glass. The last year has been very hard for us all. The waiting for the disease to come. The way it came. The loss it has left us all with. I could not create something born out of all that without signifying it in some way – showing the year 1349, and… throughout the bad times, falling feathers, my emblem, have been like messages from angels. They are my plea for the window to be blessed by God. My work is to the glory of God.'

A short, stunned silence followed.

'Aye. Right, lad.'

The Master Glaziers moved away to confer. Lord de Horesby looked unsettled. Rain began to patter the window. Father Luke lit the altar candles to lighten the increasing dimness: the colours of the glass disappeared almost entirely. Amalric, horrified at his own outburst, sagged. He watched the play of candlelight on the undulations of the glass, like moonlight on water. You can drown in water. He thought of Samson. Why think of the dog? Ridiculous!

The glaziers came back. One smiled and went to Amalric to shake his hand. 'Well, lad, you've woken us up! It's early days, still, in your expertise, but we need young folk like you. We've a mind to award you approval. We'll keep an eye on you, but… you are now a member of the Glaziers' Guild. We think you'll go far. Well done!'

Amalric was silent. Had he heard right? The faces around him smiled. The second Master shook his hand, as did Lord de Horesby and Father Luke. Nesta burst out of the shadows having seen the handshakes and put her arm in the crook of his elbow, smiling wildly. He must have heard right. He was now a glazier. Master Glazier would come later. He had gained approval, proof of his talent. It was hard to believe. If only his father could be there with a proud expression on his face saying, 'You've done reet well, son,' and if only Father Wilfrid could say, 'Well done, my boy.'

At the church door, Lord de Horesby shook Amalric's hand again and attempted a broad smile. He had no words. Then he steered the Master Glaziers to the manor for refreshment. Amalric watched them as they walked up the hill in the rain, leading their horses. Beside the two colourful Master Glaziers, Lord de Horesby looked dull and bent in his heavy, dark woollen cloak. 'Aye, he really is a grievously sad man but, despite his own heartache, he is doing his best for the village… and me.'

'I hope he'll find some happiness,' said Nesta.

'Aye.'

'Come, let's go to the feast. Folk will be keen to see you: no doubt they will have somethin' to say about your window; they'll be blunt but they'll have already heard of your success and will hope to have work come to the village. They'll not be really unkind.'

Chapter Twenty-six

The following morning in fresh sunshine, Amalric leaned on the church gate with a beaker of warm water, on the very spot where he'd met Father Wilfrid each day. His success with the Master Glaziers combined with the villagers' artless comments had left him with a jangled mind. He needed the consolation of imagining the old priest at his side – he would have helped him settle.

He heard a click from across the road and saw Nesta leave the house with Edwin. Both carried pails and went uphill towards the well. His brother really was becoming a more caring person. He tipped the last of the water away and decided to stroll into the church to offer thanks. Inside the door, Father Luke was brandishing a roll of parchment.

'Ah, Amalric, it's a good day today; the weather, that is. Yet good is always tinged with a little sadness and sadness always with a little joy.'

'What do you mean, Father?'

'I have found this.' He held up the parchment. 'It's Father Wilfrid's list of those who died during the pestilence here in the village. It confirms that near on two-thirds have gone, maybe more. A dreadful, dreadful loss. See, your friend Ned is at the top, then the twins, then your mother. He wanted them all to be remembered. We don't usually keep records of the dead. He must have bought the parchment with his own money and spent many hours recording the names. I have a mind to add his name to the bottom of the list. What do you think?'

'That would be reet grand,' replied Amalric, pleased to know his friend, Father Wilfrid, would be remembered along with his parishioners.

'I will do that today and I must then keep this document somewhere safe. I will arrange a service in a few months, where we will pray over the burial pit and read out the names. Surely, there will be no lingering miasmas by then.' Father Luke sighed. 'It will hopefully help the living. Compassion is never wasted.'

Amalric felt a little helpless as he looked at the plethora of names on the parchment. He looked up at his stoic painted friend, St Edmund, on the wall and thought that like his image, the consequences of the pestilence didn't go away. Nor did one's guilty conscience.

'Father, I have a confession but it may damage someone close to me, for he was involved.'

'Is it about your father's death?'

Surprised, Amalric said, 'Aye.'

'Then you need say no more. Edwin has been to me.' Father Luke raised his eyebrows knowingly. He put a hand on Amalric's shoulder. 'And I firmly believe Lord de Horesby will let the matter go. He doesn't have the heart to cause more upset.' Then, he picked up a broom and went off to busy himself sweeping outside.

'Have hope, my boy.' Amalric, amazed, walked towards the front of the church, knelt and offered his thanks. The unpredictability of life was… unpredictable! If only the lump of sorrow in his chest would go away. He raised himself slowly, still hampered by his scars, and took from his purse the small piece of stone that Ned had given to him after the earth tremble. He turned the carved feather in his hand until it was warm. He always had it: it comforted him.

Nesta came into the church. 'Well, that's the water collected for today,' she said, smoothing the creases in her garment.

'Edwin helped me. He's waiting for you to join him for breakfast, Master… er, Am. Come quickly.'

'Edwin can wait, I've something to show you.'

He took her hand and pulled her to the east window. A lightly clouded morning sun lit up its jewel colours perfectly. Nesta gasped. This was the window in its full glory. He looked down at the young woman by his side. Her eyes gleamed like the glass. Blue, green and gold tints stroked over her.

Amalric grinned. 'My father once told me, he wanted to make a coloured window for this church. Well, I've done that now; and it's *reet* fine. I know he would be proud of me. There was a time when I doubted I could ever make him proud. And from now on, people will know that when they see a little feather in the corner of a window, it's from the workshop of "Elias Faceby and Son, Glaziers".' Then he had a moment's doubt. 'Oh, Nesta, I wonder if now I have too much pride. I may be punished for it in Purgatory.'

He looked for denial from Nesta but she chose to ignore him and continued looking at the window.

'Master Am, is that a mouse at the bottom of the Virgin's robe?'

He studied Nesta's profile as she peered closer. Her little nose, soft lips, the plait framing her forehead. 'Aye. I painted it for you. The colour of your hair reminds me of little field mice.' Words from his heart rather than his head, burst out. 'Nesta, I love you.'

Nesta became totally still. She did not turn to face him but stared at the window. He felt crushed, awkward.

A strong beam of sunlight flashed through the glass, catching the angel Gabriel's face. 'Oh, Nesta! Did you see? The angel approves of love,' he teased, then felt like a boy again when he saw her serious expression.

'Master… Am, I do care for you, but…'

He forestalled her. 'But you are a servant.' His arms dropped to his side disconsolately.

'But other women in the village – aren't some far more suitable? Not servants. Good housewives.'

'Suitable is not enough. Once, you being a servant would have mattered to me, to my family, but not now. Things are different. We face a struggle to live.'

'In any case, I have no marriage dowry. I'm from a really poor...'

He put a finger to her lips, stopping her words. 'The dowry is you. You are all I need. The servant thing is no matter. Nesta, so many excuses. What is wrong... really? Is there something else?'

'No.' She stamped her foot, turned so her skirt slapped his legs, and ran out of the church.

Amalric was shocked at her response – her troubled expression, the way she abruptly left him. There was much more than her servant status that bothered her. It was like a wall between them preventing her from being unguarded with him – was it his strenuously hidden but increasingly passionate thoughts that she'd detected, causing her to fear him and being with child?

Running after her, Amalric saw the house door slightly ajar, even before she slipped inside. Through the window, he saw moving shadows and groaned. His hopes of talking further with Nesta were dashed. Who else could it be but Edwin and Clara, with perhaps, Lord de Horesby? Today, he didn't want to pander to their needs. Then Nesta was at the door. Her smile surprised him.

'Oh, Am, don't look so grumpy. Come inside and breakfast. Come.'

Amalric bent his head to pass under the doorway. On raising it, he peered through the smoky, soft light and saw three figures sitting at the table; Edwin and two others.

'Am!' His brother waved. 'Look who Nesta and I met when we were walking down from the well this morning.'

Amalric squinted. 'Clara?'

'No. Thurston and Matilde!'

'What?' How could they be sitting at the table when he had given up hope of ever seeing them again? It was hard to take in.

'Hello, Am, my friend,' said Thurston, wildly shaking his hand. 'It's so good to see you. You've managed to make a splendid new window, I hear?'

Matilde stood to put her arms about him. She wore an elegant all-over fine wool garment with a high neck. Her face was plump. Her arms were strong.

Matilde and Thurston told of their journey to Bruges where they had married in a church full of coloured glass. They had supported themselves for a few weeks as travelling healers, which also gave opportunity for Thurston to research the pestilence. Eventually they had realised that their real calling was back in Warren Horesby.

'I can work happily from here, Am. Travel if I must, but always come back.' Thurston went on to say they had returned late the previous day and came upon Lord de Horesby as he was saying goodbye to the Master Glaziers. He had welcomed his physician back with open arms and rejoiced at the idea of him settling in Warren Horesby with a wife as companion healer. It would bring more money into the village. And sadly... there were plenty of empty cottages suitable for a new home.

Amalric looked at Matilde. She should be happy but he knew her well.

'Matilde, is something wrong?'

Thurston reached a hand out to her. 'Am, Matilde longs for a child. I would like one too, but I believe the pestilence has left her unable to conceive. We're considering taking in an orphan and wondered if there are any here roundabout.'

'I have not heard of any,' replied Amalric. 'We have heard little young laughter these past few months and when we have, the child has always had family.'

'I know of a child,' said Nesta, as she clattered empty bowls on the table. They all looked at her. She faced Amalric. 'When you were very ill with your burns and Master Elias was ill and confused, a baby was here.'

'What?' exclaimed Amalric, mystified. 'Why didn't I know?' Then a faint memory came to him, of weeping, talk of sinning, of Swine Priory, the insistent voice of Father Wilfrid. Something about Nesta not coping with three.

'I haven't mentioned her since then, Master... Am, because I thought you would want nothing to do with her.'

Amalric became uneasy. Was this Nesta's secret, the thing she had kept from him? Had the child been hers? Edwin was lustful and near to overpowering her that night in the barn. His mother had had suspicions about Nesta, suspecting she had goaded him on. How many months ago was that? He tried to calculate rapidly but the air was too tense.

'Nesta, is the child *really* yours?'

There was a ripple of shock at his bluntness.

'How could you think that?' Her expression showed how hurt she was. 'The baby was left by our door – in a basket. Father Wilfrid said she was a bastard and let slip he recognised her as possibly belongin' to the Ashe family an' if that was so, Liza had never confessed who the father was. I called her Beatrix.' Nesta paused but had more to say. 'I thought Beatrix was yours, Master Am. Liza Ashe lusted after you. The women at the well said so.'

No one round the table spoke but all looked intently at her.

'You were too ill to tell,' Nesta went on. 'Father Wilfrid said I couldn't manage to keep the baby properly fed as well as care for you and your father. And he was right. I had to let Beatrix go to the nuns at Swine Priory. I felt guilty seeing her become thin, only just weaning, but when the nun carried her away I was...' A sob broke from her.

Matilde cried out, feeling another woman's anguish. Amalric was shaken by Nesta's comment. 'You thought I had been the father?' So this was her secret – she thought the child was his. He raised his arms, palms towards Nesta. 'No! She isn't mine. I have never even been with a wom...'

Edwin's eyes grew wide and he smirked knowingly at his brother.

'Edwin, grow up!' Amalric felt the greater man. Compassion for Nesta squeezed his throat. All the time she had been stoic and capable for him and his father, sadness had stalked her own heart.

'I believe Myrtle thought the child to be Edwin's,' Matilde suddenly burst out.

Amalric turned to her. Yes, he remembered, he had almost accused his brother, himself. All their ills had begun with Myrtle's vehemence and accusations. Naturally her grandchild would be left on the Faceby doorstep. He looked directly at Edwin but his brother showed interest rather than guilt.

'Edwin, that child is yours!'

'No!'

'That child is yours! Liza died on the birthing bed. They wouldn't let Ma save her. She's your bastard.'

'She's called Beatrix,' shouted Nesta.

Amalric stood in front of Edwin, his face twisting with anger and recrimination. 'Come on, Edwin, own up. You and the manor boys didn't care. You couldn't wait to lower your hose on your rampages. And what about that time I caught you trying to ravish Nesta in the barn?'

'But Am...'

'Oh, never mind, we'll take her in,' cried Matilde impetuously, leaping to her feet. She clasped Thurston's hands excitedly. 'Oh, I hope she's still alive.' Thurston's fingers whitened. 'A child from my own family.' But then her face drooped. 'The child belongs to you, Edwin. You and Clara will have to care for the bastard child or maybe – no surely not – you might choose to leave her at Swine Priory.'

Edwin, in the meantime stood and backed himself to the wall. 'It's not mine!'

'*It* is called Beatrix!' cried Nesta.

'I couldn't possibly have a child by Liza Ashe. She was simp... I never... Am, I was young when I... Nesta. I couldn't

hold my drink. I was miserable. Da didn't like me. You were…
Am, believe me, I've changed.' Edwin looked desperate. He spat
blasphemies.

'Stop, Edwin!' All at once, Amalric saw in his panicking
brother the remnants of a child despite the insistent growing of
a handsome man's body and nascent honesty. He put his
upright, open hand before his brother's face. 'Stop. Let's not go
further. It's too painful for us all.'

'We'll surely need to know something about her,' said
Matilde to no one in particular. 'The nuns won't let a foundling
go to just anyone.'

A few short moments of silence followed. Deep breaths
were taken. Then Amalric could not contain his thoughts.

'But why Liza? Simple Liza,' he said, sadly. 'Own up. Show
you're a man at last, Edwin. Claim the child.'

Matilde stifled a moan.

'Am, no. No! Believe me.' Edwin too, was calmer now and
eager to continue defending himself. 'When I went with the
manor boys we went to the known women of the town. To learn
how to… you know… older women. Women who knew all
sorts of things.' A leer began to play on his face but was
checked. 'You have to believe me. I couldn't have learned
anything from Liza. It was not me!'

Thurston had been silent during the squabble, looking at
Edwin with the penetrating gaze that Amalric knew well. Then
he spoke.

'What colour hair did the child have, Nesta?'

'Beatrix had fair hair. Curly.'

Edwin touched his black combed locks and shot a look of
relief at Thurston.

Amalric felt deflated. Once more he had lost a skirmish with
Edwin, yet he was relieved. He pulled at his own black locks.

'But whose child is it, then?' he asked. Then he saw Nesta's
rueful look. 'I mean, who is Beatrix's father?' His brow
furrowed. 'Ned?'

'It doesn't matter, now.' Nesta was emphatic. She shot a meaningful glance at Amalric. His torment about her evaporated. Nesta continued. 'She's a pestilence baby who needs lovin' parents and carin' aunts and uncles. She has no one else except the Swine nuns now. If Liza kept quiet about the father, as, accordin' to Father Wilfrid, Beatrix's mother did, then it must have suited Myrtle to believe Beatrix had come from this family. That means no one else'll claim her as their own. Not now.'

Sensible Nesta. They all smiled at her in response.

Hope came into Matilde's eyes. 'And what with all the trouble her birth caused, it would be good to…'

'Have her in our family as a sort of redemption,' continued Amalric. 'Father Wilfrid would have approved, I know.'

'Well,' said Thurston, 'I suppose on the morrow we will be travelling to Swine Priory.' He hugged Matilde.

Three days later in the Faceby home, Matilde cradled little Beatrix in her arms. The nuns had reluctantly let her go with the promise of financial support for the priory from Thurston. Nesta hovered, anxious to provide the correct weaning food.

Amalric and Thurston leaned on the house wall, beakers in their hands. A man carrying a sack over his shoulder passed them and waved a greeting.

'Well, Am, it's good to see folk travelling through again. Now that the path skirting the village in the pestilence has been blocked by old de Horesby's men, folk will pass, see your workshop and know you are a man of glass.'

Amalric felt happy and adult. 'That means the tavern will be more alive soon, too. I'll take an ale there from time to time. The cider and the mead were reet good too, my father said.'

Thurston took a drink and then looked into the bottom of the beaker. 'Am, I feel we have not seen the end of the fearful disease. It is said to have started in the sin of war very far away from here, spreading unstoppably within people as they travelled. I heard while in Bruges that it has already been seen again in those far places. It'll return here and we'll have to use all that we have learned in order to be able to face it once more, with confidence.'

Amalric felt both confusion and fear rising, as it had done a year before. He didn't know far places, but he believed his friend.

'With Matilde, I wish to study to find a cure for the pestilence. I must honour my learning in Oxford and work to understand the hateful disease, lest we are all wiped out. Without a cure, well…'

The lump of grief in Amalric's chest made itself obvious – he knew it would never go away. He knew his friend would carry guilt forever… and to think of it starting all over again…

'But for now, Am, there are so many good things.' Thurston raised his beaker. 'Your health, my friend.'

Amalric raised his own beaker and an imagined voice from the past said, 'Have hope, my boy.'

Acknowledgements

I would like to thank my husband for his patience when I spent hours at my computer, my daughter for an arduous first critique, and the support of my reading group friends. Thank you to Instant Apostle for the opportunity to have my work published and guiding me through the process, and especially to Sheila for her really insightful and valuable advice.